The
Mighty
Red

ALSO BY LOUISE ERDRICH

Novels

Love Medicine • The Beet Queen

Tracks • The Bingo Palace

Tales of Burning Love

The Antelope Wife (*1997; revised editions, 2012, 2014*)

Antelope Woman (*2016*)

The Last Report on the Miracles at Little No Horse

The Master Butchers Singing Club

Four Souls • The Painted Drum

The Plague of Doves • Shadow Tag

The Round House • LaRose

Future Home of the Living God

The Night Watchman • The Sentence

Stories

The Red Convertible: New and Selected Stories,
1978–2008

Poetry

Jacklight • Baptism of Desire

Original Fire

For Children

Grandmother's Pigeon

The Range Eternal

The Birchbark House Series

The Birchbark House, The Game of Silence,
The Porcupine Year, Chickadee, Makoons

Nonfiction

The Blue Jay's Dance

Books and Islands in Ojibwe Country

The Mighty Red

A Novel

Louise Erdrich

HARPER LARGE PRINT

An Imprint of HarperCollinsPublishers

THE MIGHTY RED. Copyright © 2024 by Louise Erdrich. All rights reserved. Printed in the United States of America. No part of this book may be used or reproduced in any manner whatsoever without written permission except in the case of brief quotations embodied in critical articles and reviews. For information, address HarperCollins Publishers, 195 Broadway, New York, NY 10007.

HarperCollins books may be purchased for educational, business, or sales promotional use. For information, please email the Special Markets Department at SPsales@harpercollins.com.

FIRST HARPER LARGE PRINT EDITION

ISBN 978-0-06-341040-4

Library of Congress Cataloging-in-Publication Data is available upon request.

24 25 26 27 28 LBC 5 4 3 2 1

To those who love birds
and defend their place on earth

The Red River of the North is young. From the sky it looks like a length of string arranged on a flat board in a tight scrawl of twisting loops. The river gathers in the Ottertail and Bois de Sioux rivers and runs north on a slight incline from Wahpeton to Winnipeg. The river is muddy, opaque with sediment and toxic from field runoff. Not a river you'd swim but good to fish, at least at its source. The river is changeable, a slow and sleepy trickle in summer, rampaging like a violent toddler in spring, when it sweeps across the land reflecting the sky like its mother—a vast prehistoric lake. Over millennia, the waters have given the Red River Valley earth its blackness, its life. The river is shallow, it is deep, I grew up there, it is everything.

The Night Driver

2008

Crystal

On a mild autumn night in the Red River Valley of North Dakota, Crystal pulled herself up behind the wheel of an International side-dump, steered out of the sugar processing plant, and started her haul. Out in the country the sugar beets from Geist's fields were piled in a massive loaf on the company piling ground. Crystal drove down the highway, turned onto the access road, and got loaded from the pile. She cruised back to the plant, unloaded. Repeated for as many times as fit into a twelve-hour shift.

On night hauls she always packed a certain lunch. Two sandwiches—turkey salami on whole wheat—carrots, apple chips, peanuts, two cookies. She'd attached a segmented canvas tool bag to her lunch cooler. The pockets of the bag were always filled with the same things: phone, multiuse tool, Black Jack gum, Icy Hot roll-on, Tylenol, lip balm. She brought jalapeño meat sticks, her toothbrush, wallet. In her pocket she kept a lucky hat knitted by her daughter. Crystal also wore an olive-wood cross brought back from the Holy Land by Father Flirty. She wasn't much of a Catholic, but like other people who crave order, she was superstitious. Her shift was 6 p.m. to 6 a.m. By the time she left for work, her daughter was at her homework, unless she was waitressing. Crystal got back in time to see her off to school.

At 11 p.m., Crystal ate her first jalapeño stick and used some Icy Hot. She left the plant and was going back out to the country, high beams cutting into strange mats of fog that lifted and fell, when a brilliant shadow vaulted across the road. Before she could touch the brakes, the animal was snatched away into blackness. It was a mountain lion, the first she'd ever seen. There was the flow of it, her lights glancing off its pelt, the ruthless slope of its head. Crystal rammed her elbow into the side window and slowed down. Driving over the place she'd seen the big cat disappear, Crystal felt a slight electric charge along her jaw. Even in the cab of the heavy truck something had touched her. A twinge of unease. A prophecy. She tried to shake it off. Her daughter, Kismet, and her husband, Martin, were certainly winding down their days at home. Maybe

Kismet had made popcorn and Martin had brewed himself a cup of the special bedtime tea he liked. They were safe.

'Tune your thoughts to a better station,' she muttered.

Then her thoughts were broken up as she turned down a gravel road and drove toward the powerful halogen lights out on the piling ground.

On her way back to the plant, it crossed Crystal's mind that the sighting might have to do with the grandmother who'd raised her, Happy Frechette. Happy had lugged whiskey to Fargo to sell during Prohibition. She had traveled on foot and wasted a bottle beaning a mountain lion. Good money! She had fumed about it over seventy years later. Each time she told of her walk it got longer and more eventful. Was sighting the cougar a sign she'd finally died? Avidity and cruelty had kept Happy alive, but nobody could live forever. Although if there was anyone . . .

Crystal reeled in her thoughts, drove up the lift at the beet plant. She put on the hat Kismet had made out of sparkly gold yarn; it was like a warrior helmet. A couple of the guys teased her but she mocked them back, pretending they were jealous. She was still buzzing from the mountain lion, but she didn't say a word about it. The big cat had appeared just for her. The lift rose, until the mercury switch opened the side gate and tipped out thirty-two tons of sugar beets.

By the time Crystal was back on the road, the call-in show she liked to listen to was on.

Tonight, the topic was angels. Are they out there? Are they listening to us? Answer, yes. The host, Al Ringer, was talking to an expert. They were discussing Creatures of Holiness, the Prince of Faces, Tetragrammaton, and the Order of Cherubim. The angel expert said she would break this down. If you watched the heavens, you could ask for help from the Angel President involved in governing the movement of the stars that night. For instance, the configuration of Libra, on display now, was ruled by Zuriel. Was it worth addressing Zuriel? Probably. Although Zuriel was above speech, Zuriel communicated with the Lord of Hosts by signs. Told what was needed, what was wanted, on earth. Zuriel's mute requests might be said to elicit more attention because Zuriel wore special rings that flashed and glittered.

Someone named Boris called in. Boris had been visited by an angel as a child. The angel had awakened him by calling gently from the end of his bed. When he got up, the angel took him outside, taking care to slam the door in order to wake his parents. His parents looked out the window and saw their son in the front yard.

Immediately they rushed out. The angel told Boris to run away as fast as he could. His parents chased after Boris. They were nearly down the block when behind them their house exploded.

'The angel saved us,' said the caller.

'That's what angels do,' said the nonplussed expert.

'What did the angel look like?' asked Al.

'Like a seal.'

'A seal.'

'I mean, it was kind of glowy and golden, but yes, a seal.'

'In ancient days a seal was considered a fish,' said the expert.

'You say the seal, or angel, led you down the steps and out into your front yard,' said Al. 'How did that happen? Physically?'

'A hand came out the end of its flipper and the seal-slash-angel sort of floated. It all seemed normal.'

'They do take various forms. I'll be the first to admit I have no special—'

Al cut the expert off. 'Just a minute, here's another call.'

The next call was from a person who was, or considered himself, an angel.

'Why?' asked Al.

'I was chosen. Simple as that.'

'What does our expert have to say?'

'I will try to be gentle about this, but angels are not earthly beings.'

'Neither am I.'

'They exist outside of time.'

'So do I.'

'Angels see the world from every possible dimension.'

'Same here.'

'They have direct encounters with God.'

'Obviously.'

'Well,' said Al, 'it seems that you're an angel. Thank you. Next caller.'

'Hello. I'm the mother of a son. We live on a farm. When my son was real young he climbed up and fell into a grain bin, which most people the grain would suffocate, but not him. He wasn't swallowed down. He said something lifted him up from below. Then later at the zoo he climbed to the top of a chain-link fence and down the other side. It was a tiger fence. The tiger curled itself around him and did nothing. My son's had any number of close calls. Last spring, he and his buddies went out on the snow after a party. They raced around on their snowmobiles. Well, things happened. But he was more or less okay. My question is first, does he have a guardian angel and second, how to say thank you, specifically, to an angel? Oh and third, how do we stop these things from happening?'

Crystal turned up the volume, leaned forward, stared out at the empty highway as she drove.

'Overall question. You want to know what's going on?' said Al.

'Yes, yes that's it,' said the caller.

The expert jumped in, excited.

'Obviously, yes, your son has a guardian angel! And from the gravity of these incidents I would say his guardian angel is very highly placed, perhaps at God's right hand. These instances are proof that . . .'

The expert went on for a while but by then Crystal had stopped listening. She knew the caller. The voice belonged to Winnie Geist, a member of her book club, whose family land and beet pile she had just turned down an access road to reach. Crystal could even glance across the perfectly flat fields, glistening under the moon like calm black oceans, and see that a light glimmered in a second-floor window of Winnie's house. Everybody knew about the tiger and what had happened after this party Winnie mentioned on the air. But Crystal hadn't known about the grain bin or that there were other miraculous escapes. Al Ringer moved on. Crystal turned off the radio and drove for a while in silence, headlights peacefully cutting radiant holes in the blackness. She'd never liked the kid. Gary. But people had said, the way people do, that he must have a guardian angel. Gary was in her daughter's high school class. In fact, they'd gone on a couple of dates—against Crystal's advice. She couldn't forget that Gary was one of a group of boys who'd tormented Kismet when she was going through her phase as an innocent, hardworking goth. Crystal didn't trust him and she certainly didn't trust his mother. Winnie Geist liked tragic endings, even hard history, and pretended she understood what she called the physics of farming.

Crystal had named her daughter Kismet to attract luck and lightness of heart. But fate was also involved. And the mountain lion was a hungry shadow. Or maybe—she touched the olive-wood cross that hung around her neck and remembered how the light glared off its fur—maybe she had seen a destroying angel. She thought about how another big cat had refused to eat Gary and touched her cross yet again. Crystal didn't know if there was anything serious going on with Kismet and Gary, but she did know that guardian angels only protect their special person. Getting close to someone whose angel was as powerful as Gary's was asking for trouble.

PART ONE
The Proposal

2008

The Diamond

On some days the stone was dull, as though it did not care to shine, but today it twinkled. Garrick Geist, aka Gary, eighteen years old and pressed for time, opened the little hinged box and tipped the ring side to side to catch the light. The stone winked at him. He placed the box in the cup holder between the seats of his mother's car. Many times he'd opened the box to examine the thin golden ring. Still, as soon as he shut the lid he wanted to check again. The saleslady up in Fargo had said he'd purchased a wearable fleck of eternity. He wished she had not said fleck. She could have said, maybe, piece of eternity, or symbol. People thought he was a confident person, cocky, especially during football season, which was now. His mother always insisted that from the get-go he'd been hell on wheels, though supernaturally lucky, escaping drownings, maulings, always this or that catastrophe. He had been that way until the party. He thought he'd be that way again. Still, a different word than fleck would have helped him in this moment.

While he waited for his girlfriend, who said she was not his girlfriend, to run down the front steps of her crooked old house at the end of Tabor's main street, he put out his hand, drew it back, resisted again the urge to look at the ring. Between lifting or hauling sugar beets and a home game, he had three hours. Had the stone really winked? He was beginning to feel ridiculous, but maybe he should check, at least, that it was really there. He'd bought it with his own money, not his parents' money, and Gary was pleased about that. His father had started paying him for some of the work he did on the farm. The fact was, they weren't as rich as people thought. True, he'd inherit three thousand acres, probably more from his uncle too, and at twenty-one become a full partner, but this fall they'd started on a new house and their farm debt was a source of pressure. Still, a young man needed cash, his father said. Besides buying his own snowmobile—that was last year—Gary had bought this ring. The two were more connected than anyone would ever guess, the snowmobile being the reason he had to buy this ring and to propose marriage to Kismet R. Poe. Here she was at the passenger's side window. Gary jumped out, walked around the car, and opened the door for her. His mother had taught him how to treat a lady, and Kismet R. Poe was a lady—his lady, he hoped.

Of course, she would have laughed at him and said that was fucking hopeless. Or, though she sometimes dressed tough, she was a nice girl, so she might just smile and shake her head. He felt his lips stretch in a smile so embarrassingly anxious that, as he walked back around the car, he put his hand to his mouth to wipe the smile away. He was in full control of his face as he pulled out. There was nowhere he could think of to go in town. He wanted a meaningful place, an overlook that wasn't a dam, a hill but there were no hills, a magnificent tree. But Tabor was cutting down all of its old trees. Nobody knew why. The only place he could think of was about half an hour away. So he'd asked her to go on a drive, and they started out.

After the last of three stoplights in town, they took the curve on the first overpass, went by Steve's Autobody and then lines of giant farm machinery. A seed station, stacked pallets, Pookie's Valley Steakhouse. On the straightaway Gary steered with his knees and occasionally draped a few fingers on the bottom of the wheel. Kismet's thoughts were elsewhere. They used up their conversation in the first few minutes. This didn't really bother Kismet; she liked her own thoughts and could enjoy an uncomplicated silence. Then Gary asked if she was bored. She brushed that off and said that she was a visual person.

'I mean, if you're bored, we can talk or something,' he offered.

'No, that's okay. I like watching the world go by. It's good as talking.'

In fact, it was better, at least where Gary was concerned. She liked the way the fields and ditches looked in late October, the soft scorched colors, the pale stubble left in the rows, the trees stripped bare and bristling. She counted the even peaks of pine trees that surrounded farmsteads to break the wind.

However, within a mile or two, Gary's question whether she was bored made the silence complicated and exposed the fact that she actually was bored, very bored, and being consciously bored reminded her of what her cynical best friend, Stockton, had said—how boredom was a part of small-town life that you had to get drunk to accept. She wasn't drunk now. She wasn't drunk very often. She did think that if she spent much time with Gary, though, she'd have to have a bottle handy.

Still, there was something about him. . . .

She took a deep breath, held it, and blinked at the square lake. Yes, it was a square lake. The earth had been dug from a field. The displaced earth had made the second overpass. Kismet watched the lake go by as she slowly released her breath.

'It's nice just having a quiet ride,' she said.

Kismet wanted to forestall Gary from sharing his thoughts. He might get solemn and talk about his farming ideas or his philosophy, which was that you should do what your mother told you to do. Kismet had met Gary's mother and she questioned that. Gary believed that radio frequencies could carry disease. He started many sentences by declaring 'There are two kinds of people . . .' He didn't believe in God but said he could get behind the idea that aliens had manufactured the skein of life. He also talked about, say, the Ten Commandments, and would wonder whether 'Thou shalt not kill' applied to deer. He loved deer. He cried when he saw a dead one. He also cried when he saw a living one. This was a thing about Gary that really got to Kismet. He didn't hunt. His father and uncle tried to take him out hunting. He refused. He loved animals, not only deer, but every animal. Still, she didn't appreciate it when he said that she reminded him of a deer in winter with her dark brown eyes and matching hair. Deer were lovely creatures but they were prey animals.

College will get me out of here, thought Kismet, and a tiny rush of fear made her want to sleep. She pushed her seat back. The sun was beaming through the windshield and it was autumn sun, the mellow light of early afternoon. She fell into a dreamy nap as Gary meditated aloud about whether dinosaur bones were real or had been placed there by a super-intelligent race of ancient humans, or by aliens. 'Aliens again,' she murmured.

'Damn straight,' said Gary in a heroic voice.

'You know the bones are real,' said Kismet.

'Probably,' said Gary. 'Here's the turnoff to that place. Remember Blosnik? He was a hands-on man. There's two kinds—'

'I know,' said Kismet. 'Your mom and dad . . .'

'Yeah, Winnie and Diz.'

He liked calling them by their first names.

'They always say there are two kinds of people, hands-on and hands-off. They really liked how Blosnik took our class out to dig fossils—'

'On the banks of the Sheyenne,' said Kismet. 'That was where you found the bison tooth. Which aliens didn't put there.'

She closed her eyes and wondered why she was spending her day off with Gary listening to the same things he said over and over. Though sometimes a surprising thought broke through. But not today.

'Okay. A bison tooth.' Gary nodded. 'Petrified! You know . . .'

'Turned to stone,' they said in unison. She turned away. Gary's throat shut. He was so nervous that he'd fallen into old grooves of conversation. He slowed the car. They were close. At home, he kept the tooth on his trophy shelf under a glass cheese dome. 'I love that thing,' he said every time he passed it. At present, the brown stone tooth was in his pocket. He'd brought it for luck. He and Kismet would have to walk to the place he'd dug it up. That's where he would propose. He stopped the car.

'See that?'

He pointed across a field and told her it gave on to the riverbank.

Kismet wasn't having it.

'We're walking across a field? Are you kidding? I wore my nice boots.'

Kismet lifted her foot up and rested her stacked heel on the console. 'Not budging, Gary.'

'Don't be a hardass. I wanna show you where I found the petrified bison tooth.'

'The tooth is cool, I concede that, but?' Kismet nicked her chin at some hunters in orange vests walking along the edge of a shelterbelt. Gary followed her look.

True, getting shot at wouldn't make her want to marry him.

'Hey.' She plucked the box from the cup holder and before he could speak she opened it. 'A ring.' She put it back. 'Let's go home.'

He scooped up the box and begged her to wait.

'Give that to your mom,' said Kismet.

'I'm going down on my knees.'

'In the car?'

He swung the car out and the box rattled back into the cup holder. Kismet braced herself as they fishtailed on a gravel section road and then careened into the presence of a deserted farmhouse overgrown with giant thistles. Baby trees reached through the tousled shingles of the roof. Gary stopped the car with a jolt and turned to her in torment. He couldn't speak. His agonized good looks melted her heart.

'Awww, don't look at me like that.'

'Marry me.'

Kismet blurted that she had a boyfriend, though that wasn't strictly true.

'I don't care!'

Gary grabbed the box and offered the ring to her. His hands were shaking. He'd lost weight since last March and the hollows in his cheeks gave him an eerie authority. Kismet tried to turn away, but she couldn't move. His desperation paralyzed her. He grasped her hand, wouldn't let go, and before she could react the ring was on her finger.

'Ahhh, ahhh, ahhh,' she managed.

'Yeah? Did you say yeah? You said yeah!'

Gary threw himself across the storage console and the cup holder and was on her, weeping in a frenzy, 'Yes, yes, yes, oh my god I love you I'll do anything.' And so forth, on and on, alarming her and then as he quieted, convincing her of his passion, of his commitment, of his ardor, his adoration, and his love. For surely this was love, thought Kismet, this was the heights. She had conquered him. Her heart swelled. He would do anything and everything for her. How she herself felt about him didn't really enter into it at that point. He had never gone out for long with a girl. And all of a sudden he had dated Kismet, and everyone at school treated her with a mixture of skepticism and surprised respect.

Was it true, at least, that she found him tolerable?

Or was this something pulling at her a sense of the inevitable? Gary always got what he wanted, said everyone. But did she also want to be carried off into an exhilarating madness, for that was how he was acting, an insanity of love? Was this what passion felt like?

As they drove back the same way they'd come, Kismet put on the radio and didn't listen to the music. She tried to think. Gary had said that he didn't care if she had another boyfriend. Was her other boyfriend real if she never said his name? Maybe she didn't have to marry Gary Geist but could just be engaged to him for a while. She didn't really have to wear the ring, she decided. No harm in seeing where things went between them besides, well, sex, which they'd had, or almost had, behind an old grain elevator and on his friend Charley's basement couch. During football season Gary often stayed at Charley's house so he wouldn't have to drive out to the farm.

Gary was handsome, but Charley's attractions were on a different order entirely. His looks made people uncomfortable. Charley Jura, Knieval Rappatoe, and Harlan Gall were some of the guys who had been at that party. And there was Eric Pavlecky, Gary's best friend. Eric lived on a nearby farm and had been there too. Eric drove to school with Gary every day. He was the only one of those guys who ever said hello to Kismet between classes as they passed in the hall.

'Are you going to tell Eric?'

'He already knows.'

'About the ring?'

'Yeah, we drove up to Fargo. He was waiting in the car.'

'Did you show it to him?'

'I was going to, but he said it was your business and my business and I should keep it as a personal surprise. Were you surprised?'

'Yeah, really surprised.'

'As you may know,' said Gary, as though he was some kind of teacher, 'diamonds are from the time of dinosaurs. They are petrified carbon. Old as time.' After a drama-filled pause, he said, 'You are wearing a symbol of eternity.'

'Oh my god,' whispered Kismet before her throat closed. A sudden sweat leaked from her brow and armpits, alarming her as much as the ring had. The pressure of millions or even billions of years. She slipped off the ring and silently placed it in the cup holder. She had taken Mr. Blosnik's class too and was pretty sure that diamonds were even older than dinosaurs. A simmering nausea, a twinge of headache, and flushes of fear overtook the sweats as they drove along but subsided once they reached her house. He stopped the car, hopped out, but didn't get to her car door in time. Kismet was halfway up the broken concrete walkway. She waved. He blew her a kiss, then looked around to see if anyone else was watching. So he missed that she didn't blow a kiss back at him. She was already in her house. He took out the bison tooth. Held it for a moment, nodding his head in a silent prayer. People said he was lucky to survive what happened at the party, but there were times he thought being dead might be better. He slid back in, behind the wheel, and only when he was turning onto the highway, pounding the steering wheel, moaning to the radio, did he glance down at the cup holder and notice the glint of the ring.

The Scream

'Mom . . . ! Mom . . . !'

It was Kismet's panic call, coming from the entry. Crystal lurched to her feet and rushed over from the shambles of her little work desk. It was her night off. Kismet held her arms out and walked into her mother's hug.

'What happened?'

'Gary asked me to marry him.'

Crystal stepped away from her daughter and her hands flew up to her face.

'Mom, you look like *The Scream*.'

'Don't be sarcastic,' said Crystal. 'This is serious.'

Her hands dropped to her olive-wood cross. Kismet gave a resentful waggle of her fingers. Crystal saw that at least there was no ring, and gathered that Kismet hadn't said yes. She tried to control the relief in her voice, and said, 'Let's have a cup of tea.'

'I want the tummy tea.'

Kismet's voice was peevish, like a child's, and this was irritating to Crystal but she said, 'Sure.'

There was a small pot of honey in the middle of the round kitchen table. The pot was shaped like a beehive. Kismet sat down and looked at it while the water boiled on the feeble electric burner. She spoke in a mournful, deadened tone.

'Everyone knows bees live in boxes so where does this beehive shape come from?'

Her out-of-nowhere observation seemed a cry for help. But for Crystal to jump in with her opinion of Gary might drive Kismet straight into his tiresome but too-lucky jockish arms. She stalled, poured the boiling water through a strainer full of peppermint leaves, put the mugs on saucers with spoons, and brought the tea to the table.

'Maybe, uh, village life in England,' said Kismet, using her stagy faraway look. 'You see, it became a symbol!'

They maintained a short silence, blowing lightly across the hot tea. Crystal was sipping awkwardly, as though she had forgotten how to work her lips. She could see her own teenage strategies reflected, and it was distracting to remember how she used to thrash around in the quicksand of hormones and new emotions.

'How do . . . you feel about him?'

Crystal used the most neutral voice she could manage. To stop herself from saying too much she put her cup down and pinched the side of her knee.

'It could be, I think, that I love him,' said Kismet, looking at her mother as though she was having a serious revelation. 'In fact, I may be in love. In love. How does it feel? How did you feel about Dad, I mean, when you had me? You love him, I guess, but back then were you desperately in love?'

Kismet dipped her spoon into the honey hive and stared at the tea as the honey slipped off the spoon and dissolved. Then her face opened up like a soft beseeching flower and tilted toward her mother.

I've got to be really careful now, thought Crystal. Her marriage to Kismet's father was over. Crystal had thought this before, but there had always been some reason or another not to leave Martin. But this time she was pretty sure it was for real. She'd been delaying a break until Kismet graduated and was safely in college. Her heart squeezed in, out, in, out. She drew a calming breath. She mustn't speak of this! As happened so often since Kismet had become a teenager, Crystal pictured a rickety wooden bridge and plotted her way across.

'Desperately in love? I thought so,' she said.

'Thought so?'

'Thought those were my feelings back then, yes.'

She could see that Kismet had something to say but didn't want to shock her. Please god do not let her be pregnant, thought Crystal, and closed her eyes. But Kismet only had a question. 'Was it sex?'

'Partly.' Crystal opened her eyes. 'You're still on birth control, right?'

'Yeah. How much was sex? Give me the numbers.'

'The numbers?'

'Like a percentage.'

Crystal threw her hands out, miming idiotic shock. Then they slapped their hands over their faces and whooped with laughter until they couldn't breathe. Give me the numbers! Give me the numbers! Finally Crystal gasped, 'Eighty.' Kismet screamed and pretended to choke on her tea. At last Crystal couldn't take it, just couldn't take it anymore. She put her head down on the table and mumbled loudly.

'He's not good enough for you.'

Crystal sat up. Kismet's face had hardened almost imperceptibly. Now it was like they both had poker hands and were trying not to show their tells. Kismet broke first and took the mugs to the sink. 'He really loves me, Mom,' she said, looking out the window into their scorched brown sacred yard.

I am a dumbass, Crystal thought.

They were practically the same height, Kismet just taller by half an inch. They were pliable but sturdy women, not conventionally pretty in a contemporary way but more like 1930s movie stars with curled Cupid's bow lips, eyebrows dark and flared, faces classic ovals with prominent cheekbones, sharp jawbones. Without smiling, Kismet could put to work a devastating dimple that punctuated one side of her smile with a mark of irony or complicity. She had melty brown eyes, lush black lashes. Crystal's eyes had a sharper glint, for life had taught her to be suspicious. The two of them were curvy, flexible, with small arched feet made for high heels. They could walk for miles in heels with only minimal pain. Their languid-looking, plump hands were actually tough paws. Crystal's were steering-wheel-trained by the International, Kismet's were agile from bearing plates from heat lamps to tables. They were both hard workers, descended of Ojibwe field hands, potato pickers, dedicated bootleggers. In those old films, maybe they would have played the molls of gangsters. In fact

Crystal's maiden name was the same as that of John Dillinger's Menominee lady, Billie Frechette. She'd kept that name but allowed Martin to give Kismet his last name. Poe. Another dark name with a namesake whose hair curled around his temples. Crystal's and Kismet's hair wasn't poutily curled, but flat and dark. Crystal's was cut to her shoulders and Kismet's hung halfway down her back. When Kismet wanted to end a conversation, she gave her mane an emphatic toss. She did that now and walked up to her room, leaving Crystal at the bottom of the stairs.

Memory Math

Driving home with the ring glinting at him from the cup holder, Gary decided not to make a big deal of it. His mother had wanted to give Gary the money to buy the ring. Winnie knew everything, or almost everything, because he'd talked to her right after the party. She knew who, or maybe what, had visited him when he was stuck on the branch. She knew that it kept visiting, sometimes even during games. It was really a hardship on a farm family for a son to play football during the start of the sugar beet campaign. It seemed reasonable that with all that had happened he might not play this year, but it was his senior year. And he had other reasons. So they hired a harvest hand from town and Gary lifted or hauled beets as long as he could into the night and so what if he was failing

Speck's type of math? He knew a lot more math than Speck thought. You had to know a ton of math to farm. It wasn't really his fault. The teacher had it in for him, as everybody knew.

A few months before, his mom had worried about field chemicals. Ever since Diz had started using Gramoxone, which contained paraquat, she had been paranoid that he might slip up. A mistaken taste of the stuff would destroy your liver and kidneys. Even getting it on your skin was very bad. There was no antidote. Diz and Gusty were extremely careful, but she was still freaked out. And then there was the atrazine Diz used on corn. It was a chemical that tainted well water. Winnie was concerned mainly with atrazine's effect on the penis. Shrinking it or making it womanly. Why? She was trying to raise Diz's consciousness, she said. But it bugged Gary that she'd said anything so drastic. Of course, once school started he'd glanced around in the locker room. It seemed like he was normal, but then again, maybe the chemical had affected them all. Maybe the whole group skewed. He'd gone online, a lot in fact, not because he was addicted to porn, like they thought. Probably not. He had wanted to know how he literally measured up in the world. What he saw depressed him past bearing. There were so many kinds, and which kind was his? He realized that he could only see it from one angle, looking down, and it didn't really help to use a mirror. He flipped open his prized Razr V3 and took pictures of his penis from different angles. Among other things that happened this fall, Knieval had opened Gary's phone and scrolled through his photos. Then Knieval loudly claimed that he was scared to be alone with gay Gary, which in turn caused Gary to deck him during math, and so forth. At that point, Mr. Speck walked back into the classroom.

Gary was standing over Knieval, whose nose was bleeding down his face.

'Gary, did you hit Knieval?'

'Yeah.'

'Yes, sir.'

'Yeah, sir.'

Mr. Speck, who had a square head and heavy black eyebrows that jutted over his small shining black eyes. Mr. Speck, who had a mane of hair and a super-intelligent stare and was cool, for a math teacher, said the following:

'Did you study? Do you remember what exponentially means?'

'No . . . sir.'

Knieval was still on the floor. Gary looked down and Knieval was laughing at him with blood on his teeth. 'Get out of here,' said Speck to Knieval. 'And on your way to the principal do not drip blood on the floor.' Speck walked toward Gary with a book in one hand, and stood there with an air of patient contempt.

'It means, in a functional real-world application, Gary, it means something grows very quickly, gathers force, and before you even register its existence it is beyond your control. Maybe like when you gunned it down that hill? Right, Gary? Now, say you caused the deaths of two people and maimed one, you or maybe it was Eric, but the big money is on you. And when you did this you created ripped guts, torn hearts, brains overflowing with grief in three families, not to mention huge numbers of friends and even acquaintances in this small, close-knit town. In these families you created a large dark slash of grief and that, young Gary, never heals. It closes over, but it never heals. There is always a soft crater of agony in a family after that, a sinkhole spot that people flinch from. It will always hurt to touch and always be avoided. And so many people! So the harm you caused which began the moment you went full-out down that hill, or lost control or whatever you did, became exponential. Exponential is a terrible word for you because it goes beyond deaths, too. You are responsible for so much else: the good the people you caused to die might have done, lost. The loves they might have delighted, lost.

The children they might have raised, lost. Lost, lost, lost. Exponentially.'

Mr. Speck walked away. Gary rose in the silence of his peers.

For this, he'd taken Speck's math?

Gary was wearing his letter jacket because it was a game day.

His team. The Mighty Red. 63. He turned in a circle with his arms out, waiting for someone to make a joke. It didn't happen.

For this, he'd stayed alive?

Gary left math class, walked down the hall. He was steaming. He was shaking. Nobody would ever see him shake or cry. He veered through the doors of the empty gym and sat in the stands. The nameless, unbearable sensation welled up in him. He wanted to throw himself down to break his head, but with regret he thought it wouldn't work. The gym floor was made of wood. He felt his mind rushing back to that night on the river and how he should have handled it, but those thoughts were useless, useless, useless. The only thing to do was act normal. He got up. He went out. He knew that Kismet had social studies during third period. He paused outside her classroom. Instantly, his breath slowed and his heart calmed. There was something mysterious and magical about Kismet and dating her helped Gary feel sane. He suspected it was her Indian, oops, Native American, blood—though he never mentioned it again after the first time. Gary was awed by her effect on him, but for most of the years he'd gone to school with her she just seemed weird.

Nevermore

Like all mothers and daughters, both Kismet and Crystal went through Kismet's phases. Before she took a job and cleaned up her act, Kismet was a goth, a dollar-store goth, but wasn't that the point? One bleary night she self-dyed her shiny hair a harsh lusterless blue-black, set off her narrow eyes with thick black lines, and brushed her eyelids with gradations of purple and maroon. Crystal didn't react when Kismet came downstairs the next morning and went to school. So she upped the ante. Tried to be secretive about her stick and poke tattoos. Kismet and Martin had memorized some of their namesake Edgar Allan's work. Crystal caught a glimpse of the word nevermore on Kismet's shoulder blade and a raven that came out looking like a pigeon. She pretended not to notice. In truth, she was depressed about it for weeks. Kismet's clothes were from rummage sales or Thrifty Life, all black of course. Some she shredded artfully, others were ripped or worn thin already. Kismet was sent home for the slashes beneath her butt that went too high and showed violet panties. She was sent home again for sneaking out of the house wearing a T-shirt printed with fake breasts including nipples—she'd found the T-shirt in a garbage can.

'Stop wearing garbage!' Crystal yelled at her. She was on a 6 p.m. to 6 a.m. schedule and had been roused from crucial sleep by the call from the principal.

'All we can afford is garbage,' Kismet said.

This stung and Crystal teared up.

Kismet got all hangdog and mumbled she was sorry. Crystal just kept driving, allowed the misery to sink in, and wondered where she had gone wrong. Maybe she should have married Kismet's father, but it was not good business sense. If Martin got into financial trouble, and that seemed almost certain, she didn't want to be responsible.

'Is this some kind of punishment for me not marrying your dad?'

'No,' said Kismet. 'I respect that. I think it's cool.'

'Is this about me in any way?'

'Nah.'

'Then why?'

'I just don't like the way everybody acts. So I'm manifesting my difference.'

Although she was going to be exhausted at work, Crystal couldn't deny that she felt the same way and understood her daughter's rebellion. For one thing, it didn't seem to entail much drug use (that she could discern) or drinking (easier to discern) or sex (difficult to think about). In fact, her daughter didn't go on dates often or get caught up in the massive parties that Crystal would hear about from her book club, or from Dale, who usually gave her a ride to work. No, the main aspect of Kismet's flouting of convention was heavy makeup and her choice of clothes, and what was the point of arguing about that?

Not a Sad Lump

Clothes and hair were superficial markers, Kismet knew. But they meant a great deal in high school. However, things really got difficult only when she started being openly smart. She answered every question in class, beat everyone at chess, and counterattacked in casual disagreements with those she began to call her so-called friends. Even Stockton had said she was taking it too far. This wore her down. Sitting alone at lunch and being shunned could have made her into a sad lump, but instead she became harder. For letting her voice rage out and challenging Mr. Speck, Kismet was sent to the office to sit in the chair of shame. If a popular girl was sent to the chair, it was the chair of cool, but for anyone else it was humiliating to be seen through the walls of the glass-enclosed main office.

When the halls filled with students changing classes, she got those looks of curiosity, pity, or contempt, plus the freshman and sophomore boys grinning as they gave her the finger. There was just one kid who, instead of flipping her off, got sent to the principal in order to sit alongside Kismet. This was Hugo.

The Churl

Hugo dropped out of school after sitting next to Kismet in ninth grade.

'Why are you here?' she'd asked.

'I was bored.'

'I mean what did you do?'

'Started laughing. Blosnik's ear was full of shaving cream. Every time he turned his head, well, it was amusing?'

'No doubt.'

'So that's why I'm here.'

'No, I meant why are you even here at all? At school? You're a genius.'

'Me?'

'Yeah, idiot.'

The next day, Hugo wouldn't go to school. His mother and father dragged him to the double doors a few times, but Ichor and Bev just didn't have the heart to push him through. He was smart, he was brilliant, so they applied to homeschool Hugo and whitewashed the cold basement so he could have a place to study. They began saving up to buy him a computer, but he surprised them by scrounging parts from the local library and junior college. He assembled his own computer. And there he sat, in the basement, wearing fingerless gloves and a parka as he hunched close to the screen. During the late afternoons, Hugo worked at his mother's main-street bookstore, Bev's Bookery. Some days he rode in the truck with Ichor, sanding streets and filling potholes for the city. Sometimes he went out with his father to check fields and pastures. Or they might respond to complaints from neighboring farmers. Ichor, as county weed control officer, might advise farmers on weed eradication. Hugo earned his GED and began taking college courses. He wanted to grow up and start making money so he could ask Kismet out on a date. He cleared a number of hurdles. They'd started maybe or maybe not going out. If he was honest with himself Hugo knew it was on the maybe-not side.

But more could happen. All he needed was money and a car.

One day Kismet consented to take a walk with him in broad daylight and he mentioned the car.

'I don't care if you have a car,' said Kismet. 'What's it to me?'

They were walking by the park so they sat down on some bleachers.

'Privacy. Mobility. Maturity.'

'Some of the guys I know with cars are so immature. As for mobility, I get that.'

'Privacy?'

'Oh, I see what you're saying now. C'mon, Hugo.'

'C'mon what?'

'Nothing's going to lead to what you're thinking.'

'How come not?'

'Maturity. Yours, whether you have a car or not.'

'Why not just make out?'

'Oh sure. For you that would be like throwing a match on dry grass.'

'I'll keep a bucket of water handy,' Hugo said, bending over and giving her a kiss of true love.

'Hey, what's going on,' said Kismet. 'It's like you know how to kiss.'

'I did some research,' said Hugo.

'On a human subject?'

'No, no, I dream about you.'

She laughed. 'Really.'

'Also, at my mom's bookstore.'

A moment later she asked if it was one book in particular, and he said, 'A mélange.'

'Vocabulary word?' she asked.

He looked insulted. They were sitting behind the community center on the other side of the levee, overlooking the weedy hockey rink. They were just going to sit there a minute before walking the winding path through the park to the golf course. But they kept on kissing. After they finally got up they were a little dizzy and had to sit there a while longer. Finally, Kismet said, 'Walk me home, churl.' On the front steps, she punched him in the arm and said, 'Wake up! You're just a kid!'

Bev's Bookery

Mildew. Foe of books. October was damper and warmer now. Hugo busied himself with the airflow system he'd rigged up for the bookstore. He'd met Kismet again last night, this time on the edge of a parking lot. Now he was trying to distract himself. Tinkering with a dehumidifier, he decided it might be simpler to suck air into a gentle area of warmth heated by a coil and then to breathe it out—drier, fresher, spore free—without the emptying of tanks and the frequent breakdowns and constant changing of air filters. He tinkered maternally with his invention. The shelves of books were crisper, he had to say. No curled covers or sly moldering at the bookery. He was tired of the constant battle with mildew. Or was it that the tedium of such released his thoughts, emotions, and he'd begun to fear the drift of his untethered brain. . . .

He parked himself behind the desk. Planning his future helped. Spongy at first, sloppy. But he would tend these wobbly plans until they firmed up—like Jell-O—they'd still be shaky in any case. A customer rustled about on the other side of the romance shelf. It was Mary Sotovine, a large, frisky cherub, one of the store's book club members. He didn't want to talk to her, but as always, that didn't matter. He bent, frowning, over his jotted lists. He reared around himself a wall of concentration. But as usual Mary struck right through it with her powerful rays of cornball.

'Howdy doody!' she said.

Hugo gradually raised his eyes.

'Hello, Mrs. Sotovine. How may I help you?'

'You are so polite!'

She squeaked and cooed. Her curly mahogany brunette crown, held high by a huge blue plastic claw, wobbled in appreciation. He must attend to her. For, as she was another dark-haired woman, he saw her suddenly as part of a spiritual she-pack that included his true love. His mien softened. He looked at Mary Sotovine thoughtfully and said, 'I think I have something for you. A book you might enjoy. Maybe it's the next book club choice.' He pulled a tear-stained copy of *Eat*

Pray Love from the shelf and offered it to her. He had read it as he read everything—snarfed it down. Put himself in the author's sandals. This book had spoken to Hugo in his darkness and he bowed slightly as he extended the book in both hands.

Said Mary, reading the title, 'If you added Murder it would be perfect.' She only bought Romance or True Crime.

'The human search for love,' said Hugo, 'pairs well with the human search for meaning. And maybe it could solve a murder. Here. Bev's compliments.'

Hugo added a tattered paperback by Viktor Frankl and bagged the books, folding the plastic tenderly over the hardcover with original jacket and the stained search for meaning.

The Search for Human Meaning in the Context of Geological Time

Hugo cradled his head, hands over his sensitive ears, and stared into deep time. His textbook defined a super-eon as spanning billions of years and encompassing more than one era, which were units of millions. There was the Paleozoic Era, the Mesozoic Era, the Cenozoic Era. All derived from Greek terms for Ancient Life, Middle Life, and New Life. Millions of years. Periods, the Jurassic, or the Quaternary, which we are still in, were also millions. Epochs and ages were thousands. In the face of that, what does it mean to live moment to moment, as I am living? Each instant without knowing if she loves me seems like a super-eon, Hugo thought. Then, when I am with her, time collapses. Kismet is a collapsed super-eon. Hugo was a pompous thinker. *With Kismet, there is no time. Or perhaps we shoot between epochs on a ghost ship of desire.*

'I don't know,' he said out loud. 'I'm just trying to get this straight.'

Beneath his feet were boards. Beneath the boards a basement dug from a thirty-foot-deep tranche of top-soil and reinforced with common fieldstones, or glacial erratics. In the last decades of the eighteenth century, a geologist endlessly named Henri Louis Frédéric de Saussure noted boulders of a foreign granite scattered on top of limestone high in the Jura Mountains of Switzerland. '*Terrain erratique*,' he called them, using the Latin words *erratus* and *terra* to mean 'ground that has wandered.' The term was still used to describe stones left behind by glacial ice.

That is my heart, thought Hugo. My heart propelled into place by a massive force and left here, a lonely erratic.

Hugo put down his book because tears were leaking. He felt they had pooled in his heart because of his being faced with so much meaning. Sometimes the earth would capture a volume of ice and the land would form over it, mounding to create a dead ice moraine.

Then as the earth warmed, glacial tears would water the ground from within. You might end up with a temporary source of water or a glacial spring. These were common when North Dakota was responsibly inhabited, when dinosaur bones lay on the surface of Hell Creek and the Nile of the North, the Red River, was muddy but pure.

Now, in the valley, the aquifer was being tapped out to make perfect potatoes for McDonald's fries. There were no more secret bubbling springs.

Through the spears of snake plants and gaping hearts of monstera plants in the front windows, Hugo kept an eye on traffic. Early in the day, he had seen Gary passing by alone in his mother's car. Later in the day, Gary came from the other direction with Kismet. At least they weren't laughing. There were no visible signs of happiness. Kismet wasn't even smiling, but why was she with Gary Geist?

Why was she with Gary when the night before she'd been with him?

Eric's Plan for a Bella Notte

The Pavleckys were many generations removed from the first wave of Bohemian immigrants to flee conscription in the army of the Austro-Hungarian emperor. They still farmed and some still had land. Geist's land was close to Pavlecky's, and since Pavlecky farmed no sugar beets, Eric and his brother helped the Geists out after football practice, taking turns with the lifter or hauling beets from field to piling ground, as long as the rain held off. But one day Eric drove toward the fields in a downpour and there Gary told him that Kismet had refused his engagement ring.

'After she said yes, though. Maybe second thoughts?'

'Maybe.'

'How do I get her to take the ring?'

'You really want my advice?'

'I guess.'

'Wait. Give it time. Just wait.'

'Can't.'

'God, take a minute! You take everything too fast, man, it's all downhill with you.'

Gary didn't answer. And he didn't answer some more.

After a while Eric spoke. 'Forget I said that. I didn't mean like down that hill. Give her some time.'

'How much time?'

'Shit, I don't know! Don't rush it!'

'I mean like a week, two weeks?'

'A year, Gary. What's your hurry?'

'Eric, she's it for me.'

Gary spoke in a low, intense, unwavering voice of truth. Eric was moved to pity. He liked Kismet okay, or maybe more than he could admit, but he didn't like her sudden hold on his friend, not that she seemed to like it either.

'Okay, man. Listen up. Take her someplace special for dinner. A place with candles. Italian? Fargo. Bring her a rose, just one special rose. Not a carnation from the gas station. Go to the restaurant ahead. Ask them to make her a special dessert, like a chocolate bombe or something, and give them a message that you roll up like a scroll. Tell them to stick it in the dessert.

Tell them it's not her birthday but that you're going to pop the question. Tell them the question is written on the scroll. That you'll be on your knee beside the table. They can gather around if they want to watch her read the question, and oh, give somebody your Razr with the camera open just before you go down on your knee. You'll have the ring box open and when she says yes you'll put the ring on and they'll be snapping pictures and all that. Everybody will be crying, man, I guarantee.'

Eric was himself choking up a little. He'd made up the whole scenario on the spot. It was like he was right there. And he envied Gary. He'd gotten used to Gary having certain things, like the sleek phone he flipped open with a flourish of importance, as though he was taking a call that would make him a million dollars. Eric had gotten used to the pickup and the party barn and the big-screen. All of these things weren't going to erase what happened. But Gary acted like getting married somehow would. That might be true for Gary. It would never be true for Eric. He wished it would be true. He missed the turnoff.

When Eric got home, he brought a glass of his father's whiskey out to the old barn. He'd never done that before, but now was now. He listened to the hard rain come down and leaned against the flaking paint, the splintered wood, cradling the glass. The first few sips made him jumpy, loose, like his strings had been cut. Liquor did that to Eric, which was why he rarely drank and why he absolutely hadn't since the night of that party. People thought they knew what happened, but nobody knew what happened. Eric played tight end because he was a versatile football player and thought on his feet, as he had that night. Though he was better at football, he liked wrestling more. When he was straining to break a hold, he sometimes faked a weakness in the part of his body where, in fact, he was gathering power. His opponent might relax an iota and he could with surprise effect a reversal. Reversal! Reversal! The crowd would be chanting and it was in such a moment that he made a move that caused Coach Jaws to peptalk him by insisting that he had a lot more talent than he knew and should believe in himself. But Eric thought that this capability of his—deception—only seemed to manifest when he was cornered. He had been cornered the night of the party, he had deceived, and it had been for other people, to spare them. When he reversed a near pin it was for other people too. Because they implored him.

He could hear the river now, across the field, running unusually high for fall. As usual last spring, the high school had filled sandbags and surrounded vulnerable neighborhoods and farms. He loved doing that because he loved working together with other people. In those hours, a common purpose. Nobody to deceive. Everything simple and clear, the way things never would be again, not for him.

Icy Hot

A brutal night of the worst weather possible—freezing rain. Crystal's truck bed was sprayed with antifreeze, but a drizzle combined with a hard frost turned to black ice on the road. Misery gripped her lower back. She turned down an access road marked out by huge mist-haloed halogen lights and then churned fearfully across a field of freezing mud. Crystal got her truck loaded from the five-hundred-yard-long pile, dreading how the beets at the bottom of the load would freeze to the truck bed on the way to the plant. Her neck and shoulders spasmed at the thought. Sure enough, as soon as the truck tipped on the lift and the beets didn't roll out, she had to get out the poking pole, long and heavy. Crystal started gouging at the last beets and worked until her biceps trembled and the back of her neck went numb. Finally Dale drove up in line and gave her a hand.

'That was killer,' she said. 'I don't know how I'll last the night out.'

'You still got that Icy Hot?'

'Yeah. You still got that jalapeño beef jerky?'

'Teriyaki. I'll stick close as I can behind you and trade you every time we get back?'

'Deal. And I'll throw in max Tylenol.'

'We'll get through this shit.'

Dale was good stuff, decent and quiet, a lot like Diz Geist, at least what Crystal knew from Winnie. Not a man of open feelings, but predictably good-hearted and reliable to the last. Crystal made a pit stop at the bathroom in the shop. It was much better than the Porta Pottys at the pile, but also she needed a tiny break. Driving back out this time, she felt the night warm a little and sensed grit on the road even through the heavy tires. She relaxed enough to tune in to a Ringer show she wanted to hear. It was on the economy, what had happened, why it was happening, what was in the future. She was hoping like everyone else to figure out how this could affect her family and how she could avoid the worst.

What Crystal heard made the night darker. First of all, it had snowed in the desert, though what that had to do with the economy she didn't know. Crystal heard that President Bush was little more than a bewildered bystander. The word meltdown got a lot of play. The asset drain had begun to gurgle on Wall Street. There were ironies heaped on ironies. Printing money was mentioned. The Weimar Republic. Massive bank failures and dismal Christmas retail. The U.S. going into another Great Depression. Only this would be worse because in 1929 people didn't have credit cards and the country wasn't thirteen trillion dollars in debt. Twenty-five percent unemployment was coming.

Crystal had some Halloween Butterfinger bars and ate them all at once. And that night she rolled on more Icy Hot, decided not to complain about the poker pole, and to do everything she could to keep her job.

Skillet in the Sky

Ponytail. Blue T-shirt with cloud-in-skillet logo. Black jeans and apron. If possible, black running shoes. Skillet in the Sky. Or just the Skillet. It wasn't a bad place at all if you didn't mind the food. Everything about the place was inspired by the Norman Greenbaum hit 'Spirit in the Sky,' misheard by the owner's daughter as skillet in the sky. So misheard because her father, Val Kallinor, immortalized in town lore for having brought a dildo to his kindergarten class show-and-tell, became a passionate home cook and could not bear to have his cast-iron skillet defiled by soap. It was treated like a holy object. When he heard his young daughter's version of the 1970 megahit, Val was inspired. He invested a small inheritance in a going-out-of-business restaurant at the end of main street, and from the beginning people loved it. The only problem was that Val couldn't translate his recipes from home to restaurant. He talked a lot about that with Hugo's father, Ichor Dumach, and sometimes Ichor came in to test recipes. They still hadn't perfected a signature dish. But the theme took up the slack and his place could afford to hire staff from outside the family. Thus, Kismet. During the week she waited tables. On weekends if it was busy, she filled in at the grill cooking breakfast.

Four days a week, she walked or hitched a ride from school, ate a sandwich of choice, usually the Norman (baked ham and cheese with secret sauce), and started working at four. She worked until eight or nine with a swing-shift partner, Melly or Roselle or Stockton, one of whom would close at eleven. Roselle was the daughter who'd misheard the song and said she sure as fuck was paying for it now. Melly was a young single mom whose mother could only take care of her kids in the evening. Stockton had borne the goth years and stayed Kismet's best friend, even though Kismet listened to that whiny Lilith Fair CD mix and scoffed at Britney. If things were slow, Kismet would do her homework in a booth and help Stockton close out the register, vacuum, and wipe down the booths. Then they'd hang out while one of the cooks closed up the kitchen, eating the last batch of french fries or whatever else. If Trevor was in the mood, he'd make an extra Norman for them to split.

'Gary tried to give me a ring,' said Kismet. 'Here.'

She pushed over french fries tasting of the Miracle, a deep-fried fish patty on a bun. Stockton pushed them back across the table. They were in the booth closest to the kitchen, always the booth for staff.

'Was it at least a nice ring with a big rock?'

'What? How do I know and what would I care?'

Because Stockton hadn't had an obvious phase of weirdness or rebellion, she knew more than Kismet about the boys they'd gone to school with all their lives. She knew that all the popular boys in their grade, except maybe Eric, had decided Kismet was a slag, a slut, a null, solely on the basis of the way she dressed. They were caught up short when Gary started going out with her. They'd be happy to treat her like shit again once he dumped her. Typical of boys and why Stockton had decided dating was a futile waste.

Stockton leaned over and stacked up their plates and glasses.

'Look, my friend, the world's bigger than one guy among a bunch of dumb jocks who'll be over once this season's done and there's no more football for the rest of their lives. Turn him down and move on. And don't mess with me. I know about Hugo. He's a homeschool weirdo now but he's a genius and you like him. You like him better than you like Gary.'

'Maybe.'

'Okay. You're starting to be a drag. Let's go over to your house.'

They left as Trevor locked up and took the ride he offered to Kismet's house. Her dad, as usual, was still in rehearsal for a community theater production somewhere and Crystal was hauling. Kismet and Stockton left their shoes in the cold entryway and stepped into the living room with its saggy blue floral couch, television set, built-in bookshelves, and banged-up coffee table. The big, square, forgiving cushions of the couch were comfortable and Crystal didn't care if you put stockinged feet on the coffee table or if you ate popcorn long into the night. Stockton's mother was more exacting, but she was a lawyer.

Ow

If he'd owned a car, they could have gone somewhere and had a more persuasive encounter, he imagined, a better date than they'd had so far. But he still didn't have a car so they met in the playground outside the airfield, under the carcass of a restored fighter jet that was filled with gossiping sparrows.

'I thought I should tell you,' she began.

'What?'

'Gary proposed.'

'To you?'

'Duh.'

This was a million times worse than being a lonely glacial erratic. His head began to vibrate. He eased himself onto a swing and planted his feet. His voice was a weak thread.

'Are you getting engaged to him because I don't have a car?'

'That again. No. Are you assuming I said yes?'

'Well, didn't you?'

'Not yet.'

His heart creaked open. A beam of light struck his left ventricle.

'Ow,' he said and rubbed his chest.

'What's wrong?'

He reared up like a comic book hero, gazed hotly over his shoulder, and threw off his tractor hat. His hair ruffled in the cold breeze.

'*Volim te*, my little pancake.'

He was learning to say I love you in every language he could find. He made her laugh.

'What was that one?'

'Croatian. My dad works with a guy.'

She sat in the other swing, he sat back down too, and they held hands, chatting, swinging. When it grew dark they got into the big round tube slide and began to make out at the gentle level end. He had such a delicate touch, strong hands hard from helping his dad with woodwork and sensitive from typing on a keyboard. He paused between kisses to sort of let each kiss become profound. They were wearing puffy insulated coats and hoods so they weren't cold at all, and their feet in padded boots stuck out at the end of the slide. He put his hand between the snaps of her coat and beneath her fleecy sweater. She shivered. His hand left a trail of heat. They didn't want to leave each other but she had promised to finish out Stockton's night shift. Eventually, they walked over to the Skillet.

'C'mon in. Have a coffee.'

He sat in the booth by the kitchen. She poured him a cup of coffee and took care of the other customers. She brought him the last piece of lemon meringue pie. The meringue was gummy and tipping off the lemon.

'Would you like an unclaimed bacon cheeseburger?'

Hugo looked lovingly at her. His cinnamon freckles, his long arching red-gold eyebrows and lashes, his coppery prickly hair, his skin darker than a normal redhead's, his mouth so alive and his eyes so brown and avid. He was chubby, yes, always so warm. She touched his hand, got an electric shock. They wrung their hands and pretended to wince.

'Unclaimed from when?' he asked.

'Hey, beggars can't be choosers.'

'I'm not a beggar, foolish maid, I'm a god in disguise.'

'Here. Put a lot of ketchup on it.'

Martin Poe

Kismet's father was driving an hour to rehearsals every day and could barely afford the gas. Which was by no means the worst of it. He had persuaded Father Flirty that he was an investment guru who drove an old car like Warren Buffett and had an in with Homobonus, the patron saint of stockbrokers. Then, in August 2008, the ground had tilted. On September 29 a sinkhole had opened. Now it would swallow everything—the church portfolio he'd assembled, as well as their own livelihood. It would decimate the secret nest egg Crystal didn't think he knew about. But no, she kept moving it around. It was probably safe, so why should Crystal and Kismet care? They thought they had it made. Crystal had job security. (What's more secure than sugar—nobody's going to stop eating sugar.) They thought they weren't part of the economy.

He thought these things as he drove I-29. Here and there another pile of bulldozed trees was smoldering. Wasn't burning them illegal? Or maybe not. This was a soggy fall. Every foot of farmland made money and by next spring another well-grown stand of windbreak trees would be forgotten. Ichor had told him that it all went back to Earl Butz, who told farmers to plant their crops fence row to fence row.

Economy of scale to maximize profits minimize loss. This too applied to Martin, but invisibly. He was officially a traveling theater arts teacher all through southeast North Dakota. Unofficially he was a failed actor and pretty much a volunteer. Beyond all this he was a lonely Michif. As was Crystal. They were Turtle Mountain people who snagged each other in an oxbow on the Red River and got stuck there, like trash in the tree branches, Grandmother Happy had said. But she was mean. It was more that they had followed their jobs, legal ones, he'd said to Happy. That's what responsible parents do when they have a child. Happy had tried her stink eye on him but Martin only laughed.

That was the other reason they were isolated. They did not want to be around Happy or anyone related to her or any of her husbands, and that was almost everyone. Crystal seemed to like her job well enough, and he still had hopes, though often he just kept driving around North Dakota scouting locations for invisible scenes in his head.

He loved his students, when he had any students, and they loved the stage, if there was a stage. For most of them it was salvation. Martin pledged himself to remain an actor and love the stage come what may, even with what was befalling the world. Of course, not a single young person, none of the teachers in the occasional teachers' lounge, so much as mentioned what was happening. Though they talked about housing on and on. Nobody seemed to care about the big house, the economy, even as the foundations crashed and burned.

Martin got out of the car and made his way toward a sock-smelling gym. Well, the teachers weren't financial experts. Sometimes an actor plays a part so well he just becomes it. So Martin could still count himself among the experts because like the most expert of the experts he was getting blown out of the water. He was working hard to save what he could. It was lucky for his mental survival that he could always return to his true home. Drama. And that he liked off-brand peanut butter. He slipped into the gym, sat down, and ate his sandwich slowly as he followed the scene.

He loved sitting in the front row and doing line

readings for the cast. He absolutely loved *Three-penny Opera*—how perfect for the times. He wished it wasn't. He could do this show every night of his life if he could only cast a good Pirate Jenny. Tonight, up on the stage, a scrawny, shy, wilting girl from West Fargo with her bucket and scrubbing rag was attempting the iconic song. As always, when he tried to coach ferocity out of Pirate Jenny, he thought of Crystal's audition. Their first meeting. *Crystal,* he'd thought, hearing her first delicate notes, a soubrette, *hard as a diamond with winking facets.* Then she opened her voice out and he'd felt the back of his neck tingle. She had a pure wide soprano of harrowing clarity. Not only that! She went to a dangerously weighted mezzo and blew his mind when she unloosed the black freighter he still feared was in her soul. *Turns around in the harbor, shoo. ting. from. the. bowwwwww . . .*

Ohhhh dear. He returned to the shy young woman with the adequate voice, who tried a wavery shooting-a-pistol sort of gesture.

He held his hand up. She stopped.

'Cannons would be the things shooting, you need a bigger gesture,' said Martin. But he honestly couldn't think of an appropriate one to give her.

'Just hold your arm out,' he finally said. The young woman raised a limp arm and flopped the scrubbing rag.

Martin pulled the old Mazda into the driveway. The car was buckled on one side (just a superficial crater). He got out, trudged wearily up the wooden stairs, chased by driving rain. In the entry he heard the television, and as he walked into the living room he saw lumps of girl on the couch, a movie still playing, the popcorn bowl on the coffee table, and a grocery-store jug of grapefruit juice on the floor. As he walked up to peer over the back of the couch, popcorn kernels shattered under his stockinged feet. Now the bits would stick to his socks. He hopped around removing each sock. He made a ball of the socks and went to the kitchen, threw the sock ball down the basement stairs toward a dim pile of wash. He sat down at the kitchen table and stared at a place-mat diagram of a sperm whale and a human being. He tried to think, but that was useless. He didn't know what to do, so he slogged past the balls of girl on the couch and went to bed.

The next morning Martin went to early Mass and stayed after to discuss business with Father Flirty. They had coffee in the church kitchen and discussed the plate and envelope count, pledges, bequests. Crystal always got Kismet off to school, after which she'd sleep through the day. Martin came home and crept through the door, shutting it gently so as not to wake her. He did some quiet work before leaving again for rehearsal. Sometimes he worried that he was home only to give the illusion of stability, he saw so little of Crystal and Kismet. And he knew what he called his 'vital necessities' irritated them. He'd had expensive tastes, true, but that was in the past now. He missed really good coffee. The church coffee tasted of sackcloth and ashes. His joie de vivre was fading. No drinkable wine. No song! Crystal used to sing with him. At some point it had become an effort. He missed the lightness of their early days. There wasn't even much conversation. Sometimes he felt that he'd used up his words memorizing lines and inventing characters as he anxiously drove around wasting gas and worrying about wasting gas. What a limp fish he had become, he thought. Where was his flair? He must not give in to gloom or allow Crystal to grow distant. Their ancestors had hunted on horseback, then settled down to plant gardens and beg help from the Blessed Virgin. They would have overjoyed by the Mazda, the highways, the boiler in the basement, and the popcorn in the carpet.

The Missing Cheese

There are things you never see until you're paying all the bills, thought Crystal. A small leak she had once detected in an increased water bill, but didn't follow up on, became a thousand-dollar drain over a couple years and then digging up the lawn to get at the source took up almost all of her savings. Hard to forget. Something like this was occurring now when she balanced the household account. The leak had started tiny, as before, a few dollars extra on the debit card she and Martin shared. She thought at first it was something to do with Martin's work—the necessities of drama or his personal treats. When the leaks widened to forty, fifty, and at last a hundred dollars, Crystal sat him down. She tapped on the numbers.

Martin tipped his head down and when he looked

up he was smiling gently, in the old way he used to, his eyes dreamy and warm.

Okay, it wasn't always an extraneous circumstance that made her decide to stay with Martin, one year, another year. His charm still worked. She caught his gentle excitements, his secret glances of amusement, his joking Michif ways. He took her hand and made his soul shine out.

'We're going to sing together again,' he said. 'Become a romantic duo. Tour the bars. Crystal and Martin.'

She wanted to keep this moment going, so she didn't speak. Maybe he meant it, or maybe he just didn't want to talk about money.

His hands were always warm, his feral grip like some woodland creature, maybe a bear but he wasn't hairy. She decided that the leak of money was attached to something like his craze for Red River jigging, salsa dancing, jujitsu, learning how to heal with hot stones, baking medieval style, pickling radishes, traditional beadwork. This was none of these things. He pulled Crystal outside to the shed and showed her a bicycle that was mostly green with a few yellow components. He held out his hands, palms up, and declared that the family needed another mode of transportation besides the one car. He also said that he had made the bicycle, cobbled it together from other bicycles, which were there, too, tucked behind boxes.

'Are we going to tour the bars by bicycle?' asked Crystal.

He gave her a conspiratorial smile. 'It's a very fine conveyance, only the best. I'm not going to paint it all one color because nice bikes get stolen.'

Crystal was surprised because she'd never seen a tool in Martin's hands. His fingers were made for childish card tricks, for gesturing, chin stroking, nose tapping, earlobe pulling, and intimacies. For Martin, this was a rare attempt at being practical. And he was right. The productions he worked on were taking him farther afield.

'We've got a teenage driver,' said Martin. 'We can't let her take the war pony out enough. She needs some way to get around.'

The war pony he referred to was their sand-colored beater. Kismet had her license but mainly caught rides with Stockton when Jeniver let her use their car. They walked back to the house. Martin slung his arm over Crystal's shoulders. She didn't mind him at that moment, but still thought she would leave him. He emanated a sort of hopeful sadness and contained the usual secrets. Crystal had once thought he owned some interior dramas and interesting thoughts, but then she went to great trouble to find out everything, only to fail. Martin either had no intention of revealing himself, or there was no ulterior self to reveal. He'd quote playwrights though, like Brecht.

'What happens to the hole when the cheese is gone?' he said to her now.

'There is an economic meltdown,' she answered.

It scared Martin that, after all, she knew.

The Lord's Ivy

Martin's family name had been Poésie until about a hundred years ago, when his family dropped three letters for the freedom of a single syllable. Martin and Crystal went to the same college, dropped out of the same college, and in their early twenties moved south through the cultural corridor of the Fargo Moorhead area. They followed sugar beet jobs down to Tabor, and the sugar beet plant. Martin was a boiler (of sugar beet juice) and to begin with Crystal worked office and packing jobs at the plant.

Their people had skirmished back and forth over this territory with the Dakota, and then truced just in time to have it stolen. Like the mighty red, history was a flood.

While working in her garden, Crystal had appreciated

how their families were like the Lord's ivy, a weed in-eradicable by human means. It grows low to the ground and can't be mowed. It throws its stems long and roots straight down every few inches, just like the people along the river. There seems to be a Frechette or a Poe any-where you land, but low-key, invisible. The Lord's ivy, or ground ivy, creeping charlie, thrives under the leaves of other plants and goes wherever it is not wanted. It just keeps throwing itself along stem by stem and blooms so modestly you'd hardly mark the tiny purple flowers. People step down and pass, the weed springs up, un-crushable.

Somewhere in the welter of stems, leaves, and flowers, Crystal had inherited a gene for thrift. After Martin's cheese quote, she decided that she would drain the custodial savings account she'd opened for Kismet at birth. She would deposit a lesser amount than usual in the joint account with Martin and add the rest to the secret cash she was keeping in cardboard document envelopes. They were taped beneath an old tool cup-board behind the boiler in the gloom of their damp, creepy basement. Crystal knew Martin had figured out her previous hiding places, but was pretty sure he was too fastidious to put his hand underneath the tool cupboard.

The Second Proposal

E ric's advice rolled around in Gary's head and he
decided to make a few adjustments. For one thing,
the venue. Driving up to Fargo and back plus eating
would take an entire night and that wouldn't work
during the beet campaign. The rains had interrupted
everything. You just went and went until the true hard
freeze, so there wasn't time to spare. He decided to propose at the only restaurant in town with candles, Pookie's Valley Steakhouse. Pookie's was on the outskirts of
town in a modest brick farmhouse surrounded by new
prefab split-levels and various dealerships. Inside, there
was an old-fashioned carved-oak bar salvaged from a
railroad hotel, and places set up with tables and chairs.
There was fairly soft lighting in the rooms. Lots of

plants. He made their reservation and called Flossom's
Blossoms to order the one rose.

'One rose?'

'I mean, it's classy, right?'

'Cheap. It says cheap, Gary.'

His mistake had been giving his name to sharp, har-
ried, opinionated Mrs. Flossom. She let him know that
he wouldn't impress a girl with the one rose, especially
if, as he told her, he meant to propose marriage.

'For a proposal, you want a statement floral piece.
Who are you popping the question to, may I ask?'

'You know Kismet Poe?'

'Her mom's in my book club. I don't happen to think
crap of the dad. And Kismet's always running around
in ripped clothes, including fishnet tights.'

'How about a dozen?'

'Of what?'

'Red roses.'

'And what would you like the card to say?'

'No card. I'm picking them up.'

'What time tomorrow?'

'Five.'

'You got it. She's a lucky little hush-my-mouth. No,
I take that back. Actually, I don't know why any girl in
this town would go out with you.'

'Hey, forget it. I can get flowers at the gas station.'

'Relax, Gary. Ready for your card number.'

'It's my mom's card.'

'I thought so.'

After he closed his phone, Gary fell into a sullen, defeated mood. Still, he'd gone forward with his plan the next night and dropped the roses off early at Pookie's. Now he was on the way to pick Kismet up for the dinner. He couldn't sit still, bounced around in the pickup. And when he passed Jordan on the road driving in the opposite direction, he nearly made a U-turn and chased the fucker down.

Of course, it got him thinking about the party, and how Jordan had been so happy. Also, super-loaded was Jordan at that party. But never mean or depressed or baleful, at least until they were racing downhill that night. Gary had tried to stop him, thought he remembered, anyway, hadn't he? And Travis, there was nothing he could have done about Travis, except not go on the river at all.

A Black Eye at Pookie's

As they drove across the river, Gary's fingers tight-ened on the steering wheel and his mind kept flowing the wrong way. His foot lifted off the accelerator because the sensation of speed sometimes made the pictures worse. He saw the branch poking up through his jacket, sharp, black against the snowy sky, a spear that grazed his body so lightly there was only a skid mark and very little blood when they got him into the ER. Then he remembered that Travis had worked at Pookie's. He slowed down and nearly made a U-turn. But Gary was afraid he'd see Jordan back there and the hideous mantle of fear would lower onto him. Kismet disrupted all that by reclining her seat. That's all it took. A small movement, a squeak as she yawned and dropped her head back, and he was in the present time.

This was why he had to marry her. He couldn't take Jordan anymore. Or these mental lapses either. He had to get her to say yes and he had to put the ring on her finger, tonight.

The sun was nearly down when they drove into Pookie's parking. It was a Sunday so less packed than usual. The entry was raw with the swirl of cold wet air and dripping snow; people were shucking off coats and boots, putting on shoes they'd brought along in plastic bags. When that was sorted out, the hostess, a rangy square woman with pink plastic eyeglasses and a curly brown bob, seated them. Gary had the ring in his pocket and the paper scroll tucked down the neck of his sweater. He excused himself and went back to the kitchen, a madhouse. He wanted to ask for a special dessert. A bleak, stringy fry cook at the griddle looked up. He recognized Gary and gave him a glare of contempt, then turned back to his work and ignored Gary's words.

Gary went back out front and found the hostess. 'Where did you put the roses?' Now she too had become hostile, as if she'd thought things over.

'Behind the bar,' she said in a low voice. 'You have your nerve coming in here.'

Gary walked toward the dining room. He was beginning to feel unreal. Maybe they should leave. The red roses were behind the bar, though, so that was good! He paused. The servers were charging back and forth across the industrial carpeting. Pressed against a pastel wall, Gary waited until he saw the one who'd given Kismet the menu.

It was Grace Stigley, a girl he'd gone out with as a freshman. She had slapped him for some reason when they broke up. Also, he remembered she'd gone out with Travis. Passing him in the hall, Grace looked surprised, then screwed up her face with either grief or spite. His plans were fucked. In fact, when he got back to the table Kismet said she didn't want to eat at Pookie's. Grace had jokingly told her she might throw rat poison on their food. Kismet worked at the Skillet. She got the message.

'Seriously,' said Kismet. 'We shouldn't be here.'

'How about,' said Gary, inspired, 'if we sit at the bar?'

Kismet was reluctant, but Gary managed to convince her it would be okay. The old-fashioned bar was in a different room entirely, and for the time being it was quieter. It wasn't a table where they could gaze into each other's eyes, but maybe he could wink at her reflection in the mirror. It would be just the two of them at one end and beyond them a dark picture window. Distantly, the sugar beet processing plant with its plume of steam was framed, spectral against the dark sky. They took barstools and he insisted that she order a steak.

'I don't like steak.'

'We can drink wine now. We're eighteen.'

'I know,' said Kismet. She'd been a few weeks shy of voting, and she'd wanted to cast a historic ballot. Gary didn't care.

'I'll have a glass of house white,' she said.

'Say, bartender? Do you have champagne?'

'Ooooh, the bubblaaaay. Let me look out back.' The bartender flung down his rag and clomped away.

'I won't drink it. Why champagne? Is it that ring again?'

'We can't make him go out back for nothing.'

'Don't propose to me, Gary.'

The bartender brought back something with a wired-on cork and put two wine goblets and an ice bucket on the bar. He carded them, stared at their driver's license pictures, snorted, threw the bottle in the air, and barely caught it. The ice bucket said Holiday Inn on the side.

'Like my wine bottle trick? This champagne is a first!' said the bartender as he exuberantly twisted off the wire and forced the cork, which shot off violently and struck Kismet beneath her left eye, knocking her off the stool. Gary jumped down to help her up, but she had already rolled over and was standing.

Grace just happened to be passing through the bar. She leaned against the wall with her arms folded and saw the whole thing. She gasped and doubled over, hitting her thigh.

'Sorry,' said the bartender, clearly not sorry. 'It's on the house. We only had this one bottle.'

'Did you hear that?' said Gary. 'On the house.'

'Oops,' said the bartender. The bottle slipped out of his hands but didn't break; he picked it up and tried to pour.

Kismet moved Gary's glass and the bartender kept pouring onto the bar. She wrenched the bottle from his hand and said, 'Bring me a Diet Coke.'

'With ice, ma'am?' asked the bartender, round-eyed with fake solicitude.

'Fuck yes, you turkey,' said Kismet. She'd had enough and had now gone outside herself with fury. She leaned over and started to pour the bottle into the sink.

'Let's not . . . ,' said Gary.

'And I'll take steak after all,' said Kismet, righting the bottle, pouring the last of it into Gary's glass. She settled herself back on the stool. 'The top sirloin, also on the house. Raw.' She told the bartender, 'I mean cold raw. If it touches flame I'll burn you down. I'm going to hold it underneath my eye.'

'Awww, really?'

Grace was still propped up against the wall.

'Shut up and die,' said Kismet to her. Grace mooched away, still laughing but with an undertone of hysteria, as if she might break into tears.

Gary reached out and squeezed Kismet's fingers. 'Oh, honey.' She flung his hand off.

At least the bartender brought the cold red top sirloin. Kismet looked at herself in the mirror behind the sparkling glass bottles, holding cold steak underneath her eye with a napkin. Going out with Gary was, she now saw, hazardous. She had to share his perilous position here in Tabor. It was dawning on her that what she thought of as surprised respect from other people in town might be just surprise.

'We shouldn't have come here,' she said.

'We'll be okay!'

She examined her reflection more closely in the bar mirror.

She could have gone to the ladies room, but who knew what would happen to her in there? Her hair was still piled in a topknot and it looked like her eyeliner hadn't even smeared. She was wearing a cap-sleeved black 1950s cocktail dress and a boa of iridescent black rooster feathers. Her sheer black stockings had seams up the back of her legs and her slingback kitten heels were mint condition—all thrift finds. This outfit had sunk her mother's heart when Crystal realized that Kismet was wearing it out on a date with Gary.

'I don't want you to propose, Mr. Gary Geist,' said Kismet, swinging her leg. She kept the steak pressed on her eye and sipped the Diet Coke. 'But you can tell me of your undying love all you want while I sit here. Where's this coming from?'

Gary, nervously smoothing down his gray crew-neck sweater and charcoal gray dress pants, caught his breath when she said his formal name—it felt flirty and he slugged down the dregs of the sparkly wine to steady himself.

'What can I say? I guess you know everything,' he said.

'I don't know where the ring, where that was coming from.'

'West Acres.'

'Give me a break, Gary. Why me?'

'Because you're the most beautiful—'

'Yes but no I'm not.'

'The smartest—'

'Yes but no I'm not.'

'Because I like your feather scarf.'

'Okay. I'll accept that.'

'And you excite me.'

'Oh god, you heard that in a stupid movie. Can't you say something original?'

'You give me a mental hard-on,' he said.

'No, no, no, no.'

Kismet pulled the feather boa over her face to hide her horrified expression. Gary continued, 'You complete me. You give me a funny feeling that runs up my spine and around my neck and down my chest and squeezes the breath out of my lungs. Um, you make me crazy! Um, Miss Kismet Poe.'

Gary went around the back of the bar, picking up the dozen red roses in their thick glass vase. He removed the plastic sleeve and put them on the bar in front of Kismet. Then he spoke, looking straight into her eyes.

'What can I say? I'm scared and you make me feel safe.'

Kismet dropped the boa back to her shoulders, reached down, and accepted the dripping roses. She put them back in their vase. The way he'd spoken to her straight on had at last touched her. Maybe she was beginning to get the picture. Safe. Somehow she made him feel safe. Funny thing, she also felt safe with him. Their food came. Gary ate with sad-eyed intensity. She kept the meat beneath her eye with the napkin over it as she ate. The baked potato was a little difficult to manage one-handed, but she easily forked up each tough green bean and gnashed it to a stringy pulp. They didn't speak. Kismet knew she'd gotten the truth and was trying to think what to do with it. Gary was appalled he'd told the truth and afraid of what she would do with it. Gary looked into the mirror to try meeting her eyes, and saw Jordan behind them, passing by outside in the hallway, wearing his football jersey with the upside-down number. He was carrying his helmet too, but at least he had his head on straight.

The Scroll

When Gary turned back to his ravaged T-bone and the second glass of beer he'd ordered, he remembered the scroll. This wasn't over. No, no! Dessert was yet to come. Kismet still had the steak beneath her eye and she was looking at herself in the bar mirror and laughing as she sang *M-m-m-m-ma poker face.* He looked at her the way he'd seen his father look at his mother, with fond indulgence. She seemed a little tipsy, because now she'd added to her soft drink a whiskey shot or two.

'Let's get some chocolate cake,' said Gary. He'd used his best handwriting for the proposal and the scroll was actual stationery.

'No thanks. We should go.' She put the steak down and dug in her little handbag. 'Here's my half for dinner.'

'They already took the credit card,' said Gary.

'Well, be sure you get it back. And take this anyway.' She gave him two tens.

'I won't take it.'

He stuffed the money back into her bag and reached down the neck of his sweater. 'C'mon, have some cake.'

He pinched the scroll up through the neck hole of his sweater. Kismet eyed the creamy rolled paper.

'What's that?'

'Read it.'

She wouldn't accept it.

'Look, Gary. You told me your reasons. I guess I have some questions. I mean, how come you need to be safe. Are you scared?'

'I shouldn't have said that. I can't really explain it. Just trust me.'

'This is all kind of sudden, Gary,' she said, carefully. 'Plus, I mean, that cork hurt. Maybe we should just be—'

'Don't say it!'

He'd shouted. He put his hand over his mouth and looked around the place. People were leaving now, throwing on their coats and jamming their feet into boots. Still jabbering and laughing, some were coming into the bar. They were all grown-ups and so Gary felt like he and Kismet were still alone. He looked earnestly at her and put the scroll down before her. The roses blazed behind the green-black curved feathers that framed her face. Gary blinked away his emotion. She took the scroll and a tender, warm safe feeling invaded her. A scroll, how ridiculous, but also sweet. Kismet told Gary that she'd read the scroll when she was alone. She said that they had to go now. That she had promised her mother she'd be home early tonight.

'Why, were you out late last night?'

'I was at work,' she said, lowering her chin. It was hard not to flirt with Gary when he looked at her from under his lush eyebrows. She had to keep her guard up. And she had to remember about Hugo.

'Okay. Read the scroll, huh?'

'Hugo was there last night,' said Kismet. Saying his name felt momentous, but she had to do it.

'Oh him,' said Gary.

That maggot, he thought in relief. Nothing to worry about.

Hugo

He looked forward to his driving test. He'd buy a car. Maybe he would go out to the oil patch even before he finished his college courses. With a pending diploma, he'd get the job that he'd seen advertised—reading core samples. Mud engineer. Mudlogger. It was one of the best jobs out there. Still, the thing he needed was an older self-presentation. He was sixteen now, well, seventeen in his mind, but even so, people sometimes mistook him for a middle-aged man. A dumpy, harmless soul. He'd capitalize on that.

Hugo had been saving the money he made selling rare books online. He would purchase a car that went with the slackness of middle age. Some kind of clunky manly ride, nondescript as a car can be. Or maybe not. He had a dream car in mind. Why not go for it?

As for his look, he'd banish T-shirts, wear a light blue oxford shirt, tucked into staid blue jeans. He'd sacrifice, cut his hair and brush it to the side. He'd wear eyeglasses and carry pens in a pocket protector, very retro and distracting. Instead of his beloved Pumas, boots. Steel-toed boots. He'd purchase a few worn-in items of work clothing at the thrift store and maybe score a Members Only jacket. Finally, he would learn how to write and punctuate. For too long, he'd relied on a keyboard. A man of dignity would have legible script. Small, evenly spaced printing was within his grasp, but his cursive didn't flow. Once he'd conquered all of this stuff and bought a car, he'd drive out west. Camp in his car while he secured a place to eat and sleep. Make money and claim his future, if she would have him.

The House

Crystal owned the house. Hers was the only name on the deed. She, not Martin, had bought the house from the town for three thousand dollars, because it was becoming derelict and the town would otherwise have had to bulldoze it. The house was an ordinary two-bedroom clapboard house with a boxy entrance and awkward square windows. She loved every inch of the place and had done everything a person with no building skills could do. It was held together with paint, wallpaper, duct tape, wood putty, and Crystal's will. Every room in the house was lopsided. The foundation was like a mouthful of broken teeth.

Crystal had caulked together places where cracks appeared, painted layers over buckling walls, scraped down floors, propped up doors, lovingly jiggered windows back into rotting frames. She'd sanded down and restored the decorative lintels and turned banisters. Out in the backyard, Crystal had planted large plots of squash, corn, pumpkins, pole beans, basil, mint, as well as a thorny hedge of blackberries and raspberries. She had a feral plum tree in the back that grew an exquisite fruit. Kismet loved the garden and the house as much as her mother did. They both loved the house. It was the thing they had going for them, an address.

The Cream Puff

Hugo stuck his hand in the recycling bag and pulled out the local newspaper, hoping to buy a car with the two thousand dollars he'd saved. He kept his eye on bulletin boards and daily ads in the newspaper, looking for a seller with a certain amount of desperation.

There it was. His actual dream car. Cream puff! Loaded. 1997 Toyota 4Runner. Silver gray. Newer tires. Low mileage. Nice interior. Sound. NO ACCI-DENTS. Best offer.

Hugo called the number and on the third ring a man picked up and moaned. It was a hello moan, like a root pulled from the earth. Hugo got the address and the moaner agreed that he would be there when Hugo showed up. It would take half an hour to walk there from his house, Hugo figured, what with the cold wind maybe less. Hugo put his checkbook in his back pocket and started out. From his parents' gravel drive onto a scrap of dead black highway. From the highway into the mournful tree-lined secret streets of the lost south side of the tracks, small houses and big box elders, maples, Siberian elms, a few massive indomitable oaks shaking their branches at the iron sky. The houses wore a hundred layers of paint, or were re-sided in sturdy plastic. Candy green, white trim. Maroon, brown trim. Most of them were carefully looked after but every so often there was a dismal and official-looking bank notice tacked to the front door. Or just an air of sudden emptiness, as if the owners had fled in the night.

At last he came to the house, which was next to the levee. The old white clapboards were peeling and there was cardboard in the front windows. He didn't even try the front door. There was one of those official notices on it. He walked around the side of the house. An air conditioner was built into a side wall and there were blankets behind two windows. The backyard had a high fence and blue tarps covered the contents of the yard.

'Hello? Anybody home?'

Only the clatter of wind flipping back loose shingles, the remaining cottonwood leaves, and other unraked deadfalls in the unmowed grass sticking up against the house. He felt the vibration of the river freezing against the earthen berms of its bank.

'I'm here for the car,' he said in a lower tone, stepping back near the lifeless air conditioner, speaking near the broken edge of a window.

The blanket was pulled incrementally aside. There was a streak of grayish face. Then the blanket, pink and stained, dropped back into place. A door squeaked and he heard someone rustling beneath the blue tarp out back. An emaciated man with long brown hair and the pallor of a midnight creature held the tarp up and nodded at Hugo, who ducked under it as into a cave, and waited for his eyes to adjust.

Hugo shook hands with the skinny, barefooted man, who pointed to the car, its color pale gray, hulking in the icy blue light. It wasn't a silver gray; rather, the color was flat, with an uneven finish. Beyond the car, three children played silently in a pile of dust. They were wearing shoes, at least, and thin coats. The oldest boy crouched over the others, picking up toys, taking them away, murmuring to each of the younger ones in tones so low Hugo couldn't make out the sense of the words. The too-quiet children seemed in a spell of dread and the man seemed polluted by anxiety. He wheezed as he showed Hugo around the car, pointing out its noble features with a shaking finger. The leather seats, nicely worn in, the woodlike resin of the steering wheel, the adequate sound system, the engine which, as far as Hugo could tell, looked like it had all of its pieces. According to the pale man, the car's air-conditioning worked, the power steering worked, the seats reclined, there was a driver's side airbag. The mileage? One hundred twenty thousand.

'Not exactly a cream puff then,' said Hugo, growing a little dizzy.

'This truck will go to three-fifty, easy,' said the man, twisting and untwisting his fingers. 'I mean, it's a 4Runner, built on a truck bed. Great car.'

'Does it come with a title?' Hugo had to ask.

'No,' said the man. He looked stricken, but assured Hugo that it wasn't stolen. After a while he made an odd strangled sound and blurted out the truth.

'I repossessed it.'

'From where?'

'The people who repossessed it in the first place, from me.'

'Won't they just come and take it back?'

'I changed the color. I changed the VIN. You can get a title from the DMV for a few dollars. Say you lost the original in the flood.'

The car was a 1997, so that was plausible. That year the flood had swallowed everything along the Red

River's banks and outside of its banks. It was amazing that this house had survived that year in any shape at all. Yes, the title could have swirled off in the current. Hugo looked at the VIN. The guy had done a great job on it, if he had indeed changed it. Only a tiny nick that could have come from anywhere.

'Would you take two thousand?' asked Hugo.

'I was hoping for four.'

'How about twenty-five hundred?' said Hugo. 'I could owe you the rest.'

The thin man gave Hugo an assessing look, deep and fixed. His openmouthed wheezing raised the effect alarmingly.

'Look, we lost everything. How do I know you'll pay me?'

'I'm a man of my word,' said Hugo. 'My plan is to go out west, get hired in the oil patch, not just a low-level job either. I am studying to be an engineer. So I will be able to take on the debt. Until I get going, though, I've got two jobs and I'm living with my mom and dad. I can pay you a hundred per week.'

It was getting colder now. Hugo felt a shudder starting. He slapped his hands across his chest. They both started hopping up and down a little. And what about the children?

'How old are you?' gasped the man.

'Twenty-eight,' gasped Hugo.

'Really? I took you for twenty-three at most.'

'Okay, you got me. I'm twenty-six.'

The man gave a soft little moan that indicated assent or surrender. The sun blazed through a threadbare place in the tarp and cast a round halo of chilled light on the children. Reassuringly, they wore sock mittens. The oldest brother was a calm magician always changing the scene.

A sort of apparition came through the door. She was a normal woman. Her dark hair was neatly pulled back and she had a professional air about her.

'Hi, I'm Melly,' she said, no nonsense, extending her hand. Hugo shook it. Her hand was so warm he found it hard to let go.

'Hey, I saw you with Kismet at the restaurant. You're here about the car?'

'Yeah.'

'Good. Don't tell anybody we're living here, okay? I park my own car a few blocks away. I gotta go now.'

She ducked away, under the tarp. Her husband or boyfriend or the father of her children went through the back door and Hugo followed him inside. They were in a dingy old clean kitchen. Little beds and mattresses backed up against one wall. From the room beyond, a space heater was huskily whirring. The cold was bearable.

'You got cash?' said the man.

'A check,' said Hugo.

'Well, I can't cash a check. Maybe Melly can but then somebody might look at her account. We're sort of in arrears at the moment. Trying to dig ourselves out, you see, so I only take cash.'

'I'll be back then,' said Hugo. 'With cash. Cash down. Then I'll pay you every week.'

'Actually, cash every week, too,' said the man.

After a glass of warm tap water to seal the arrangement, Hugo walked out into the street. An hour and a half later he drove the car, its tank nearly empty, down the south-side street he'd walked earlier that day. The steering was a bit loose and maybe it needed new brake pads. His mother would not approve, but his father, Ichor, whose name meant 'blood of the gods,' would love that his son had broken some rules.

Before he drove home, however, he picked up Kismet. They folded down the backseat, started making love at dusk, and didn't stop until after the moon came up. Their phones had died and they had no idea what time it was. They drove back to town. Hugo dropped Kismet at her door and she bolted up the steps. Someone had perhaps hauled fiberglass insulation in the back of the car and her skin was horribly alive with the pricking of tiny needles; also the heater didn't work. Her teeth clacked together as she unfurled a sleeping bag into her bed, crawled in, and pulled a blanket over her quilt and the sleeping bag. She lay there shuddering until her blood warmed and she drifted into a messy cave of sleep.

Blood of the Gods

Ichor Dumach was a big, rangy, raw-boned, awkward-looking man with long arms and hard hands. His face was expressive and friendly. Sparrow-colored hair bristled off his brow. Ichor had given his massive shoulders and general coloring to his younger children, two girls aged eleven and twelve, who fought like gladiators for their parents' attention. Hugo's mother, Bev, had kept her flawless complexion and sharp entrancing lip line, but had endowed their oldest, Hugo, with warm skin and reddish hair. Also her dark eyes and long arched brows. Hugo had his mother's interests—books and bookish pursuits—though like his father, he enjoyed tinkering with clocks and vacuum cleaners. Bev and Ichor were beginning to think their daughters' violent intensity might lead to crime—theirs or their own. Hugo was their sensible hope flung out into the world.

Ichor was a fervent man. In the year 1991, Ichor had hitched a ride down from Canada for the Labor Day special—the yearly Canadian at par sales in the Grand Forks malls. Bev had gone in for an Orange Julius and came out with a man she loved. When Hugo drove up, Ichor saw the 4Runner and charged out of the house. Learning that his son was actually acquiring the car, he flung himself upon it in a frenzy of enthusiasm; he began examining the car inch by inch. Hugo was at his side.

'Listen and learn,' cried Ichor, slapping his powerful hands together.

He pointed out each part of the engine and described its purpose. He made an assessment of what parts were in good shape and what must be replaced. Ichor nodded in satisfaction with each discovery. He was so pleased with his son's first major purchase that he loaned Hugo the money to buy it outright. Ichor offered to show Hugo how to do a tune-up, fix the brakes. Together the next day, they rumbled down to the blue-tarped house. Hugo paid off the rest of the car with his dad's cash. He was overjoyed. When they were home again, Bev asked to see the title.

'It was lost during the flood of ninety-seven,' said Hugo.

'In that case, you'll be applying for a new title,' Bev told him. 'For the insurance.'

'Of course!' Hugo gave signs of vigorous agreement. But he preferred not to take any steps to press the issue of the car's paperwork, not right away.

It was Bev's rule that the family sit down to dinner together every night. Ichor usually cooked. There weren't many surfaces in the house, they all got used, and it didn't matter how much stuff was on the dinner table. They pushed aside books, newspapers, magazines, bills, socks, broken toys, to make room for food.

Gerta and Trudy were supposed to set the table, but they usually started a fight to avoid chores. They were powerful children with baleful stares. Gerta had cut her hair so it stuck out all over, like her father's. Trudy had kept her hair long so her mother would help her brush it. Gerta's eyes were troubled pools, the brown of leaf mold. Trudy's eyes were a strange, alien, ultramarine blue. Somehow, their eyes belonged to Ichor, although his were hazel. The girls had the same blunt noses and prominent teeth.

'This is yours,' said Gerta, shoving a mirror with a purple plastic handle at Trudy.

'No, it's not,' said Trudy, slamming it out of Gerta's hand.

The mirror flew across the room and shattered against the television.

'Seven years of bad luck!' They shrieked in fury and launched themselves, but Ichor grabbed the backs of their shirts and separated them.

'Go to your rooms,' he said. This happened several times a day.

He had divided one medium-sized room into two tiny rooms. He'd even put another door in so that they could each have a door to slam. The doors had locks so they could lock each other out. It cut down on physical attacks. There was a thumping exit and the slam of doors reverberating through the walls. Muffled yells. Silence.

Ichor brought the Dutch oven to the table. Bev had sliced a loaf of bread and covered it with a dish towel. She put a glass dish of butter beside the bread.

Ichor crossed himself four times, one for each child and Bev. He'd started doing this when they first married. But he couldn't stop as the children mounted up. He did it now so quickly his shovel of a big hand blurred while he mumbled an indecipherable plea for mercy.

'I'm going to the oil fields,' said Hugo after grace, as they each took a piece of bread from the basket.

There was a long, fraught silence.

'No, you're not,' said Bev.

Ichor frowned into his bowl, spoon poised, as if he were seeing a vision. Maybe he was hearing in his son's voice the command and certainty that had caused him to leave behind his own home as a young man. But not this young.

'Not before your car is top shape!' he said at last, thinking he could draw the repairs out until Hugo came to his senses.

They were eating a mushroom and cabbage goulash with several types of meat. Ichor loved to cook his variety stews. He calmed himself by making egg noodles from scratch. He hunted pheasants, deer, and had even killed a wild boar. Every time he made a complex stew, its leftovers trailed richly into the week. After each meal, there was one of Bev's desserts. Rhubarb crumble from frozen rhubarb this time.

As he ate, Hugo launched into an alarmingly detailed plan for how he would complete geology and engineering courses over the winter and spring and then drive out to the oil fields around Williston. There he would obtain one of those outrageously lucrative jobs he was looking into online.

Bev stood firm, shaking her head, first with exasperation and then, when nothing moved Hugo, despair.

'You are far too young! They'll eat you alive out

there! There's no housing! No safety protocols! You'll get a crap job. A dangerous job. No, no, no.'

Hugo tried to coax his mother downstairs to show off the online degree he was pursuing, the courses he'd already passed. She refused to descend. He had to talk to her back while she loaded the dishwasher. Speaking in a calm and sensible manner, he completely failed to persuade his mother that he knew what he was doing.

The Cheap Sectional

Football season was over. Christmas and New Year's were over. Valentine's Day was on the horizon like a high pressure system. Kismet told Gary that she hated Valentine's Day and told Hugo that she was working at the Skillet on Valentine's night. It would be a big tip night, anyway, so she wanted to work. Then Gary asked her to a party that would take place the weekend before, at his house, which seemed safe enough.

'I want you to see my party barn,' he said.

In fact, the party barn had been shut down for the past ten months. Nobody had had the heart to go inside. Cleaning it up, Gary had stopped many times to catch his breath and slow his racing heart.

'I don't want to see your party barn.'

'This is going to be low-key.'

'Will there be dancing?'

'Well, yeah,' he said, after a moment, still hesitating although he rallied with a flourish of certainty. 'That's a given!'

Dancing. Her mother had an old-fashioned pressure cooker with a twirling metal disk for blowing off steam. Wow! Kismet saw it going off in her head.

Gary picked her up and they drove out to the Geist place. Gary's party hangout was a pole shed that had been fixed up with a wide-screen and a heated area with couches, a bathroom, a small stretch of floor, a fridge and bar. He didn't tell her that she was the only one invited to the party, but once she walked into the echoing place she turned on him.

'Where's everybody else?'

'It's just you and me and this twelve-pack,' he said, and his grin froze. 'Kidding. Sorry.'

He'd learned that the lines that made other girls smile did not make Kismet smile.

'This is, like, abduction. You kidnapped me, Gary, under a false pretense. Take me home.'

'Mom and Dad are right over there,' he said, nodding at the house, 'so nothing's gonna happen. Don't be a hardass.'

'There's that stupid word again.'

Gary raised his hands and gave her a pleading look.

He said the sectional couch was really nice and asked her to try sitting on it. She looked at him suspiciously and had barely touched down when he landed beside her. She sprang up.

'Sit on your own side,' she ordered.

'Okay. And I promise I'll never say hardass,' he said. 'I swear.'

He was smiling in a fixed way he hoped might get to her. Kismet was spooked by the vacant unfocused look in his eyes, like there was something creeping up behind her. She turned, and he made his move, which was to be magnetized by her purple sweater while inching across the cushions and up, over her, until she had to lean back. Now was the crucial moment. He leaned even farther, intending to lower himself onto her, murmuring. Incoherence might hypnotize her. But his knees were on a section of the couch attached by Velcro to another section. Maybe the stuff was an imitation brand, because with a weird farting sound, it gave out. *Rippppf.* Suddenly Gary was sliding away from Kismet, then he was on his knees, on the floor, and she was scrambling away. Gary crawled back to her, but she kicked him away and started laughing. 'Awww, Gary, new twist on couch surfing. Forget it.'

'No, no, please,' he begged in a husky voice.

He pushed the couch pieces back together and got in

position, lowered one knee between her legs, intending to start undressing her. Then he stopped and withdrew his knee. He realized that she was wearing maybe the worst clothing for sex ever invented, the skinny jean. The denim bit impossibly hard into a girl's hips, so had to be tugged down inch by inch, and the extremely long tight ankles were almost impossible to pull off. Even if she wanted to pull them off, the jean ends hardly fit over socks, and she was still wearing her lace-up boots. He would have to seduce her so thoroughly that she would rise and remove the jeans herself, and he'd already blown it by leaving on the overhead fluorescents and not moving the remote, which was underneath her. She shifted, blasting on the golf channel, hushed voices at full volume.

'Nice tempo, caddy likes it, dog likes it, my stone mother, it's gonna go outta frame now, watch. There it is!'

'Where's the remote?' cried Gary.

Kismet rolled off the couch and stood up, hands on hips. The commentary continued.

'And there's the danger, he'd gotta be, no sweat, yes sweat, and the longest putt ever. . . .'

She left for the bathroom. All was lost.

'And my sorry looks like he's gonna use the toe of the putter to strike the parakeet. Ohhhhh!'

At last Gary found the remote between the cushions. Just before Kismet returned, he managed to find an old movie, lower the sound, and turn off the overheads so that the only light on the couch came from outside radiance, the moon, and snow. Again, she wasn't having it.

'No, Gary. Too late for romance. C'mon. Take me back home.'

'I will. Let's just sit here and have a beer and enjoy this old movie. It's black and white, see?'

Kismet tapped her foot with an ironic flourish and glowered.

'Okay. Wait a sec. Pretty sure Dad's stuff is up for grabs.'

He walked over to the bar, bent into the darkness, and came back with a pint of peach schnapps.

'Here.'

They sat down. She uncapped the plastic bottle, tipped it up, then put the cap back on and nodded thoughtfully, swinging her hair across her breasts. The next time she took a drink she left the cap off. After the third drink she threw herself backward and the whole sectional couch suddenly moved apart, the first section again, the next section, the last section, until it was three tiny couches and Gary thought with despair, Fuck yes, and threw himself down on the floor.

'I can't believe this,' said Kismet from the floor beside him.

He pulled down the cushions. She stood up and shucked off her boots. Some music floated toward them, a soothing theme from the old movie, a murmur of genteel conversation. The remote was probably under the rug, doing him a favor. She began to dance, fluid and unselfconscious, in her own little bubble. Gary got busy. He arranged the cushions. After the fourth drink, she hopped around in a circle; was she pulling her jeans off? He lay back and she got on top of him.

'Oh no, oh god!'

He sagged.

'Awww, well, that's okay, Gary.'

'Wait! Lemme get it back.'

She sipped at the rest of the pint. There wasn't much. She sat on the rug and again tipped backward, gasping and laughing. He jumped on her and tried to save his new stand in a blur of motion, but it was too soon.

'What was *that*?' said Kismet. Scooping up her socks and jeans, she went back into the bathroom. Why had she suddenly slugged down the peach schnapps?

'Because you're bored,' she said, looking at her face in the mirror with the words Miller Lite across it. But I must still be sober or I wouldn't know I was bored, she thought. I'd better get more drunk.

'Actually, you're scared of going to college too,' she told the mirror, but this was the sort of boozy honesty a person says or hears and forgets, until much later.

'Gary, so borrrringeeeee,' she creaked out with a strange heady excitement.

Nevertheless, when she went back to the party area and he went down on his knees before her, stripped naked, and said that he would never lie to her and please, oh please, would she marry him, oh please, Kismet bent over in the magnanimity of peach schnapps, kissed him on top of his head, and said, 'Aw right.' Then she kept crumpling deliciously forward, ended up on the floor, fell asleep, and he curled around her and put his face in her hair.

Showdown at Bev's Bookery

Why can't she just get rid of him? thought Hugo. Am I not enough? He went to the store's minifridge and removed one of his mother's containers. He'd been trying to cut back on his mom's treats by telling himself the truth. Sugar, though sparkly white, is a dirty substance in regard to its effect on the brain. As usual, having had this thought, instead of avoiding sugar he ached for it.

Ah, happy moment! Here was Bev's spécialité. Bumble. Her own homemade dark chocolate and lemon bars, striped like bees, famous enough to have been listed in the parish cookbook, a recipe collection sold to make money for the renovation fund that now, he suspected, had been sucked back into that region of mystery, the stock market. The bumble bars always brought people closer. They were for sharing after life's large events. Tiny fragile baby creatures trailed clouds of glory into the ruined universe. Bev's bumble bars appeared. Matriarchs and patriarchs crossed the black river. The taste of Bev's golden stripes manifested. Bumble bars on the tongues of the living told them sweetness, tartness, gravitas of good dark chocolate— these attributes survived. Hugo sighed.

It seemed to him that his mother's preparations had been very serious, and the use of waxed paper, solemn and consolatory. It wasn't plastic wrap, so cheap and casual, strangling the world. It was old-school waxed paper, which responded to its surroundings, stiff and businesslike when cold, supple when warm. Bev had used it to layer the bars in Hugo's smaller container, too. He removed a bumble bar and took a bite. The dark chocolate spoke of lush equatorial heat. He thought of Proust, and how he got a rush of times past, memories activated by the taste of a pastry. But the bumble bars were more about forgetting. An intense rush of sugar, circumventing the brain's reward system, helped a person live in the present. As Hugo pressed up the bumble crumbs and licked them off his fingers, the door chimed. He looked up dutifully, to greet. The customer was Gary Geist. Hugo choked. Gary stared in surprise at the shelves of books on books, and stayed surprised, also, when his gaze shifted to Hugo.

'Hey, maggot,' said Gary.

'I don't answer to that,' said Hugo.

He was calm. At least outwardly calm. Oh my god, what was it to be? Was Gary there to kill him as he'd killed the heroes of the football team? Hugo wouldn't even be one of the empty helmets that had kept watch, last fall, from the bench at every game. He would just be a maggot that Gary crushed. And the worst thing was, he couldn't really blame Gary because he, Hugo, had willingly joined his body to the body of Gary's intended, over and over, and Hugo was fully committed to keep doing so unless Gary managed to kill him. Beneath the counter, there was a personal Taser, which belonged to Bev. It was for her self-protection as a woman alone in retail. It had its own plug-in dock and Hugo could grasp it easily, without even bending over. The thing was now in his grip, hidden, as Gary pretended to peruse the bookshelves.

'It's, yeah, not that great a nickname,' said Gary, mildly.

'I don't have a nickname,' said Hugo.

Gary looked at him in surprise.

'What should I call you, then?' he said. 'Hugo, like, *Hew-go*?' Gary shook his head as though this was impossible.

'Leave this place,' said Hugo, with dignity, he thought.

'Okay then, Ghostship,' said Gary.

'How'd you know?' said Hugo.

'I'm Avenger995.'

'Huh. You're not bad.'

'I'll own you one of these days, Ghostship.'

Gary was smiling down at a copy of *Play It as It Lays*. He paged through, put it down quickly.

'Not to your liking?' asked Hugo, curious in spite of it all.

'Thought it was a different kind of book,' said Gary.

'Are you looking for something special?'

Gary gulped and his face turned a deep color, almost purple.

'My folks think I have a problem. Put a lock on my computer. I kinda need some help, see, I'm looking for, like, not porn or anything. I'm just not good at'—Gary gave a yelping laugh of despair—'you know. Looking for an instruction manual, like, for sex.'

Hugo's grip on the Taser tightened. Fury gripped his dantian. Absolutely against his will, and without a shred of volition, his voice emerged from his center of being.

'Top shelf, left back corner. Popular before the aughts.'

Gary turned away. Hugo muttered, 'Aw fuck, she deserves to be happy, but where's my icy left brain?'

How could his bookseller self betray his real self like this? Yes, Hugo had pledged, lived out a vow almost mystical, to help those who entered this domain find the book they needed. But to aid and abet the enemy was beyond the beyond. What he was doing cried out for common sense. Someone should stop him. Someone like himself. But there was only himself, and Gary came back to the counter with *Clinical Sextasy*. The subtitle read: *By Lesbian Doctors for Men*. Gary put a twenty beside the book and didn't wait for change. Just bolted. Leaving Hugo there at the counter. Maggot. Well named, thought Hugo. Just a blob at a desk helping my rival find the key to actually pleasing the woman I love. Which means Gary probably wasn't pleasing her before. And now he'll go back and god, oh god, he'll try page 82. Of course he will! Who wouldn't? Madness! Hugo banged his head down on the desktop and, still gripping the Taser, applied it to his left thigh. There was a terrible, singeing crackle. A scream lifted out of his head. He found himself on the floor, discharged Taser flung beneath a shelf. As he lay there, engulfed in sensation, staring up at the stamped tin ceiling, the pain gradually diminished and he felt better, so much better. Hugo waited until his heartbeat slowed, then he rolled over, raised himself on all fours. But tabletop position reminded him of page 90 and he threw himself back down.

'You've ruined your life,' he said aloud. 'Ghostship. You have only yourself to blame.'

It helped to address himself, conferring distance, and because he had survived, Hugo eventually saw that he should have the wherewithal to treat himself with a bit more kindness.

'Actually, as a bookseller faced with a request from a customer, I did an honorable thing. I can live with that.'

Still, the Taser tears kept trickling from the corners of his eyes and down into his ears.

Hazards and Benefits of Self-Tasering

Hugo decided to accelerate his plan because he heard himself say to the empty store, 'I can't go on in this fashion!' If he didn't shock himself to death, it was sure to be something else. Proximity to Kismet, his luck and his fate, was too painful, and too dangerous. He lay on the floor behind the counter for a long time. Fortunately, in a way, no customers. At least his brain worked. At least his brain could think. At least his brain could see ahead into the distance. In his vision a year passed. He was rolling in money. Already driving home.

His thoughts rainbow-wheeled on the ultimate question: How to steal her away from Gary? Maybe meet her at an appointed place on the highway. Pick her up and keep driving. Maybe she'd climb out a window, into his arms. Or maybe he'd sneak into their agribusiness dwelling, into their bedroom, apply the recharged Taser to sleeping Gary. Except that as Gary had signaled his vulnerability to Hugo, and now that Gary was a bookstore customer, perhaps he had immunity. Plus, Hugo now understood the effect of a Taser on a human thigh, and to apply such heartless cruelty was more difficult to imagine. Could he do it?

No. Hugo retrieved the Taser from beneath a bookshelf and returned it to its dock. Decided that his mother's safety was assured. He patted the small pile of travel books that held promise. He loved to pore over their descriptions of bistros and tavernas. He touched the glossy photographs of bedrooms and cathedrals—to him both places of worship. Any country would do, actually. In Europe, in the Mediterranean, or maybe they would go to Bali. What did it matter when destiny would crash the party anyway?

Still no customers, but there were a few online requests. Hugo got busy.

Maybe self-tasering works like electroshock, he mused. Maybe the jolt to my brain has mysteriously banished my dismal sorrows. I feel unusually upbeat and cheerful! Anything is possible!

Winnie

People in towns and cities had strange ideas about farming. People thought you just put a seed in the ground and it grew. Winnie Geist's husband, Diz, called farming a war, but Winnie said it was a conflict. True, something was always trying to kill your crop, but there were ways and there were ways . . . she drifted off thinking of her parents' ways. Driving to town over the summers, she had looked out to either side and seen that a field of sugar beets was going to be a good stand, that corn was growing unevenly, that soybeans had been planted too early or too late, that the sunflowers were outstanding. She knew who owned each field too, and so she was glad for or irritated by various families along the way. Now, driving toward the book club meeting, she let her mind relax.

'We haven't lost Gary,' she heard herself murmuring. Then she cried out and was in that void she knew well.

After the accident she'd stayed in bed. She knew she would be able to function, but not yet. Every night, she promised that she would pop to her feet in the morning and start doing what she had to do. But her eyes would open in sunlight and she would feel her bones turn to lead. Yes, she had wanted to let the world go. But the accident was not the first time. While she was in high school, the government accelerated her family's loan payments and blow after blow had landed. They'd lost their home, their farm, everything. Except one another, they kept saying, except us.

Sport Geist, father of Diz, had bought Winnie's family farm from the bank for half of nothing. Her parents had sold their cattle at a loss, the equipment at an auction, moved out of their hand-built home into a rickety little white house in town. Her father had held her shoulders, looked into her face, said that as long as they worked, no job too menial, they'd hold their heads up. She held her head up. And anyway, in town people didn't care. Most of the town kids had no idea what life on a farm was like. Losing a farm had no meaning for them. Winnie had kept her girlfriends and stayed Diz's girlfriend, in spite of everything. She'd always loved Diz as much as she hated his father. Sport had mostly regarded his sons as free labor and rarely addressed them except to give an order. All through high school, Diz asked her to marry him. She said the best she could do was go to the local junior college and take bookkeeping so she could keep books for the farm. It was a kind of promise but she wouldn't marry him until after Sport was dead and buried—in the earth he didn't deserve to inhabit.

She turned into Bev's drive. She cut the engine, but her hands were stuck to the wheel. The others lived in Tabor and saw one another all of the time. She had gone to school with Bev, though, and stayed friends with her. Bev had been a Pavlecky before she'd married Ichor. Bev would stick up for her. Still, Winnie Geist sat outside in her car. She'd arrived early to the book club and had to gather her courage before facing the women who would walk into Bev's house. This was only the second meeting she'd made it to since the accident, and at the first meeting she hadn't said a word. So she needed to see who was coming before she entered.

Many women she knew from church would be at the

book club meeting. She knew that some actually prayed for her and her family. But on dark days Winnie believed that some prayed against her. She found it hard to bear the sting of their eyes when they'd watch her enter a room, and it was even more difficult to open her mouth and speak.

It was going to be stressful, but not as bad now, not after Gary had told his mother that Kismet had said yes. Yes to his proposal. 'Mom, I'm so happy.' He'd said that. Kismet wasn't going to wear the engagement ring, maybe, but he'd told her he could live with that as long as they could be engaged. Winnie felt a sifting of hope and pulled down the mirror to see if she'd bitten off all of her lipstick.

The Meeting

S oon more cars turned onto Bev and Ichor's driveway and parked on the grass alongside the gravel. Women emerged, bearing covered pans or platters, squinting in the unfiltered light. The cold wind whipped each guest toward the front door. As they passed into the flat-roofed entryway porch, Bev greeted each woman. She guided them into her no-nonsense living room and gestured past the mismatched facing couches toward the dining table, polished by Gerta and Trudy to a ruddy gloss. Mary Sotovine, red and shiny with excitement, took off her double-knitted brown mittens and extended her pink padded palms toward the fireplace. She said, 'Look at your house, it's so homey!'

Homey as a living hell, thought Gerta, passing resentfully into the kitchen. A living hell was a favorite phrase of her mother's, as in *You girls are making my life a living hell.* Gerta believed her hands were chapped from scrubbing countertops. She looked critically at her fingers and thought her knuckles looked dry and wrinkled. She turned her fist from side to side. Anyway, they'd do for beating up Trudy.

'Good gravy,' said Mrs. Flossom, who always brought wilting flowers. 'At least the table's cleared off. Here. Put these in a vase.'

While Mrs. Flossom's back was turned, Gerta tossed the bouquet in the kitchen sink and slipped beneath the table to brood. She tried to rekindle her satisfaction at how Trudy had been caught running the vacuum cleaner angrily across the carpet, slamming it up and down with brutal glee. 'Stop it, Trudy! Or I'll give Gerta the rest of the ice cream.' Trudy wouldn't stop. The memory of the ice cream she received in order to punish Trudy made Gerta dreamy-eyed. Strawberry. Trudy had also been ordered to unclog the vacuum cleaner. While their mother was busy scooping out the ice cream for Gerta, Trudy started slicing away at the hair twined around the vacuum roller, using their father's keenest paring knife.

Ichor had come upon this outrage and admonished Trudy, causing her to slip in her work (on purpose) and cut her own finger. That baby, what a screech. Yes, there were still some darker spots where Gerta had rubbed the blood into the carpet instead of lifting it out with blood remover (it was stain remover but with them in the house it was always used for blood). Gerta could still see the shadows. What satisfaction. Gerta watched Mrs. Flossom's gray shoes take root in the carpet. She was probably smearing the table up there with her moist fingers. How infuriating that these grown women would destroy her mirror shine. It was really too undignified to even bear.

Her mother asked Crystal to pour wine and lemonade. Gerta saw Crystal's cool army-style women's lace-up boots. She wanted them.

'Trudy, Gerta, where are you? Come help me put out the chips and three-layer dip.' Bev gave the order in her nicest voice, which meant they were under threat. Trudy lifted the tablecloth and was underneath in a flash. The two sisters sat in the center, arms around their knees. Although Bev would have to bend over and drag them out to press them into service, and probably wouldn't do that, Gerta and Trudy were still trapped. However, there were also possibilities, like stealing wine. That would mean teaming up, but for the greater good perhaps Gerta would declare a truce.

'Truce,' said Trudy, reading her mind.

'Let's steal wine,' said Gerta before her sister could say it. Crystal was pouring wine for Winnie Geist.

'Thank you,' said Winnie. 'Will you sit beside me?'

'Thanks,' said Crystal, who had no intention of doing such a thing. Her feet moved away.

Trudy crept out and hooked down the newly opened bottle of riesling. There was a fuzzy old television downstairs in Hugo's lair, and the girls slipped down there with their bottle of wine. Each took a swig. 'Sweet,' said Trudy. 'Not bad,' said Gerta.

'Jeniver!'

Crystal hugged Stockton's mother. Jeniver was mixed-blood too, Irish and Dakota Sioux. Gravity had always drawn them together. The two women broke apart and eyed each other. Jeniver nodded and said, 'Chin up.' She would not let Crystal leave, even if Karleen Krankheit, mother of Kismet's classmate and frenemy, Ally, challenged her in some way, as she usually did. And here Karleen came—stocky, rock-jawed, blond-bobbed, in an apricot tunic, fluffy white vest, and white leggings. She was in her late forties, with sun-damaged skin and small cold eyes. She entered right behind Jeniver and said, 'You missed your town council meeting.'

The two women had bashed against each other for what seemed the entire history of Tabor.

'I was away on town business,' said Jeniver, who had been visiting her mother.

'Oh reeallly,' said Karleen. She wagged a pointer finger and made a mischief face. 'That's not what a little birdie told me!'

'What kind of little birdie? A cuckoo?'

'No. No.'

'A dodo bird?'

Oh, things were really heating up.

Electrified by the sound of disagreement, Bev barreled toward the two with a plate of mini-tacos. 'Come in! I thought you were conferencing!' she said to Karleen. 'Weren't you conferencing? Didn't you go down to the Cities to get some kind of major conferencing award?'

Smothered in questions, forced onto a couch, Karleen then sat pinioned by Tory Whitson White and Tania Whitson White, identical twins with serpentine bodies and sleek prematurely gray hair. They had both married men with the last name White. On the coffee table, platters of sandwiches were set, ham salad, egg salad, chicken salad, pimento cheese. There were small platters of sliced vegetables, dip, and, on the dining room table, chips and bumble bars.

A few stragglers edged in and then the couches and chairs were full. People came in from five to five thirty for a dinner/happy hour, then the meeting started at six. Bev called the meeting to order, a tradition because the meeting was at her house. She welcomed everyone, applauded their new member, Melly, from the Skillet, then went down the checklist and called out names. Nearly everyone was present, which discouraged Bev. She'd sold only six books and thirteen women were there, meaning they'd bought them from Amazon. Bev held up *Eat Pray Love*, chosen by Mary Sotovine. But before she could open her mouth, Darva Geist held up her hand and said they really had to address Gusty's digestive issues.

'Fiber,' said Tiny.

'Moving on,' said Bev.

Moving On

I have a question.'

Karleen Krankheit raised her hand.

'Here we go,' muttered Jeniver.

Everyone remembered Karleen's attempts to jettison them for one reason or another and they lay in wait, eyeing her, breathing silently. In some hearts there was anticipation. Who would she target this time?

'My question is, are we just going to ignore things?'

'What things this time?' asked Jeniver.

'You know very well.'

Karleen looked around the room, attempting to fix each of the women with a probing stare. Some eyes slid away from hers. Others brightly widened.

'All right, Karleen,' said Jeniver, wearily. 'Let's address things.'

138 • LOUISE ERDRICH

'There's a real-life *Eat Pray Love* going on right here, in this town,' said Karleen. 'Only pray is spelled with an e.'

She looked around triumphantly, pleased with her planned pun. There was a sigh of exasperation, but also appreciation. The room was evenly balanced. The stakes had risen. Karleen pinned her eyes on Winnie's face, which was, as usual, beautifully made up and at this moment perfectly controlled, like a morning-show hostess ignoring a guest throwing up behind the couch.

'It's about Gary,' said Karleen, opening her hands with a theatrical flourish. 'Gary pushing Kismet Poe to marry him.'

'Let's move on,' said Jeniver. But there was a murmur of opposition.

'My sister-in-law's niece Grace told my daughter Ally that Gary was at Pookie's pressuring Kismet to marry him,' said Karleen.

Winnie continued to gaze impassively at Karleen. The book lovers stirred with interest.

'Well? Well?' Karleen's voice rose.

'I don't see where that's any concern of yours,' said Tiny Johnson, who made special-occasion cakes out of her kitchen. She noted a possible cake opportunity and was, anyway, always in favor of weddings. 'I haven't heard anything. And it's their business.'

'Not when Gary hasn't been charged yet!'

'Charged!' The White twins gave soft, excited gasps.

'Charged? He paid for the flowers, anyway,' said Mrs. Flossom.

'Charged with what?' asked Jeniver.

Karleen faltered. 'Something.' She tried to revive her eager attack. 'Does this poor young woman even know what she's getting into?'

'Let's talk about the book,' said Crystal, although in essence, and maybe for the first time, she agreed with Karleen.

'I'll start,' said Jeniver. 'This book meant a lot to me. I see myself in her, doing all of those things she does, especially the eating.'

'And the loving.' Crystal laughed. 'Way back when.'

'Before the flood, yeah,' said Jeniver.

'Well, they took two in the ark,' said Crystal. 'High old times.'

'It's always better on a boat.'

'Cut this out!' cried Karleen.

'Cut me in,' said Tiny.

'You two,' said Mary Sotovine. 'As for the pray part, I kind of asked myself, why go to India to get enlightened when you can stay home and be a Catholic?'

'The book is *Eat Pray Love*,' Bev started over. 'I'll go around the room. General impressions, two minutes each.'

'I'd like to talk about the pasta,' Tiny said.

Winnie sat forward a little. 'Excuse me. Just a moment. I do have something to add.'

Everyone turned to her.

'A few nights ago, *not* at Pookie's, Gary did propose to Kismet. And she did him the honor of accepting.'

Winnie leaned back, her face glowing with an imperturbable warmth. 'Needless to say, I'm delighted,' she added.

Crystal stood slowly, all eyes on her. She looked down at Gary's mother, then stepped forward and leaned toward her with a dangerous glare. 'That's not true!'

Winnie tried to contain her disappointment, then alarm at the way Crystal continued staring, her eyes hot and narrow. Hands at her sides, Crystal clenched and unclenched her fingers. Winnie's lips opened to softly placate.

'No, no, don't you speak,' snapped Crystal. 'My daughter is too young. She's going to college. And even if she wasn't, Gary's not right for her.'

'To say the least!' said Karleen Krankheit, vindicated.

Crystal turned from the room and walked into the kitchen. She realized that she was overcome, breathing too fast, her thoughts darting around. Why hadn't Kismet told her? It couldn't be true.

Back in the living room, Winnie recovered her aplomb. She lifted her hands and gave a soft, indulgent laugh. 'Yes, they're young, like Romeo and Juliet. What can you do? Young love!'

She was about to try connecting the engagement to the group's book somehow when from the basement there came a series of shrieks. The screams intensified, became a laughter of loons or a violent pack of wild curs. There was a roil of noise as though barrels were being slung into the hold of a ship, and then the crazed clomping and thumping of feet on the stairs, the burst of an opening door, and more shrieks from Gerta and Trudy.

'*Mom, Mom,* get down here! You have to see this!'

The Cutie Pie Bandit

Just before the First Bank branch in West Fargo closed on a Friday afternoon, a man dressed in a green housecoat and a fake white beard held on to his ears by rubber bands peered at a bank teller through tiny round sunglasses. He wore a green peaked hat and maybe also a fake button of a nose. He was adorable, said the teller, Bella Courtier, a pudgy curly-haired woman of fifty-seven who was pretty cute herself. The criminal pushed a note at her that told her to put the money, all of it, in his shopping bag. His bag ('Get this!' she later said) was from a Toys"R"Us. She had just counted, so she knew it was eight thousand dollars that she put into the bag.

Bella gave the shopping bag of money to the gnome

but was so nervous that she forgot to add the marked bait money in a separate drawer.

'Thank you e-e-e-e-ver so much,' the robber said in a squeaky voice.

He left. Bella pushed the silent alarm. Maybe she waited a little longer than she should have because the squeaky voice just killed her. And that was the only danger, as it turned out—laughing too hard—now that the whole thing was over. Whew! She was so grateful for life!

Yes, he had a gun of some kind, she was sure that she'd seen a gun, but no, she couldn't describe the weapon. How he'd vanished, she couldn't say. He went out the door and after a little while the manager and the other teller came out of the back office. They'd seen nothing. They were even skeptical, like maybe Bella was joking, until they looked at the security camera footage, along with the police, and everybody tried not to be the first one to break out laughing. Nobody admitted this later, but when the robber did the squeaky voice they all did start laughing, so hard it became uncontrollable. They gasped and cried, choked a little, had to wipe their eyes and drink cups of water.

'Wasn't he just the cutest?'

'Cutest cutie pie?'

'We should shut the fuck up. He took *money*.'

Bella said this in the squeaky voice and this time they rolled on the floor.

It was on the news that evening. It was on the next morning too, and also on the weekend evening news. It was on for five days, the announcers leading with 'no sign of the Cutie Pie Bandit' and then cracking up, shaking their heads, asking for tips from viewers, but obviously rooting for the bandit.

Winnie

Driving back to the farm, Winnie seized on the wedding. How to make it lovely, quiet but somehow spectacular. It would be tasteful, memorable, complete. When she thought of how happy Gary had been when he told her that Kismet had said yes to him, an unfamiliar sensation pervaded her. A twinge of anticipation. She was so grateful that she nearly had to pull over. And the announcement hadn't gone so badly, had it? Nobody had left. Well, Crystal had bowed out. But surely she would come around. Winnie would be in touch with her. They'd work this through. And thank god for the Cutie Pie Bandit. Everyone had trooped down to watch the repeat of the story, and afterward discussing the bank robbery had taken their minds off both the book and the engagement.

Peach Schnapps

Her mother was sitting in the living room staring at the door, so when Kismet got off work that night and walked inside there was no escape.

'Are you engaged to Gary Geist?'

Kismet shook her head, shifted her eyes. 'Noooooo.'

'Are you sure?'

'Well, I, well . . . I had too much peach schnapps, Mom.'

Crystal turned away, squeezing her eyes shut.

'God. Kismet.'

There was a space of growing dismay between them.

'You can't get married. You've applied to colleges. Kismet! I raised you better!'

'I know,' said Kismet, sinking onto the couch. 'I'll talk to Gary and call it off. But you know, Mom, he really loves me.'

Crystal brought her head up and looked into Kismet's eyes.

'A lot of men are going to love you, Kismet. Hugo already loves you too.'

'How'd you find that out?'

'By not being stupid. Look, just go tell Gary it's off. You're too young. He'll be okay.'

'Okay, I'll call it off,' said Kismet.

And she tried, she really did, she tried.

Spaghetti Squash

One night, they were eating a giant bowl of spaghetti squash sautéed with onions at Hugo's house. Again, his sisters had been sent to their rooms.

'What is this?' asked Hugo, suspicious of the noodly squash.

'I got it from Crystal,' said Bev.

'Your friend will never let us starve,' said Ichor, digging in. He had cooked the squash with an entire stick of butter. Ichor picked mushrooms that grew around fallen trees down by the river. He often dropped off bags of them—hens of the woods, even precious morels—on Crystal's doorstep in return for her garden wealth.

Hugo forked the limp heavy strings onto his plate. He lifted a wad gingerly onto his tongue. The clump tasted like sour paper. He tried to tell himself that this was the taste of love, but he'd told himself that about the unclaimed bacon burger too and it had given him an unpleasant stomachache.

'I'm sure it's super-nutritious,' he said.

Ichor got up to forage for some hot sauce.

Upstairs, the girls were pounding on the floor. This meant they were hungry now and wanted to come down. But Ichor called from the bottom of the stairs that they still had half an hour of detention. Hugo wanted to talk about his plans again. He hadn't yet come to his senses.

'One thing bothers me,' said Bev, in a low voice. It had taken her all this time to broach the subject that most worried her. 'I am afraid that you're thinking of leaving because you want to impress Kismet. I know you like her.'

Hugo placed his utensils carefully upon his plate. He folded his hands, looked his mother in the eye. There was a short, momentous silence. Ichor sat down with the hot sauce and glanced from Bev to Hugo.

'Love her,' said Hugo. 'The truth must come out. I love her. I'm in love with her and I'll always be in love with her.'

'Oh no!' said Bev, sinking back in her chair. 'I heard she's engaged to Gary.'

'It's temporary, Mom. You know my plans. I'm

going to make money. I'll come back for her when I'm rich. We'll see what happens then.'

Bev stared at her son, heart sinking. Obviously, he thought he knew what would happen.

'People don't just run away together,' she said. 'Not anymore. Why don't you two get engaged and stay here?'

'She says I'm too young.'

'You are!'

'Money is not the only thing,' said Ichor. He tapped a few spoons of sour cream onto the squash noodles, shook on the hot sauce, added a collop of meat.

Bev got up this time, went into the kitchen to rummage around for a bottle of red wine she'd hidden. She opened it and drank a glass right there, alone, looking out the window into a blustery wall of darkness. She loved Hugo with that superb kind of love a mother has for a male child, a love that is deeper and more pure for knowing that he'll more than likely turn out a fool.

Back at the table, Ichor was about to make a pronouncement.

Hugo steeled himself.

'As I say, the important thing isn't money,' said his father. 'It is when a man cooks for a woman and later makes heated and trustworthy love to her.' Ichor leaned toward his son. 'These are the things that bind a woman to a man. Not money.'

Panicked by his father's unwanted advice, Hugo meekly croaked out a word.

'Stew?'

'Braise your cabbage first,' said Ichor, narrowing his eyes.

'The way you make mushrooms is really tasty,' said Hugo, emitting a high-pitched sound of pleasure, hoping to divert his father.

'The mushroom is well-known as an aphrodisiac,' said Ichor, sagely nodding. 'You must use dried as well as fresh.'

'I know how to pick mushrooms,' said Hugo, who'd gone mushroom hunting with his father many times. Where was his mother? He continued trying to steer the conversation away from physical love.

'Take no chances,' said Ichor. 'You don't want to kill your lady. Pick no mushrooms on the edges of the fields around here. They absorb poisons.'

'I don't suppose I will be cooking out in the oil fields.'

'You must always cook!' said Ichor in a scandalized tone. 'Which is why you must live here, or at least where you have a kitchen. They are living in toolsheds and Porta Pottys out by Williston.'

Bev came back into the room with the wine, sat down. Then she rose and took down the glasses of red and white crystal, antiques from Ichor's family, used only for special occasions.

'Don't go, Hugo, please stay,' she said, lifting her glass.

'If only I could stay,' said Hugo, after a moment of thought. He shook his head. 'You know I can't.'

They sipped their wine, picked their glasses up, and put them down. A sense of mountainous impossibility bore down on Hugo's parents.

'Let's not be sad sacks,' cried Ichor. 'We should celebrate that we have a genius for a son!'

'A genius with no common sense.' Bev nearly sobbed.

'How can you say that, Mom,' said Hugo, his heart pierced. 'I have saved my money, got a GED, figured out how to go to college, forged an ID, got a car. I have a ton of common sense.'

'Our son is now a man,' said Ichor, lifting his antique glass. 'Which is to say he's now an impetuous . . .'

'. . . pighead,' said Bev.

'He can no more give up his love than I could give up my love for you, Beverly.'

Bev refilled their glasses. With great emotion, the three drained their figured cups and set them down among the papers and tools.

'Still,' said Ichor, 'you can stay a pighead right here at home. You don't have to go out there and get blown

up. Or worse.' He opened his mouth to list the horrify-
ing possibilities, but choked.

Ichor gripped his chin as if in pain, and Bev sobbed
out loud. Hugo watched them with the distant sympathy of a young man who knows what he's doing is
stupid only to the people who love him, therefore of no
consequence.

PART TWO

Vows

2009

The Mighty Red

On the night before her wedding, Kismet Poe and her high school girlfriends walked over to the train bridge. It was early June. The air was sweaty and thick, uncooled by the moving water. The bachelorettes dangled their feet over the end of the bridge and drank vodka shots out of soggy Dixie cups. Maybe it was Stockton who dared Kismet, or Ally or Brianna who dared Stockton, but somebody dared somebody. At some point they stripped to bright lace underwear. The Red River was still swollen with spring flood, ice cold, and filthy with debris. They didn't jump. They weren't suicidal enough to spring directly into the current, but they did let themselves fall off the bridge, which everyone later agreed was idiotic beyond belief.

The bridesmaids managed to scramble out of the

brown muscle of water and cling to the rocks bermed up against the dike, but Kismet floated on. She let the current clutch her and carry her to the main street bridge, but right there it took her under, whirled and rolled her. The feeling was not unpleasant, as the shock of cold had worked with the vodka like a stun gun, but soon Kismet knew she would have to breathe. She didn't want to die but also understood with perfect clarity why she'd let the current grab her.

She absolutely could not marry Gary Geist. No, not at all. In a white flash, she saw everything. How after she'd said yes, except she hadn't actually said yes, Gary had clung to her. He'd tucked her close to his body—the way he would run a football through a mass of crazed teenage defensive linemen. And Winnie! With savage determination she had planned the wedding—a limousine rented out of Fargo, an elaborate cake made by a show baker who'd won prizes on a TV Bake-Off. There would be a reception at the church event room, then another reception and a fancy dinner at the golf club. She described slow dancing, whirling lights, a Cabo honeymoon. Winnie's fixations on these ever more complicated plans had exhausted Kismet. Crystal, in her distress, kept trying to talk her daughter out of getting married, but she didn't understand the dazzlement of cakes and lights. Winnie had plunged forward while Crystal was on night hauls. The Geists were paying for it all.

All of these plans had wrapped around Kismet strand by strand until she slipped one tenth of a grade point down past salutatorian to merely graduating. She'd been accepted by every college she'd applied to but the emails panicked her. She threw acceptance letters in a heap. As the wedding plans intensified, all of the correspondence got smashed into a corner. Kismet even quit working at the Skillet. It started to look like it would be hard enough work just dealing with Winnie, who sent email after email, with complicated attachments. Kismet opened the messages, skimmed, clicked them shut. Mesmerized by dread, she'd gone forward. Or not stopped things.

Perhaps because if everything stopped she might have to confront the truth about herself. She hadn't meant to fall in love with anybody, and was she even in love at all? To be sure, something had clicked. Hugo made her laugh. Laughing made her delirious. In Gary's case, there was nothing like being rejected and then embraced. She'd been invisible, at best sneered at by most of the cool guys, then suddenly adored by Gary, who'd been way too anxious to marry her. Even desperate. Kismet knew that there was something wrong with herself, and something wrong at home. And maybe she was getting married because she wanted to have better sex than Hugo could give her, not just in an itchy car, or maybe she was getting married to Gary because there was something wrong with Hugo, or maybe there was something wrong with Gary and that's why Winnie was so eager for Kismet to marry her son and was throwing this lavish wedding. Maybe she had no business getting married at all. These wrong, unsettling elements were about to present themselves—she had sensed this would happen. She'd been waiting for it, even. But here and all, numb in the river, she remembered she must live, even though she was pretty sure that all the wrong things were gathering into a big ball that would come rolling at her, maybe crush her, and her chest was already bursting for air.

The Red Ladder

First responder Odie Rappatoe saved Kismet. Eric Pavlecky, training with Odie, was right behind. She was flailing by the bridge, where the two had been sent to look for her. Odie flung out a personal flotation device and Eric reached down, hauling her in. Kismet's mother had sent them out because, when she'd bolted from deep prayer into her daughter's bedroom, she found plastic bra hangers, panty tags, and the other bottle of vodka. What scared her was the train bridge and the river close by. Kids partied by the river, but it was unthinkable that they might have gone in. Kismet was urgently needed because of the shattering drama unfolding at her house. Odie wanted to be part of that drama almost as much as he wanted to save Kismet's life. He would be part of the biggest scandal to hit the town since . . . maybe there had never been a scandal this big. At least not a scandal that wasn't an accident. He wasn't sure. But there was no question Kismet's mother needed her at home, needed her badly, for already there were police and soon a state trooper, maybe even FBI, and certainly the newspapers.

As for Eric, he was mainly thinking about how Kismet's death or what might have been thought a suicide just before the wedding would have affected his buddy-like-a-brother Gary. Later, he was ashamed of his first reaction. But it would take a while for him to break the habit of thinking of Gary first.

At the house, Father Flirty, who was anything but, leaned over the kitchen table to steady himself. He was pretending to be sane, but behind his bewildered, soft blue eyes he was disintegrating. Poor Flirty. The question came again.

'You were acquainted with Martin Poe?'

'Correct.' He tried to gather himself. 'I knew the man in question.'

Then he choked on the context and could not go on. He wished he could just pass out. This was too much. Poor Flirty. Grappling with Martin Poe's numbers. Scheduled to wed the Poe daughter, Kismet, to Garrick (Gary) Geist at 11 a.m. the next morning. Maybe, the priest thought in sudden desolation, he would send them to a justice of the peace. Not have this wedding in his ready-to-renovate church. Not bless their union in the void of Holy Rosary's bank account. Astounding and wounding, the bold cruelty of the betrayal. The blaring vision of the $1.5 million, represented by the red blaze in the giant money ladder painted on a plywood rectangle in the church community room, gone.

'I'm . . . yes . . . I must sit down.'

Thoughts of the red rising slowly up the rungs sank Flirty into a chair. All that money scraped from bitterly small sugar beet campaign checks, clerk and teacher and grocery bagger checks, bartender and grain elevator operator checks, slipped from worn plastic wallets dollar by dollar since the year 1998 and worthily invested, practically growing by the minute. This money had been carefully heaped together by Martin Poe, investment counselor, trusted servant, tireless fund-raiser. Martin had kept the money in a dedicated series of accounts that were no longer. No longer anywhere. Impossible to imagine how all of those handfuls of change and wads of small bills could simply, unspeakably, disappear. Father Flirty's heart began to flutter and weakness seized his gut. He sought the scratched kitchen chair in the corner. Nodded. Sipped from a glass of water. A jelly jar, he saw, an old Tom & Jerry glass, cheap.

Of course, there were big donors too. Like the Geists, for instance. (No, no, he had to go through with the wedding.) But he would wear a threadbare simple robe to symbolize humility. He had done no wrong. And yet Father Flirty's friend, yes friend, Martin, was a very well-liked man who had never done a wrong either, up until now. And he was married to a woman who also had never done a wrong. And their daughter too, an outstanding girl although with a non-saint name, this good-hearted little family had just deep-sixed the grand renovation plan for the church and new priest's residence, for preschool and Catholic kindergarten and truly, thought Flirty as his throat squeezed shut around his memories of the culprit, what Martin Poe had done might sink forever the town's regard for the prestige of local Catholics, or their faith in humanity, perhaps even their trust in Father Flirty.

When Kismet walked dripping and shivering into the kitchen—so cramped, so shabby, her mother's valiant little touches apparent in the handmade teacup-print curtains and the overscrubbed floor—oh, when Kismet walked in she knew that the marriage she had nearly drowned herself to avoid was inevitable. There was that sense—of general disaster mixed with the horror of shame—signaled by the grim or gaping police officers, by the slumped priest. There was her mother's smeared eye makeup. Her aura of furious tension. But also—and Kismet knew her mother very well but this surprised her anyway—a whiff of savage jubilance in the way Crystal Frechette sat at the chipped wooden table, staring at the wedding ring she'd pulled off her finger and set on a saucer. She'd done it right away, signaling that she now abjured her slim, swivel-hipped, salsa-dancing husband and his lifetime of pieties and surface charm. She had cast away Martin's expensive shirts while she sewed kitchen curtains, his insistence on steaks while his family ate grains, his iced coffees and artsy jobs, which were mostly parts in local plays. She told herself that she had stayed with him for the family, as a woman of faith will. Also, his charms ran deeper, into the murk of mutual history. There was his certainty, his confidence, his sweetness, his . . . but if only she had followed her gut instincts and, somehow, she couldn't imagine how, gotten rid of him! An excited regret smothered her thinking, and a forgetful fury obliterated the exhaustions of their love, which was like no other love on earth, he had always insisted. Quite recently, Crystal had decided otherwise. It was exactly the same as most marriages that included an utterly self-absorbed man. At least she had named her baby

Kismet, a name to attract luck, and at least Kismet would have security. She had refused to decide on a college, yet, yet, she was marrying a Geist.

'Let's go upstairs,' said Crystal to her daughter. She stared pointedly at the men.

The two police officers, and Odie, shuffled around and then filed toward the front door. Eric was waiting discreetly in the ambulance. Odie was extremely disappointed that there hadn't been sirens and TV cameras lined up in the streets.

'Are you sure you don't want me to stay? I could give you some oxygen,' said Odie to Kismet.

'Give it to him,' said Crystal, nodding at Father Flirty.

Flirty would have actually liked the oxygen, but he shook his head and allowed himself to be shooed sorrowfully after the other men. Crystal followed, closed the door, and turned the dead bolt, which reminded her of Happy, who'd kept a dead bolt on every door in her mansion. Crystal knew that, like her grandmother, who was very smart, she was also smart, but that also like her grandmother she had a weakness. Her grandmother had lost her position in life by paying off a husband's debts. Now it seemed Crystal might be on the hook.

'Tell me what happened!' Kismet clutched her mother.

Crystal told her about the money and how Kismet's father had disappeared. In one blow, everything. Kismet closed her eyes and saw the same painted ladder that had tormented Father Flirty. It gave off a terrible radiance, the heat of shame, and because of its ghastly red bars (which she had helped her father paint, even), she did not tell her mother that she'd been pulled out only after she'd been swept under and nearly drowned. She said nothing about how she didn't want to marry Gary Geist. Her father had demolished everything familiar, the shock eating up all sensation. The town outside the walls of their modest old board house was already buzzing. As she began to absorb the implications of what her father had done, Kismet slipped toward a notion that by just getting on with it and getting married, she would be the hero of the wreck. The wedding would divert attention. She and her mother would not be defeated.

But her mother sensed the struggle. Nobody let themselves fall in the river, not this time of year, not ever. It was the region's life giver, but also it was a treacherous brown vein of trifluralin, atrazine, polychlorinated biphenyls, VOCs, and mercury, not to mention uprooted trees and sunken cars.

'In the river. Ohgodohgodohgod.'

Crystal hugged and rocked her daughter.

She whispered against Kismet's wet hair, 'You stink of booze, too. Goddamn bachelorette party. You could have drowned.'

Kismet still didn't tell her mother how close she'd come, but she gripped Crystal tighter, sagged against her. If only Crystal hadn't been distracted by Martin's crime, she might have realized that now was the time to act, to say something, to stop her daughter from making a serious mistake. At Kismet's age, being open to reason from a parent comes in slim windows that slam shut fast.

'Something else? Honey, are you scared? Cold feet?'

That her mother could even think of her feelings in the crazy shredding of their lives moved Kismet so much that she decided to do the last thing her mother would have wanted. Kismet would sacrifice herself.

'No.'

The whispery tremor in the no should have told Crystal. But she was drenched in shock and shocked relief. Crystal dried her daughter's hair with a dish towel and tried to stop her thoughts from seizing on what could have happened in the river. She tried to talk about the wedding plans but, as always, the groom's name stuck in her throat. Gary was a lazy talker, drawling with his blue eyes vacant. So what if he was Mr. Right for so many girls, not only rich but there was

his football captaining and student council president-
ing and his fake-looking white teeth. There was last
year's tragedy, which she hated to blame him for as he
was young, but he didn't seem in the least remorse-
ful. Not Gary. Still, Kismet had professed to love him,
love him, love him. So many declarations, like she was
trying to convince herself.

'Are you sure?' Crystal asked now. Her voice cracked
a little.

'Yes, for sure, it's decided,' said Kismet.

'Only if you love him,' said Crystal.

Kismet didn't answer.

Crystal walked up the narrow staircase with her
hand on her daughter's back and then, as Kismet lay
safe beneath the flowery bedspread, Crystal stroked
the hair along her forehead. A streetlight blinked off
and night entered the dim room where the layaway
bridal gown hung like an apparition on the outside of
the closet door. Crystal's heart leaked love and warning right along with her daughter's heart, but she didn't
insist that her daughter call the wedding off. She told
herself it had to be Kismet's choice, though perhaps,
just maybe, there was some scared frozen part of her
that thought Kismet could save her too.

Dangercat

The weight of first light, the struggle not to rise into consciousness knowing bad things waited there— the vodka headache, the bloating, the potential misery of her period starting on her wedding day, right out of the blue, wouldn't that be just . . . the wish, oh just the subtle green wish that slipped alongside Kismet's cheek like the tendril of a climbing plant, that Hugo would enfold her to his comfortable bulk and make her laugh. She could hear his whisper, she breathed his cleanly OCD smell of fresh soap, his shy armpits, because, yes, could it really be? She startled, heart zinging. Yes, it was Hugo. He was calling her softly from under the bed.

It was 4:39 a.m. and sometime in the night he'd made it through the minefield, past her mother's first-floor bedroom, up the creaking stairs, into Kismet's bedroom. Had he actually wedged himself beneath her bed? Well, she had put risers on it to increase the potential storage space and removed the boxes of school notebooks and awkward drawings just last week in order to destroy all evidence of her past life. Her stuff was now piled around the room. She hadn't done a thing. But anyway, there was enough room under the bed and yes, in fact, Hugo had hidden there most of the night. He had stretched out on his back, right underneath the bedspring and mattress and Kismet. For many hours, Hugo had been staring up into the dust-ball gloom, allowing the flow of tears to slide from his eyes into his cupped ears. Thoughtful Hugo had wanted to let her get some rest before the stress of the day's events. Those events. Now she forgot all about them for he was crawling up the side of her bed and sliding beneath the covers. She rolled into his soft freckled arms and crushed her face into his blast of gold-red hair.

'Hello, Dangercat.'

He had many pet names for her.

She began to cry and their feelings overwhelmed all judgment. They made the delirious last love of lost destiny. There was so much emotion in that room that it poured off Kismet's old mattress, out from under the quilt her mother had pieced together from Kismet's favorite T-shirts. That emotion altered the surfaces in

Kismet's childhood bedroom. The shelves of treasured books, jewelry boxes, and wire daisy-shaped earring hangers all shuddered with fateful pleasure. The many collages she had made from magazines—collages of eyes that were sightless, lips that couldn't speak, hands that couldn't touch—suddenly came alive and there was babbling, blinking, whispering, touching. Life was all around them in a whirling haze of heart-lifting happiness. It could never be replicated. It could never come true. That's what made it so powerful.

'Your marriage is an ephemeral blip,' said Hugo, as they lay together, in fraught peace, at dawn. 'I do not believe in it. We are bound by fate.'

'And surrounded by junk,' said Kismet, looking at her clothes, her stuffed animals. 'Has this ever happened before? Us?'

'Maybe our ancestors had a thing.'

'We should trace it back,' said Kismet in a weak voice. It was true that both their families had been in the valley for centuries.

'Books,' said Hugo.

'Which books?'

'Uh, classics? I guess after today—'

'Adultery,' said Kismet. Her voice was hushed.

They kept saying the word because it sounded so

weirdly grown-up. It did not occur to either one of them to stop having sex after Kismet's wedding.

'Let's read the same books,' said Kismet.

'I'm sure we've got copies. I'll pull them.'

'And then we'll go to all of the places in the books. And have adultery.'

'Don't you commit adultery?'

'As in commit to, or as in a sin?'

'Both.'

'Right.'

Kismet saw a wide dry desert of time and Hugo tiny in the distance. She pushed her childhood quilt into his arms and kissed him. His lips were soft and full like a woman's and his eyes were muddy hazel brown, completely vulnerable. So young. Nothing could be done about the fact that he was only a homeschooled kid, no matter what he said, and she was a recently graduated senior taking on the cross of womanhood before her time.

High Ceilings

Truly, the cross. Hours later, she stood before the giant wall cross and writhing crucified Christ as Father Flirty's voice tremoloed along through the marriage service. His voice was amplified by the tiny mic clipped to his stole. In his distress, while donning his vestments, Flirty had pulled his cincture too tight and now he felt it digging into his tummy, a fitting penance for the double breakfast he'd eaten in despair. He had worn the gorgeous white brocade chasuble of course—what else was he going to do?—and it fell symmetrically as his thoughts went up and up. One reason he had become a priest was the feeling of comfort these high ceilings gave him. There was room up there for thought, for memory, for prayer, for emotion.

During the ceremony people mumbled responses and joined reedily in hymn singing, but really they too were thinking. Beneath that glorious ceiling they were feeling, they were remembering. They were mulling over their mistakes and hopes, private madnesses, or worries about money.

No Halo

Martin had promised to walk his daughter down the aisle, that's what got to Crystal. He promised, then scampered off. And would she have to pay back this insane sum of money? She would be night hauling for eternity. She began to pray to St. Christopher, who'd crossed a river carrying on his back a very heavy baby who turned out to be a grown man. Jesus had skipped down and put a bright halo on St. Christopher. Would anyone put a halo on Crystal? *I damn well deserve one*, she thought.

Love, Reality Shows, Greasy Pizza

At a certain point, it had stopped being the three of them anyway. Or so Crystal thought in her collapsed consciousness. The wedding seemed to be taking forever. It had been Martin and Martin. It had been Crystal and Kismet. Martin spent his time on his own pursuits and Kismet did her own homework and was self-reliant. When the family went on little trips, never real vacations but just overnight trips here and there, they'd book one room and Kismet always shared a bed with Crystal. Martin needed the other bed to himself.

Martin. He needed to stretch out and zumba in his sleep. To put in his night guard so he didn't wear down his molars. To paste across the top of his nose the sticky butterfly that would open his nasal cavities. To ceremonially don his silk pajamas and sleep on his special pillow. He had many rigid sleep preparations and every so often he added another. It was all to ease his descent into unconsciousness, that scary place. He was filled with anxiety about nodding off, but also about not sleeping. Waking up during the night would ruin the next day.

While Crystal could sleep in a ditch. On those family trips, Kismet and Crystal would ball themselves up in twisty sheets, eat chips from the vending machines, drink root beer, share a bag of red licorice vines. Sometimes they would even have a decadent cardboardy cheese pizza delivered to the front desk. They both loved the grease pooling in the cheese. When they switched on the motel television, Martin would sigh, pull down his eye mask, screw in foam earplugs. And so love dies, Crystal thought, pulled down to earth by the tedious weight of a partner's habits.

Or at least love hibernates. Because to tell the truth, Crystal was finding that she still had some feelings for Martin, even when surrounded in her own kitchen by police.

Once Martin had passed out in his motel bed, Kismet and Crystal could watch *Dance Moms* or *Chicken Hoarders*, low volume, exaggerating silent guffaws and elbowing each other. They wore long saggy T-shirts and leggings to bed, soft old clothing that washed up in the laundry year after year. It wasn't just economy; they took delight in worn things, burnished things, objects with scars and repairs. To be in a motel room, especially a cheap, new chain motel room, was moving to them in a way. It made them feel giddy, trashy, temporary. A person wouldn't read in a place like that, wouldn't think, wouldn't even have an affair with a man they were in love with. Those new crappy rooms were for being normal.

They knew they were not normal in real life, where Crystal made bread from scratch not because it was artisanal but because it was cheaper, where all their clothes were 75-percent-off clothing, from Alco, or from Thrifty Life, which after the fall of 2008 was less embarrassing, just the place people shopped. The town or farm rich went to Fargo or Minneapolis, to the Mall of America, bragged about it. It used to be that the town well-off were considered the normal ones. They were like the people in movies and TV shows so it seemed they were Americans but lately Crystal and Kismet had come to know on some level that they were the real Americans—the rattled, scratching, always-in-debt Americans. It was okay with Crystal because she had her job, her house, and knew she and Kismet would rise. Somehow, they would rise. It was never all right with Martin, though, who couldn't put a jaunty face on desperation, who was sometimes rageful about having to do without his special items of comfort, and who would have loved the fancy wedding reception, also loved the second one, scheduled for this evening and only hours away.

The Teacup

Winnie closed her eyes. There would be plenty of time later to cry with relief. Here, in the church where she liked to be, old shocks caught up with her but they were muted. She got lost in the scenery of memory. She'd married Diz at this very altar, carved with clover cutouts representing the Holy Trinity. Right there where Gary and Kismet were standing. Then, as now, she hated Sport Geist for buying her family's farm and bulldozing the entire homestead.

The ceiling went up and up and pictures crowded into her mind.

After they'd moved into town, her mother had worked in the dime store, when the town still had a dime store, on a main street of thriving shops. Her father had driven a beet truck—hard, bone-rattling, seasonal work. Off season, he delivered appliances and sold window air conditioners until the appliance store went out of business. More people lost their farms. And the farms that survived got bigger, so fewer people to shop and those who survived wealthier, so traveling out of state. After a while there came the dollar stores. Walmarts opened in the area. Downtown began to look haunted and hollow. And her family also dwindled. Her brother and sisters moved from here to there, from there to where? Sometimes they didn't send more than a Christmas card. She had stayed, though, and married Diz. They had brought her parents out to live their last years on the land. That was all they'd wanted, to be on the land. She was proud of having given that to them.

Then, last March. Weeks must have passed before she remembered coming downstairs. By then she had weakened more than she thought and landed on the living room carpet. Vividly, she remembered picking a piece of fluff off the carpet and putting it carefully on the sofa. She had crawled onto the living room couch, where she saw blips of light, heard the shift of Diz's gears squeaking, and the pump of music as Gary pulled the car into the yard. The carnival. She remembered thinking about the county fair and being confused. What kind of carnival ride am I on right now? She'd loved the teacup. She had thought she was on a very slow teacup, so slow that she'd be able to drink a cup of tea without a dribble. She saw herself spinning incrementally across the field to the horizon.

She picked herself up, but something had changed.

Diz and Gary decided to build a house for Gary's future. They didn't seem to notice the powerful mess in the house they had. They could only think about the house they were working on. Once it was time to plant, they hired a few subcontractors. Although it seemed she was moving through heavy syrup, Winnie stayed upright for longer and longer amounts of time. After a while, she noticed that Gary had stopped looking scared, miserable, wasted, hollow. He began to look like himself. He mentioned Kismet Poe and Winnie got her phone number. Winnie called Kismet and offered to drive her to Gary's away games. The girl declined, but her voice was polite. Winnie knew Kismet's mother but hadn't seen the girl for years. She looked Kismet up in Gary's old yearbooks. In one photo Kismet sneered from under what looked like a nest of black sticks. Next year, she was wearing a black ribbon around her throat and her hair was pulled back except for one curl, an arabesque, in the middle of her forehead. The next year, she looked normal. Not one of the class beauties, exactly, but there was something about her that jumped off the page. A bit of force, some extra life.

Now, in the church, she heard the *Do you take this man* spoken.

It was done, oh, now it was done. Winnie let her tears fall and smiled.

Do I

Here it was, the hour of truth. When Kismet could have risen in her tear-stained gown and bolted out of the church. When nobody would have stopped her or blamed her. She'd had to walk down the aisle with her mother. I tell you, they'd say, that was when the girl just fell apart. It would have been Poor Kismet this and Poor Kismet that. Her father ruining her life discussed with excitement, then within a couple of years a legend, like other town disasters. Possibly, in Kismet's alternate future, she didn't get married at all but went to a friendly college and her father somehow returned the money. Possibly, Gary Geist would then marry one of the two remaining bridesmaids. Or maybe the third, Ally, who had been locked up in her bedroom under parental guard—it was Ally whose parents had given the most money to the church fund. Ally or Brianna could marry Gary. Not Stockton though, because she did not like Gary. But, hmmm, it did make Kismet uneasy to think of Gary without her. Sometimes he said he would have to kill himself without her. However, that was just in the heat of the moment, right? Well, Gary could mysteriously disappear—let us say, into a fabulous existence. Yes, imagine if he really disappeared! Not murdered or anything, of course she wouldn't wish that, but why couldn't Gary simply happily vanish?

'Yeah, that would be great,' said Kismet. She blinked, coming back to herself.

'*I do* would be more correct here,' said Father Flirty in his most catechismal voice.

Kismet stared into Gary's face. He was looking away, a knowing glance at his best man. But Eric was looking at Kismet, nodding encouragingly, mouthing the words. He gave a nod and a lift of his sandy brows and stared at her with worried brown eyes.

'Do I?' said Kismet, looking at Eric, whose face cleared in relief. 'I mean, I do.'

She had the disorienting thought that Eric was the one she would actually be marrying.

Her eyes shut. Alas, it was done. Her mind raced off.

She imagines that Gary follows in his parents' footsteps,

back to Russia, to join some rich and powerful sugar beet farmers his parents have kept in touch with. He doesn't know they are actually criminals, but once he goes there, they won't let him return. Or maybe he joins their sugar cartel by choice. Kismet smiles, her blunt vampy features and tender eyes glowing with the joy of Gary living a continent and more away. It is a surprise when he kisses her.

Splendor Stripe

Meanwhile, in Holy Rosary Church, everyone who witnesses the newlywed couple walking back down the worn carpet of the middle aisle, away from the peeling altar, goes away saying how radiant Kismet was, a normal bride, how she must love Gary so much that the embezzlement thing didn't register above the flood of joy she had experienced right then, although in actual fact her mind kept assembling an inner narrative. When Gary grabbed her arm too hard, pinching her, he whispered, *Hope your mom has a good lawyer,* and Kismet's thoughts surged. Large men baring golden teeth suddenly plunge Gary headfirst into a huge barrel of vodka! They keep him down. Gary's legs kick straight out until his whole body relaxes in a horrible way and he is dead.

Why, she wondered moments later, showered not with rice but with sunflower seeds on the church steps because this was also sunflower country, why did this disturbing fantasy take hold of her when of course she loved Gary so very much, loved him enough to have let things go on and on when he asked her to marry him, and now, such thoughts having taken hold of her mind, at that crucial time, his lips pressing against hers unwelcome, the taste of his stale beer and brat breath from his last night as a bachelor covered with mint gum, why did she feel only worried amusement? And why did she not feel the head-ringing explosion of her father's crime, either? She picked a sunflower seed from her veil. It was a plump Splendor Stripe. The capacity to make any sense of her own emotions had deserted her. Once, months ago, she had told herself that she loved Gary, and everyone said love was eternal, so what had happened to those feelings?

Ephemeral Blip

After the ceremony there was the immediate reception in the church event room, perhaps doomed now to its perpetual gloomy food window, its collapsible tables covered with tablecloths of disposable eternal plastic. Mrs. Flossom had provided centerpieces of white roses and baby's breath. Also there, the first wedding cake, the much anticipated famous wedding cake, barely fitting into a large white van. It had been delivered on a pallet by the baker and her terrified husband. The cake had wobbled, but not broken. It was a castle, story after story of frosted towers, a fairy palace of sweetness. There were the photographs, taken with knife poised over the cake's white-flagged towers, and there was a splendid devouring of the cake on wedding-bell paper plates with metallic-look plastic forks. The napkins were printed with more bells, their names, the date. This first reception, meant to be public for the town, went on for quite a while. People praised the fluffy, exotic crème anglaise filling, the superior sugar in the frosting, the intricate sugar roses that twined on every layer. There was also (under special dispensation from Father Flirty) champagne. At the pop of the first cork, Kismet flinched and touched her cheekbone. Then more corks popped and the stuff was poured.

Kismet raised the skinny glass to her lips and the gentle bubbles grazed her nose. She took her first-ever sip of champagne. The ghost of a taste, an emotion in her mouth, unreadable. She drank again to try and understand. But it was too fleeting. Then she got it and smiled. *An ephemeral blip.* She drank until the champagne stopped thought, stopped taste, stopped emotion. People whirled, talking in her face. People watched from the sides of the room. They were talking about her, talking about her father, trying to corner Crystal, who eluded them all.

After a brutal set of photos, Kismet's mother squeezed her arm and said that she had to leave. Early.

'Are you going to see a lawyer?' said Kismet.

'Oh, honey, yes,' said Crystal.

They wrapped each other in a silent hug with eyes squeezed shut. Getting a lawyer? It had never happened to them. It was as apocalyptic as Kismet getting married. They hugged harder, trying not to cry. Everybody looked away.

The Golden Light

The church reception ended and the newlyweds drove out of town in Gary's pickup, rattling cans off the back fender, followed by honking cars. The receding floodwaters, which had crested at over forty feet, still stood in some of the fields nearest the river, reflecting sky so the world was confusing and horizonless. Once they turned onto the highway, Gary pounded on the steering wheel, swore at his friends for having written Just Married in shaving cream on his FX. He was afraid it would eat the paint away and those words would be permanent. After his tantrum about the shaving cream, they didn't speak. Kismet was frozen. She'd never heard him in a rage. He reached out, grabbed her hand, placed it on his zipper. Kismet stared out at the fields that had dried out and were newly sprouting sugar beets planted with industrial exactitude, field after field. Gary sped up some more and the beet rows rolled by like the green spokes of time. He pushed her hand. *Pet me.* Oh, okay, what a baby, maybe it would soothe his stupid anger. As long she was giving Gary attention with her hand, she decided to let her brain relax by thinking about Hugo. Directly, she was filled with such joy that she squeezed. Gary yipped like a cowboy and turned down a side road.

'No! You'll ruin my dress!'

He did a U-turn, raising a splatter of wet grit.

'Okay,' he said. 'Just go back to what you were doing.'

She put her hand where he wanted it. He swerved, hit the gas, and rolled the truck. There was an unreal slow-motion airborne time as the truck slipped through air. There was an obliterating smash, a roll, a flash of upside down. Then she was looking out through the windshield as before. Only the truck was beside the road instead of on it and in a planted field.

'This is Pavlecky's field,' said Gary. 'It's dry. Good thing.'

Kismet took a breath. Her chest was okay. She examined her hands, her arms, checked in with her legs, reminded herself to breathe. She touched her face, her head, her hair. No blood. She seemed to be all right. The sun was on her, shining with a soft afternoon intensity. Nothing had been dislodged, except, wait, something had definitely been dislodged. Yes. Something that had perhaps been too loosely attached in the first place had been dislodged.

They bumped down to an access road and kept driving toward the house.

'Aren't you going to say something?' she asked after a while.

'About what?' said Gary.

Diz had dropped off a huge suitcase that Kismet packed that morning. Gary helped his wife out of the car and shook his head, but the side doors were barely warped. Holding hands, the two walked up a dirt path.

'Don't worry,' said Gary, frowning at the dirt.

The couple stood in the mud dust before the brand-new tan house with brown trim, Gary scuffing at the dirt with the toe of his polished shoe. 'There wasn't time to put in a driveway.'

Gary scooped her up and staggered a bit as they crossed the threshold. This house was the wedding gift from Gary's parents. He'd told her about it, over and over, but kept the actual sight as a surprise. He'd explained that the house was a high-end customizable prefab. It had been plunked down on the outskirts of the farmstead on the other side of the old lilacs, and he'd worked with his dad on special features. Yes, Gary's parents lived across that hedge, maybe not ideal. But now it occurred to Kismet that her mother could maybe live here too, if things got worse. Gary stood Kismet on her feet, like a doll, right there on the mellow wood-look floor of the entryway. Unexpected tears pressed behind her eyes. Oh yes, Crystal could get used to this place, if she was driven out of town, that is. Kismet walked in and thought that she had never seen such light. Or known that this was what she'd always craved—western light pouring into a house in this way. Transfixed, she watched the slow sinking expansion of radiance across the damp weed-proof soil. She looked around and her heart slowed in helpless pleasure. Mellow golden sunlight flickered through tall rhomboid windows, spilling across the walls. One wall was still Sheetrocked and taped, waiting for paint. Here and there, cans of paint and magazines—agricultural ones—were stacked. A few trees had been left in the yard, cottonwood and ash. Shadows of their leaves, faintly blue, roiled across the creamy plasterboard and up the stone, or maybe fake stone, fireplace and chimney. Kismet walked into the room, tranced by the fireplace. Each rock was perfectly split to harmonize with the next rock in mica-flecked pink or gray or tawny yellow. Cheery little flames licked behind glass and she stretched her hands out before she could help herself. The fire disappeared, sucked back into the logs. Behind her, Gary laughed—in that way. What way, she asked herself, exactly did he laugh? He laughed like a *stupid cow*. And yet he loved her! She turned and saw that he held a remote control to the gas insert, and she shrugged as if she'd been kidding too.

Kismet flung herself down on a dog-smelling sectional—reassuringly not new—but he grabbed her arm and pulled her up. He dragged her into the kitchen—showed her the gas range and the new refrigerator with the options for ice and water right there in the door. It was too much for her and again tears assailed her, but this time it was grief, for Crystal, who always filled her plastic ice cube trays so carefully and sometimes placed a tiny mint leaf in each ice cube, or made coffee ice cubes for her father's iced coffee or lemonade ice cubes for lemonade, or froze grapes to dunk in glasses at, say, an imaginary party where frail glasses of wine would be served from a silver platter.

Gary rummaged through the fridge. Pulled out

THE MIGHTY RED · 197

cold cuts, groaning with hunger. She made sandwiches for him. Brewed coffee. For herself, a bowl of corn-flakes. Afterward, she did the dishes, put things away, turned the pans over, as she did in thrift stores, to see the manufacturer's marks, and gravely looked at plates and cups, seeing that everything was made in China, and new.

Gary had gone up to the bathroom to shower. He told her that if she wanted, she could go upstairs and take a bath while he was taking a shower. She went upstairs. She heard the water going behind one door and saw that there was another bathroom, which contained a suave commode and an oval bathtub. The floors were covered in digitally distressed linoleum floor tiles pretending they were from an old castle.

Kismet started running a bath and went to the walk-in closet, which was the size of her old bedroom, to get out of her wedding dress. She got the satin down past her hips and slithered like a shedding snake over to her belongings. When she unzipped and opened her suitcase, the smell of her old life wafted gently out. Her mother had slipped a bottle of her own perfume into the suitcase. The frosted glass stopper of the tiny vintage bottle was shaped like a flower petal. Kismet patted her throat and rubbed a tiny droplet between her wrists as she used to do when she stole into her mother's room and used Fleurs du Monde. The perfume wilted her down onto the carpet.

Kismet dug her hand into the packed pile of folded jeans, through her balled socks and tangled underwear. She pulled out an XL T-shirt of faded bronze featuring a sword-wielding, sexily ripped, bikini-clad angel beneath the word Magic. She put Hugo's T-shirt around her head and passed out for a moment. Then in the bathroom there was the turbo whine of a hair dryer. Uh-oh. She threw off the T-shirt and tried to struggle back into her wedding dress, lying on her back, squirming it over her hips. She was pulling up her panty hose when Gary walked out of the shower, into the closet. Naked, with a hard-on, he said, *Let's ball.*

'I'm running a bath,' said Kismet.

'Hey, I married you, didn't I?'

He grinned at her, slowly raising his lip to show his teeth. 'Plus this house? I laid the floors in. I taped the Sheetrock. Gimme the candy.'

He sank down where she lay, tried to pull down her panty hose, push up her satin skirt, and kneel between her legs. It didn't work, but he seemed undaunted. She reminded him her bath was running. He said absently that there was an overflow gasket. A strange expression crossed his face.

'You're so beautiful,' he said. 'I'm sorry, slut.'

'I don't like that,' said Kismet.

He was holding her arms down. He threw himself on top of her, moved jerkily, in a kind of fit, went slack, then inert. She gave a hard push and staggered upright, kicking off her dress.

'You know when you rolled the truck? I lost something,' she said. 'I lost my love for you. Whatever I thought was love is back there in Pavlecky's field.'

She scrambled around and pulled on the big T-shirt. He didn't move and she bent over to make sure he was breathing. Had he taken some drug?

Maybe an overdose. But he was indeed breathing.

Damn, thought Kismet, sinking back down into the carpet to catch her breath.

He stirred and shook his head as if to clear it. When Gary heard what his new wife had said, he'd fallen a great distance, into a lightless pit, and gone inert.

'Did you take something? A drug?' she asked.

'Hey, we're married.'

'Did you hear me?'

Gary tried to rally his wide, lazy grin, just like in his high school senior portrait. His teeth were movie-star straight and brilliant. He'd had his jaw broken and his bite messed up in a football game. Some of his teeth were implants from corpses, he had told her. His grin had cost a fortune.

'The bullshit is over, babe.'

He reached over suddenly, swiped her hand in his, and began to stroke himself with her hand, gently, as if her hand were a piece of cloth.

'You're creeping me out,' said Kismet.

'But you sorta like it, am I right?'

'No.' She snatched her hand away.

Gary's self-assured grin turned, for a moment, mean and furtive, then the anger passed and a bewildered look settled there. He gazed at her like a child stumped over an arithmetic problem. To steady herself, Kismet called up, as she had several times in the past few weeks, the moment last fall when Gary had nuzzled her collarbone and told her in a husky slurred voice that he loved her, that he'd die without her, that nothing else in this world mattered, that they had to get married right after they graduated.

'So you don't, that's not, hey . . .' Gary was still trying to reset his brain when she walked into the bathroom and locked the door behind her. He gave the door a light rap. She turned off the bathwater and hit the tub drain, then wetted a cotton ball to begin the process of removing and reapplying her makeup. He gave a softer knock and said, 'What will it take to make you open that door?'

'You outside in the truck, waiting for me.'

'I did bad,' he said after a few moments. 'You didn't like it.'

'You got that right, Gary.'

'I won't . . . ' He started to speak, couldn't go on. She kept squirting foundation on the side of her wrist and patting it on with the tips of her fingers.

'Okay, I won't be that way again.'

Kismet stopped and looked gravely at herself. She saw that she looked scared and something else. She looked desperate. Why, she could hardly force a dimple to her cheek.

'Yeah, you won't do that again. You acted disgusting. Where'd you get those moves?'

'Uh, well.'

'Gary!'

'Off the internet.'

'That's what I thought. I'm not going to have sex with you tonight, Gary, just prepare yourself for nothing. I might never want to have sex again, ever, after what you called me.'

'No, no, let's not start that way.'

'You have dishonored me,' she said. Her voice was

queenly. Where had that come from? She wasn't really all that hurt, or insulted, but with the word slut he'd given her the upper hand.

She sharpened her eyebrow pencil, lined it up with her tweezers, square compact of eye shadow, liquid waterproof eyeliner, and blusher. Blocking out everything else, she slowly began her ritual.

Perfect Advantage

Crystal fell into a trauma sleep right after the church reception. She had to ravel her unstrung brain. She had four hours before the 6 p.m. dinner. But after only an hour she woke, swimming into consciousness, and the awful sensation broke over her. Martin. Then the ache over Kismet.

Crystal took a painful breath and decided to meet the afternoon. At least she now had the whole mattress to herself. She did not have to sleep in the shallow furrow her body had pressed into the various foams, quilted cottons, and whatever else had taken the impressions of her and Martin's sleeping bodies. At least now she could rest on the firm center. She sat up. Her backache was gone.

'And here I thought it was the driving!'

She was thrilled for a long second. Then a little of the ache returned. But the center of the mattress had definitely helped. Crystal swung her legs over the side of the bed. The floor she'd sanded with a rented sander and coated with a toxic poly was smooth and cool. She needed coffee. To have it, now, she still had to go through the lengthy procedure Martin had instituted. She walked out to the kitchen, put a kettle of water on the boil, and shook magic beans from their airtight jar into a white grinder. The droll club-shaped machine cracked the beans and began to whir. The scent of ground coffee and then the first taste of it bounced her up. While she had slept, the mail had come. She fetched it from the box and set the envelopes in a crisp pile.

It was 3 p.m. Her daughter had been married for a total of four hours. Already Crystal regretted having let the marriage just . . . happen. Couldn't she have done something? Meanwhile, the police had been to the house again. She'd heard them knocking, but put a pillow over her head. Why should she talk to them after last night? They did not seem to believe her and implied that they would be watching her. But the marriage, this was the main thing that bothered Crystal. Somehow she hadn't fully connected the wedding with the loss of her daughter. Somehow it ached that Kismet hadn't come home with her today. Crystal paced through the house, impatient to talk to Kismet, to go over the events of the ceremony, the reception, minute by minute, to dissect the behaviors and the possibilities, to figure out what to do next, to plot a strategy before the wedding dinner. She'd left messages on Kismet's cell phone. She had emailed. Still no word from Martin. Everything she wrote was sucked away but no messages came back. Of course, coverage was probably sketchy out there on the farm. Looking in the slender old phone book for the Geists' number, she came up with only the beet factory offices. She supposed their home number was unpublished. And with her own house staked out by the police (she noticed that a white Camry was still parked across the street, an unknown man behind the wheel), she didn't exactly want to jump in the car and drive to the farm. To show up with a police tail—how would that look?

She dragged herself over to her plain desk, set in a corner of the living room. Nothing on the desk was of any sentimental value whatsoever, except, taped into an aperture, the last payment she had made to extinguish the mortgage on the house. Crystal had usually worked two jobs. Weekdays she used to be a receptionist for a construction company in town. On weekends she worked on the main floor at Penneys, right downtown and only a few blocks from home. She saved and scrimped, loved to see zeros in her amount-owed boxes. Late fees sickened her. The other slots in her desk were there to hold current bills, fresh envelopes, and stamps. The drawers held checks. Paper clips. Yellow sticky notes. A letter opener with an enamel bluebird handle, from Kismet.

Discarding the junk mail and credit card offers first, then using the bluebird opener, Crystal slit open every envelope. One by one she slipped out the bills or notices and studied them. Medical insurance. She wondered how to handle Kismet's coverage now and put that aside. Electric was satisfyingly low because the furnace was turned off and no air conditioner in use yet. May, June, and September were low months. When it got really hot, no watering, except she saved her bathwater for the flowers. She'd get by. Her family phone plan. Should she call to remove Martin? No. It would look suspicious. And again, Kismet, who had just bought herself a cell phone. Should she pay for her daughter's phone plan, which was attached to hers, or would that change? Would Kismet now enter Gary's family plan? It gave her a little pang. She paid the bill. Her account was sinking. Her subscription to the local newspaper had lapsed and she wrote a check out, paid up. Huh: Martin had scheduled a physical before he ditched—such foresight—there was a copayment due.

Maybe she'd have to pay that. Perhaps he would get caught if he tried to use his insurance card in an emergency. The final envelope was from a bank, some sort of offer to open a new sort of checking account, she imagined. But it was not. She had to read every word of the notice for mortgage payment many times before she even understood.

There was suddenly a mortgage on her house. Impossible. She jumped up, walked in circles. Considered the situation. No! This would not stand. No! The explanation was too obvious. Martin had gone behind her back. Somehow he had tried to mortgage her house. When the truth hit her a red film dropped across her vision. Her head buzzed with adrenaline. The sickening nerve. How this was even possible she had no clue. But there it was. Not a large amount by some people's standards. An impossible amount for her. It would take the money she'd saved for Kismet's college fund, at the very least.

She stood, sat, took hold of herself. But of course he had done this illegally and she would straighten it out. She would drive—no, walk—immediately to the bank. She snatched up the scrap of paper. But there the problem magnified itself—the name of this bank or this mortgage company was unfamiliar. Perfect Advantage. Only a post office box in Omaha for the place to send her check, not even a physical address. There was, however, an 800 number.

She dialed the number. A young male voice answered. 'Perfect Advantage. How may I assist you?'

'I am a representative of the Better Business Bureau,' said Crystal. 'I have a complaint from a member and I would like to investigate that complaint.'

The voice didn't miss a beat.

'All right. May I have the name or account number?'

'The name is Crystal Frechette. But there is no account number on the letter that she received.'

'Spell that please? If you will hold for a moment, I will check out her information.'

Crystal held for three minutes and the young man came back on the line.

'I have a number for you. Are you ready?'

'Yes.'

'Great. If you would take this down . . . 2879499 4832020384756109 dash 3. Don't forget the dash. That is the account number. According to our records, the first payment of $823.34 is due on June 20. In order to avoid any late payment fees, your client can use a credit card. Would your client like to do that?'

'No,' said Crystal. 'Because she did not take out a mortgage on her property.'

'I'm afraid she is mistaken. Our records show—'

'I would like a copy of your records.'

'Certainly. I will put you through to our records department.'

The line went dead.

Crystal laughed and threw the paper down. A scam! A phishing scheme. Sending out phony mortgage bills hoping someone on the other end was stupid enough to pay—what gall. She fumed. She paced from the desk to the kitchen to the front window. The white Camry was still out there. She snatched the mortgage bill and again turned it over as if in secret writing an explanation would appear. She sat down at her desk, tapped her bill-signing pen on the sturdy edge of her jaw, then called Jeniver.

Half an hour later, Crystal entered an office building constructed of textured brown cement blocks. She checked in with the poker-faced receptionist (part-time, Crystal knew) and took a seat in the generic beige waiting alcove of Longie and Longie Attorneys at Law. The double Longie sounded good, but the only Longie there was Jeniver. She was a salty freckly brunette who wore sharp jewelry and bold colors. Jeniver burst into the waiting area, grabbed Crystal around the shoulders, hauled her into the office, and shut the door.

'Here.'

She poured a mug of coffee for Crystal and pushed it across her desk, then sat down with an expectant look. Jeniver was wearing a purple jacket and turquoise knit top. Her earrings were silver scimitars. Her narrow brown eyes glinted.

'Really glad you came in. You're going to need some legal protection. Has anyone hinted that they might hold you in any way responsible for the money Martin stole?'

'No!'

'Let's make sure that doesn't happen.'

'We have to talk about that, yes, what Martin did, or didn't, do, with the church fund. I mean, we'll get to that. But now there's something else—this letter I got. To preface this, I paid off my mortgage ten years ago and a line of credit two years ago. I own my house, as you know!'

'All too well,' said Jeniver, who'd listened patiently to many a D.I.Y. crisis.

Crystal slid the letter across the dull laminate surface of the desk, and Jeniver examined it.

'So you didn't take out this mortgage?'

'Martin must have forged my signature, everything.'

'The shit. Let me keep this. I'll do a search on this company and try to find out the scoop. You haven't paid of course.'

Crystal cocked her head. 'Of course not?'

'Well, some people just pay anything that comes in the mail. You'd be surprised. I'd say ignore it but with this Martin thing you never know.'

'That's what I thought.'

'Okay, I'll get to the bottom of this. No charge.'

'That's all right, no really, I can—'

'Haven't you been screwed enough for one week?'

Crystal teared up, put her hand to her throat.

'Not just by Martin either, honey, I have this foreboding feeling.'

'Foreboding? About?'

Jeniver looked wary, coughed delicately into her fist.

'Stockton tells me that Kismet says she really loves Gary, but I still don't feel good about the wedding. And I have not gotten over that weird announcement at the book club.'

Crystal had the dreamlike sense that everything that had happened this morning had occurred on a conveyer belt. And that she should have hit the red emergency button.

'I should have stopped it somehow,' she said to Jeniver. 'But I can't even begin. Also, you know,' she blurted, 'Kismet fell in the river, last night.'

'Stockton too. All of them. What dipshits.'

'They're idiots.'

'Not like we were, right?'

To laugh felt good, though Crystal feared that once she started she might never stop. Crystal's laugh was rich and warm, a whiskey-soda laugh, though she rarely drank. Jeniver's laugh had been a raucous bray in high school, but practice of the law had squeezed it to a sharp series of knowing woofs—not dog woofs, but another kind of animal. A night animal. Jeniver's laugh was the sort of laugh that might emerge from dense shrubbery and sink your heart. Her laugh always impressed Crystal, comforted her. She was in capable, clawed hands.

Green Silk

Back at home, Crystal's breath clogged and her brain buzzed. How could she possibly go to the golf club and celebrate? She sat on the edge of her bed and tried to just take things one minute at a time. After a while she managed to calm her heart. At least she had something marvelous to wear. From an upscale Fargo thrift store, Crystal had purchased a dress for this occasion, a very nice dress, but maybe now a bit too nice. It was not a dress she could ever have afforded new. But somehow it had been marked down enough for her to have it. Crystal went to her closet, opened the saggy door, touched the glimmering cloth. Yes, she thought, this looks like an embezzlement dress. However, it doesn't look like the dress of a woman who is in danger of losing her house.

Crystal brought the dress out into the light and tried it on. It was slippery green silk shot through with golden threads. Tiny linked initials of the designer were embroidered into the pattern. The dress was lined with heavy satin. The hem was weighted. The sly neckline lay flat just below her collarbone. Three-quarter-length sleeves, fake cuffs, small gold initial buttons. The dress was immaculate, yet it had been worn, for it bore the trace of an unusual perfume, which hadn't cloyed, but retained a hint of freshness and life.

She had fastened a mirror inside her closet door. She searched a few moments for the green silk jacket that was supposed to go with the dress, but then decided that the dress was better on its own. Kismet had often slipped in to check her outfits in that mirror. Crystal smoothed the dress along her stomach and studied her profile. Nothing can touch me in this dress, Crystal thought. I can walk through this shitstorm and I'll still look perfect.

'You're a devastating love witch,' she said, out loud, to her reflection.

Tears pressed up because this was the sort of thing

she and Kismet had said when they looked into this mirror together. Only of course afterward they hugged and laughed, and now Crystal turned away from the mirror and had to cover her face.

Why, oh why, oh fucking why on god's earth had she let her daughter marry Gary Geist?

She tried not to cry on the silk as she slipped out of the dress to take a quick shower. There was a trace, like the perfume, of the spirit of the woman who originally owned and wore the dress.

Whoever you are, Crystal thought as she stepped into the shower stall, you are surely dead, for although we don't acknowledge this, most of the best thrift shop clothing is bequeathed to us, not transferred from the living. She turned on the water. Still hot. Hello! You with the good taste! This is me, Crystal. I am asking for your help. I need to walk through holy hell and still look good. I need to get my daughter out of a questionable marriage if she needs to get out. And also, I need to keep my house.

Be of good cheer, the spirit spoke as soothing steam. I have suffered and am now on the other side, but I will help you. I know some people.

Crazy, thought Crystal. But thank you. Somehow, she felt better.

I have to go through with this, thought Kismet. *There's no out.* She gathered up her graveyard-shift self bravely greeting a party of ten at 2 a.m. and managed to joke about rain on her wedding day. She liked the sound of it on the pickup roof, the comforting sweep of the windshield wipers.

'Hey, we're married,' said Gary.

The words. The nod. The slow wide grin. The perfect teeth of the dead.

'Time's wasting,' he suggested.

He reached for her hand but she moved it away. They rolled along without speaking.

'I have to do one thing,' said Kismet. 'I need to order a book.'

'Order one?'

'Or get one. Stop at Bev's Bookery. I'll only be a minute.'

'Okay,' said Gary, looking away.

With spring and rising temperatures, last year's harvest of sugar beets, stored in loaf-shaped piles giant against the horizon, were rotting. And now it was raining, though too late to ruin the wedding. The bottoms of the beet piles were mush and the lakelike bodies of the holding tanks were filled with what sugar beet farmers always called organic material. For instance, the head of PR, as he spoke to the many complaints: *I am sorry, but the organic material is simply vulnerable to degradation in spring. We are always working hard on the problem of fragrance.* The complainer would say it was a stink, not a fragrance, and the head of PR would say that, to himself and so many others in the valley, that stink was the fragrance of money. Yes, the rain smelled like rotten eggs because of the hydrogen sulfide produced by the deteriorating sugar beets. Yes, the air over the fields and into town and along the river smelled like old cooked broccoli that you have forgotten in a bowl in your refrigerator, or maybe like burnt coffee run through the wrong end of a dog. Yes, there was a penetrating unpleasantness. The smell affected everybody's outlook. Even for the good of the economy, it was a thing that some people could not easily get used to. But although you weren't used to it, you had to accept it if you wanted to live along the mighty red. Hugo sloshed through the stinking rain and took his mother's place in the bookstore.

'I left you dinner,' said his mother.

He checked as soon as she had gone. There was wrapped food in the clean little white store refrigerator.

Threads of outdoor fumes caused him to reflect. Here was some of the most fertile land upon the earth. The owners of this treasure were various farmers whose bill-paying cash crop was sugar beets. Many considered it a point of pride that their area was number one in the country for the production of sugar. But although sugar is a useless and even harmful substance, and although this nutritionless white killer is depleting the earth's finest cropland, you forget that when you are eating blueberry crumble, thought Hugo, sweeping his finger across the blue stain and sweet crumbs on his plate.

'Better money in the oil fields,' he said, out loud, thinking of his next move. 'But there won't be blueberry crumble.'

The clouds sank and opened, the storm slashing down, beating upon the empty storefronts, pelting the random arrangements of fake flowers in the windows, rippling across newspaper covering the glass. The bookstore had no customers. Hugo had accomplished the next phase of his studies and now had some engineering classes under his belt. He hadn't told any of this to Kismet because the timing was all off. He was smart, not smart enough to get Kismet, but he was sure that he was smart enough to use the courses he had finished to get a job in the science of fracking. He had gone to microscopic trouble to meddle with the dates on his old birth certificate in order to get a properly dated driver's license so that he could get hired. By summer's end, he intended to have made a big pile of money, enough to support himself and Kismet. Of course, he would have to steal Kismet from Gary Geist, to whom she had now been married for six long hours. He washed his plate in the bathroom sink and emerged again to sit behind the desk. Instead of going to the oil fields, he would have preferred continuing to work where he was working now—he loved this exquisitely crammed, pleasantly dry little bookstore on main street. Hugo bent close to the computer to try and figure out his mother's new style of keeping inventory. He squinted at the tangle, drifting, as water darkened the sky and the sky poured mightily down. If only Kismet . . . he glanced at the door.

She blew in on the sour rain.

Stood on the absorbent mat just within the entryway. Dripped and spoke at the same tempo, which is all Hugo saw. The sense of things Kismet said? The gist? Nothing. He could see her lips move and hear the sounds of her voice and the pounding rain. He couldn't register meaning. The air between the two of them, the swirl of headlights in the misty murk, the peaceful whine of tires rolling by on the wet asphalt of main, outside, and just Kismet and Hugo in the dim bookstore, and the many titles, *Anna Karenina* among them, which mirrored their ecstasy and now their plight, and Chekhov, 'The Lady with the Dog,' ending at the moment where their difficulties also had begun, and contemporary novels of betrayal and adultery and sin, which Kismet and Hugo would read for confirmation of themselves and which often ended with death the justice, but most often only for the woman. These books they had sought were all around them now and Hugo wondered if Kismet felt, as he did, their power at that moment; she was wiping the rain from her cheekbones with the palm of her hand, blinking, continuing to emit hazy white noise from her bare lips and holding the very tip of her tongue between her teeth as she concentrated on his face.

'I have to tell you,' said Hugo, in a state of urgency. He'd been thinking. 'Like maybe your dad did not embezzle the money.'

She watched his moon-round face in the grainy dim light.

'Maybe didn't steal it. Maybe he lost it.'

Hugo said that the money could have vanished last fall, in the crash, along with so much other money, and that Martin had been desperately pretending ever since then.

'Was he weird?'

'He was weird,' said Kismet, shaking water from her hands.

'Yeah,' said Hugo. 'Even I could feel it. But now that

the building season's starting, see, the money isn't there. Maybe it was all spent on the design and there's nothing left. Maybe Martin's gonna turn up with a scorched-earth portfolio, and it will be awful, sure. But it won't be a criminal proceeding or prison or whatever.'

It was awkward now.

'So,' he said.

She began to weep as she walked backward, mumbling incoherent phrases of longing and regret. Then she was out the door. Hugo stood between the romance and nonfiction shelves watching the pickup leave and the rain skitter down the plate glass. He thought maybe she had needed him to say other words, words he could not produce. Or not in time anyway to stop her from walking back out into the rain. She had asked him to save a book, hadn't she? And said that Gary was waiting in the truck. Yes, she'd said that. Was the book *Madame Bovary*? He'd give her a copy. They had laughed about how they would read their way through Europe before they ran off together. Had she also said, could he have misheard or did she actually say: Wait for me?

PART THREE
The Wedding Dinner

2009

Damaged Goods

G ary pulled around to the golf club entrance and got out to help his bride. Kismet took his hand as she stepped out of the pickup and shuffled along beneath Stockton and Ally's moving roof of umbrellas. Crystal was waiting in the doorway, wearing the green dress with its pattern of tiny golden symbols. Of course, word got around, before the truth of the dress came out, that Crystal had spent a ton of stolen church money on designer clothing. Crystal fixed her daughter's dress and hair, then they held each other in the hallway, where the photographer had set up flowers and lights.

Crystal whispered, 'You okay?'

'Mom, he didn't steal the money.'

Crystal put her arms around her daughter and said, 'Let's smile.'

Kismet's face already hurt from hard smiling, and Crystal was so disoriented that she hardly knew where to put her feet. Winnie Geist appeared holding her arms wide, posing sideways to emphasize her slim hips. Here she was, tense in a suit of textured linen, her eyes and hair the color of dry sand. She was ready to kiss her son on the cheek and pose for more pictures.

'Where's Diz?' she cried.

The photographer posed them, sorted them, ordered them here and there. It was a relief to have directions to follow. Kismet joined a lineup with her bridesmaids and when Stockton said, 'Oh, puppy, let me hug you,' Kismet wanted to sob. Ally said she'd left the radio on in her room, playing music, and sneaked out. Her mother would be furious, but she'd deal with it. 'She can't take my phone away because I don't have a phone,' Ally said, as she had said many times. Brianna was the one locked in her bedroom now.

'Let's have the bride and groom,' said the photographer. Watching the two take their places, Winnie said, 'Won't their children be the most handsome?'

Kismet hitched her breath in as Gary put his arm around her waist. She tried to control her slow roll of dread as the photographer's camera mechanically stuttered. Children! Gary let his mother grab his head, arrange his hair with her fingers. When he reared back, she tucked her chin down, teared up and said, *Gary, my boy, oh, Gary!* He moved her hand off his neck and went to find his best man, Eric.

'C'mon, guys, pictures.'

Knieval and Harlan sauntered over. Charley, watching the crowd from the bar, clawed back his brown-gold mane, aware of eyes on him. For he had been favored by fortune although his beauty was only recently apparent. A year ago he'd been awkward, too skinny, tentative, but after near death he'd become an arresting creature, lynx-like, with muscles of hard wire and jutting cheekbones. His skeptical, sweet smile ended in thin white scars like whiskers.

The groomsmen were wearing their powder blue rental tuxedos, and also stunned forced smiles because, although they were comfortable with one another as teammates, their friendships had been strained ever since the party. They drifted apart as everyone moved into the banquet room and with laughs and calls searched for their name cards.

There was a table for Uncle Gusty, Aunt Darva, the Pavlecky and Spiral families, who were all more or less related by blood or proximity. There was a table of assorted friends, the parents and siblings of the wedding party. There was a young people's table and a table of Crystal's friends, including Jeniver and others in the book club, except Bev, not Bev, since her son had blurted that he longed to challenge Gary to a duel. There was a table of Skillet employees, including the Kallinors. Closest to the bathroom there was a motley table of children who looked like everybody in the room and still managed to seem random. All of these tables were draped with round sky blue tablecloths and decorated with centerpieces of white carnations, baby's breath, fake rosebuds, white tulle. The head table was a regal rectangle studded with small bells of silver plastic. The families of the wedding party came and went, chatting with excitement and elaborately pretending not to eye Crystal. As soon as Gary and Kismet sat down, people started tapping knives against water glasses and the newlyweds kissed, a neutral lip-press. Cheers went up. The servers came around with red and white wine. On each table there was a platter of cheese, crackers, and fruit. There was a bowl of olives and a basket of bread. The servers returned with kebabs of chicken and vegetables, strips of marinated steak and peppers, and more bread.

Winnie put a cloth napkin carefully over her dress. She looked brightly around, poked up a black wrinkled olive with a toothpick, and tried to pass the bowl to Diz, who frowned as though in pain. On a wide side table there were plug-in pots and steel steam trays. The servers lifted the lids on a three-main buffet: chicken breasts doused with tarragon sauce, pink salmon with dill, sliced roast in gravy, mashed potatoes, steamed green beans, carrots, pearl onions. There were giant bowls of salad with shaved carrots and cucumbers, and smaller bowls of rotini salad with broccoli, pepperoni, pickled peppers. Winnie elbowed Diz and he stood. She handed him a cordless microphone, he tapped it and spoke.

'Welcome, welcome!'

Diz gestured expansively and sat down.

'That's all you're going to say?'

'You said to welcome them.'

'You have to be more festive, Diz. Congratulate Gary. And Kismet too. Then make everybody get up and eat!'

This was the only wedding they'd put on, the only wedding they'd ever put on, and it struck Diz that he had to give this moment all he had it in him to say. He gathered his courage, wrested the microphone back from Winnie, and stood again. 'The wife says I wasn't festive enough!' Diz paused and the room hushed. He was a commanding, uncomfortable presence. 'You understand,' he began, and now the room grew tense. 'We love our son.' He stopped, searched the ceiling, gathered his words. 'And now we will surely love his choice. I mean, love Kismet. For love in the beginning is a downpour. Over time, like me and Winnie, it is a good soaking rain.'

He made a gesture toward heaven and sat down, sweating.

Winnie clutched his arm. He had never said anything so poetic.

There was a general run on the buffet table. Someone was supposed to bring plates of food to the head table, but nobody came so Kismet and Stockton stood up and took orders from the parents. Told the rest of the bridal party they were on their own.

'I'm on my feet so much,' Winnie said. 'I'd enjoy a plate.'

Kismet arranged a plate of food for her. As she set it down, Winnie oohed at the way Kismet had tonged up a sprig of dill onto her salmon.

'It's a picture. Like in a restaurant,' she said. 'You're the perfect daughter. You're just scrumptious!'

Crystal's and Kismet's eyes met over Winnie's softly burnished hair. It was a troubled glance, of no great meaning, but there it was. Then, in a whimsical voice, Winnie said, 'I hear Gary rolled the truck again! Are you okay? Tell me if you still feel dizzy!'

Crystal jumped up, staring at Kismet. 'Rolled the truck? The pickup? Were you in it?'

Kismet looked guilty, then thought, why?

'Oh, just off the road into a level field,' said Winnie. 'Hardly even dinged the sides. Do you feel okay, Kismet?'

Kismet went to her mom and put her arms around her golden green silky shoulders, kissed Crystal's cheek, and whispered. 'I'm really okay.'

Things are sliding, thought Crystal. 'Come home with me,' she said. 'Don't be married anymore.' She touched her olive-wood cross as Kismet gave her a tense smile and sat down again.

After the gabbling and eating and laughing, so satisfying, such a relief to Winnie, the time had come for people to say something nice, to bless the wedding. She waited for someone to start, maybe Eric, as the best man, or maybe Uncle Gusty, but nobody seemed to think of it. So Winnie rose with the microphone in one hand and a glass of red wine in the other. People scrambled, laughing, to put wine in their glasses.

'I want to make a toast!' she cried.

People tapped their knives on their glasses. Winnie raised her wine and before she could say a word, tears surged up and thickened her voice. 'Gary and Kismet are the most loveliest couple the world has known! I am the lucky mother. Oh, I'm choking up. I can't talk. I love you. Where's Eric? Eric! You are up!'

Glasses clinked and Winnie sat, dabbing a tissue beneath her eyes. Eric rose, his voice shy and strained. He made it carry, though.

'Where's the good stuff? We should be drinking Diz's best champagne, not this box wine!'

A laughing cheer went up.

'But save that for later,' said Eric. 'For now, just let me say what an honor it is to be Gary's best man. Partly because it gives me a chance to warn the bride. She's got a lot on her plate right now.'

The guests shifted and looked around, uneasy. It was clear that Eric had had an early start on the partying, which was unusual for Eric. Not that he always held back, but he was known to be disciplined, usually sober, careful to make his weights during wrestling season. Of course that was over now, for good. These days, he was training to be a medic. There was a murmur of *Okay nows*, encouraging him to stop, but his glance swung wildly to either side and he took a deep breath.

'I can see it from here—a lot on her plate. She's got every kind of kebab, plus the olives, plus the cheese. She couldn't eat yesterday. She was nervous. Her maid of honor, Stockton, told me—wait. Those girls are crazy! But I'm the best man so I need to tell you that Gary is my truest and best friend.'

A patter of applause began and went on, as though to cut him off, but stopped when Eric held up his hand.

'And I say this because I love Gary like a brother. He's got some issues.'

Everyone who'd begun to clap or had laughed in relief at the food description instead of some embezzlement joke again went silent.

Eric laughed and pointed at Winnie. 'Hey, she's white as a sheet underneath her spray tan, friends, thinking, *What don't I know about my son?* Winnie, you are passing damaged goods on here, palming Gary off on an innocent young woman. I see some eyes rolling out there! Eyes rolling! Not my speech. Stockton and Ally can fill you in on Kismet's innocence and all that. I'm just here to talk about Gary's issues.'

Everyone knew that Eric was Gary's ever loyal childhood friend, so they'd expected a heartfelt set of platitudes. But pockets of silence fell now, people shushed one another. Winnie's mouth opened and shut twice. She took a long drink from her wineglass. Smiled from side to side.

Eric nodded, breathing hard. A red flush mottled his neck and crept up his cheeks.

'So what's it like to be a Geist, huh? To come from a family where this town is in your back pocket? What's it like to be Gary? He's not allowed to have an issue. He is not allowed to fuck up. So when he does fuck up, right? Because we all fuck up. What happens? Like on the team, Gary calls the plays and the rest of us take the hits. So I took a hit for Gary.'

Tension ramped up in the silence that enveloped all of the tables. Even the children quieted, their eyes darting around the room for the cause of the mysterious frozen pall. Eric lowered his head and glared around the room, his mouth tight.

'Took a hit for Gary last year,' he said again, not drunk at all now, his diction precise and clipped. 'The man planned a party and took the team off a cliff.'

Knieval, another roan giant in a room of several, walked to Eric's side and gently put an arm over his shoulder. Eric made to shrug it off but the arm came down like an iron bar.

'Next speech,' Knieval said, and led Eric out the Alarm Will Sound exit, but no alarm sounded except the silent ones in peoples' thinking. It was unknown whether Knieval meant to comfort Eric or smash him around out there. Bill and Bonnie Pavlecky had been out in the entry and came back to the tables with puzzled looks. The wedding guests were all tight smiles, waiting to see how Gary would take it. With gritted teeth, giving space the long stare. At last he shook himself and grinned more naturally and there was some tentative laughter. Harlan, dark and thin, took the microphone and pretended to check it before he spoke. 'Hey, congratulations, man. The other issue, folks, I'm serious here, is sexual.'

Winnie rose in alarm, but he waved her down. Charley raised a devastating eyebrow, took a plastic vial off the table, and blew a line of soap bubbles. Winnie turned and fixed him with a glare. Charley froze, hand lifted for effect. 'It's a party favor, right?' He blew into the wand again. Harlan waved away the bubbles.

'I've got this, Winnie. Kidding. The other issue is I love this guy, not that way of course. He's a stand-up friend to me, to everyone. As good a person as you'll find in the whole state. He'll make a husband to his lovely bride. They are a fairy tale romance, aren't they?'

A flutter of applause.

'Holy shit, aren't they? I can't hear you!'

Some roars, whistles.

'I can't hear you! What'd you say?'

Big noise. Harlan raised his glass and drained it with a desperate, thought Kismet, a not happy gesture.

'Hear hear! Hear hear!'

The glasses clinked hard for a real kiss and then

Kismet couldn't see anything because Gary pulled her up, bent her over backward on his arm, and ground his lips onto hers until the cheering lapsed and the mothers-in-law had to pull him off, a time-honored wedding dinner ritual.

Alarm Will Sound

Out in back of the golf club, in the glare of a halogen floodlight, Knieval and Harlan were slamming Eric back and forth between them, letting out a
syllable with each slam. 'This. Is. His. Wed. Ding. Day.'

Charley stepped out of the emergency door.

'Awww, you guys are so sentimental.'

Charley flicked soap off his bubble wand and
clenched it between his teeth. He slouched up to the
three of them, draped his arm over Harlan's neck.
Harlan stepped back, sighed, didn't shake him off.
They had all started playing football back in junior
high and had a physical ease with one another. Knieval
generally played guard and center, conditioned to protect his quarterback. Harlan played running back,
protective of Gary unless he was carrying the ball

himself. They were okay with fake fighting one another, or Eric. But even then they went easy on Gary.
Now, their tight friendship group had two big holes in
it. One filled with sorrow, the other rage. When things
went upside down, the anger seeped out all around
like acid from under a loose lid. Knieval shrugged his
jacket back into shape and shot his cuffs. He'd always
had little issues with Charley, who cocked an eye at
Knieval's movie gesture—the stock image of a tough
guy held back from violence. Knieval gave a tight-
lipped grin and tipped his head to stretch his neck, a
movie gesture too. Charley took the bubble wand from
between his lips and used it to emphasize his words.

'You know what's happening, right?'

'What's happening, Charley?' said Knieval, stretch-
ing his neck the other way. Charley wanted to reply,
Stop doing that shit, but checked himself and spoke in
a mild tone.

'You're missing the point.'

'What point?' said Harlan.

'The point is,' said Charley, 'you should be applaud-
ing our man.'

Charley tossed the wand over his shoulder, straightened up, and started clapping slowly and emphatically.
He stared soberly at Eric.

'It's about time, Eric. Yeah, you do it all. Including

take the hits for Gary. You're still taking the hits for Gary from these jerk-offs.'

'Hey,' said Harlan.

'No offense,' said Charley. 'But you guys, Gary's a mess. So you whale on Eric, that's how I see it.'

'So what?' said Knieval.

'For once, Eric's not taking the hit. For once, Eric's real.'

Eric glared at Charley from under his brow, breathing hard. He wasn't drunk anymore. 'Thanks, man, I've got this.'

'Okay, you're the best man,' Charley said. He gave Eric a sad, true smile. When Charley smiled, the scars went up his cheeks. He hadn't caught a barb so the clean cuts had become white lines and over them his calm lilac eyes shone. There was something deep and innocent, always, about Charley. His eyebrows had always been the eyebrows of a *Vogue* cover model. He'd grown three more inches. Everybody knew he was going somewhere.

Knieval and Harlan glanced at each other and hunched over. They stared at the tips of their black dress shoes, which belonged to their fathers.

'Eric,' said Knieval, looking down but offering his fist, knocking knuckles with Eric.

'I don't know what got into me. I'm not that guy,'

said Harlan. He raised his eyes to Eric's and said, 'You fucking saved my life.'

Harlan stepped forward, put his hand around the back of Eric's neck, and brought their foreheads together. The two leaned thought-to-thought in a fierce embrace, then broke apart. Knieval stood beside them, murmuring like an echo, 'Lives, our lives, lives.' This was the most they ever said, but to Eric it was everything.

The Funeral Cake

There were more toasts, increasingly strained, every one of which fell flat or came out garbled. There was so much that could not be said but was being said anyway. Eating was the thing everybody could do, and everybody went back to devouring a sensational amount of food. The groomsmen appeared again, their faces open and relieved. Charley tapped on the microphone to get people's attention. When everyone was looking at him, he leaned forward, and slowly in a ringing voice said, 'Cake.'

There was a sauntering rush toward this second cake, the evening cake, set out in the entryway. Kismet walked out with Eric, who had become quiet and thoughtful. Wandering casually toward the cake, she noticed that it bore no resemblance to the cake she and her mother had planned out with Tiny Johnson. Kismet stopped, stared at the cake, looked around. Tiny was nodding at her. Winking. At some point, Tiny came over and whispered that the cake would be free.

'Free?' said Kismet. 'But it was already paid for.'

'It was for Cal Buddy's funeral this morning. They wanted three white cakes for the dinner after, fancy sheet cakes,' said Tiny. 'But nobody even touched the last one. It's one of my best cakes. Two-layer vanilla sheet cake with raspberry filling. Free. I'll refund your mom for the other one.'

Kismet stared at the funeral cake. You couldn't tell with the white piping and wreaths of white roses added by Tiny. But it was an omen. A thought began, and although Kismet tried not to let the thought surface into words, it did, momentarily. *This marriage will end in death.* The strangeness and the wrongness was again catching up with her and she thought of running out the door. The golf club was a hundred yards from the Red River. If she kicked off her heels, she could sprint up the levee and jump back into the river. She did want some kind of oblivion that was not more booze. There was a dreadful shredding sensation in her chest, where her heart used to be. Later, she would remember the words 'Until death do you part' and realize that marriage is ideally supposed to end in death. Nobody really talks about that after the ceremony. But Kismet had already thought about it and she thought about it a little more when Val Kallinor took from a zippered case an enormous chef's knife that he'd brought for the purpose of cutting the cake.

Val pressed the handle of the knife into Kismet's hand. For a moment she felt the weight and lethality of the blade. A sensation of hot red rage filled her and she squeezed the handle. Then Gary stood beside her and put his hand over her hand. His hand was sweaty and too warm, as though he'd been making a fist. His palm was padded and sticky, like a child's. Her fury adapted to his need and she was swallowed, first by disgusted resignation, then by sudden loss. She nearly cried out with longing for her own anger as they pressed down on the knife.

'This cake sucks,' he said in a shaky voice.

'Because it's a funeral cake,' she murmured.

Winnie was instructing the photographer not to send pictures of this cake to the newspaper, but to use a picture of the elaborate cake earlier that afternoon. There was no Martin to take the traditional second dance with Kismet, so Diz gave her a wink and held out his big mitts. They danced at arm's length to 'Three Times a Lady.' Charley had taken charge of loading the sound system and knew to start with tunes for the parents. 'Sugar, Sugar' was next and everyone pepped up and moved to the floor, waving their arms and shuffling. After a few more tunes, the music got smokier and heavier. The children of the mixed-bag table became a frenzied mob on the dance floor. Kismet shuffled around with Gary, next with her mother, swinging her arms, then with Gary's mother, then with Diz again, doing the swim together, then with Gusty, with Dale Himmelkampf, then at last with her bridesmaids, who were both tearful and somewhat drunk. Stockton cried and cried, wetting Kismet's neck.

'What's gonna happen?' she kept saying.

Kismet patted her back. Kismet had changed into a slinky red dress and four-inch heels, black, shiny, giving her a nice arch. Stockton held her so tightly, on her own four-inch heels, that they tottered comically on stiff legs, like dolls.

Eric tapped Stockton out and took her place. He was eye to eye with high-heeled Kismet.

'You mind?'

'Gary send you? He'd not much of a dancer.'

A slow dance came on, which felt a bit awkward until Eric said, 'What a relief. The kids are gone.'

'They're probably in the bathrooms clogging the toilets up with huge amounts of paper,' said Kismet.

'Yeah, it's what I'd do,' said Eric.

'So, what was with your speech? What hit did you take for Gary?'

'I kind of want to apologize for what happened at Pookie's,' said Eric, ignoring her question. 'Gary wanted some advice about proposing and I told him to take you out to an Italian spot in Fargo. He picked Pookie's.'

Kismet laughed, then felt she could easily get hysterical. She gulped back her reaction. 'So it's your fault I got a black eye.'

Eric breathed in and turned down the corners of his mouth. 'I heard it was a champagne cork? Really, I'm sorry.'

'Did Gary tell you about it?'

'It was Grace, we're cousins.'

'You're cousins with everybody.'

'Just about everybody in the room anyway.'

'I'm so tired,' she said. 'Did I make a mistake?' She stopped and put her hand over her mouth. 'I can't believe I said that. Forget it.'

He looked at her in a way that gave her vertigo. Maybe it was the colored revolving lights. She really hadn't looked at Eric before because he was always near Gary and everybody looked at Gary. The lights passed over Eric's impassive face, the banked energy behind his eyes. He showed his teeth and Kismet realized he wasn't smiling. He was baring his unremarkable teeth and trying to speak. At last he managed some words.

'That hit I took for Gary? Maybe I can tell you about it.' The song ended. 'Sometime.' He stepped back. 'Thanks,' they said to each other in unison, and turned away.

Gusty, Darva, and Diz had come over to sit with Eric's parents, Bill and Bonnie Pavlecky. Winnie came over too, but kept getting up to check on the kids, who were throwing cake.

'You're micromanaging,' said Diz, when she'd barely touched down and popped back up.

'Take a load off,' said Gusty. Darva punched him. 'She has to micromanage. That's Winnie. She won't stop until she's worn down to the bone.'

'It was a lot to plan,' said Winnie. She jumped up and got a cup of black coffee from the urn set up in one corner, by the cake. Back in the day, she had smoked, and she wanted a cigarette now. Or another drink, but she'd had two and that was her limit. She sat down and decided to drive the family home. They were all drinking too much. Diz had put away how many beers?

'A couple,' he said.

'A couple and a couple more,' said Darva.

'Well you did a good job, Winnie, here's to you,' said Bill, raising a can. He and Bonnie were like people carved from soap—their general outlines fitting into the blocky rectangles. They both had sensitive mouths, worried eyes, and the exact same color of hair, once brown, but now turning the color of tree bark. Their bland skin charmingly blotched when they were startled or uncomfortable. Bill's skin was starting to blotch as he raised his can again.

'To the newlyweds.'

'And Father Flirty.' Bonnie barely moved her lips when she talked, so it appeared that she was imparting secret information. 'He's not here tonight.'

'He never goes to things like this,' said Diz.

'Yes, but he was going to make us an exception. He must be in shock.'

'Hell, I'm in shock,' said Gusty. His head was big and noble. The Geist men were typically handsome. 'Some a that was my money.'

'We're all tied up in it,' said Diz.

'If I ever get my hands on Martin, he's done for,' said Bonnie. 'And you, and you'—she pointed at the men—'you're backing me up.'

'No question,' said Gusty.

'We promised we wouldn't get into that,' said Darva to them all, ruffling up like a plump little angry hen.

'I know, I know,' said Bonnie, with a grim seizure of her lips that could have been a smile. 'It's just hard.'

'One thing,' said Darva, her small, black, unblinking eyes fierce and glinting. 'Nobody's gonna blame Kismet in my hearing.'

'They'll answer to me too,' said Gusty, nodding at Diz. 'That boy of yours looks relieved. Happier than I've seen him for a long time. And I'm glad about that.'

'Agree,' said Bill. 'A wedding is to the good. Maybe this rubs off on Eric. I'll be a happier guy too. Am I right, Bonnie?'

'Absolutely,' said Bonnie, sipping on her tequila sunrise. She said this in a light, calm voice but flexed her jaw muscles, watching the dancers.

'This girl's gonna be a farm girl, you'll see,' said Darva. 'Nothing like her dad. Ever seen her work the Sunday rush? Well, you gotta surprise coming. This girl can hustle.'

'But can she clean?' asked Diz. He showed his slash of a grin, rolling his eyes. ''Cause we need that. Winnie's up to her eyeballs.'

'Oh, I should think so,' said Bill, looking carefully around for Winnie. 'Did those kids leave any cake?'

There was still more crying on the dance floor. Ally started weeping and she got Melly all emotional. She was only three years older. Stockton and Ally smiled at each other with dripping faces and Stockton whispered to Ally, *We could have died last night, you know.* Which started them again and even Melly cried, bawling out *You idiots* above Lady Gaga. They were all wearing Wet n Wild mascara so they could cry all they wanted. After each luxurious bout the girls went into the bathroom and reapplied makeup, tipping up their faces to concentrate on lip pencil, turning back and forth to study the contour of cheekbones, the flare of eyeliner, the arc of eye shadow. They sprayed their hair back up in artfully messy chignons. Then gave one another brave shrugs and stepped back out, tipping forward in their agonizing heels. Suddenly, Stockon threw her shoes at the wall and whooped. The music intensified. There was a disco ball for fun. Silver ovals spun through the air, traveling across the walls, passing over the dancers' bodies, touching shoulders, hair, elbows, breasts, knees, skinny shanks or full hips, boys and men in saggy pants, slightly hunched in off-the-beat motion, all the same, all with delicate approval. The ovals of light caromed off the walls and bobbed in darkness, lending to the room a ghostly underwater calm. Kismet's heels were quite comfortable and she twisted and turned with the music, sometimes alone. If she had stayed in the river, maybe it would have looked like this as the oxygen left her brain. The swaying swirl, the slow progression of danger in the music, cut with Jell-O-y sentiment as she walked toward the light, which of course came on at midnight when the band left and she and Gary were driven home by Winnie to supposedly pack for their honeymoon. That was off now because of what her father had done. The second good thing to come out of that.

Mushroom Love

Although she did not fully recall her last sighting of Martin, there had been a fight. Over money, as usual. He'd taken a job, a volunteer job. His income in the past year had been barely three thousand dollars, of which only six hundred had appeared in their joint bank account. Now Martin was gone, at a huge cost, but gone. There was no violence in Martin but the hurt from their fights lingered.

'You always throw money in my face,' he'd said.

'Because you spend all your money on yourself. You're stingy with your family,' said Crystal.

Stingy was the worst thing you could call a Michif. She'd hoped to shut him up. But he hadn't even blinked before he said, 'Better stingy with money than emotion. You're coldhearted.'

Coldhearted was the second worst thing you could call a Michif. And it was true. She was sometimes too tired to have emotions and had started acting rationally. She knew how men hated rational women. Crystal stopped showed her feelings in an argument. She was done with second chances, done with the opulent mercy of women. Unaffordable mercy. For years, no matter how hard she'd saved, she'd been overspending. She forged onward and it finally ended with Martin saying, 'I'm outta here.'

He'd driven off. She had been relieved because he always came back. But then instead of Martin coming back it was the police, knocking on her door, and the others, too, then at last Kismet, drenched. And in no time she was married. Crystal's postponed shock buoyed her through the wedding dinner. After kissing her daughter, she slipped out before ten. Her reflexive thoughts kept telling her that Martin couldn't have mortgaged the house. And if they only delayed the renovation, that money in the church fund was sure to turn up. There was just too much of it to hide. It was all too absurd, too wrong.

Crystal made it home, stripped her dress off onto a padded hanger, crawled beneath a quilt. She watched the news, hoping to hear Perfect Advantage was going down the drain. But she hadn't taken out a mortgage in the first place. No she hadn't. She persuaded her wracked brain to stay awake, or at least not doze. She had to start back on her night haul schedule.

The telephone, oh god, the telephone.

'Sorry, I know it's late.'

'You know I try not to sleep nights anyway.'

'Well, this will keep both of us awake. I couldn't tell you at the dinner. But I thought you'd want to know.'

It was Jeniver, her voice compressed around a snarl. Crystal's heart jumped to life. 'Just give it to me straight.'

'Your signature is notarized. He must have found someone who looked enough like you, borrowed your driver's license or some other ID, plagiarized your signature, and fooled the notary who signed off.'

'So what does this mean?'

'It will be hard to prove the forgery and you might lose. People are trying everything possible to convince judges that they didn't sign mortgages or understand the fine print. Plus, Perfect Advantage was bought by one of the giant banks and not only are they getting bailed out but they have more lawyers than the population of our state.'

'But you'll take the case?'

Jeniver paused, and her voice changed.

'Of course I will and I'll give you a huge discount.

But now that I know how hard this is gonna be, I'm sorry, I can't work totally free. The fact that Martin absconded with the entire church fund makes our case more plausible, but it will cost you.'

'Plus the mortgage. Should I pay that?'

'Absolutely not. But you'll be bombarded with foreclosure notices and they will try to bully you into vacating. Just hang on.'

'They who?' said Crystal.

'I don't know which bank yet, but it will be a legit bank. Legit in quotation marks. I'm going to try to get an injunction. Otherwise, the sheriff.'

Crystal hung up the phone and stared at the walls of her bedroom. She herself had repaired the Sheetrock, screwed, taped, and mudded the walls smooth. Then she had painted the walls a color called Mushroom Love because she wanted to be reminded of the floor of a forest. She had babied the ostrich ferns and pothos by the south window. She went over to her plants, lifted her money plant off the floor, where it wasn't doing so well.

'Get crackin', little pal,' she said to the money plant, setting it on the broad windowsill where, beginning tomorrow, it would catch more sun.

The Hit

The hit. Something about it. Strange thing to think of on your so-called wedding night. But Kismet's thoughts have been out of control the whole wedding. She dozes, wakes, pages through those thoughts until with a jolt she is fully awake. She reaches over to the bedside table for the water glass. Questions. The hit that Eric took for Gary. It was something that Eric couldn't get into, not yet. Her thoughts hum over the town. To her knowledge, nobody had suffered a mysterious crime. Except. Except there was the accident that happened, March before last, a thing nobody wants to talk about or think about. Even the people who blamed Gary knew that it was nobody's fault. Especially not Eric's fault. And now the other thing, her father running off with the money. Or running off with a depleted portfolio, according to Hugo. None of that had to do with taking a hit for Gary, but she and her mother were taking a hit for her dad. He'd left them to deal with the massive fallout, which was just beginning.

How can she sleep under the pressure of such thoughts?

Kismet slipped out of bed, into the bathroom, gulped more water, and made a nest for herself out of towels on the bathroom floor. Maybe they'd had some kind of sex after all. Between her legs, a purgatorial burn. She needed an ice pack. If only she was eating greasy pizza with her mother. Instead, a mental cave-in occurred. It started slowly with a few hiccups, then accelerated until Kismet was freaking out with sick futility, laughing so hard that she had to stuff a washcloth between her teeth. After a while she sat up. Removed the washcloth, glanced over at Gary's crumpled suit, and rummaged in his pants pocket for the key to his, no, their, pickup.

The Offering

After Kismet left the bookstore for the wedding dinner, Hugo could have closed up the shop, but he was loyal to the Bookery's customers. These books must be available and nobody would be shut away from their influence. He kept the store open for a while. Scattering water from their umbrellas, two regular customers entered, as they did every few days, to sell back the romance books they'd bought the previous week and buy new ones from the crammed shelves devoted to that genre. They grumbled a little about not having been invited to the big wedding dinner at the club. Then touched the sprung spines of romance. Bev's made enough cash on that one shelf to almost pay the (cheap) rent, and even though some of the books were tattered, bathwater bloated, soft as butter, nobody complained.

'I'll take these,' said Iris Carmody.

Savage Bliss. Savage Nights. Beloved Savage. Hugo rang up the sale.

'Have a nice night,' he called after Iris and her friend. 'Happy reading,' he added. He was pretty sure Iris had bought, read, sold back, bought again, these exact same books a couple of times before.

After they left, Hugo watched the water sluice down the window. *Wait for me*, had she said it? Had he imagined that she said it because he so unbearably wanted her to come back to him?

Eventually Hugo closed the shop and wandered back, past the crooked little bathroom, to another crooked little room that he'd fixed up for himself. Perfect for naps. But tonight he decided to sleep there, keeping a sort of vigil. She had definitely said *Wait for me.* She had a cell phone, but now she'd be with Gary, and of course her reception was iffy. Anyway, Hugo preferred to rely on the psychic magnetism between them. The room had no window, which was a good thing. He had made it very clean. He liked to feel the cleanliness of a place. Even though it was an old building, the floor was sound. The walls were sturdy. He read for a while, then rose and dusted the room, wiped the woodwork.

He adjusted the antique prints of birds. He'd slipped those prints from a secondhand book box that came in an estate bin, then centered the prints in cheap wooden frames. He'd placed them all around the bed. It was his childhood bed, narrow blocky wooden planks. As a boy, he had scarred up the headboard, gouged arcane symbols of protection and power. When he moved it to the bookstore, he'd brought wood oil and polished the dry old boards. The mattress was thin and lumpy, the sheets limp and faded. The quilt upon them, however, possessed in his mind an unspeakable energy.

For it was Kismet's quilt, sewed out of her favorite T-shirts. The One had given it to him upon their fateful morning. Which, he glanced at the clock, 11:45, was still just that morning. The quilt held a history of Kismet from the time she was a child. The first T-shirts she wore were stamped with unicorns, dolphins, white-maned ponies, and ballet dancers. Next came the Powerpuff Girls and Sailor Moon. Harry Potter. Her favorite cereals. The Lucky Charms leprechaun. Tony the Tiger. Then Lord of the Rings. Rihanna. Pink. Katy Perry. Destiny's Child. Beyoncé. There was an NDSU Bison, a Golden Gopher, a Husky. Her college picks. The quilt was framed by blue jersey material and backed with a blue jersey bedsheet. Kismet and Crystal had hand-tied the squares with bits of white yarn. It was a puffy quilt.

The inside was a special polyester filling. Hugo retreated beneath the covers. It was not a warm quilt, but the lightness of it had a cozy feel, especially over a blanket. He had a nice old rummage sale reading lamp. A wooden crate for a bedside table. He had pulled a hardcover copy of *Madame Bovary* to give to Kismet.

It was a sweet, clean, old book. The pages were deckled and the print crisp. An Ex Libris bookplate with a brown sailing ship and compass rose identified the book as having belonged to Barbara Thrall. There was no date whatsoever in the book, just title, author, and SOCIÉTÉ DES BEAUX-ARTS, Paris, London, and New York. Hugo opened the book and slowly inhaled. You could tell things from the smell of the pages. For instance, this *Madame Bovary* had been kept in a dry, bright room on an unpainted wooden shelf. The spine was slightly faded to a lighter blue, so there was the scent of sunlight, but the shelf lacked height. The top of the book was scraped, its indigo binding a bit frayed. This book had been regularly dusted and read at lengthy intervals. A few times only. The owner had used a bookmark, had not owned a cat, and had no sloppy eating habits. This book had a good life. Hugo chose a page at random and read. *She could not detach her gaze from the carpet where he had walked, from those empty chairs where he had sat. The river still*

flowed on, and slowly drove its ripples along the slip-
pery banks.

Chemistry, math, geology, and even World of War-
craft weren't enough, though in the last, he'd traveled
to distant realms and experienced the simulacrum of
death and resurrection. He had to read novels in order
to understand the sensations that engulfed him when it
came to Kismet. This passage reassured him—he was
not alone in his devotions. For he treasured an ink-jet
copy of the palm of her left hand, carried a singleton
earring of hers in his pocket. A few hours before, after
she had walked back out into the rain, Hugo had stared
fixedly at the drips on the mat and at the streaming
window of the door, much as a dog stares after its de-
parting human. Now Hugo flipped the lamp off, closed
the book, and set it gently upon his heart. Perhaps
it was dangerous to love as a dog loves. To love with
canine devotion was to live in a state of miserable ex-
hilaration, to exist on a knife-thin edge of joy.

'So be it,' said Hugo.

The river still flows on, and slowly drives its ripples
along the slippery banks.

An hour passed. And another. He dozed. At last
there was a tap on the back alley door. It was she. Hugo
let her in. The rain had erased the violent odor from the
air and there was only a sort of feline smell to nature.

'My fate,' said Hugo, holding her.

Her night hair streamed down her back.

They walked into the tiny room and sat down on the quilt she had crushed into his arms that morning, now yesterday's morning, a thousand years ago.

'Gary's sleeping. I came into town to get a pizza.'

'What kind?'

'Meat lover's.'

'Let's not talk about him.'

'Well, you asked.'

'I did ask. I un-ask.'

'I can only stay a minute. Let's lie down and hold hands.'

'Yes, my fate.'

'Quit calling me that,' she said, cradling his hand to her face. As she toppled down, a swoop of delight threaded through them and gathered their hearts up and tied a bow. They lay there together as an offering, a bouquet for the gods.

PART FOUR

Honeymoon

2009

Short Order

The day after the wedding, the rain stopped and the sun came out. A few sparrows from the grain silos down the highway popped over to chatter in the lilacs. Kismet had cranked the window open. How pleasant it was to wake to their high-pitched gossip, if only . . . Kismet's skin still prickled from lying near Hugo. At the thought of what he'd said last night about driving out to the oil patch, her heart lurched. After she'd left Bev's Bookery and driven to the farm, sneaking up the stairs, she'd wrapped *Madame Bovary* in Hugo's T-shirt and put it in her suitcase. Now she slipped out of bed and into the closet to find the book, touched its dark blue-black cover, and replaced it. She pulled on jeans and a sweatshirt, smoothed down her hair, and with a quick twist banded it off into a ponytail.

Kismet padded barefoot down to the kitchen, removed a can of Folgers from the cupboard, made
coffee in the Mr. Coffee. Dazed by how swiftly life was
changing, pouring coffee to help her brain adjust, she
heard Gary slouch down the oaken-look stairs, turned
to see him yawning and scratching his head. He stuck
out his hand for a mug of coffee, and just like that their
young days of life were over.

Kismet's training took over. She downed a swig of
her coffee and rubbed her hands together.

Diz loomed in the back doorway, then walked across
the linoleum with muddy boots and sat down with
Gary. Kismet didn't like the muddy tracks. She tipped
her head down, studied Diz, her brows lowered. The
two men began to plot out the day's strategy. Diz had
already been out testing the fields—some wet and some
dry. Kismet investigated the refrigerator, found eggs,
sausage, bread, then the freezer, found frozen hash
browns. She put the sausages in the cast-iron skillet to
brown, heated butter in a Teflon pan, and asked the
men how they wanted their eggs. Over easy for Diz.

'Over hard,' said Gary. He blinked into his coffee
cup. Three eggs apiece for the men. Kismet toasted and
buttered the rye bread, flipped out sausages and then
the hash browns, slid the eggs on last. Set two plates on
the table.

'Ketchup?' said Diz.

She got ketchup out of the refrigerator and set it on the table. Diz took a bite of crisp potatoes. Nobody said thank you.

'Hey, you guys,' she said, sliding into waitress banter as she stood by the table with her hands on her hips. 'Can I get good morning and a thank you, gorgeous?'

'You sure can,' said Gary, startled, choking a bit on his mouthful of coffee. He lifted the mug with a gallant gesture. He gave a magnanimous smile, then fell on his eggs, proud of himself and proud of her for being what his dad would probably call a pistol.

'You picked a good one.' Diz winked at Gary. 'She's a pistol.'

'I was a short-order cook,' said Kismet, wishing immediately she hadn't said that. She could see a lifetime of three-egg breakfasts. 'And I still didn't get a thank you.'

'Hellooooo?'

Winnie entered the house with a songlike hoot. She looked at the two plates of food set out before the men, then at Kismet, who poured her a cup of coffee.

'Scrambled,' said Winnie, before she took her first sip.

Kismet made Winnie's eggs. Then she made eggs the way she herself liked them, sunny side up, and sat down across from Winnie. The men left their plates on the table, got up to go outside.

268 · LOUISE ERDRICH

'Kizzy,' said Winnie, 'could you clear those plates?'

'Kizzy? Nobody has ever called me Kizzy.'

She put the men's plates in the sink and sat back down. 'I can't say your full name. It hurts my tongue, Kizzy,' said Winnie. She waved her fork. 'You mind? I like to eat alone. It's a thing I have.'

Kismet stared at her new mother-in-law.

'Do not call me Kizzy, Mrs. Geist,' she said. 'It's a thing I have.'

'Mrs. Geist? You can call me . . . oh.'

Kismet was happy enough to eat alone and took her plate outside to sit at the picnic table by the dirt driveway-to-be. Looking out at the struggling grass and tiny border of dirt, she decided to plant petunias and marigolds. The yard was small for a yard in the country. The front door faced the sunset, not the highway like Diz and Winnie's. Ten yards from the garage, boundless fields began. The rain was gone, evaporated, but leaving a promising scent. Kismet looked at the rows that looked like the ones her mother had hoed. The plants were still tiny. Though she knew the crops were rotated, and Gary had said they also planted some wheat and corn, this was a sugar beet field again. It felt like someone would come along soon and tell her to get back in there with her hoe. And she'd meet her mom walking beets from the other end of the rows.

There were big-time owners and there were workers. It had been like that since the Red River Valley was settled. First the land was taken from the Dakota, the Ojibwe, the Métis, by forced treaties. Then the original people started working on the land they had once owned. Sometimes Native people farmed, which made the taking more complicated. Sometimes owners were also workers, now, with giant pieces of computerized equipment. Kismet's family had always been on-the-ground workers. Her granduncles, Happy's brothers, had followed the wheat and corn harvests up and down the valley. Even Happy had picked potatoes before she made her fortune running booze. When sugar beets got big, Crystal had worked alongside the Mexican families who traveled a yearly route. Those families had stayed in the migrant housing, gone now. The little houses had been burned and the land lasered smooth to grow a few more rows of crops. Now there were as many retiree white workers as Mexican workers and they all lived in RV camps. Winnie called and Kismet walked back in.

'Thanks, honey,' said Winnie, gesturing at her plate. 'If you don't like Kizzy, I'll just call you honey! Cause you're a honey!'

Kismet had no answer to that. She sank a stopper in

270 · LOUISE ERDRICH

the drain, ran hot water, and added translucent purple dish soap. But she wasn't going to bus for Winnie.

'Can you bring the dishes over, please?'

She asked this politely. Winnie pretended she didn't hear and just sat there with the dirty plates in front of her. She launched into a reverie about her dogs while Kismet did the other dishes.

'Poots has gotten so crazy. Maybe it's the pesticides. He barks at every single noise in the house. Then Jester goes nuts too. The phone rings. Yap yap yap. The microwave. Yap yap yap. And the doors—if you go through a door, open a door, he barks. But then he looks at you with that *expression*, you know, as if the little tyke is seeing right through your chest bones and into your heart! So I can't just put him down, can't extinguish him like Diz wants. I give Poots his sleepy pills in the evening when Diz needs to watch TV, and then, oh my god, that little dog snores like a lumberjake.'

This was the first time Winnie had spoken to her about something other than the wedding. Winnie sounded slightly off, but maybe she just needed more coffee. Kismet left Winnie to her coffee and walked out the kitchen door, saying she needed a breath of fresh air. But the wind had switched direction and Kismet breathed again the sweaty air off the rotting beet piles. Past those piles was town, and her mother. Oh god,

Mom! She should be there with Crystal. She should be there to help her mother. And she couldn't even talk to Crystal because of her phone. Maybe she could get on Gary's computer and send her mother a message. Kismet's head was a hive and all the bees were landing. Maybe it was the sudden jolt of caffeine, or maybe it was everything.

Magic Beans

One of the best fields had taken on a lot of water and been too soggy to plant, until now. Diz and Gary made their decision. This year new Roundup Ready GMO sugar beet seeds, very special, had cleared a preliminary level of government approval. To acquire the seeds, Diz had signed a stewardship agreement that was a legally binding pledge never to buy these same seeds from an unlicensed dealer and not to sell or share his seeds with another grower; he'd agreed to top or rogue any bolting sugar beets, to follow all pesticide labels, to use recommended herbicides on other Roundup Ready crops, and also not to plant or put seeds in wildlife feed plots.

Although, thought Diz as he looked around, all

fields were automatically wildlife feed plots, there was no avoiding that.

The seeds were small golden orange balls, cheerful and glowing. They were created to be immune to the killing powers of Roundup. Diz and Gary lined up the buckets of seeds outside the shed where they'd backed up the planter. They took the tops off the buckets and poured an equal amount of seeds into the row of big drums on the back of the machine. They didn't generally talk about their feelings. They didn't go deep into things. Their bond was work. Gary had always loved hearing the rush of seeds into the drum. Today it soothed away his wedding night of what seemed like heavy sleep instead of happy sex. He wasn't sure. He could hardly remember what had or had not happened. His disquiet soon vanished. The two men were in such a good mood, smelling damp earth and old chaff, that they decided to ride in the cab together. They started the engine, adjusted the settings to 22 inches for the rows and 3.5 for the seeds, set the controls, started rolling. As they cruised up one row, enjoyed a graceful turn, went down the next, land gulls drifted down and scattered up, catching the sun. Gary's heart warmed. The constant motion of white wings, the smell of a working engine, the sunlight on the clean, bright green hood of the machine where they'd tucked a can of brown sugar baked beans to heat, all was good. They glanced at each other, then squinted at the field, nodding with upside-down smiles as if to say, 'It doesn't get any better than this.'

When they stopped, Diz produced his can opener and they took two spoons out of the lunch box. As they ate the beans, Gary thought about how Kismet had cooked the best breakfast they'd had for a long time. That was something. It was really something. You couldn't deny it was something.

As they ate the rest of their lunch, the day started heating up. Gary loved how the shimmer of heat took up the whole horizon like a vast lake. He loved how the trees on the farmsteads looked like islands hovering over the water. Whenever he'd pointed out those islands as a child, and asked his mother what they were, she'd always said, 'That's the happy lands.'

They were out there, oh yes, the Happy Lands were out there today.

Across the Lilacs

Hellooooo!'
Winnie had left and was again calling from the other side of the lilac hedge.

'Come on over! Time for a tour of the big house!'

'I need to go to town, Mrs. Geist. Is that okay?'

'Sure, but later. You can even take my car, honey. But I need you for something first.'

'Okay, later then.' Kismet stepped through the lilacs. It was like a magic gate, but where you came out was unmagical as possible.

The big house was indeed a much larger house, and older, but still very much like Kismet and Gary's wedding house. There were more of the perfect stones, some fitted to the outside foundation as trim. The windows were more elaborate, and there was a sort of turret from which it looked like the house could easily be defended. Kismet took her shoes off at the door and walked in behind her mother-in-law. She filed away the fact that boots Diz's size were kicked off onto a rubber boot tray. Next time, she would make him do the same at her house, her and Gary's house.

Poots was a small rust-colored dog of indeterminate breed—probably miniature pinscher. Jester was also small, indeterminate, black; his ears flew back and he bounced across the rug. The two dogs ping-ponged at Kismet in a frothing frenzy, nipping at her legs, but she was wearing jeans. She ignored them. They circled swift as squirrels, dashing at her ankles, hanging on to the denim by their teeth. She continued to ignore them. Soon they quit. Comforted by her indifference, they claimed her, trotting beside her on dainty legs, taking quick sniffs. They could smell her unconcern, and then maybe they could smell her astonishment.

First the kitchen, mounded with unscraped dishes and pots. A sour, sourceless reek. Black and amber drips baked onto the stove. Winnie gestured proudly as though nothing was out of order. Then on a long dining room table, plates of half-eaten food, bowls of dried pasta, as though a family had been forced to jump up from dinner and run for their lives. The kitchen was the same—as though disaster had struck and the people had bolted, leaving everything. The tour ended with the basement—the brightly lit laundry room, heaped. The only orderly place was the closet containing the vacuums, the various mops, the buckets, the shelves of cleaning products.

'Okay, honey. Here we have the blow-by-blow!'

Winnie described the use of each cleaning instrument and then gave Kismet a computer printout—each room had a cleaning calendar and a set of directions for what should be done each time.

'You have a calendar,' said Kismet.

'We're way behind, as you can see! Haul up this vacuum cleaner, will you?'

'Why are you so behind?'

'Wedding preparations, you know?'

Kismet had always had the feeling she would pay somehow for Winnie's fevered wedding work. She carried a maroon vacuum cleaner upstairs and set it on the living room carpet. But this was too much. She tried to shake off a nightmarish fog. Winnie showed her the various buttons—for wood floors, for delicate rugs, for heavy carpet. Then she walked away. Kismet picked up piles of magazines and newspapers. She stacked them on the lowest shelf of the bookcase. *Agrotech Quarterly,*

Farm Life, Agweek, Valley Life. She went back to the vacuum cleaner, plugged it in, started it up with a roar. Kismet ran the vacuum expertly under and around each article of furniture. Soon, her training took over. She and her mother had made their way through their house cleaning carefully, exclaiming at dust balls, marshaling their brooms, mops, buckets, and vacuum cleaner. In fact, Kismet now began to take satisfaction in the way the suction eagerly took hold of the carpet, energizing the petrochemical nap, bringing up sand from under the carpet in satisfying grainy gasps. What a machine!

Winnie knew that late last night Kismet had driven the truck into town. She was also awake when Kismet returned, a couple of hours later. 'I'll give you the benefit of the doubt,' Winnie said, and walked upstairs.

'What doubt?' Kismet called after her. Kismet finished the carpet, then started on the rest of the room. While she was removing wads of dust and muddied glasses and cups from the living room windowsills, she heard water running upstairs. Winnie had disappeared so suddenly. It sounded like she was running a bath. Kismet walked to the bottom of the stairs.

'Winnie?'

The dogs yapped wildly in alarm when she raised her voice. Winnie called down.

'Throw Poots out the door. I'm just taking an eety-beety bath! Finish the living room, okay?'

Winnie wasn't taking a bath. She sat on the edge of the tub with the water running. The sound hid her low heart-ripping sobs. The water ran for a while more, then Winnie turned it off. Poots smashed himself at the bathroom door and Winnie let both dogs in. She was having one of her attacks. Winnie's mind was filled with pop-bottle rockets. Her thoughts fizzed out or sparked ferociously.

She picked up Jester and held him tight until she could breathe. Then she slipped into the bath.

Nobody had really cleaned the house since the accident. But now that Kismet was here, they could start over. Winnie already loved Kismet, couldn't get enough of her. Kismet was polite and kind. She cooked and she was cleaning. Everything would be splendid, shining, godly. Things would be the way they used to be. Winnie would walk into the kitchen every morning and her feet wouldn't stick. The dishes would return to cupboards and the spaces would be reclaimed, tables would be cleared. Winnie's heart lightened.

Kismet was a hero, but if she knew her value, Winnie feared, she might escape.

Kismet finished the living room, wiped off each surface, polished the glass coffee table with vinegar and the Sunday *Forum*. Still, no Winnie. She started on the kitchen, immediately filled the dishwasher, started it, hoping maybe Winnie would run out of hot water. In her house, her mom's house, she would. Kismet continued to wash dishes. She filled the drainer, then smoothed out a dish towel and set more dishes out to dry on the towel. Another towel. The counters filled with clean dishes. After a time, Winnie tramped downstairs, giving off a floral scent.

'Oh golly,' said Winnie, hands over her heart. 'You are a wonder. These dishes are left from our Easter Day feast. Can you believe it?'

'It's okay,' said Kismet. She was mystified, but transforming this level of disorder into order was rewarding, too, in a kind of brutal way. 'We're on a roll here.'

Winnie began to work with Kismet, clearing the kitchen surface by surface, scrubbing carefully at the drips baked onto the blue enamel of the stove.

'I'd like to get into town,' Kismet said. 'I'm really worried about my mom. Maybe I could use a computer, at least, to check my email? My phone doesn't work.'

'You gotta baby this stove!' Winnie answered, her head deep in the oven.

Kismet stood back, resisting the fairy tale urge to push Winnie in, close the door, hit Bake, and steal her car keys. No, no, how can that be in my head? Kismet's thoughts momentarily cleared. After all, maybe this was a trap. Maybe getting me to clean was the reason Winnie had pulled out all the stops for the wedding. Maybe when I am done they will fatten me up and eat me for their Fourth of July feast. At least afterward I won't have to do the dishes.

'I need to call my mom,' said Kismet, her voice shaded with desperation. 'Do you have a phone that works? A landline?'

'It's on the fritz,' said Winnie, pausing and then putting her sponge down carefully. She took slow deliberate steps out into the living room and sank down on the couch from which Kismet had just vacuumed a bag of dog hair.

'Oh, thank you,' Winnie whimpered. 'I can't thank you enough. It is so clean here. It is a true marvel.'

Winnie plunged into a motionless slumber. Kismet joggled Winnie's shoulder, and helped her over to the stairs, even placed her new mother-in-law's hand on the rail.

'Maybe you need more rest, maybe you're under the weather, maybe you need to go back to bed? Can I take your car while you're napping?'

'Not yet,' yawned Winnie. 'When I wake up, we will both go to town. I'll drop you at your mom's house. And oh, the computer? It is kaput.'

'Okay. We'll go in when you wake up. Promise?'

'Promise, honey!'

Truly, thought Kismet, walking outside, it had probably been a fabulous wedding, if only she hadn't been the bride. It was hard to know if Winnie was always like this, so wary of her car being borrowed, making these excuses so Kismet couldn't call her mother, basically trapping her, or whether she had done something. Had she done something?

Well she had, this was true, taken Gary's pickup into town and spent some hours lying beside Hugo on a bed. But Winnie couldn't know that, could she? Winnie must have been asleep. She seemed exhausted to the bone and she must have slept hard. Still, the way Winnie acted—it was disorienting. And the wreck of the kitchen—where was that from? This disorder that Kismet kept working at seemed deeper than a month or two. The pockets of grease in the corners had an ancient, sullen quality. There was a level of despair to the mess that pierced Kismet's heart. She and her mother maintained a level of cheerful order in their house, so to Kismet, the uncontrolled buildup spoke of personal disintegration. What she found shook her up. Cutlery glued together with molasses. An unopened bag of birdseed devoured by meal moths that had feasted and died within the sealed plastic. Knives rusting away in wet pans. There was an unreality to each discovery that pointed to a terrible underlying cause.

The Pasture

Winnie could see the site of her family's old farmstead from her bedroom, but only she knew where it was because the buildings had been pulled down, the trees bulldozed, and the fields planted. Sometimes as she fell asleep she imagined walking there.

During those final years on that farm, Winnie had grown up hard. Nobody knew how that stayed with you. She'd been hungry back then so she was avid for food now. But she often stopped eating for the secret horror at the plenitude of her life—surrounded by easy food. Her parents had been third-generation farmers caught in the cost-price squeeze of the 1970s, when the income from crops and livestock was less than they cost to grow and produce. Her folks took out a government loan with the Farm Home Administration, an FDR-era lending agency established to safeguard farmers from the devastations of the 1930s.

During the Reagan administration, budget director David Stockman decided to suddenly accelerate, or call in, loans that farmers had previously had decades to repay. Winnie's family hung on, hung on, barely climbing out each year, until at last they went under and the family farm, bordering on Geist's, had been foreclosed and was bought by Sport Geist.

Winnie had a brother, Clark, who came back to Tabor and bought a bar. Sometimes during the beet campaign he came out and topped or lifted beets. He had been the youngest and hadn't been there when their farm and all of the equipment was auctioned off, but Winnie had.

Diz knew, but he didn't really know, the secret shame of losing all you love—the clapboard house, its back room the original logs, the white barn with the fieldstone foundation. The neat coops, the grain bins, the sheds, the livestock, the truck, the combine, the tractor, the horse, the livestock. They even lost their dead, who lay nearby in a country graveyard with a small Lutheran church beside it. The church had also failed after the whole community had withered. Trees now grew through the roof of the K–12 schoolhouse, the swings dangling, rusting on their chains, the monkey bars hauled off and sold for scrap. There were still a few houses, a gas station, a bar, and the main road was gravel. It was all gone but here she was. Winnie's parents wouldn't talk to her for a year after she married Diz, but she was the only one of their daughters who hadn't left for the Cities.

Since then, she had pretended to be a Geist, to live at a level of prosperity that she didn't believe would last. Stability—she didn't trust the word. She knew because she kept, or rather juggled, the farm's accounts. Winnie scrapped, she bullied, she argued with Diz about what to plant, which fields, when, how much, how to balance, should they chance soybeans and sugar beets when they had to be harvested at the same time, should they try sunflowers, wheat and what kind of wheat. She had fought her way back to a functional life, and had weathered (literally) the many times she and Diz had misjudged or hit a long drought or heavy flooding and gone into debt. But when Gary had nearly died and Travis and Jordan . . . well, when they died, some part of her had plunged down that pasture that once belonged to her farm and she'd gone into the river with those boys.

Two Little Dogs

When Winnie looked at her life, oof, two little dogs. When the dogs set each other into hysteria, Winnie thought of the utility tub downstairs. Filling it. Did they even know? Of course they didn't. They trusted her with their very lives. So there it was. Poots and Jester. She couldn't call the cat by name, although it gave her the least trouble. This was supposed to be the time in a woman's life when she cut the shit and went for broke. Instead, Winnie picked up, or left, all sorts of shit on the floor. These little dogs had been invented many centuries ago for rich people who had servants to deal with their waste. Now everybody kept these dogs because they were cuddly alarm systems cheap to feed. Desperation gripped her when people told her that small dogs could live as long as twenty years. Then she looked into the dogs' young and trusting eyes and was ashamed.

Winnie walked back downstairs and the dogs went into a tither.

'Ready to go to town now?' Kismet asked.

'Boy-yoys, come to mama,' cried Winnie.

From the end of a brand-new charging cord, Winnie pulled two tiny collars attached to citronella spray bottles. The bottles would be positioned below the dogs' chins. The bottles were fitted with noise-activated nozzles. When the dogs barked, there would be a puff of harmless citronella, a smell that dogs apparently liked or disliked. Who could say.

'Finally, there will be peace in the valley,' said Winnie.

She winked at Kismet and filled each tiny bottle with the penetrating citronella oil. She seized the collars and buckled one of the contraptions around each dog's throat, assuring Poots, then Jester, that the collars were humane and the latest in humane technology.

There.

She stroked and patted the dogs. Set them gently on the floor. As soon as she backed away, Gary came into the house. The dogs, who adored him, began to bark. As advertised, the citronella bottles puffed. Bark. Puff. Bark Puff. BarkPuff. BarkPuff. BarkPuff. Pffffffffffffffffffftaaaark. The dogs went batshit, popping and puffing. Maybe, no for sure, they were actually getting high on the citronella. Winnie was hungry and went to the refrigerator. It was 4 p.m. She sat down, popped a beer, and watched the tripped-out dogs skitter in circles across the linoleum. Winnie watched the dogs until three beers washed her brain clean and she was utterly calm.

'You are sheer entertainment,' said Winnie.

'Mind-blowing,' said Kismet. She gulped her own beer, icy cold. 'Now let's take the collars off.'

Gary bent over and gently removed the collars. The dogs rolled their eyes at Kismet in such horror that tears started into her eyes.

'I'm sorry,' she said to the dogs.

'Winnie, you were torturing them,' said Gary.

'Those are humane society approved,' said Winnie, tipsily complacent.

'I have to use your phone to call my mom,' said Kismet. 'Then we're going to town, right?'

'For sure.'

Winnie went out for a watering can walk around the yard. She loved pampering her rows of flowers.

When she came back, the dogs were stretched out, silent on the floor, and she thought for a moment, with hope and horror, that she'd killed them. But no, their legs jerked spasmodically, so they were still alive and dreaming, their gums flared back, yellow teeth clenched in ecstasy.

Dust vs. Dirt vs. Soil

Kismet pulled a plastic armchair from a stack in the garage. Although she needed to go to town, she also needed to drink a beer, even though she didn't like beer. She set the chair on the concrete floor of the garage with the double door open to the west. What was to be the driveway was water-resistant, clayey gray silt. She sat down, snapped open the beer, gazed out. Everything was lined up across the horizon, the dark purple and magenta clouds in stratified layers. Light burned in strict rays through the top and bottom. You could see the day going out as the sky slowly ate up the light. The wind came up, a strange, unnatural wind, burning hot, whipping up the dirt, coming from the southwest. Tomorrow would be a furnace. Any flood-waters would vanish. Any rain would evaporate, as if it never had fallen. The heat would shimmer atop the earth, an unbound malevolence. Every step or movement would kick up clots of mud that turned instantly to dust. Kismet's thoughts, slightly beer-soaked, were once again under the influence of the funeral cake. She dreaded tomorrow. The fields would suddenly be so dry that this dust would fill Kismet's nose, her mouth, her lungs. If she stayed here, eventually it would stop up her guts. She would be composed of dust, her brain an eggshell full of dust, dust her thoughts. She would serve the Geists her whole life and then at last she would be dead, contributing her atoms to the dust, the giant fields of it that stretched to the horizon.

She reached down. Scooped up a handful of dirt from a pile set next to the garage.

What was this stuff?

The God Stuff

The moist dirt that clumped in Kismet's palm, a friendly weight, was different from the gray silt rising in the field. Her fistful was dense, rich as chocolate, turned up when the basement had been dug beneath the new house. The contractor had scraped off the topsoil and made a mound of it. This very old dirt had collected on the century-plus-old island of Geist homestead. It was ground that had never been plowed. It was soil. The homestead topsoil reached down twenty feet. In places, the Red River topsoil had originally gone down to sixty feet. Everything was happy in that godly stuff. You could leave a stick in that soil and it would grow. She walked out into the driveway and looked past the lawn, into the dense and tangled strip of trees that formed a backdrop for the houses.

Along the edge of the woods, there were tufts of the ancient grasses—bluestem, switchgrass, porcupine grass, wheatgrass, and fescue—that once had covered the entire valley. The old grass still lay flat as it had been beneath the snow. New growth was swiftly bursting up from beneath. Kismet's dirt was a fistful of the primeval loam that had accumulated epoch on epoch of floods and receding floods. She opened her hand and looked at the bit of soil.

Really, what was in this stuff?

She lifted her hand and peered into the bit of darkness. It was a jumble in there—insect husks, fluffy particles, nutlike crumbs, infinitesimal threads that looked like the branching dendrites she'd once seen in a microscopic illustration of a human brain. It was like some kind of tiny forest in there, all packed together. There was movement. A millipede and then a red speck, a mite, crawled out.

She could hear the pickup rumble off the highway. Gary pulled up in the truck, honked at her, started to pull away, but suddenly Diz plunged from somewhere in the big house, through the front door, out, onto the cement walk.

'Go back in town an' get me a pizza pie!' he bawled at Gary.

Kismet ran toward the truck, but with a salute, Gary

made a U-turn and pulled back out on the long drive. There went her ride to town. Diz lumbered back into the house. Kismet went back and picked up another handful of dirt. There was a shell in the loam, a tiny white scallop, delicately ridged. A memento of Lake Agassiz. Her high school science classes had visited the ancient beaches along the sides of the valley, where the waves of unthinkable age had washed and crashed, dunes of grassy sand now. These shells, forced up through the freezing and melting of the soil, eventually found the surface of the land. She let the mite crawl back into its hiding place and put the dirt back but kept the shell, putting it in her pocket. She'd had so many omens. This was the first good one.

Kismet walked toward the shelterbelt trees and spied a place where the tall grasses had been pushed aside, perhaps the beginning of a little path. She stood at the entrance to the path. Sipped the beer. It was a thin, green walking path, kept clear, no fallen branches or sprouting trees to block it. This was a path someone could walk every day, she thought. Stepping into the tangle, her heart slowed. Walking among trees was her favorite thing. Here at the edge of the homestead there were large cottonwood trees, some scruffy box elders, roiling masses of chokecherry, even wild plum and old apple trees with bitter, gnarled fruit still clinging to the branches. She stopped and leaned against a tree, listening to the clatter of the cottonwood leaves, staring at the flat gray fields. The baby beet plants, coddled in their chemical dust, stretched row after laser row into the shimmer of tomorrow's heat, and she thought the order of the earth, beneath the unpredictable sky and the tangle behind her, was exquisite.

Happy's Walk

In February 1933, a meeting between the farmers of Tabor and representatives of the Chippewa Sugar Company took place in a barn and was attended by a lonely spirit. Shortly before that meeting, two booze-packed Reo Roadsters, rampaging south on the Meridian trail, had wrecked in a ditch, killing a young male driver with no identification on his person. He was the ghost. The driver of the other vehicle, a determined young woman named Happy Frechette, was barely scratched. She climbed out of the wreck with two suitcases of Canadian rye whiskey and walked to Fargo. At the scene, the first people to discover the accident were busy snatching up every bottle scattered through the grass. They picked clean the crash site well before Sheriff Brownie and Mr. Sotovine of the Sotovine Funeral

Home arrived to collect the dead driver. But within those contraband bottles tucked beneath their coats, the spirit of the nameless driver had taken refuge. So at that meeting, where young Otto (Sport) Geist persuaded his grandfather to pledge two hundred acres of cropland to the sugar company, accepting the terms under which the sugar company would supply the proper machinery, seed, and even assist with labor, a good many of the farmers imbibed the whiskey runner's soul. Afterward, as the celebratory lemonade was spiked and poured, members of the Chippewa Sugar Company joined them. Jubilant toasts were made to the effect that the sugar beet aimed to rival wheat, then surpass wheat. Although it would have thrilled, nobody could have foreseen that sugar would also surpass sunflowers, corn, potatoes, soy, flax, and everything else that grew in the Red River Valley. The soil would be chemically altered to grow the beet, and industrial factories would spring up to make the beet into sugar. That meeting, however, was why one fierce summer, many years later, Happy's granddaughter Crystal was climbing aboard a sugar beet truck in the dim fresh hour before light.

Beet Field Bones

The truck was parked in the Piggly Wiggly parking lot, across from the county courthouse. Crystal was twelve years old. She was relieved to escape from Happy that summer. She groped her way over the bare legs of her girl crew to a hay bale in the corner, then slumped over, taking up two bales, and put her head on her balled-up sweatshirt. She tried to doze. When the truck stopped, brakes gasping, Crystal got out and sharpened her hoe. The boss, John Track, a Sisseton Dakota, took out his clipboard. The girls unfolded from sleep, knotted their shirts around their waists, and stowed their lunches in a box underneath the truck. John Track assigned the rows and the girls began to walk beets, thinning them lightly. The weeds were just now invading the fields, still tender. There wasn't much strenuous chopping to be done except where there was a dip in the field, allowing rain to collect, growing the sudden thistles shoulder high. Crystal wore canvas gloves and swung her hoe from the left, like a sickle, letting the bright sharp edge do the work, keeping a regular pace. She wore a two-piece swimsuit, a pre-bikini, so that she wouldn't get a farmer tan. Though here she was—technically, a farmer. And she liked the work. The only thing wrong with the job was how her feet sweat. Otherwise she could have walked for years in the fatal sunshine, over the poisoned earth, occasionally blessed by the acid rain, chemically altered by an occasional crop duster.

At noon the crew of girls sat in the shade of the truck. Crystal opened an olive green plastic thermos, and drank some vegetable soup. Track teased her, gently, the way Indian men do. He knew the Ojibwe ladies of the generation who had benefited from Happy's long walk.

Happy's boyfriend had died of windshield glass, bled out beneath a pearl dawn sky. On her walk, Happy shed hot tears for his ruin, but this was mostly because she'd discovered he had made her pregnant. Unclaimed, he was buried in the corner of a field donated by the Geist family to the penniless dead, who were forgotten in a generation and plowed into the earth. If there were fragments of her grandfather's bones in the beet rows that Crystal walked, she didn't notice. Why should she notice a bone when she was looking for a thistle?

And why should Kismet notice a bone, either?

But she did. Drowsing against a cottonwood, she looked over the same field her mother had once hoed, and noticed something pale, incongruous, a white stick in the corner of the field. Perhaps a rib, a femur, turned up by the movements of the stars, or a frost heave more likely, or the tilling and the planting and the wrestling of food from the earth. Kismet held the shell of unspeakable age and started at the white scratch she didn't recognize as her great-grandfather's bone.

Bone Black

After crossing the Red River sometime in the 1830s, a priest climbed a tree seeking a spot where he could safely observe an approaching herd of buffalo. There he witnessed a deranging spectacle—the buffalo stretched all the way to where they disappeared into the line between sky and earth. He was forced to stay in the tree for three days as they passed, passed and migrated, three days of horizon-to-horizon buffalo. He nearly died of thirst. 'You may judge now the richness of these prairies,' he wrote later. There was no end to the beasts. Just like it seems there is no end to us, in our billions. But everything on earth can be eliminated under the right conditions.

The conditions for the buffalo were slaughter by hunters, slaughter by traders, slaughter by tourists, slaughter by train, slaughter by the Winchester Repeating Rifle, slaughter, slaughter, again slaughter, disease maybe, mostly slaughter, and then there were only bones. By 1880, the prairie and prairie breaks, the sloughs and grasses, horizon to horizon, were decked with bones so thick a person couldn't walk in the tall grass or sit on the bank of a river or slough without stepping over, sitting on, pushing aside the bones. They were snagged high in the trees after floods, and piled along the riverbanks after the living buffalo had sunk and served as rafts and bridges for their own. There seemed no end to the bones. But there would be an end.

One day a young man stood at the foot of Shackamaxon Street in Philadelphia, sugar town, 1882. Folded into his vest, a letter of reference. He had an idea that involved a railroad ticket and the millions of dead buffalo out west. If he could get those bones into railroad cars and ship them to Philadelphia, they could be heated in a sealed vessel at 700 degrees Celsius, which was 1292 degrees Fahrenheit, not easy to imagine. The super-heating would drive off the organic matter in the bones, leaving activated carbon, composed of tricalcium phosphate, calcium carbonate, and carbon. Bone charcoal. Bone black. Ivory black. Animal charcoal. Abaiser. Pigment black 9. Bone char. Carbo animalis.

Buffalo black. This substance could be used to refine crude raw sugar processed from sugarcane, slave sugar, although of course the slave trade had been abolished, then as now, but there still were enslaved people, then as now. Bone char worked better than bull's blood or egg whites or any other substance to bleach the sugar white. And the bones! The bones were everywhere, he'd heard, littering the ground, so thick that a farmer couldn't plow without stacking them beside the fields. He went into business. The bones were picked up by human hands and transported by animal effort, eight dollars, ten dollars, sixteen dollars a ton. They were piled beside the railroad tracks as each section was built farther west. Hills of bones, mountains of blind skulls, loaded onto railroad cars and shipped back east to process sugar. So it was, every teaspoon of sugar that was stirred into a cup or baked into a pudding was haunted by the slave trade and the slaughter of the buffalo.

Just as now, into every teaspoon, is mixed the pragmatic nihilism of industrial sugar farming and the death of our place on earth. This is the sweetness that pricks people's senses and sparkles in a birthday cake and glitters on the tongue. Price guaranteed, delicious, a craving strong as love.

The Cakelet and the Keys

Winnie woke at night and went over to the window to make sure Gary's pickup was still in the drive, make sure Kismet hadn't taken the keys. She had told Gary to hide them and he'd looked at her like she was crazy, which he did all the time anyway. But maybe he understood. Every time she imagined Kismet leaving and going back to her mother, maybe even her tribe, if she had one, Winnie felt a terrible urgency come over her and she checked to see that Kismet was still on the property. Winnie imagined that Gary would disappoint Kismet and she would run away. Or that she herself would disgust Kismet and Kismet would run away. She worried that Diz would let Kismet down even though they seemed to get along better than anyone else. And at last, Winnie knew that the way she was behaving might even cause Kismet to bolt. But she couldn't help it.

Winnie had saved the tiny top tier of the cake with the little plastic man and woman on it. They stood in a lush garden of frosting roses and sugar vines. Winnie had nested the top of the cake tower in a small box and put it in the freezer. Now she crept down to the kitchen freezer, opened the cake box. She plucked up a few bits of frozen icing and slipped the sugary specks onto her tongue. As she was shutting the box and arranging it among the other wrapped foods, she heard Gary's truck drive up on the other side of the lilac bushes. If it was Kismet, sneaking out again, Winnie decided she would go back and eat the whole damn cakelet. She slipped outside, into the yard, and peered through the lilacs at Gary's driveway.

It was Kismet. Gary had let her take the truck.

Winnie faded back. They were newlyweds, she shouldn't be watching them all of the time, but the fact that Kismet was slipping off into the night again was so upsetting. And now Kismet was carrying something. What? Winnie's thoughts branched out. She padded back upstairs, where she had a better view. Diz was sleeping on his back. He rumbled and whistled when he snored, a lonesome call like a freight train in the dark.

Kismet and Gary were talking on the back steps. Winnie opened the window a crack. She heard the words of a fight.

'Chopped black olives?'

'So pick them off.'

'No.'

'Here. I'll pick them off for you.'

'Don't treat me like a baby!'

'You're acting like a baby. Just pick the olives off!'

'No!'

Then they vanished into the house. What now? Winnie thought.

Gary lunged through the kitchen into the dining room, across the space where they were going to put a large table, a space beneath a low chandelier. He struck his head on the light fixture. The large metal cones crashed from a socket in the ceiling and sagged, cockeyed, swaying on a wire.

'Don't touch it!' yelled Kismet.

'Don't shout. You could fry yourself,' he said, sullen.

Gary dragged a smaller table over, stood on top, and tried to stuff the wires past the dangling rim of the socket, back into the ceiling. He asked for a slot head screwdriver and she brought it. He began to prod around in the wires.

'Stop it, you'll electrocute yourself!' Kismet said.

'I know exactly where to poke,' he muttered.

The air in the nearly empty dining room was buzzing with resentment. Their hearts were beating hot with adrenaline. Gary's voice was choked off by fury. He wobbled and Kismet held his leg to steady him. Then her hand tingled with the shock of electricity conducted through his body. The screwdriver flew out of his hand and he yelled for her to give the screwdriver back.

'Did you feel that?' She wrung her hand.

He jumped down, grabbed the screwdriver, and stabbed it deep into the black crevasse next to the swirl of colored wires. There was a crackling sound. From the dining room ceiling, an electronic voice, faintly British and faintly female, spoke. 'Warning. Warning.'

'What's that?' asked Kismet. Again she touched him and felt the prickling of electricity.

'Gary, drop the screwdriver!'

The alarm went to its next level.

'Oh fuck me,' said Gary.

He sprang off the table and stood beneath a smoke detector that had been placed out of reach on the vaulted ceiling. The alarm was now emitting a spectacular, ear-mangling screech. They ran outside, fingers in their ears.

'You set it off!'

They were on the back steps.

'Where's the circuit breaker?' Kismet yelled.

'Basement!'

They ran back inside, milled around in the basement, wincing, opening and shutting doors. Kismet vaulted up the steps and yanked open the kitchen closet. There it was. She jerked the fuse box open and snapped off the main circuit. The house plunged into darkness and the screeching quit. After a minute, she heard Winnie calling from next door. There she was, leaning out the open window of her bedroom in silver light. At least the moon was out.

Kismet waved up at Winnie.

'False alarm!' Kismet shouted.

'I don't think so,' Winnie muttered, but she closed the window and slipped back into bed beside Diz.

Gary plodded up the stairs into the kitchen. He saw the rest of the pizza sitting on the counter.

'Come on,' he said, picking up the box. 'Let's sit out back.'

Kismet groped around in the fridge, snagged two sodas, a jar of red pepper flakes, and followed him outside. They sat across from each other at the picnic table, the box of pizza between them.

Gary forgot about the olives and put two pieces of pizza together into a thick pizza sandwich.

'That was the stupidest fucking thing! I worked on this house! But the circuit breaker's in the basement at Diz and Winnie's, so I ran down there. Anyway, did you see your mom?'

'She was at work.'

'I gotta get some help on this. I don't know what I did. I was so mad at that cheap chandelier thing. Shoulda never gone poking around with the screwdriver. Coulda lit myself up!'

'You did light yourself up,' said Kismet. 'I felt the electricity go through you.'

Gary shrugged.

The moonlight cast severe shadows across his slanting cheekbones, deepened the hollows of his eyes. He fell silent, eating wolfishly, drinking his soda, casting a sidelong glance at Kismet from time to time. A moon breeze rattled the cottonwoods.

'What the hell,' she said at last. 'Let's leave it all for tomorrow morning and go to bed. The fridge and freezer will stay cold. We don't need lights.'

She rose, tipped down the rest of the soda. He got up and closed the empty pizza box.

'You ate the olives,' she said.

'It's too dark to pick 'em out.'

'How were they?'

'Disgusting. Like dead snails.'

'Your mom likes olives.'

'She likes anything Italian. You know, sometimes I think she wants to ditch Dad and me. Sometimes I think she wants to flee us, go there.'

He said this so solemnly. His earnestness surprised Kismet. She walked into the house, grabbed a flashlight from the kitchen drawer, and went upstairs. She didn't want to think about the electricity that had gone through Gary or about what he'd just said, but she couldn't help it.

'Is that why she wanted us to get married so bad? So she could get out?'

'Oh no, I don't think so,' said Gary. 'Mainly, she wanted us to get married because of me. I told her how I felt about you. In love and all that.'

'Are you really?'

'Guess,' said Gary, turning to her in the silver light, touching her hair. He began to stroke her face, then made his way down her neck, her arms, down the sides of her legs, to her feet. He began to massage her feet.

'Wow,' she said, in hope. 'That feels really good.'

Gary dropped her foot and threw himself on her, ground against her hips. She held on to his back and looked up into the fuzzy air. Darkness bunched up against the ceiling, draped silkily in the corners, darkness translucent in the window radiance. He was

312 · LOUISE ERDRICH

wound up like a circus toy. She rolled out from under him, scattering his magazines.

'I'm beat,' she said, in such a sorrowful voice that Gary thought she was going to cry.

'And there's probably more cleaning,' she continued. 'Does your mom always leave things in such a wreck?'

'She's been, you know, busy with the wedding and all,' said Gary in a low voice. 'Plus she went through a lot.' Now he wanted to cry too.

Outer Space

There wasn't much left of the season, and now they would be driving in the yard of the plant, getting loaded up and bringing the beets over to be boiled and processed. The piles had begun to smell so bad that some of the drivers had quit for the year. But there was money in plugging your nose. Crystal was also still driving out of solidarity with Dale, who needed the money and called this part of the job 'feeding the monster.' He was helping two kids through college and wanted to make enough to take a car trip with his youngest and his wife. Sarey rarely came to the book club meetings but still read the books after Crystal left them with Dale.

'So are you and Sarey planning your vacation like in *Eat Pray Love*?'

'Yeeaaah,' said Dale. 'We're eating to get up our energy for the love part and praying it happens. But I suppose we'll only get as far as the Dells this summer.'

The Wisconsin Dells were a family playground full of water parks and big cheap hotels. Dale had grown up in Wisconsin, near the Chippewa Flowage.

'God's country, not like here,' he said.

'Are you insulting my homeland?' said Crystal, getting out of the car with her cooler.

'Put your glow vest on,' said Dale.

Crystal put on her safety vest. She walked over to her truck with Dale.

'You know what would be nice right about now?' she said. 'Getting abducted by aliens.'

Dale looked at her sympathetically. 'Outer space would have to smell better. Also, you know, they're out there.'

He'd seen a few spaceships and described them, hovering, shifting, light glancing around below a huge shadowy circle. And he and some of the other drivers had seen a meteor blaze down in a mane of light that lit the fields and highway. He'd seen a wolf by Tintah and thought he'd seen a plane from the air force base up by Grand Forks shoot down a satellite.

'You're doing good,' he said. 'You'll live this down.

I hope you stashed the church money someplace real secret.'

'Shut up,' said Crystal. 'Or I won't give you any.'

'Seriously,' said Dale. 'You'll be okay.'

Crystal opened the cab of the truck. The inside smelled like sauerkraut so she knew it had been Reggie Wholler's. He kept himself going on hot spicy sauerkraut and giant dill pickles. The next shift of drivers after him had gotten together and presented him with a bag of Gas-X.

The Farmer Car

The next morning, Kismet slept until seven and then got up and dumped away the dregs of coffee the men had left in the glass pot. She made herself a nice fresh cup and went to what had become her spot—the shade of the open garage. All her life, in Tabor, she'd had to leave town to see the horizon, so having the horizon outside the door and drinking a cup of coffee looking into all that space was unexpectedly compelling. She hadn't imagined that the horizon would be something to get up for. Her back was to the east and the house cast a long cool shadow. The sky had that hot blue eloquence of early summer, the heat pleasant now but already gathering. She watched a few clouds take shape out of nothing. That was another thing. In town you never got to see them form in the distance. At present they were small and friendly.

The men came back. She made Diz take off his boots, cooked the usual round of breakfasts, and made them a bag of sandwiches from a package of ham she found in the meat drawer. They left. When Winnie came in, Kismet made them both breakfast and went back out with her plate. The clouds she had watched before had recruited more clouds. They were large, puffy, sailing grandly out of the southwest, glowing white. When she went back inside, she saw that Winnie was gone but that at least she had brought her plate and cup to the sink. It was a start. Kismet ran water over the smears of egg yolk and left the dishes to soak.

'Hellooooo,' she heard from beyond the lilac bushes.

'Hell nooooo,' she sang back, softly, and laughed.

They worked until noon, and this time it was just a sorting project. They had made it through the whole house. Kismet didn't bother trying to call her mother yet, because Crystal would be sleeping after her night shift. She had to catch her mother in the window between 3:00 and 5:30. Kismet went back to the wedding house and read for an hour, then brought *Madame Bovary* downstairs. She ran the vacuum cleaner around the floor, reading as she went. At last she got her purse and went over to the other house. She called out, heard Diz tell her to come on in, and went through the kitchen door. Winnie, stooping into the cool glow of refrigerator light, jumped.

'Hey!' she said. 'Knock?'

'I did knock,' said Kismet.

'Hey there!' cried Diz, his big face creasing in pleasure.

'Let's go to town now,' said Kismet.

'I've had a beerio,' said Winnie.

'I will drive.'

'Maybe I need to take another little rest, though.'

'That's okay. I'll take your car. I'm a good driver.'

'You can take mine,' said Diz, holding out a set of keys. 'It's the only farmer car we have. The rest are all agribusiness.'

'Diz, you are a laugh.' Winnie started to chortle. Couldn't stop. Maybe, after all, too many beerios.

'You'll find it in the back shed,' said Diz. He called every outbuilding a shed, no matter how big.

Kismet thanked him and took the keys. She grabbed her blue fringed purse and flung a buffalo plaid shirt over her T-shirt. Then she used the opener on the key chain to raise the door to the equipment shed. It slid creakingly up to reveal Diz's farmer car, a pleasant-looking green vintage tractor looking tiny beside the mammoth equipment used now, probably the one Gary had once mentioned, belonging to Diz's father. So this was a joke.

'Cute,' said Kismet.

She hopped on the tractor, turned the key. The tractor started up after a few cranks and coughs. It was parked snout out so off she went, bouncing on the tattered scrim of padding, hitting the steel beneath, which hurt. The wind hurt too, flinging grit. But it was better when she got to the highway. An hour or so later (thank goodness Diz had topped the gas tank), she pulled up in front of her mother's house and shut off the tractor. A man in a white Camry got out of the car and stretched. Kismet waved at him and gingerly let herself down. Wind torn, sore of butt, hungry, she walked into the house and there was her mother, hunched over at her pigeonhole desk.

Crystal was readjusting numbers and trying to get the zeros back into the amount owed column. The two walked into each other's arms the way two people do in mourning. They tried to cry but soon they were tearily laughing.

'How'd you get here?'

Kismet brought her mother to the door. There was the tractor, blocking the view of the white Camry.

'Check out my ride.'

Crystal raised her hands high and slowly lowered them onto her head.

'No way.'

'Way.'

'You rode that into town?'

'Diz gave me the keys. I think it belonged to Gary's grandpa or something. They keep it tuned up, full of gas.'

'It's the kind of thing they drive in parades.'

'Used to. There's no more parades in this town,' said Kismet.

'You sound like Bev.'

'How're Bev and Ichor. And Hugo?'

Kismet strained to keep her voice casual. She'd quoted Hugo about the parades, actually. They walked to the kitchen.

'Fair.'

'That's nice.'

Crystal shot her a telepathic glance.

'Hungry?'

'So hungry.'

'Spaghetti? Or beans and rice?'

'I could go for a bowl of spaghetti. That would be great.'

Crystal put a pot of water on to boil and peeled

some carrots. She'd boil the carrots in salt water, mash them up with fried garlic and onions, add some basil, oregano, a can of tomatoes, a few spoonfuls of tomato paste, red pepper flakes, a dash of cinnamon. *Voilà*. Sauce. They almost never ate meat because meat, even misery meat, cost more than carrots. Nobody else made this sauce, and Kismet loved it so much that she put her face in her hands and began to weep, for real.

'Mom! Why'd he *do* it?'

'I have no idea!' Crystal's voice was too light. Her good cheer was a little spooky, but being overly cheerful to absorb shock was her way. 'There's no sign of him, either. At least not that they're telling me. But that's not the main thing.'

'Not the main thing?'

Now Crystal wiped her hands on a kitchen towel and became grave.

'I let you get married to Gary. You didn't want to.'

Kismet and her mother locked eyes, but only for a moment. A mother-daughter eye-lock got witchy so fast.

'Let me? Mom, I was going to do it no matter what. Really, do I listen to you?'

'Sometimes! So listen now, please. You said Gary rolled his truck. He's always getting out of danger but other people aren't so lucky. He has a guardian angel.'

'So do I, Mom.'

That stopped Crystal, but after a pause she said more softly, 'Will you stay here? You can divorce him, just get away from him.'

'Maybe,' said Kismet, slowly. 'Come to think of it, there was last night, too. He stuck a screwdriver in a light socket.'

'What?'

'I had my hand on his leg to steady him and I felt him get shocked, but he didn't feel it.'

Crystal spoke in a subdued fearful tone: 'Case in point. Do you still love him?'

'I *did* love him, I remember loving him, *knowing* I was in love, feeling like I was crazy about Gary, at some point anyway. I thought it would come back. But no, I've just been nonstop cleaning.'

Kismet said this with a mournful shake of her hair. She let her lips turn down, and tremble.

Crystal said, 'Cleaning? Did you say cleaning? On your honeymoon?'

'Well, Gary's out planting so . . .'

Crystal put her hands back on top of her head and began to walk around the kitchen in a little circle. She went faster and faster.

'Please stop, Mom. You're making me dizzy.'

Crystal halted and frowned at her daughter.

'Stay here.'

'Well, you're my role model. You made it work, Mom, you stayed with Dad.'

'I mean, obviously, we got together when I was your age. But your dad's not dangerous, I mean, okay he's not safe around money and all but he never, oh, never mind. For a while it was so beautiful, Kismet, we had you. It was all meant to be. My life seemed magical once you were here.'

'Magical? Me?'

Kismet's chin was still trembling, but she loved hearing that. With a hero's compression of her body, she gathered herself, lifted her head, and pushed her hair away from her face. Her eyes were skittery. Maybe she was more shaken up from the tractor ride and the rollover and the electricity than she'd thought.

'I guess you were right, Mom.'

Kismet put her chin on her fist and thought. She shook her head, then squeezed her mouth up and squeezed her eyes shut to demonstrate hard thinking. 'Well, I don't feel in any danger, except from overcleaning and the tractor ride. I mean that rollover was just *boom*, and I was right side up. My hair wasn't even messy. And maybe that electrical thing wasn't all that bad. I know he loves me, too, needs me. When I first started loving Gary, it was the way he would look at me, sometimes, like I was the coolest, the best. He'd marvel at me.'

Crystal bit down on her lips and said nothing for a minute. Finally she shook herself and said, 'I don't buy that he's safe. And you loved him because of the way he marveled at you? What about character?'

Kismet didn't speak. After a while Crystal felt the need to prompt her.

'What character traits made you love him?'

'You never asked this before,' said Kismet.

'Don't put this on me,' said Crystal. 'I assume you have the good sense to examine a person's character.'

'Like you did? With Dad?'

'That's a fair point,' said Crystal. 'All the same.'

'Character. Character. Well, I don't know. The way he moves is really graceful, he's strong.'

Kismet closed her eyes, mumbled that she knew looks weren't character, then suddenly burst out, 'Oh god, I make three-egg breakfasts every morning for all of them.'

Crystal frowned, a little jealous. The only time Kismet made breakfast for her was Mother's Day morning. She'd had no idea that her daughter was capable of this on a daily basis.

'And I'm cleaning Winnie's house that hasn't really been cleaned since before the accident,' Kismet went on.

'That's over a year ago.'

'Mom, it would break your heart.'

'Cleaning on your honeymoon.'

'Like I said, Gary's out in the fields all day.'

'Some honeymoon.'

'No, it's better he's out of the house, although I did love him, I really think I did.'

'Dear god.' Crystal waved her hand as if to push away nonsense. 'All right. You managed to duck the issue. So what about Hugo?'

Wow, her mother really zinged that one in. She was so good at that.

'Hugo?'

Kismet attempted a look of confusion.

'Oh, right,' said Crystal. Now they'd hit an impasse. But Crystal was an adept U-turn conversationalist. They began to dissect the wedding ceremony, the fabulous cake, the dinner and the dinner speeches, the long maud-lin dance. Kismet told her mother about the second cake, the funeral cake. Then she told her mother that she was no quitter. She couldn't leave because she couldn't just give up.

'Yes, you can,' said Crystal. 'You give up when it defies common sense to stay.'

'That time hasn't come yet,' said Kismet.

'It will,' said Crystal. 'And when it does I'll be here

for you. And until then . . .' She took a stone off the windowsill and threw it out the back door. That was her way of warding off bad luck. Kismet got up and also took a stone off the windowsill and threw it out the back door, across the yard. She threw it so hard that it hit a tree and made a tiny *thunk*. Crystal took another stone, threw that one out. They cleaned off the whole windowsill.

'We don't have any more stones,' she said. 'No more bad luck.'

Crystal put another pot of water on for the pasta and began to mash the boiled carrots with mad alacrity.

'Although there's something else,' she said to Kismet. 'It's about our house. Your dad put a mortgage on it.'

'What's a mortgage?'

'Yeah, right? You don't know because we never had one. Because I paid it off. Now this. One more damn thing and I'm gonna blow.'

Crystal explained a mortgage, then about the mortgage, what had happened. She tried to say how bad it was, but started laughing, hard, which made Kismet laugh, which is when they started with the hysteria, such a relief. Eventually they threw themselves on their bowls of pasta, gummed up the pasta with Parmesan cheese, sprinkled on more red pepper flakes, kept eating.

'We'll get out of this, my girl,' said Crystal. 'We'll get out!'

Later, Gary called Kismet. At least his phone, a fancy one, worked from the farm. She talked to him from her old bed in her old bedroom, where she'd gone to have a sobfest on top of the faded purple comforter. However, Kismet couldn't get herself to cry.

Maybe the tank was dry. Gary asked her to come back and said Diz didn't even know she'd taken the tractor into town. Diz was really sorry when he found out. Winnie was asleep (the beerios, thought Kismet).

And he, Gary, had a new book he wanted to read together.

'Read together?'

'Yeah. I bought it for you and me.'

'Where?'

'At that place, you know, where you went to order that book.'

'Bev's Bookery?'

'Yeah, that one.'

'Did you buy it from Bev?'

'No, from that kid.'

'Oh, wow. Okay. Well, look. I need to stay with my mom overnight. She's had a bad thing happen, you know, with my dad and all. We need to strategize.'

'I guess. But we're newlyweds.'

'Yeah. I guess?'

'Well, we *are* newlyweds.'

'Doesn't feel like it.'

'Why don't you just, like, ask about my day?'

She said nothing.

'I planted, fixed some broken teeth on the harrow, went in with the backhoe to dig out a rock we're sick of, junk like that.'

'I cleaned your mom's whole house. So I deserve a night at my old house with my own mom. And she only has tonight off.'

Gary was silent, trying to concoct an argument. But he'd seen the effect of her cleaning on the big house. A god-given miracle. She was right. 'Just the one night, though?'

'I'll come back after my ass stops hurting, Gary. You'll have to pick up the tractor.'

'No problem. I'll borrow Eric's dad's flatbed.'

'Tell Diz it runs great.'

'Dad!' yelled Gary. 'She said the tractor runs great!'

Kismet was being sarcastic but Diz was gratified.

'You picked a winner, boy!'

'Tell your dad I heard that.'

'She heard that!'

Kismet hung up. It was hard to be mad at Diz because he liked her so much and, maybe, she was beginning to like him back.

'**I need** an emergency meeting,' said Kismet to Stockton. 'I rode into town on an old tractor. I'm at my mom's house. Come right over.'

Within fifteen minutes there was a knock on the door, a pounding up the stairs, and Stockton pushed her way into Kismet's bedroom. She jumped on the bed, grabbed Kismet.

'What the fuck, what the fuck? Did all that happen?'

Kneeling on the bed, hands on each other's shoulders, they stared into each other's eyes and let their mouths fall open. Stockton had long strawberry blond hair and a round, scowling, cowgirl face. Her voice was squeaky. Her eyes were made to stare up from under her pale brows. Her snub nose was made to snub. Her mouth, drawn upon her face with a pin, curled down at the edges in a natural frown. When she was overjoyed she looked underjoyed. When she was unhappy you couldn't tell. She and Kismet were the two smartest girls in their class. Then came Ally and Brianna. The four of them had not been the most popular. But they were the most formidable.

'I swear by all that's holy,' said Stockton. 'I will kill your dad.'

Stockton's dad really was a cowboy, in the Indian Rodeo Association, or had been until he flew off one too many bulls. Still, Jeniver was the source of her attitude.

'Get in line, right? And Mom and me. What are we supposed to do? I'm pretty sure the whole town's gonna get drunk, surround the house, and, like, get out the tar and feathers.'

Both were silent. They'd read *Huckleberry Finn* together in seventh grade. They'd done a lot of other things too. Their favorite candy was Pixy Stix. After watching *Blow* on VHS, they decided to pour the powdery sugar on a mirror, cut it with a snitched credit card, and snort the sugar powder through the biggest bill they could find, a limp tenner.

'Ooooh,' said Stockton, slowly sinking back into the pillows and tapping her chin, 'so they'd get tar at a road construction outfit or something? That would be a stretch. And feathers. They'd have to kill a bunch of chickens—somewhere—I'm thinking the nearest chicken farm's down by South Dakota. And plucking the dead chickens. Who's gonna do that?'

'Duh, there's machines. But they don't just give away their feathers. Father Flirty would have to take up a collection, and who's gonna listen to him anymore? Or the Geists, maybe. They gave a lot of money.'

'Then the rail. Rode them out of town on a rail. What kind of rail?'

Stockton rummaged around in her backpack and took out a package of Red Vines. They stuck a vine each in their mouths and used them to ponder.

'There's not rails just lying around.'

'True. Not like in the old days.'

'Were they railroad rails?'

'They used to make all their fences out of wood then. So fence rails.'

'I've never seen one of those in my life.'

'I would say the hazards are more social?'

They nodded and fell back on the bed, chewing thoughtfully.

'Of course,' said Stockton, 'your mother is a saint.'

'That's why your mother has to rescue her all the time.'

'You know what would be nice?'

Against the wall of Kismet's room, across from the bed, there was a long low chest of drawers, painted eggshell white. Upon the chest was a small VHS player from Radio Shack. Stockton lifted the frilly blue doily off the top and pushed in one of the movies they had watched together hundreds of times, *The Saint*. For a while they sat on the bed eating red licorice and reciting the lines with the characters.

Crystal yelled up the stairs.

'Girls, girls, come down here right now!'

Kismet rolled over and groaned. Stockton pulled her up. They went downstairs into the living room, where Crystal was standing in front of the television, watching the news.

Rasputin

It was an hour from closing time on a sleepy after-noon at a Bank of the West when a frightful person glided up to a teller's window and demanded all the money. The teller behind the chosen window was Rosy Peoples, a young mother of two who was motivated to survive. She tried not to look at the robber, only at the note, which was printed in black stick-on letters from a drugstore. The bag he shoved at her was made of re-cycled plastic cloth and came as a freebie from Bank of the West itself. Rosy had prepared for this moment. She shoved in the money, which amounted to fifteen thousand dollars. She would have remembered the bait money if she hadn't glanced at the robber's teeth.

Long, brown, fanglike, and spotted with blood! After the teeth, she couldn't help looking at the rest of the robber. Black matted hair hung in ratty sheets to either side of his glowing eyes. She said later that his eyes were mesmerizing. That they were blue with black rings, like husky eyes. He wore dim, tattered clothing. A glittering medal. She thought perhaps a cape. For sure, black leather gloves. There were no fingerprints. His voice was low, harsh, and hollow, like it was coming from deep in the earth. Did he have a gun? He didn't need one.

'I think he was a demon,' said Rosy.

Her voice was still shaky, but also, now that she had survived, she was thrilled to be the center of attention.

Nobody saw him leave. Downtown wasn't empty but he seemed to have passed unnoticed out of town. Rosy said that she sank down to pray for deliverance before pressing the alarm.

'He wasn't of this earth,' said Rosy, now earnest and self-important. 'He just took the money and went straight back down to hell.'

Later, the evening news report pulled up a historic photo of Rasputin, which the police believed had inspired the robber. The security camera footage played again.

Something about the way the mad monk walked, or gestured, or turned his scraggly head, or perhaps something he was wearing, scratched at the edges of Crystal's perception, but she didn't let it in. Kismet felt it too but she only muttered a line from *The Saint*: 'Can't spend hard currency in hell.' And the three of them laughed.

The Mad Monk

Rasputin slipped behind the post office dumpster and immediately someone else, a meek fellow wearing heavy black-rimmed eyeglasses, a boiler suit with the name Curtis embroidered on a pocket patch, and ancient loafers, was dragging a black bag of garbage along the side of that dumpster. Curtis opened the lid and was about to toss the garbage in when the police car passed. Curtis gaped at the car, put the garbage into the dumpster, and rummaged around a bit. Curtis then strolled out to the shuttered auto-body shop at the edge of town, holding a paper bag of groceries in his arms. Cool Ranch Doritos, a loaf of bread, and a large head of lettuce could be seen if a passerby would chance to look over the edge of the bag.

The old-fashioned wooden garage with a rusted car still on blocks outside it faced the cemetery, deserted today. Curtis ducked into the lean-to, where odds and ends had been abandoned. Shortly afterward, a slender man in biking clothes emerged with a water bottle in his hands. He wheeled along a vintage ten-speed outfitted with waterproof saddlebags. The bicyclist hooked reflective sunglasses behind his ears, fastened on his helmet, fiddled with the gears, pulled on padded gloves, and at last climbed onto his bicycle. He began to ride with a trace of that intense self-important air professional bikers emit. He seemed to be warming up for a longer ride, just passing through town. He nodded slightly at the streets he passed, smiled somewhat patronizingly at the municipal plantings of flowers. The bicyclist reached the town bank and to his evident surprise, and his disappointment too, the bank was closed. For a while, he stood with other onlookers, watching and commenting on the robbery. Apparently, the bank had been hit about ten years ago, so was supplied with security cameras that had captured the robber quite well. At present the staff was being questioned. There was nothing to see. Everyone went home. The bicyclist thought it best to get back on the road and took a minor highway west toward a town with a small steakhouse and a Super 8 motel on its outskirts. The wind was against him and his legs were beginning to hurt. When he saw the town on the horizon, he allowed himself to look forward to a hot bath.

Diz and Gusty

As boys they were husky. As men they are bulky. They loom like monoliths. They are chainsaw art. As Diz and Gusty lumbered across the yard, strong bulwark guts atop leg beams, they talked. Their thin exquisite lips barely moved. Their handsome wind-whipped faces were impassive in the shadow of billed caps. They had survived their father by sticking together. They never discussed the past. To speak about the way their father, Sport, had treated them, would be like grabbing an electric fence.

The sun was fierce, the ground already kicking up heat. Their narrow blue eyes of Roman generals glinted as they entered their shadowy arsenal. Diz unlocked the back room of the tan and green metal pole barn, switching on the light, and the brothers frowned at the supply. Gusty lifted his hand and counted containers, which were kept in a chain-link enclosure with a padlock.

Dual Magnum. Roundup. Warrant. Outlook. Chloroacetamide. Betamix. Ethofumesate. UpBeet. Gramoxone.

'We should scout again. But I know what we're gonna find,' said Gusty.

Diz switched off the light and they adjusted their hats before they walked into the field planted with his non-improved seeds. In that field the beets were past the emergent stages, the soil dry and powdery despite the recent flood and rain, and the sun was now relentless as hate. But worse than the glare of sunlight was the presence of the 2009 weed of the year, *Chenopodium album*, one of the most noxious and difficult to eradicate.

'Hot damn,' said Diz.

His shoulders sagged, and Gusty even took off his hat. They'd sprayed proactively, pre-emergence, using the big guns. But lambsquarters was back. Such a meek name, but their devil had a lot of names—goosefoot, pigweed, shitweed, baconweed, wild spinach. Cheerful shallow lobed leaves, silver undercoat winking in the sun. The men turned. Trundled or strode back toward the same outbuilding and the ninety-foot-boom self-propelled sprayer they had gone into deep debt to purchase.

In some places, lambsquarters is considered the Prince of Greens, one of the most nutritious greens ever analyzed; it was one of the earliest agricultural crops of the Americas. It also resembles amaranth, but the brothers rarely spoke of that. The rough-cut men were preparing to eradicate one of the most nutritious plants on earth in favor of growing the sugar beet, perhaps the least nutritious plant on earth. Evolution thought this was hilarious.

Lambsquarters

Meanwhile, Crystal's garden was full of the tender little leaves. She got up at her normal waking hour, 2 p.m., and around four she walked out into her early summer garden. Lambsquarters, with their pleasant silvery undersides, came up at just the right time, when you needed to eat something fresh and green. There was a rumor around town that Crystal was so poor she ate weeds. If only they knew. She clipped the youngest plants, pulled off the leaves. Then she went inside and sautéed them in her most extravagant household purchase—extra-virgin olive oil. They were good. Extremely good. If you really really like greens.

The Rasputin robbery was repeated on every news cycle. Crystal watched, amused. After all, what with the CEOs of banks getting millions of dollars in bonuses instead of arrested and thrown in jail, who cared? At least somebody was making a withdrawal from a bank instead of forced deposits, instead of losing their retirement accounts, instead of getting fake-mortgaged and foreclosed. She ate another bowl of greens with smoked salt and olive oil. If you're eating weeds, you can afford extra-virgin olive oil and fancy salt. Supposedly. In fact, however, the eighty dollars that Martin had left in their joint checking account had to last the rest of the month. Crystal regarded her secret stash (still there) as a sacred trust. This was Kismet's college money. Later, after Crystal washed her face, she dabbed on a little olive oil and massaged it into her skin. Cheap but effective! She seemed to glow. Though maybe it was the lack of air-conditioning.

Crystal had several fans placed strategically throughout her house. Her cooling strategy was to take a shower with her clothes on, then work in front of a fan. She had an hour, now, and she had gathered a pile of things to sell on eBay—vintage plates, baskets, ceramic pots when she'd been in that throw-pots phase, some old sheet music, a dress with the rainstorm pattern, the dress with the golden chains that she'd worn to the wedding dinner.

As she put together the wording for each item, the phone rang. It was Jeniver.

'I've been doing a deep dive into this,' she said. 'Martin must have had your driver's license and worse than that, you were apparently there. The officer who handled the mortgage said he met you. In fact, there were multiple meetings.'

'No,' said Crystal.

'Of course not,' said Jeniver. 'The nerve. He probably found someone who looked like you.'

'But this other woman—she learned my signature?'

'Why not? A signature is pretty easy to imitate, though I've got a forensic graphologist on it right now.'

'Oh god,' said Crystal. 'Is this going to cost?'

'My forensic graphologist is also a palm reader. Very reasonable. Don't tell anybody. For the rest I'll put you on an installment plan. Don't worry.'

'Thanks so much, you are so kind, but what's the ballpark?'

'It will be thousands,' said Jeniver. 'But I hope not tens of thousands.'

With a keen pang, Crystal resigned a portion of her hidden cash to lawyer fees. She looked at the neat arrangement of eBay items on her kitchen table. Right then, she mentally added anything that belonged to Martin. After she hung up the phone, she went into their bedroom. For the first time since he'd left, she opened his closet. A hint of Paco Rabanne and his leather goods, the shoes in their shoeboxes, drifted out. He'd left behind almost all of his carefully chosen clothing. His cherished designer topcoat. She touched the soft navy blue wool, pulled it from the closet. A button dropped off. Just like that. Its threads had held until that moment. The surprise of it made tears jolt into her eyes. Why would she cry? She hated him. Look what he'd done. Still, she found herself pressing her face against the coat's heavy satin lining and trying to control an overwhelming spasm of sobs.

Here, here! None of that! No snot on the eBay coat!

She brushed her tears off and continued looking. There were also keepsakes, items he'd picked up on their local travels, stored in clear plastic bins. Ceramic cream pitchers. Wooden eggs. Maybe she could get something for those. There was a box of old camera equipment. A bin of pictures. She took the pictures out of all his picture frames. She would sell a box of picture frames. Silk ties from Italy—he'd gone through a phase. The ties were beautiful, handsewn strips of luxury. She stroked the ties, lifted them out on their special tie hanger. He had some good shirts. And what about the shoes? She had a phone to take pictures, a fairly reliable Dell to post them. Things were looking up, right? She had stuff to sell and she still had a physical address.

'There's just a lot to do,' she said, holding her fingers to her temples. Again, tears washed up. Tears of panic and also, well, did she miss Martin in some way? No, she'd decided years ago that as soon as Kismet was grown she would leave him, somehow. He was the type who would ignore her and then cling to her ankles. Maybe she would fake her death and tell only Kismet that she was alive. No, it wasn't that she missed Martin, it was the thought that he'd gotten another woman to mimic her so well. The fact that maybe he'd been seeing another woman all along suddenly occurred to her. Outrage squeezed the living heart in her chest. Yet he had always maintained that he loved her, adored her, she had always been his one and only. He said these things to coax her back to him after he'd blown money on ties.

Well, maybe they'd fetch something now.

Crystal sat down on the bed, sweating so hard that beads of water dripped down her face, ran down her throat, between her breasts. The truth was, even though Martin was melodramatic and ineffective, she didn't believe he was an embezzler. He wasn't a criminal. He was too scared to be a criminal. Too afraid of getting caught. She thought of his interests. Was salsa dancing a crime? His love of high school and community theater? In the closet was his Willy Loman suit.

Pinned onto a hanger his Puck leotard. That leotard stabbed her heart a little. She never told him that the sock in his jockstrap kept crumpling, rearranging, and even popping up during his speeches; he didn't know and thought he was killing it with every line. Had she not told him in order not to burst his frail ego bubble? Or did some resentful iota of her heart enjoy the derision behind the audience's laughter?

The memory almost made her laugh now. He had redeeming qualities. She knew he had been proud of the church renovation fund, that he'd worked harder than anyone to raise the money. Although his efforts looked suspicious now, it had been all in earnest at the time. She knew this because she'd been there, working beside him on the benefit shows. The choir concerts, *The Pirates of Penzance, Joseph and the Amazing Technicolor Dreamcoat.* He'd knocked himself out. But what about the house? Maybe he really thought that in secret he'd pay the money back before she'd noticed. She frowned, fell into a drift of thought. Actually, that was his way. He'd borrowed from their small joint account before, but he'd always paid back the amount. And although he had these expensive tastes, he'd never racked up credit card debt. The worst kind. Even now, the credit card had come back clean. Oh, she'd canceled it, but it had come back clean. That was something he hadn't done and he could have done it. He could have maxed out those credit cards before he skipped town, leaving her with 25 percent interest and no hope of ever, ever getting out of debt.

The fact that Martin had spared her that particular form of hell made her think. Credit card debt was their baseline, the thing they promised against, a sort of death-do-us-part thing. They would never use the credit card except in a dire emergency. And this was a dire emergency and he hadn't used it. Perhaps this was a sign. She wiped the sweat from her face and held the rack of ties away from her body as she walked out of the bedroom to photograph the glistening figured strips against a neutral background. People always looked for signs when all was lost, but these were very good ties and all was not lost, not yet.

The Bones of Venus

The evening before he was to leave, Hugo went for a goodbye walk. It was 9:30 p.m., the dark sifting from the east, a golden line of fire still marking the western horizon. He intended to stroll down to the bridge from which Kismet had accidentally flung herself into the river, but the cemetery stopped him. There were only a few graves. The grass was long tonight. Local legend had it that a beautiful female giant from a passing circus in the town's early days was buried in a certain spot. That patch of shaggy ground always affected Hugo, and he stopped there to say goodbye, struck as always by the thought of her large bones floating in the earth. He stood a moment, then sank to his knees. Slowly, he toppled sideways so that he was coiled in a fetal ball.

'Don't be weird,' he muttered, thrashing his arms and legs around until he lay on his back, comfortable under the first star. 'Hello, Venus,' he said, 'above and below.' For the legendary woman's circus name had been Venus. She had worn a blue and silver headband with a star on her forehead. Her wavy blond hair had flowed down to her waist. And now her namesake star rose, pure and modest in the blue-green sky. Everything down here on earth was shattering, yet pointless. He heard his younger sisters in the grass, spying on him, creeping closer.

He knew they'd jump him. They'd nearly wrecked his reproductive future the last time, so he turned over on his stomach. They tried slithering like snakes but snorted like feral swine. Suddenly they made their break, scrambling toward him with whining puppyish ardor. They plopped themselves rudely all over him with salty legs and hair that smelled of dirt and rain.

He made the right sounds, 'Arrrrhhhhh! Gaahhhh!,' to satisfy. To bring them joy he cried, 'Ow, ow, ow.'

His sisters beamed. Then they fell asleep. That's how they were. One minute overwhelming, the next unconscious. Hugo left them there with Venus.

He packed two sleeping bags, a ground cloth, a foam mattress, and his favorite pillow. He packed a cooler with sandwiches and Dr Pepper. Bev gave him a bag of grapefruit and five hundred dollars. Ichor gave him a set of work clothes, warm jackets, hats, boots. Besides the clothing, Ichor gave his son a bottle of lavender massage oil (massage was another of Ichor's side gigs), a tub of frozen soup, a loaf of sourdough bread, dried morels, a wrench, a multicomponent screwdriver, a hammer, and a very sharp knife.

Just at dawn, Hugo pulled out of his parents' driveway. Numb with wonder at himself, he gritted his teeth in an effort not to look back. He looked back. In the rearview mirror he saw all four of them, up far too early, waving. They were like people from a fairy tale, bulky sweet-faced people standing together in baggy pajamas that looked like the clothing of peasants.

'Don't feel anything yet,' said Hugo. His eyes welled with tears, and spilled over. 'There's no shame in it,' he said, wiping at his cheek. The road blurred, but it was a totally straight road. Hugo took a right on I-29, traveled on up past the industrial beet plants enveloped in steam and endlessly processing sugar. At Grand Forks, he exited I-29, took a left, gassed up, and kept going. Every so often he slowly ate a sandwich. Bev had made them for him, using peach preserves. They were holy sandwiches, he thought. The chunks of peach were heavenly. The traffic thinned. The land opened up in rolling swales, rows of tall swaying trees. This was shelterbelt country. The trees stopped the dirt from dissolving into the air each spring, and kept the water from washing into the ditches, draining the fields. There were sloughs and small lakes on this route, a whole other tranquil world. Hugo didn't listen to the radio. His mind was still overflowing.

Kismet

Kismet started by raking the dirt in the yard smooth. The nice loamy soil that she'd clutched earlier on had disappeared. Scratching at field dirt, she broke up clumps of gray grit and spread the dust around. She was wearing lots of sunblock and a big straw cowboy hat. She would need more sunblock to live out on the land. And for later, she would need more beer to reward herself through the long evening and keep herself in a trance.

'Honey, that won't work,' said Winnie, coming up behind her.

Kismet straightened up, holding the rake.

'What won't work?'

'That dirt.'

'What do you mean? It's dirt.'

'It's not real dirt. It's that dirt.'

Winnie pointed out into the field. 'This is sugar beet dirt. Don't you see? To plant anything else we have to get a pile of real dirt.'

'Dirt's supposed to grow anything,' said Kismet.

'Regular soil dirt, sure, but this is sugar beet dirt, like I said. Diz and Gusty get this fertilizer that helps the dirt work for the seed. The seed is fixed up so the beet won't die when it's sprayed for weeds. Also, bugs. See, it's all a system they have with the companies.'

'Okay.' Kismet threw down the rake.

'My farm had a lot of real dirt,' said Winnie vaguely. 'When I was a kid, my mom had us spreading chicken shit on the garden.'

'Let's go in and make iced tea.'

'It sounds ridiculous,' Winnie continued. 'But we can call up Prairie Lawn to get the dirt. I was going to make a garden someday. But you can do it. I'm going to the grocery so let's make a big list.'

Winnie hooked her arm into Kismet's and they walked inside.

Kismet took ice from the freezer's ice bin, put it in a glass pitcher, added water, stirred in a powdery iced tea substance. There was added lemon flavor so she didn't even need to add lemon. The two sat down with the pitcher and two glasses for the iced tea. Winnie pulled

the plastic off a foil pan of store-bought frosted cinnamon rolls. She had half a freezer full of these little
pans. Gary walked in and Kismet barely acknowledged
him. Bringing her back from town, he had driven with
batshit insouciance.

'Have a cinnamon roll,' said Winnie.

Gary gave Kismet a despairing look and walked out.

'What's going on?' asked Winnie.

'Nothing,' said Kismet.

The Death of Emma

Kismet was reading in bed. Gary crept up to her foot and cradled it against his cheek. Kismet let him keep her foot while she read furiously, one paragraph over and over, because she was too mad to make sense of the description. After all this fruitless romance, Madame Bovary was actually poisoning herself, and as any fool must know, being poisoned was a horrible death to die. *Emma, her chin sunken upon her breast, had her eyes inordinately wide open, and her poor hands wandered over the sheets with that hideous and soft movement of the dying, that seems as if they wanted already to cover themselves with the shroud.* Suddenly Kismet sat up straight and threw down the book. What on earth had she been thinking? Hugo was an idiot. Why had he given her this book?

The next morning, Kismet asked Diz if anyone was using the pile of boards behind the equipment barn. 'Have at them,' he said. She yanked out seven two-by-four-by-eights and one she would have to saw. She pulled some shorter boards to reinforce the sides. She would have liked four-by-four-by-eight cedar posts and corner clamps. Or something like that. What she wanted she was only imagining. In the tool room she found screws, a cordless drill and driver kit, hammers, nails of all sizes, and some corner braces. She found everything she needed and hauled it to where she wanted it. She started building her boxes on the cement slab by the garage, and got one done. Diz helped her place it beside the garage. He told her that the deer would eat everything.

'I suppose that means we need to build an eight-foot fence with four-by-four cedar posts and tie it into the garage then,' she said.

'Told Gary he got a good one,' said Diz. 'You growing tomatoes or what?'

'What kind do you like?' said Kismet.

'My, my, what do I like. Can't remember! Those big red juicy ones. Those little yellow ones shaped like pears.'

'I'll grow those,' said Kismet.

Diz looked down, squinting at the gravel. He adjusted his cap.

'You know, that car business got a little out of hand. Tell you what. I'll give you a ride next time.'

'When?'

'Next time.'

'How about now?'

'I gotta do things now.'

'Can I take the car?'

'Okay, I'll get it.'

He went into the pole barn, came back out, presented Kismet with the keys to the old tractor.

'You earned it. You're a good one,' he said.

His laugh could only be called a chuckle, a word she hated. No way was she taking another sore-ass ride to town on that tractor. Unless she could sell it and buy a clunker.

'I'm not riding that.'

Diz looked stricken. His narrow-eyed gaze faltered. He glanced from side to side. His big red cheeks and firm lipless mouth sagged. He actually gulped.

'Sorry, honey, the wife has spoken.'

'Tell her I'm going to hitch. And when I get to town I'm pressing charges. You can't keep me here against my will.'

'A serial killer could get you if you hitchhike,' said Diz.

'A kidnapper has already got me if I stay here.'

'You don't have to say that,' said Diz, in a truly wounded moment of distress. 'Tell you what. I'll take you with me. We'll get everything we need.'

Kismet drove into town with Diz and spent an hour with Crystal. Diz waited in the truck, parked behind the white Camry.

'This sure isn't normal,' said Crystal, standing at the window with Kismet.

'Two men watching our every move, and it's not like we can go to the police,' said Kismet. 'They aren't going to interfere with the FBI.'

'Or Geist. Can I sell your prom dress?'

'Please. And my homecoming dress. And the weird patchwork wool cape Dad gave me once.'

'That cape with its display tweeds might fetch something!'

They went out the back door and sat on the steps. The raised beds, surrounded by carpet samples to tamp down weeds, were backed by a chain-link fence threaded by purple morning glories, the sort that blue seeds reverted to—Grandpa Ott's. Weeds, but so sweet. They were starting to bloom.

'They're choking out my cucumbers,' said Crystal. 'I should rip them out.'

'Leave a few,' said Kismet.

'That's what always gets me into trouble.'

'We could make a run for it,' said Kismet, nodding toward the alley. Her problems seemed trivial compared to her mother's situation. 'Have you heard from him?' she asked in a whisper.

'No,' said Crystal. She took Kismet's hand.

Kismet's heart was starting to pinch. Her breath was trapped. The plum trees to one side of the yard were thick and glossy. The little catalpa tree a neighbor had given them was putting up a leader. It would soon shade the back steps. They were such graceful trees, and their flowers were little orchids.

'I like their big leaves,' said Kismet, nodding at the catalpa, tears in her eyes. She gripped her mother's hand harder.

'Has the time come yet?' asked Crystal. 'Seems like you've given this a shot.'

'Not yet. And I'm putting a garden in, Mom. Can I have a few seeds?'

Crystal kept a plastic tub of seeds. Inside were packets she hadn't used, seeds she'd kept from the best squash, the best tomatoes, the best pole beans. She had purple beans, foot-long beans, and hollyhocks, all colors. The seeds were in labeled envelopes, in tiny mustard or custard jars that sometimes turned up at the food shelf, slightly expired luxuries. They hugged for a long moment and parted. Kismet got into the truck with Diz and then they bought what they needed for the fence. While they were at the tractor store, Kismet saw some oval-ended, galvanized-steel stock tanks. They bought four—two for herbs and two for flowers. On the way back Kismet asked Diz all about farming—how they decided which crops to plant, when to rotate the fields, what pests and weeds were problems to which crops, what the government had to do with all of these decisions, what it meant to belong to a sugar beet co-op where membership involved owning a piece of every stage of production.

'Sounds like you're a bunch of Communists,' said Kismet.

'Don't tell anybody.' Diz laughed. 'Anyway, you have to buy your way in. So . . .'

When they got home, the two unloaded everything. The pile of topsoil from Prairie Lawn had been delivered. Diz told her where to find a wheelbarrow. Then Kismet went inside and made a tortilla casserole, put it in the oven. She went out to the future garden plot, sat down on an island of stiff weeds, and watched a colony of ants at work. They were the tiny golden brown kind, intensely disciplined, carrying crumblets of pizza crust they'd sawed from a piece that Gary had dropped. Down the hole of their colony into a secret warren of passages they went.

Like me, thought Kismet. We never give up. Not Mom, not me. Maybe her dad hadn't given up yet either. All this listing of tasks, of planning gardens, fences, future dinners, was a way of maybe getting trapped but at least not giving up. This made her think of Madame Bovary, the giving up. The death scene still upset her. Emma's screaming, her sunken eyes, her black gaping mouth. Kismet gripped her hair in her fist and pulled it over her shoulder. She began to comb through the dark tail with her fingers, frowning. Like her, Emma had been bored and furious. Except she wanted romance and Kismet had too much of it. Kismet wanted other things. But until she knew what she wanted she wouldn't give up on what she had.

Clouds sailed west, blazing white barges conducting passengers over to the badlands and along the powerful, brown Missouri River. The horizon cast up a transparent curtain of radiance. It parted and a fountain of red-gold light struck the house and trees. Her skull felt too tight for her brain and her heart too big for her chest. That I should be alive, she thought, with everything to live for, and all this boundless sky.

'Whatever Emma would do,' she said out loud, 'I should do the opposite.' The last thing Emma would have done was put her hands in the dirt and start a garden.

So, she thought, I'm on the right track.

'I'm going on strike after this,' said Kismet that evening, taking out the casserole and putting it on Winnie's counter.

'Okay, that smells soooo good,' said Winnie, chipper, breaking out in obliterating applause.

'That means I'm not making dinners or breakfasts,' said Kismet.

'Oh, Kizzy,' said Winnie in a sagging tone, walking up to her and putting her head on Kismet's shoulder. 'You know you don't have to. I don't want to be a burden. I don't,' she mumbled. 'Just don't abandon.'

Kismet slowly raised her hands and patted Winnie's back. Stood there holding a stare of hushed suspension with Jester and Poots.

'I have to go now, Winnie,' she said.

'How come? Stay for dinner.' She turned her mouth down in exaggerated sadness. Her mouth, with its perfect matte lipstick. Today she must be feeling better.

'I have to go now, Winnie,' Kismet said again.

'Oh, Kizzy—oops, honey—look, let's go on a mission okay? Bill and Bonnie invited us over tomorrow. They're gonna grill. Let's go over to their place, okay? You will for sure like it and you can see their garden.'

The Vesper Flight

Winnie and Kismet drove over late in the after-noon with two versions of potato salad. Winnie swore by her mother's warm potato salad, made with red potatoes, a dressing of white vinegar, bacon fat, bacon bits, parsley, salt, pepper, sugar. Kismet swore by her mother's recipe: golden potatoes, parsley, sliced boiled eggs, chopped onions, and a dressing of may-onnaise, oil, vinegar, yellow mustard, salt, pepper, and cayenne. Paprika to decorate. The bowls were covered with Saran wrap. Kismet's was in a cooler, Winnie's was best slightly warm. The day was mild and sunny. The road to the Pavleckys' was gravel, and they raised dust. Winnie slowed down so they could open their windows and Kismet could watch the swallows perched in rows on the power lines. Killdeers veered from the ditches, uttering their shrill keering cries of alarm. Doves pecked up sand in the road and scattered before the car. The ditches were unmowed. Redwing blackbirds sang in the cattails.

'I like coming to Bill and Bonnie's,' said Winnie, 'because our farm was kind of like theirs. My dad and mom had a kind of circle going, chicken for eggs now they are called free-range, but then it was just the way you raised chickens—and some cows and pigs. A pile you loaded into a manure spreader for the fields. And other ways of farming—cover crops and such. Things Diz won't hear about.' Winnie fell silent. 'I mean, it's the scale of things, says Diz. But the Pavleckys are working on getting their ways up to large scale. It can be done. I like your garden idea, Kismet.'

'You do?'

'I just have trouble when things remind me too much. That's why I never kept a garden.'

The clouds were lined up in rows that afternoon, like the sky was furrowed with a fleecy cloud crop ready to harvest. The Pavlecky farmstead was circled with plum and apple trees, mowed between rows, and then close planted pointy pine trees for windbreaks. In the yard there were basswood, maples, big old cottonwoods where their land went to the river. Eric was there, and when Kismet and Winnie stepped out of the car he came over, hair rumpled, hat on the back of his head, T-shirt streaked with grease. He was so different from his usual contained, almost military correctness. Kismet was surprised to see how relaxed he was, apart from Gary or at school or in Gary's yard. His movements were fluid and his face was changeable, goofy, engaging. He walked with them to the backyard, which bordered on a shaggy field of harebells, globe mallow, Queen Anne's lace, blanketflowers, new milkweed, and unmowed grasses. There were plank tables and some chairs around a firepit. And more birds. Woodpeckers laddering up and down the box elders, swallows tending nests under the eaves of a wooden shed, flickers, robins, thrushes.

Kismet put her cooler on the table and stood in the gentle noise.

'So many birds,' she said to Eric.

'They need bugs to eat, and we got 'em. We don't spray much of anything but ourselves.' He handed her Off and citronella. 'But between the chickens and the swallows and the nighthawks there aren't, you know, hordes of mosquitoes. Just annoying clouds. And gnats.' He put his hand to his face and his fingers came away smeared with grease. He pulled out a bandanna and wiped at his chin and cheek. 'Did I get it all?'

Kismet pointed to her forehead. He swiped at his.

'What's going on there?' she asked, pointing at the disheveled grass and flower field. 'It looks wild.'

'Maybe someday, but to get it back to wild takes work. I mean, we started this a while ago. It's prairie planted but you have to weed out the invasive stuff forever to get prairie reestablished. I think it almost broke Mom. But you should see it in spring when the prairie lilies come out. Every single plant has its own pollinator so you have to coax those in too. Like, well, it's not for the faint of heart.'

Bill now had the charcoal lit, and was tending his grill the way men do, with self-satisfaction and command. Bonnie was inside the house with Winnie. Eric's older brother, Torrance, came out of the tractor shed wiping off his hands; their younger sisters emerged from the horse barn behind that shed. They ran at Torrance and started whipping him with their braids. He twirled to avoid them and cried out when their hair touched him.

'Ichor and Bev are coming over too,' Eric told Kismet. 'If they bring their girls it will be holy hell. When my little sisters get together with those two, it's unbelievable.'

He groaned half an hour later when the Dumachs drove up, followed by Diz and Gary.

Later, as the girls whirled around, the parents talked, and Torrance was getting help with some mechanical problem from Gary, Eric said to Kismet, 'Bring your chair over here. I wanna show you something.'

They took their lawn chairs over to the prairie field that Eric and his dad had been working on for years. Barn swallows, tree swallows, swifts, were plucking insects off the tops of the flowers and grasses. The sun was low and the light was a golden barge floating through the trees.

'Now just watch,' Eric said.

As the heat rose off the earth the insects rose too, and the black arcs of birds began to feed with such swiftness and intensity that Kismet's eyes could scarcely follow. They outflew their shadows, veered so close and at such a rate of speed it seemed at every second they would collide, but only their shadows merged and came apart. Their intricate blur of flight rose to a frenzied joy so dark and dazzling that Kismet was lost in emotion. She sat under a spell. By the time the air cooled and the swallows began to swoop away to their nests, she felt wobbly and strange, as though she too had been flying.

Eric's dad called him over but although the mosquitoes were avid, she didn't leave. She continued to sit there alone.

The light softened and shadows crept out of the trees. The evening breeze in green twilight set up a soft clatter in the cottonwoods. She gasped, suddenly, for pain shot through her at the widening arc of her knowing. She had seen a lot by now—the deadened dirt, the perfect row crops without bugs or weeds. She had talked to Diz about how this perfection was accomplished. She could see it now. Practically everything she and the Geists did, and even her mother's job, was destroying what she had just witnessed, the joinery of creation.

Eric

There was always an excuse for Eric to drop by Gary's house. Eric told himself that it was because the Geist place was on the highway and he passed it going into and out of town. There was always something to tell Gary, something to borrow, a message. Sometimes Gary was there, but Eric wasn't actually stopping to visit. In fact for the past year he would go out of his way to stop when nobody was around. He'd park outside the party barn, which was now a storage shed, though there was still the big-screen TV and the couches out there. He pulled up beside the big shed and allowed himself to go over what had happened. If he did this every so often, the pictures didn't take him by surprise as much. It was like, he thought, therapy—a distant thing that happened somewhere vague but which his mother and father sometimes mentioned, offered it to him if he needed it, which he probably did. Today he had set his mind, always under pressure, free to let the pictures flow. But maybe he also knew Kismet would be there when he drove into the yard and cut the engine. In his rearview, he saw Kismet put down the power drill and walk over, shucking off her gloves. She was wearing a red-billed hat and she'd stuck a kerchief in the plastic sizing notch to keep the sun off the back of her neck. The hat read SNAP-ON TOOLS. Her dark slick hair was tightly braided down her back. Her shoulders were strong for a small person, the short white T-shirt sleeves rolled up over her biceps. Her baggy jeans hung oddly off her hips, crimped up at the waist with a belt, like maybe she was wearing Gary's jeans. She looked at home here, Eric thought with surprise. He swung himself out of the truck. He was wearing a white T-shirt too and he was so fit he almost looked like a toy man, his powerful torso smoothly pegged into his belted jeans. He wore dark brown work boots and his hat cast a curved shadow across his eyes.

'Gary home?'

'Not yet. Come on in. He'll be back in a few.'

'Nah, that's okay, I'll wait out here,' said Eric, looking off to the side.

Kismet appraised Eric's careful manners. He'd turned

back into the away-from-home Eric she'd known before yesterday. But maybe it was just that he didn't want to be alone with Gary's new wife in their new house.

'No really,' she said. 'He'll wanna see you. Look, you can sit out back on the deck. I mean, it's not a deck, maybe it'll be a patio. I'll bring iced tea.'

'Okay then.'

Kismet went into the house and Eric sat at the weathered old picnic table next to the dirt drive. He'd eaten at the picnic table plenty of times before, when he worked on the place with Diz, Gary, and Gusty. He was curious to see what the house looked like inside, once it was lived in, but he wanted to wait for Gary to show him around. She brought a pitcher of tea out and three stacked gold plastic glasses. She unstacked the glasses and poured real tea, brewed tea, for herself and Eric.

'We're out of lemons,' she said.

He shrugged and drank. 'It's good.'

'So, before yesterday, where were you hiding?'

Eric gave her a wary look.

'I don't mean that literally.'

He gave a short laugh. 'Actually, I'm getting a higher certification up in Fargo.'

'For?'

'First responder. EMT. You know. I have to, like, put in over a hundred hours.'

Kismet peered down into her tea.

'Thanks for saving me that time. I mean, you and Odie.'

'It wasn't a big . . . I mean, that was my job.' He shifted his feet, uncomfortable. 'It was just my job to do that.'

'I would have drowned.'

'You would have got yourself out.'

'Probably not.'

'How come you jumped?'

His panicked look told Kismet that he wished he hadn't asked.

'Oh never mind,' he said.

'No, that's all right. I didn't jump, okay? I fell. But maybe I was clumsy on purpose. It's not like it isn't obvious, right? I didn't want to get married.'

Eric was very still. He didn't move a muscle. He didn't blink. He kept his expression neutral, but said, 'That was, you know, the general . . .'

'The general consensus.'

'From people who knew you jumped, fell, in the river, yeah, but . . .'

'Didn't everybody know?'

'Well, I never told anybody. Odie, he probably forgot it even happened. That's Odie. Your friends didn't want their parents to know. If parents found out, they didn't want anybody else to know. It didn't get out there, not really.'

'Then my dad split.'

'Took up the town news cycle for sure. He must have planned it pretty good.'

'I'm surprised. I mean, surprised he isn't caught.'

'Yet.'

'Right. Not yet.'

They swirled their tea and the ice clicked dully, pleasantly, against the sides of the plastic glasses.

'Funny to call them glasses when they're plastic,' said Eric. Oh for weak, he thought.

'I wonder where he is,' said Kismet, 'and how he actually got away. If he does get away. My dad never seemed that organized—I mean, not on a criminal level.'

'They found his car, right?'

'I hope my mom can get it back.'

'She's living her life. She's a cool lady.'

Kismet looked straight at him for a moment, pleased. He met her eyes but looked away in alarm.

'You know, Eric, what you said at the wedding dinner?'

'I was super out of it.'

'Yeah, maybe, but you said you'd tell me what you meant. You said you took a hit for Gary. What'd you mean by that?'

Eric tried to laugh, fell silent. He gripped his hands together, tightening and untightening his fingers.

'You meant that night, didn't you? The night of the accident.'

'What? No. Why would you even think that?'

'It just seems like something more happened than what did happen.'

'More happened than what did happen.'

He spoke with light disregard, as though he was just repeating what she'd said. But Kismet saw how hard he clutched the glass. More happened than what did happen was also a statement. She could feel his foot bouncing up and down. With a seemingly conscious effort, he stopped his foot. After a while his foot started jiggling again. He looked out, across the fields, took a gulp of tea, and started gnashing the ice. Stopped. Kismet was at a loss.

'It's okay,' said Kismet after a while. 'I know you. Whatever happened, you did the best you could do.'

Their eyes stuck on each other for just a second too long, then they both looked down at the sweating glasses in their hands.

'Yeah it was,' he said. 'You're right. It was the best I could do.'

They sat with that for a few seconds, then Kismet said there were cookies. She went back into the house and Eric was left there alone with the crack in his mind. He tried not to fall backward, through the aperture into his memory. Kismet came back just in time.

'There's no cookies. Gary and Diz ate 'em all.'

'No worries.'

'Hey, are you gonna make a job of it? Like become a paramedic?'

'Gosh, no, it's just that we live so far out here, but I'd like to get to paramedic level, yes.'

'Good skills to have,' said Kismet.

'So you're a carpenter!' Eric nodded at her work.

'Diz cut the boards for me in the shop. All I know how to use is a drill.'

'That's something! Someday I'm gonna find me a handy woman,' said Eric, then coughed to stop himself. A flush rose from the neck of his T-shirt and bloomed up his throat. His ears went rosy, his face began to flush. Kismet watched it happen and it reminded her of Hugo. The two were cousins after all. She saw the flush retreat until the last of it stuck around his eyebrows. Kismet and her mother always took careful note of the way people blushed. They hardly ever did blush, but it wasn't, said Crystal, because they had no shame.

'Heard anything from Hugo?' she asked, then horribly, she felt a rare blush pour up her neck, too, heating her face. See there? she thought, and was annoyed. They sat there blushing furiously together, crunching ice.

'I guess he's out there,' Eric finally said. 'I mean, it's money if he gets a job. But can he really, I mean really, pull it off?'

They both began to laugh in a strained way.

'He bought that car with his savings, and he's got this resumé he concocted from air,' said Eric. 'But what do I know. He was my little buddy when we were kids and all. Hard to think of him as, you know, a professional of whatever kind.'

'A mud engineer, like a field engineer, is what he said.'

'So he told you? I mean, I doubt it. But I didn't think you knew him that good.'

Kismet caught herself, looked down. 'Oh, you know, Bev and my mom are friends.'

'Right, right.'

But the way Kismet had blushed and then lowered her eyes made Eric curious. Sometimes he couldn't help himself. 'Is there something I should know about?' he said in a teasing voice, trying to hide a sudden pang of jealousy—on behalf of Gary, he told himself.

Kismet faked a look of confusion. It was a convincing fake. She brought the bill of her cap down and gave a kind of smile that was just a dimple on one side of her face. It was a little unnerving.

'Sir, what are you implying?'

The way she said that, just so bold and smart, gave Eric a fizzy jolt. What had he been implying? Dumb jerk, he thought. Yes, he'd like to find a woman who knew how to use power tools, and who was quick on the uptake. Who was sort of funny. As if she'd read his mind, Kismet said that Diz was going to teach her to use the Skilsaw so she could make whatever she wanted.

'What I like about living out here is you need a whole array of skills. I wanna be like my mom. Ahhh.'

She stopped suddenly, let out a breath, gulped tea, and put down her glass.

'You gotta be upset,' said Eric. 'About what your dad did.'

'I feel crazy. I think I've accepted that it's happening. But still. Where is he? I mean, my dad's not'—she gestured, loose-handed—'not . . .'

'Good at hiding?'

Kismet shook her head. 'No, I mean he's not that kind of man.'

Eric tried to keep emotion out of his voice, but his dad and mom had put a lot of money into the church fund and his voice sharpened when he said, 'Or maybe he is.' Kismet took her hat off and put her hands over her face.

'I'm sorry,' she said.

'It's not your . . . you don't have to . . . I'm sorry too.'

After a while she dropped her hands and looked at him, openly looked at him. Eric startled. It was as though behind her hands, she'd taken on a decade. Her eyes were like his mom's when she was weary, hollow and dark with tiny puckers at the corners. He looked away from Kismet without speaking and then looked back, unaware that his own face struck her the same way. Weighed down. Completely weary. Seen a lot.

'What's going on?' he said. 'You look sad.'

'I'd like to come back to your place and watch the birds fly up. I mean, sometime.'

'It's called vesper flight.'

'Oh, I like that.'

'Come over anytime you want,' he said, and panic rose in him because she was married to his friend. 'And bring Gary,' he said in a strangled croak.

The Grown-Up

He stopped in the town of Devils Lake, ate at the Main Street Café. Then on to Minot, where he gassed up for the final leg of the journey. The sky lowered as he headed toward Williston. Continual lines of oil trucks roared past in the other lane, blinding him with sinister awe. The sun sank in a neon blaze. Here and there, he saw plumes of flame in the black fields. Hugo had never seen a landscape so starkly alien. By the time he made it into town, he was a dumbfounded mess. He pulled into a church parking lot. Cut the engine. For a long time, he vibrated. Then tipped back his seat and lost consciousness.

Early the next morning, there was a tap on his window and he was asked to leave the parking lot. So he drove to a strip mall and entered a diner. After he'd washed up in the battered men's bathroom, he ate a pancakes 'n eggs 'n steak breakfast. He drank some black coffee, like a full-on grown-up. He picked up the help-wanted section of the newspaper, looked at the bulletin board in the entrance. He retied his fledgling ponytail, put on his father's jacket because the air was cool, and went out hunting for employment. He had a job by noon—not the perfect job, but a starting job. Now the problem was a place to live.

Hugo knocked on doors all that afternoon, traveling up and down the once sleepy streets. No vacancy, anywhere. On the outskirts of town, he turned into the driveway of an old farmhouse. A woman was watering the lawn. He asked if he could fill a water jug at her hose.

'Help yourself,' she said.

Hugo introduced himself and told her he was looking for a room to rent.

'I'm Janice. My husband is Melford. We call him Bud. We're the Bergs. And I'm sorry. Everything's rented. The basement, the driveway, even the garage. We had to put the old outhouse back into commission. This hose doubles as an outdoor shower.'

'What about that piece of lawn beside the driveway,' said Hugo, pointing. 'Can I rent that? I can sleep in my car. The problem is getting kicked out of a parking lot, you know. An outhouse and a cold shower are all I need, except for maybe keeping my ice packs in your freezer?'

'Do you have a tent? A car's uncomfortable. It starts to smell in there. You'll get real hot.'

'I'm saving up for a tent,' said Hugo.

'In the meantime,' said Janice, 'I guess you could use the refrigerator box. We just got a new refrigerator and you could set up the box beside your car. Put your camping bags inside. That way you could at least stretch out.'

'That sounds great,' said Hugo. 'How much?'

'Ten for the refrigerator box. Two hundred a week for the spot and the amenities—outhouse, hose.'

'That sounds fine,' said Hugo, too tired to be awed by the price of what didn't seem like amenities.

He parked his car and pulled the refrigerator box out from the Bergs' backyard. It was industrial cardboard. It would do. He positioned the refrigerator box next to his car, then packed it with his foam mattress, pillow, and sleeping bag. He unfolded his camp chair and set it up in his living room, a patch of grass in front of the car. He drank some water and ate a few nutrition bars. At last, after sunset, Hugo crawled into his cozy den. He nodded off, slept deep into the night. He woke when a couple of pickups roared in, heard some men talking, fell back asleep in the silence that followed. He woke again when three raccoons squabbled with one another down by his feet. They uttered sharp, low-pitched noises, garbled, like human speech. Hugo drew his feet up. They moiled back and forth across the open end of the box. Hugo tried to be scared, but he kept drifting off. Eventually, grumbling, they trundled away. Hugo slept. Before dawn, the pickups roared to life. They would be his alarm clock. He used the out-house, then went to seek his fortune.

Three Heists and One History

1

Darth Vader strode into the First Citizens Bank in southern Minnesota on Friday afternoon. The disguise was childish, the cape awkward, the mask difficult to see out of, and he had a feeling there was something else wrong. So he merely stood in line, trying not to disturb the force. Suddenly he began to search his pockets, hidden under the cape. Darth appeared to have forgotten his wallet. He turned around with a swish and left the bank. The undercover guard followed Darth out the door. But too late. Behind the bank, in an alleyway, the guard found Darth's mask, cape, gloves, and boots together in a melted pile, just like in a movie.

2

A week went by and this time a harmless old man moved slowly into a Gate City Bank, resting from time to time on the seat of his walker. He made it all the way to the teller, where he passed a note with the usual directions. It was Friday, nearly closing time, and the teller, Bailey Farr, couldn't have cared less. She filled the plastic bag he gave her and said, 'Lotsa luck, old man.' The robber slung the bag from the handles of his walker and made his way out the door. The police, summoned by the silent alarm, shoved the elderly man to the sidewalk in their hurry to catch the robber. A shopkeeper helped the old man to his feet. The fellow reached into a flimsy bag, pulled out a thousand dollars, and gave it to the good Samaritan. 'This way,' said the helpful shopkeeper, opening his front door and guiding the robber out the back.

3

The week after, a nun in a navy blue knee-length dress, short veil, and sensible shoes came to First Citizens Bank and collected the cash on hand.

'For the poor,' she said softly. 'God bless.'

Aliens

I think it might have been a mistake,' said Kismet to Gary.

She hadn't planned to say this, but she did say it. Ever since she'd watched the vesper flight, an overwhelming sense of life was in her, stronger even than her stubborn conviction to not give up on her choice.

'What are you talking about, a mistake?' He didn't look at her.

'Getting married straight out of high school,' she said, trying to say this in her kindest voice, although she felt it might only make it worse for Gary.

But he laughed as though she'd said something mildly funny. 'Oh, well, it's still too early to know. We got off to a rocky start. Never even got a honeymoon.'

'That's not it, no. I think we don't have that much in common.'

Gary was very still. They were sitting on the doggy couch in the living room, together, and she had turned off the television.

'Kismet?'

'Yeah.' She looked down at the brown pillow she was clutching.

'I've got something to tell you that might help. I don't believe in aliens anymore.'

'Really. What about radio waves causing diseases?'

'Actually, I said microwaves, low-voltage waves, and the studies show—'

'You read studies?'

Gary looked at her in hope. 'Of course, yes, or I hear people say that studies reveal this or that.'

'Remember what Mr. Speck said, though. You should find the actual study that people reference and check it for accuracy.'

'Oh, Speck.' Gary's voice was desolate. Kismet knew they were straying further and further from what she wanted to say, but she was compelled to console him.

'Yeah, Speck was brutal that day. I mean, he's a good teacher, but I felt bad for you. I know he was still broken up over Travis. At the same time he shouldn't of singled you out. It wasn't your fault.'

'I used to say that too,' said Gary.

Quietness hung between them. Somewhere in the house an appliance kicked in, maybe the water heater. It wasn't the refrigerator. Its ice-making clatter was now familiar to Kismet.

'I think—' said Kismet. She stopped. What could she say. 'That's too much to take on yourself. It's just too heavy.'

Gary swung a little, side to side, and shook his head.

'What you say does not exonerate me,' he finally stated.

Gary lay down on his side and put his head on the pillow in her lap. She put a hand down and stroked his hair, pushing it gently and rhythmically off his forehead. What he'd said was so sad.

'All the same, it wasn't your fault.'

Her hand was so merciful that it seemed each stroke unstrung a bit of tension in his body. He began to float. All the same, what could she know.

Frozen Grapes

Perfect Advantage had become testy, adding late fees, making ever-so-sorry threats, ramping up the interest rate, even sending around a representative at 3 a.m. to silently leave a note on Crystal's door. After she rose in midafternoon one day, Crystal fumed and weeded her garden, killing only the inedible weeds, using her bare hands. She almost always wore work gloves to save her fingernails, but today she wanted the full satisfaction of pulling out the roots, firmly but slowly, to get all the smaller fibers. Every time she tried to hate Martin, she caught herself imagining him holding her hand at night. No sex. Just hand-holding. She needed that. She needed to share this catastrophe with him, even though he'd caused it. She needed him to solve this, even though she knew for sure he couldn't. And he was so very gone. They couldn't find him! Their frustration cheered her up. She was perversely proud—he who seemed so finicky and fragile—Martin—an embezzler capable of eluding a nine-state dragnet.

With her middle finger flipped up underneath her kitchen table, Crystal had endured interview after interview with various state, local, and federal agencies interested in catching Martin. She told the FBI about her unmarried status because she was terrified she might have to pay back the money Martin had stolen. She couldn't remember telling Father Flirty, but over the years she'd lost track of who knew and who didn't. It wasn't exactly a secret and also, to confuse matters, she'd worn a ring.

During these interrogations, she got to know her questioners and watchers. She was now bringing mason jars of cold water out to the man in the white Camry. She included her special minty ice cubes or the grapes she froze by the pound when they were on sale. The man, Bing Cox, loved the ice cubes. He told her she was creative. He mentioned that he wasn't married. Once, he apologized and told her that she should remember to close her curtains at night. He might have given her the creeps, except that for a week after that he couldn't meet her eyes out of embarrassment. She put coffee beans in the ice cubes and brought him iced coffee one morning. He gasped, smiled, and glanced up at her with a look she knew well—the doggish joy of a man pampered by a woman. Crystal smiled back.

There was also Father Flirty. After a few weeks, he resumed his visits, which had formerly been conferrals with Martin. Now, Flirty knocked at the door while Crystal was washing her hands. He came in and she brought him back to the kitchen. He sat down. She rummaged around for a treat—he had a sweet tooth. He needed to talk with Crystal about the betrayal.

'I forgive him, of course,' said the priest, taking a delicate bite from a frozen grape. She'd put a small bowl of them on the table. His closely clipped hair was receding in a perfect zigzag, like a vampire's. His skin was extremely pale and his eyes were rimmed in red. A teary vampire. His canines were even a bit prominent. Did other people notice? Crystal nodded in sympathy, offering iced tea to Father Flirty, who added spoonfuls of sugar to his glass and stirred it briskly. Of course, he was dumpy and round, not lean and vulpine, like movie vampires. Though wouldn't a bit of tummy be a sign of his vampire success?

'I will be the first one to visit Martin in prison,' Flirty said with an air of resolution.

'If they catch him,' said Crystal.

'Oh, they will,' said Flirty, 'they always do.'

'On the cop shows. That's fiction.'

'Is it? Surely if he isn't caught, he'll repent and return? Surely his conscience will torment him?'

Flirty spoke as if there was a code of honor somewhere and Martin had signed it.

'Mine would,' he said morosely, pursing his lips as if to whistle.

'I suppose mine would too,' said Crystal.

But she wondered. Her views had soured on community trust and hardened on everything to do with banks and money since she had been scammed on the mortgage.

'You have a lot of things piled up here,' the priest observed, pressing a clammy hand to his neck.

Crystal had scavenged boxes, newspaper, and bought rolls of packing tape. She had begun packing objects before she even put them up for sale, leaving the boxes unsealed. She lived two blocks from the post office and went there every day. She was clearing over a hundred dollars per week. The house was looking more arranged. All the knickknacks were gone. The extra dishes. Martin's collections of landmark spoons and his beautiful cashmere socks, still in their packaging.

'Yes,' said Crystal. 'I'm trying to clean house. I'm selling a few things online.'

'Martin's things?'

Out popped a lie.

'Of course not.'

Flirty bit his lip and Crystal glanced casually at the pile of cardboard and paper. There was a wooden box with a sailboat painted on top. *Handmade cedar box perfect for keeping treasures!* Martin's cuff link box. Though it was a rare man who wore cuff links anymore. They just weren't moving. She had been about to mail the cedar box to a woman in Tennessee.

'If you do sell his things, I would expect that you would deposit the proceeds into the church collection plate,' said Flirty. He flipped a whole grape into his mouth and crushed it angrily between his teeth. Then he sagged.

'Does Martin even care? Does he even realize what he's done? Such a disaster. I don't know where to turn!'

'It will be all right,' said Crystal. As a mother, this was something she had learned to say with conviction.

Father Flirty dashed a few tears from the edges of his eyes, which had sunk deep into his plump cheeks. He shook his head and began to laugh with sudden false merriment. 'Oh, look at me. I'm supposed to be the one consoling you. You've suffered too. The loss of your hubby.'

He said this with a twist of his rosy mouth and went on.

'The abject humiliation. Oh dear. The loss of regard in town. Your friends turning against you. From what I hear, people despise you now! All this, and round-the-clock surveillance!'

'It is a hardship,' said Crystal. Her voice was serene. She had a full-price taker on two Italian silk ties.

'Not only that,' said Flirty in a lower tone, his creamy jowls quivering, 'I wonder if I should have allowed the wedding? They are so young. To be honest, I thought that she was pregnant, and didn't know how to address that subject, given the circumstances. I've learned since that she is not.'

'You shouldn't pry into a young woman's privacy,' said Crystal. She took away the iced tea. Flirty reached for another frozen grape, but she moved the red pottery bowl from beneath his hand. The bowl was a long-ago gift from a friend. Nice enough to bring between ten and twenty dollars, she thought. *Handmade rose-colored pottery bowl, signed by artist. Perfect for frozen grapes.*

'I must get back to work,' she said to the priest, but he didn't move.

'There is talk about starting the renovation fund again,' he said. 'I am finding that idea totally beyond me.'

He leaned over, put his forehead down on the kitchen table. A pond of tears gradually formed on either side of his face. By then, Crystal was cleaning the kitchen. She wiped the table around his pallid head. After a while, he sagged into sleep. When he woke up, disoriented, his forehead creased and red, she helped him up out of his chair and walked him down the front steps. Father Flirty was rather spiteful, but she had sympathy for his desolation. In the Camry, there was movement. Bing's crumpled face came up off the steering wheel. He got out, gestured. Should he help?

Crystal shook her head and waved him away. He was adding pollution to the block by idling his car with the air-conditioning on. After Father Flirty walked sleepily away, she told the agent that he could sit in the front yard, underneath her tree. She had a folding canvas camp chair—a bit stained with mold, so not for sale. He might as well be comfortable. She even brought him, at 5 p.m., a wine spritzer (box wine, but who'd know) with frozen grapes, which were becoming her signature.

'I probably shouldn't accept this,' he said, taking the glass.

'It's nothing,' said Crystal, disappearing into the house.

He was a big solid guy with a shock of colorless hair

that cowlicked in front. His features were bold and his smile came easy. His eyes were an exciting contrast with his hair—dark, with rich eyelashes. His eyes were shy.

She packed up a vintage Fair Isle sweater and two pieces of Syracuse china, then looked around the room. Maybe she could sell the old brass library lamp she'd scored, years ago, at a garage sale. It was in her bedroom and she liked it, but it was solid brass. Perhaps she should sell her television. The last things she would get rid of were the electric fans, blowing over pans of water, swamp coolers that kept her brain from overheating.

Crystal went into the living room and looked out the window. Bing and his white Camry were gone. On her days off, someone else took over at night, but she hadn't yet figured out who was watching after dark, or from where. Maybe there was someone in the house across the street, which had been deserted, but now looked nominally occupied. She sat down to the news.

Crystal

Security across the tristate area was stepped up on Friday afternoons. Still, there was a robbery in Langdon. This time the cameras caught the clear image of a woman with shoulder-length black hair, wearing a short green jacket with bright gold buttons, a flared skirt in business black, stockings, low heels. Crystal leaned toward the television. The robber wore aviator sunglasses and carried a leather tote. Hot red lipstick. Necklace of freshwater pearls. Crystal sprang up, gasping, then put her hand over her mouth.

The teller was loyal, determined, a bank employee through and through. She filled the tote bag, ducked behind the counter, crawled under a desk, hit the silent alarm, and called 911.

Although the well-dressed robber fled, the police

were reported to be hard on her trail. The security camera footage played again.

Crystal had sunk to the couch, hyperventilating. She recognized her missing green jacket, her tote bag, and her skirt. She recognized her hair. The footage ran again. The woman even walked like her, gestured like her, and the pearl necklace had been an anniversary gift. A signal? Again, the footage.

Crystal scrambled off the couch and walked outside into the street. She stood in front of the blank-windowed house. After she stood there long enough that her location would be noted (hey, look, she was not on the lam!), she walked up the stairs she herself had repaired, into the door she'd painted blue, and sat down in the chair. She switched channels. Watched again and again. So that's how he'd signed the mortgage papers. That's how he'd ruined her life. And now she was wanted for robbing a bank.

PART FIVE

Marriage

2009

Crystal

Martin had her down cold. In the security footage, Crystal was a friendly pony, shaking her head as if nosing forward to a feed bag or a teller's window. She'd grown her bangs out long enough to tuck behind her ears, but Martin's wig gently swooped in front, enough to hide his face. He brushed the pearl necklace from time to time just the way Crystal thought she would, to make sure it was still on. It was a freshwater pearl necklace he had given her two years before. Crystal looked in her jewelry box and it wasn't there. She'd kept the necklace in a little white velvet bag and that was gone too. It was strange seeing yourself do something that you hadn't really done. Martin had to have been wearing shapewear under that skirt. He had no trouble with heels—they were low heels, not Crystal's. But his walk was her walk. She'd never watched a video of herself but she just knew. He'd taken the green jacket to her mother-of-the-bride dress. Crystal had to admit he wore it well. In some barely admissible way, she was touched by how well he'd imitated her. It proved, at least, that he'd been paying attention.

Also, she realized that Rasputin had been wearing one of her St. Christopher medals. That's what had bothered Crystal when she watched the footage from that robbery.

Harsh twinges of pain pulled at Crystal's heart. She put a hot pack on her chest and threw herself onto the couch. The stabs took a while to pass and she used the time to fortify her outrage. Or tried to at least. The thing was, she started laughing. In her laughter there was a note of something that made her stop. The laughter bubbled up again. She was laughing at his audacity. How wrong she had been. She had never imagined he had this in him. Crystal stopped herself again and listed all the ways he had threatened their stability and gotten them shunned, and worse. If he'd not absconded, Kismet might have had the good sense not to marry Gary Geist. Crystal might have had the brain cells left to insist on it. This was all on Martin. She couldn't actually still love him, could she? No. She would not allow it. She would not have a stupid heart. A weed is just a plant that grows in the wrong place, and Crystal decided that if she had any sympathy for Martin, that feeling was a weed.

North Dakota Weed of the Year

The dandelion was chosen by North Dakota State University as Weed of the Year in 2009. Cheerful, indomitable, persistent (seeds stay viable for at least five years), poetic, hermaphroditic, edible, medicinal, bitter, and enduring. Ichor had always loved dandelions even as he forked them from his lawn and encouraged farmers to spray them dead. He didn't use dandelions in salads or make them into tinctures or wine, but from time to time he wished on them.

As with every weed Ichor encountered, he admired their strategies for survival. Dandelions had spread across every continent because their wind-borne seeds were tiny; they sank deep taproots, and they did not require pollinators because they were both male and female. They persisted also because of their habit of bringing sunny cheer after winters of exhaustion. Some people and most parks gave up, simply welcomed them in spring, and mowed them down before they made seeds. They were the sun when they bloomed, the moon when they formed seed heads, and the stars when you blew on the fragile globes. Ichor threw a pile of slain dandelions on the weed heap.

He stood up with a blown dandelion. *Dandelion, into the wind you blow. Take my wish and make it so.* Ichor blew on the airy globe and the seeds floated away on oceans of air. He watched them drift toward the road until they disappeared. Walking back to the house, he saw Bev at the window, drying her strawberry blond hair with a pink towel. He saluted her.

'What did you wish for?' asked Bev when he came inside.

'The usual,' said Ichor, folding her into his arms.

Toast

Every night she turned on the news and waited. But nothing happened. Sometimes there was mention of an ongoing investigation. But then the newscaster would move on to how many banks got bailed out and how many people lost their homes and interview those who could never retire and declared they would have to work until they keeled over on the job. She was surprised at how quickly Martin's series of crimes dropped off the news cycle. Well, not the local news cycle. Martin's most heinous crime was still referenced every week in Father Flirty's sermons, where he urged the congregation to pray to St. Nicholas, known for forgiving sinners, to intercede with Martin to repent and return the money. Crystal didn't go to Mass anymore, of course. How could she have withstood the pressure of peoples' eyes on her? She was still being watched at home, but the interviews in her kitchen had ceased. And Bing continued to merely wave or say hello. One afternoon, Bing did ask her, in a seemingly casual way, why she went to the post office so often. She told him that she was selling things online.

'Can you actually make money?'

'Why, do you have things you want to get rid of?'

Bing opened his mouth and then paused. He shook his head and said, 'Everybody does.' Crystal got the clear impression he was going to say something else. She kept talking.

'Selling things gives me a focus. I don't see many people outside my job.'

Bing nodded. Of course he'd noted this. She was being watched by a tag team at the beet plant.

'I'm toast in this town, except for my old friends.'

'Toast,' said Bing.

'Would you like some?' said Crystal. 'Then I can show you why I go to the post office so often.'

She asked him into her house. He'd been inside before, but to ask questions. It gave her an odd feeling to actually invite him to enter. Crystal gave Agent Cox the smile that, in high school, she'd practiced in the mirror because it showed off her dimples. Now she did it without thinking. Actually, she didn't care. Her hair was up in a disordered knot. She had on a pilled white blouse and a pair of baggy denim jeans. The only nice thing she was wearing was a beaded belt buckle, which she had decided not to sell. Red, black, white, of glittering cut beads. She didn't even have on mascara. But again, she didn't care! Crystal waved at the corner where the boxes on the floor, open, held a set of fancy bird-themed mugs, cuff links (still not selling), a fedora Martin had used in gangster roles, a small statue of Diana the Huntress.

'Those are the things I'm selling,' she said.

'What are they worth?'

'Is that an official question?'

Bing actually fidgeted, startling Crystal. She couldn't recall a man becoming that uncomfortable at a remark she'd made. His eyes darted from side to side, his fingers twitched, and a blush started. It went from his chin to his forehead, then seemed to rush into his ears and dissipate from the edges of his ears into the dim air of her living room. Aha, thought Crystal.

Then she suddenly noticed how thick his white-blond hair was, how tall he was, how strong his shoulders and sensitive his wrists. She looked down in confusion. How big his feet.

'I have iced tea.'

They went into the kitchen and she opened the refrigerator, which was ancient and didn't seal well. She opened the little freezer at the bottom, which made good ice. She lifted out the trays with the mint leaves, twisted the plastic trays, and tumbled some cubes into the pitcher of sun tea. Also the glasses. They were dollar-store glasses. She'd sold her vintage iced tea glasses with the White Rock fairy on them for a tidy sum.

Crystal put two green cardboard coasters on the table and then the glasses on coasters, with some green mint leaves. The table was painted white, and she thought coasters emphasized whatever was put upon them. She poured the iced tea, sat down with Agent Cox.

'Cheers,' he said, raising his glass.

'Cheers,' said Crystal. 'Oh, I forgot to make you some toast.'

'I don't really need toast. I was thirsty.'

'That's good. I don't have any butter. I use olive oil. People expect butter on toast.'

'People?'

'I guess you're the only people who've been here. Other than Flirty. He likes butter.'

'What about Jeniver Longie?' said Bing.

Crystal set her glass down, hard. Bing started slightly back because she'd changed her gaze from soft to hard. 'I invited you in as a person, not as the guy who's scoping me all the time. You can take your iced tea to the car.'

'Hold on! It's hard to . . .'

He was fidgeting again.

'And quit that fidgeting. Quit blushing. You're not that awkward. You can really turn it on and off, can't you?'

'It's impossible to fake blushing,' said Bing with some dignity.

He also apologized, which Crystal thought was the mark of a secure male, though she also thought involuntary blushing should disqualify him from the FBI.

'I am attempting to be what you might call a regular person,' he said. 'But anyway, don't answer the question. However, if someone does ask you why I came into your house, please say I had a few questions for you, all right?'

And then he let the corners of his regular-looking mouth turn up as in a different sort of question. He raised his eyebrows and waited. She couldn't help but reassure him a little. It was a weakness, she thought later. This responding to a man who asks for approval had been her downfall in so many ways.

The Waistcoat Trove

The next afternoon, Crystal began to go through layers of extraordinary vests—Martin's treasure trove. There were formal and knitted vests, Victorian waistcoats, as well as silk foulards and scarves. He'd kept them in a plastic storage tubby in the tiny crawl space of their attic. She was striking deep into his possessions. As she unfolded, refolded, divided into piles, she tried to grasp Martin's actions. He'd surely had a nervous breakdown. Given the drawbacks to robbing banks in North Dakota, only a person cut off from reality would try. In country flat from horizon to horizon there was simply nowhere to hide. Plus North Dakota was known for the citizen posse—bloodthirsty, armed past description. Given righteous cause, the family-values people of field and town became a pitiless

414 · LOUISE ERDRICH

one-minded beast. Even (or perhaps especially) in the present day, this happened. So how could Martin, of all people, defy known logic and danger?

The waistcoats, sensible vests that kept his weak lungs cozy in the icy blasts, testified to Martin's instinct for self-preservation. His Victorian vests, particularly a prized one of rose brocade, often appeared in productions that required a monied gentleman of a more graceful era. He wore his scarves tucked into the vests to hold off throat-chilling winds. Crystal hardened her heart and brought the vests and scarves down to her staging area. One by one she photographed them, concocted a description, and put them up for sale. *Broke-in leather cowpoke vest. Citizen posse vest. Sherlock Holmes smoking jacket vest (with pipe). Lord Byron would have worn this!* She deleted Lord Byron and wrote in Mr. Darcy, then deleted Mr. Darcy and wrote in Mr. Right.

Still the question persisted. Why was Martin, of all people, so far successful at eluding capture? And as he was successful, how could he also have lost his mind? Crystal was losing her own mind over this. She was having an irrational, grieflike reaction.

She tried not to think about a posse. But her own words kept coming back. *Bloodthirsty. Armed past description. Pitiless one-minded beast.*

Hugo

Pre-Worm

Again, he was eating in the Porta Potty. Hermano, his new buddy, had laughed when Hugo got out of the company pickup and took the cooler into the Porta. But Hugo needed privacy to eat, he'd already lost his sense of smell, and his physical boundaries were broken down. Also, he hurt all over. Demands of the job. What went out of his body and what came in were just animal facts. It was more important, for a few minutes at least, to be alone. He needed something to take him out of the day, so he plugged his nose with a paper napkin, stuffed two peanut butter and jelly sandwiches into his mouth. Motrin went down with a long slug of Gatorade. He was soul-whipped and desolate, but the pay was crazy. The pay was tops.

His job was squeezing into tight places, putting his hands into hand-crushing machinery, unjamming things that might snap off his arm, cleaning up unspeakable toxic filth, lifting heavy objects, dropping heavy objects, filling holes, retrieving objects stuck in holes, hauling bags marked with slyly tiny warnings and skulls, slitting open the skull bags, mixing chemicals, pouring dangerous liquids into the abyss, obeying any order shouted by another man.

Yes, the job was foul, dangerous, humiliating, delirium-inducing, unsettling, enraging, boring, impossible, hellish. Was it hellish? There were better jobs. Hermano's job, for instance. But Hugo had skills and hopes. His doctored-up resumé was sitting on the office desk waiting for someone with authority to read it.

Worm

This was Hugo's next job. He moved up. The Worm collected core samples so that either an exploratory well could be situated or a record of drilling activity could be prepared, the mud log. The Worm was supposed to be an assistant to the petroleum geologist.

But Hugo never saw this phantom geologist. Hermano drove a truck with the drill to a designated spot. They operated the drill, which went millions of years deep into the earth. The drill backed out with a sample that Hugo helped place in a wooden case built to spec. He labeled it and on it went. At other times, Hugo was assigned to take samples from well sites and bring them to the laboratory, a camper kitchen. His high-tech equipment consisted of a bucket, a tea strainer, and the camp sink. He was always worried about cross-contamination with coffee grounds.

Soon a microscope and a UV light box appeared where Hugo washed and prepared the well grit, which he spooned into neat sandwich bags, thence into manila envelopes. He inscribed each envelope with the depth at which the sample had been found. Then he entered all of the information into a rattletrap PC. He left the samples on the kitchen counter of the camper, and by the next morning they were gone.

At the end of each workday, Hugo ate at the same poky diner he'd investigated on day one. The diner had expanded, taking up a parking lot. Now people parked on side streets, boulevards, and sidewalks. Every other night, Hugo drained his cooler and bought more ice. He bought peanut butter, jelly, bread, and Dr Pepper. Then he went back to his scrap of lawn. He dragged his refrigerator box out of the side yard, shook out the sleeping bags and foam mattress, plumped his pillow. He surrounded his sagging box with a tarp he had scored, took a cold refreshing shower behind the garage. Then he crawled into his box and tried to sleep through the churring and hissing of raccoons as they playfully attacked his feet. At 5 a.m. he'd enter the drive-through line at McDonald's. By six he was at work with his second coffee and his third Egg McMuffin. In fulfillment of his dreams, this routine became his way of life.

Peace in the Refrigerator Box

Next there was a magical development. It seemed that the wildcat outfit that Hugo was working for was unable to keep up with itself. There never had been a real geologist, but it seemed Hugo's samples had been acceptable to whatever authorities were looking at the samples. He was promoted. Nobody called him a mud-logger yet, but that's what he was. He gaped at his paycheck. Deposited it. Then paid to be next in line for the space in the Bergs' garage, which came with access to hot water.

Hugo's bank account began to flow toward five figures, so he also paid Janice Berg to make him real lunches. He began to find his work mildly addictive. And he made some friends by sharing Janice's lunches, which were packed in Bud's old fishing cooler. Hermano and the guy who'd taken Hugo's old job, Florida, came together at noon every day, when he opened the cooler. They ate in the camper, which was now, sort of, Hugo's. Janice did not prepare just any lunch. Cold pop swaddled in Ziplocs of ice when it was hot. Hot chocolate and coffee in a thermos when it was cold. Sandwiches with cheese, heavy on the meats, the lettuce kept separate and crisp. The bread thick and soft. Squares of cake in a Tupperware box, a dozen boiled eggs, cookies. Sliced apples with lemon squeezed over them and cinnamon sugar to dip them in. Peeled oranges, baby carrots, ranch dip. Home-canned pickles. Janice was a goddess. She was even letting him take hot showers now. And there was a lock on the outhouse door. He could shit to his heart's content, a thing he'd always taken for granted. Although he was still sleeping in the refrigerator box, there was peace, for Bud had shot the raccoons.

Magic Seeds

Diz wore a respirator and a pair of overalls, gloves, and boot covers to load the plastic drum with glyphosate, which would flow into the wing bones of the sprayer. He was extremely careful with drips and spills. Once the spray was aerosolized, out of his control and on the wind, it could land anywhere. Diz always waited for the stillest moment on the least windy day and went out. This was the hour just before dawn, when everything was suspended in expectancy of light, when the hush was disturbed only by the broken cries of a few birds.

Or sometimes no birds at all, he thought as he pulled himself into the cab. The absence of birds made Diz uneasy but he wasn't spraying birds, was he? Yet there were fewer birds around his farm. Used to be robins hunting worms in the furrows. Used to be blackbirds around the grain bins. Owls at dawn, rats in their claws. Well maybe, he had a sudden thought, those could have been the rats and mice he'd had to poison. He thought back to how birds used to chatter as the sun rose. Now, a few sparrows, maybe, or more often just the hiss and boom of wind. He closed himself into the cab and adjusted the screen, turned on climate control, rode slowly and carefully down the section road.

As he made his way to the field, Diz saw that Winnie was up too. She was on the cement slab in the backyard playing with her dogs. Earlier that morning, when he'd reached over to embrace Winnie, one of those little dogs had bitten him. But now as he passed they were running back and forth, chasing a striped ball. Winnie was running after them, in circles too, and Diz melted. Look at his wife! Chasing around the place like a hooligan! His girlfriend, still. He punched in the adjustments he needed to make, started the application. He kept the sight of her in his thoughts. Winnie in a silky green bathrobe, twirling and laughing, her hair sticking out like a boy's. She was getting better, feeling like her old self, he was sure of it. Yes. He looked down at the purple indentation of teeth on the back of his hand. Their jaws were so cute and tiny, she'd said earlier that morning, as she put some ointment on the little circle of purple holes.

'You love those little shits better than you do me,' he'd said.

'I do not,' she had answered.

'Can I say four words?'

'Okay.'

'Put dogs in kennel.'

Sometimes she acted like she didn't know what he was getting at. But this time she brought her little dogs downstairs with their chew toys and then she came back upstairs, slid into bed next to him, and said, 'Whatcha got for me, Dizzy?'

Now the world was his. Everything was functioning and his wheels were guided down the rows. He barely had to steer except to come around at the end of each row. There was no hurry. Nobody to bother him. The field was dry even in the spot that sometimes welled up with moisture. Maybe an old spring there once upon a day. For some reason this morning, as he and Winnie were lying drowsily together, she had said something about what they didn't talk about. She'd said she was so grateful to Kismet because she could already see that Gary was better. Which meant there had been something wrong with Gary before, which they'd had trouble admitting. So he was better. And Kismet was helping.

'It was kinda just left out there,' said Diz aloud.

Diz had his thoughts in the noise of the cab while he was working. It was where he figured things out, had emotions, loved his place on earth, worshipped the sky. Sometimes the banks of clouds, their color and purity, made him turn his mouth down, take a deep breath, and shake his head. He would occasionally talk to himself. 'Thing she said about *helping* maybe, like as if there was something we never got to after that night.'

His mind jumped to the wedding dinner, the speeches. He and Winnie had never discussed what Eric meant. Diz continued to move his lips.

'What was that about Eric taking a hit for Gary—as in football maybe. Or could it have been *that* other night?'

The night over a year and a half ago now. The night his thoughts still refused, though pictures often flooded his brain. When he let down his guard, he'd relive the little of what he knew had happened, in every detail, over and over. And always it seemed to Diz like something more happened—even more than what did happen. Or what he was told happened. More than the police report. More than the boys were saying. Unspoken matters.

He couldn't talk about this to Winnie, or certainly Gary. Diz just didn't have the words. He solved things by working on them with a wrench. He showed his love to Gary by building the new house. But there were times he became agitated inside. These episodes came upon him more often now that Kismet was there. It was as if her presence softened him, opened a door, stirred up things he didn't want to relive. Those unspoken matters.

March 27, 2008. Even at the time, Diz sensed that he might be crossing a divide. When he had no idea what would come next. But ever after there would be a before. There would be an after. When he truly allowed himself to remember all of this, Diz felt like his heart was pouring blood.

Coming home from a meeting in Fargo, driving slowly through a ground blizzard, powder snow airborne just a few feet above the road, Diz and Winnie had seen lights flashing, dim through the worsening snowstorm. They were first curious, then alarmed, then silent and overpowered by dread as they realized the lights were at their house. An ambulance pulled out of their driveway and drove cautiously past them, siren blaring. That's when they couldn't breathe. Winnie clasped her hands in prayer, closed her lips, muttered deargod, deargod, deargod. Another ambulance was idling in the turnout. Then Diz was inside the equipment shed they'd outfitted for Gary. Police were suiting up and going off on commandeered snowmobiles. Someone said Knieval and Harlan were in the ambulance. Eric was inside the house wrapped in electric blankets.

'And where's Gary, where's Gary?' he asked.

There was a sensation, a quiet buzzing, a droning. Everyone was saying something with their avoidant behavior, with the way their eyes slipped over him and over Winnie when she followed him inside. She lost her balance, tipped over, and screamed, *Tell me!* It felt like death, it could be death, because nobody would say Gary's name, but they didn't know there were other names not being spoken.

Gusty and Darva appeared and Darva ran to Winnie. Held her around her waist and walked her over to the house through the snow. Someone leading the way with a halogen lantern. Diz had to sit down. Beer cans all over the party shed. Uncapped bottles. Cigarette butts and an empty handle of vodka. Rug crumpled, chairs tipped over, stuff just tossed. Gusty came over and sat beside him.

'They're going out to search for Gary,' said Gusty. 'They'll find him. He went down the river.'

Diz was numb, stupid, head in a jar.

'They'll find him.'

'Yeah they will. He knows that pasture.'

'Winnie's old place?' Diz asked. 'They drove over to your pasture?'

'Yeah they did.'

Gusty was looking down at his knees. Diz noticed that the stubble on his brother's face was growing out gray.

'They drove down the slope?'

Gusty didn't raise his head.

'Over the bank?' asked Diz.

Gusty nodded and they just sat there. They sat there. Nothing.

Eric

Eric turned off the highway because he saw Kismet wearing that red-billed hat with the bandanna to keep the sun off her neck. He thought it gave her a somewhat goofy look that was somehow also cool, like all the things she wore. She walked up beside his window.

He rolled down his window and squinted at her.

'Looking for Gary?'

'Yeah.'

Kismet nodded and looked away. 'He'll be back here any time now. Come sit down. Want a sandwich or something?'

'I wouldn't say no.'

This would be his last visit for a while, he promised himself. He got out of the truck, walked over to the picnic table, and sat down. He tried to take hold of himself. But Kismet came back in only a short time with a sandwich on a plate. Wheat bread, turkey, ched- dar, mayo, mustard, lettuce.

'My favorite kind of sandwich,' he said.

'Oh yeah? This is my favorite too.'

'Are you a good cook? I mean, besides everything else?'

'What?'

'Like, besides you being smart.'

'Smart.' She said this with an eyebrow raised. 'Smart. Oh okay. I filled in short-order cooking at the Skillet, so I can put sandwiches together. And breakfast.'

'Man, it's hot,' he said.

'No, it isn't. Not that hot.'

'Geez, oppositional.' He laughed. His laugh seemed forced, to his ears. High-pitched.

'Oppositional? Me? Where'd you get that?'

'De-escalation training.'

'Oh, right.'

'Yeah, things can get out of hand pretty fast.'

'You said it. Out of hand pretty fast.' She seemed to read something into his comment. Then she shook off her serious tone and said she'd make him another sand- wich. He nodded. He was surprised the sandwich was gone. He was still hungry, as if the sandwich he'd just eaten had not filled him but made a hollow in his belly.

She rose and went back into the kitchen. He got up to follow her because he didn't want to be alone behind that house. But he stopped because he didn't want to be inside the house, either, or be anywhere around here. He shouldn't have come to Gary's at all. Eric walked to the kitchen door and opened it a crack. Then he shut the door and would have sneaked off but she was making him food it would be rude of him not to eat. Eric walked back to the table. He tried not to stumble into that dark space in his thoughts. But of course he was already there.

The Party

March 27, 2008. A fall of new snow had settled over a crust of ice and the sun was sparkling down on the fields. Eric, Harlan, Knieval, Charley, Jordan Darioux, and Travis McNaff had ridden or trailered their parents' snowmobiles to Gary's place. They parked outside the party shed and started partying, just beer and weed at first, then later on shots and harder stuff, but that was after the sun was low. Diz and Winnie wouldn't be back until after midnight, and the boys' plan was to take a snowmobile ride and then crash overnight in the loft.

'Let's get moving, ladies,' Harlan said every so often. They kissy-faced him or agreed but then they kept talking because they weren't just bullshitting around, they were dealing with some very heavy stuff.

Was Mrs. Gorowski the sexiest chick who'd ever lived and once that was affirmed why was she teaching high school geography when she looked like Jessica Simpson? How had ugly Coach Jaws attracted her, married her, and why had he allowed her to keep her maiden name? But most important, was that shadow just below the base of her throat a tattoo and if so, what was the rest of it?

'Tail end of a viper,' said Harlan, who had again forgotten his impulse to get the party moving. 'What's the longest river in the world, Jordan?'

'The Jordan,' said Jordan.

The others stared at him in wasted surprise until they realized he didn't know he'd made a sort of joke.

'It's the Nile,' said Charley.

'You're full of shit,' said Jordan Darioux. (Dah-roo!!! Howled at games when he made a tackle that opened a highway for Harlan or Gary to run or nabbed a receiver, even a pass, for he was quick.) 'And Gorowski doesn't have a tattoo. She's not the type. She's class.'

The others treated Jordan with care. Unlike some middle linebackers he wasn't aggressive, but sweet and weirdly mild. He was necessarily very big. He loved geography, had the hots for Gorowski, and maybe even a little altar to her in his basement bedroom or next to his game console, where he pretended to play

Assassin's Creed and *Halo* but secretly played *Super Mario*.

'It could be just a trick of the eye,' said Jordan. Turning to Harlan, he began to lean over, slowly, down toward the brown-gray indoor-outdoor carpeting, with his eyes locked on Harlan's face, scanning for Harlan's eyes, as if to focus. Charley carefully pushed him the rest of the way over with his snow-booted foot and Jordan made the slow-motion fall last another few seconds to get a laugh. All of the guys loved Jordan, but maybe Gary loved him most of all. It wasn't just that he kept the big rhinos off Gary on the football field, it went back to when they were kids. Gary jumped up. Yes yes yes he was the handsomest and most obtuse.

'If it was a snake . . .' He used his hands to illustrate its slide down the center of his body and was lifting his forked fingers to stick his tongue between them but Harlan slapped his hand away in time.

'A rose,' said Charley suddenly, with feeling. 'If she had one it would be a rose, like, to commemorate.'

'Commemorate?' Jordan leaned forward, brow lowering. He was almost as protective of Charley as of Gary, and had a pact with Eric and Travis never to let anybody pile on Charley.

'Someone she loved,' said Charley.

'Fuck you, pussies,' said Gary.

'Because it ain't Jaws.' Knieval got up and plunged his hand into the cooler for a Bud. Jaws was the perfect name for the coach because not only did Jaws have cold little pebble eyes and too many teeth but his smile was upside-down. As coaches go, he wasn't the best, wasn't always fair, played favorites, and of course did not deserve his wife. They didn't play for him, though. They played for one another and always had.

Harlan stood, tipped his beer to Jordan.

'Doubtless, sir, if she were the type, *you'd* be her type.'

Harlan drank, gave everyone his thin-lipped lopsided grin. Jordan slowly and tragically raised his eyes. He was a poppy-pink blond hulk. His lower lip was sticking out. He was going to be one of those gentle crushers who has six towheads, three on each side, sitting in the church pew.

'Let's get moving, ladies,' said Harlan.

'I'm not a lady, I'm a feminist,' said Gary.

'No, you're not, you're a wuss, and you're only saying that because you want Goth Girl to like you,' said Knieval.

'She's an alien. You guys are hot for her.'

'Shut up. You're getting on my last nerve. She's just not that into you,' said Eric. He was already vaguely aware that he didn't want Kismet to like Gary or Gary to like Kismet.

'You're on my last nerve. That's what moms always say,' said Travis.

Eric walked off and pretended to rummage in the cooler. He wasn't drunk enough to deal with this conversation. Gary yelled after him.

'Of course she's into me. Anybody with half a pussy's into me.'

'Half a pussy! Half a pussy! Man, that's you, Gary,' Knieval yelled back.

'Fuck you. I could get her.'

'Well, do it then, you loser,' said Harlan, but in an affectionate tone. Calling Gary a loser or half pussy was a haha joke because Gary was such a winner they could only hope to take him down a little.

'You're always watching her,' said Jordan.

'She's crazy,' said Gary.

'Pussy's pussy,' said Knieval.

'You've got a point,' said Charley. 'Like, a tiny little point.' He waved his pointer finger from his crotch.

'I will get her. I will use her.'

'Shamefully, so very shamefully,' said Knieval.

'Panties,' said Jordan, very drunk now. It might have been the raciest thing he'd ever said.

'I'll find out about her,' said Gary.

'Report back, you pathetic dick,' said Eric, pushing on Gary's shoulder.

'Let's get moving,' said Harlan. And now he stepped into his suit and his insulated boots, donned his helmet and at last his gloves. He started walking out the door. The others watched him disappear and fumbled around, suited up. Then, as if drawn along by a tightened string, they rose and walked dimly or staggered off after Harlan. Jordan held the wall for support. Gary crawled to the door and dragged himself up, but then the cold hit him and he revived. On the way out, Jordan yanked the leather football helmet off the wall, the one that had belonged to Gary's grandfather when they won state so long ago. Eric told him the helmet wasn't a real helmet, but Gary was already across the field and Jordan followed.

'Jordan followed?' asked Kismet.

'Jordan followed,' Eric said out loud. He was dimly aware she had returned, and tried to stop himself from talking. But he felt something odd happening as his mouth kept moving and he couldn't stop his words. It was like the party had seized control of his voice box and he kept on talking when Kismet put down the second sandwich and a plate of pecan sandies.

'Then we cranked up and flew,' he told her.

Their Godlike Trance of Speed

The fields flat, slick, glistening. The pounding in their heads a joy indecent—to be shit-faced drunk and traveling with gorgeous force and speed. Darkness pouring behind them like a cape of energy. All his team, floating, smashing, floating up and smashing down. It's me, me, me, leading them, thought Gary in his heart. Snot smeared his face shield and he slowed until he stopped. Were they all crying? He looked around. Maybe just him. Eric put his visor up and yelled, 'Slow the fuck down!' Gary grinned back and saluted him, *Okay, Mr. Everything*, then cleaned his shield off with snow and counseled himself, *Get it together*. But once they took off again, Gary could not slow down. Just could not. He was gone—they were with him or they weren't. Follow me or don't follow me. He was going sixty, eighty, a hundred easy, a thousand maybe. Only Jordan was going as fast, racing him across one of Gusty's fields. But Gary beat him easily, pulled way ahead. When they came to the slope he was surprised. He'd forgotten. It came so soon. But they were a team and this was ice and glory. Unexpected, yes. Sheer kinetic force hurled him down the incline through the gap in the old fence he knew of and spurting through out onto the river. And you had to lean into an air turn right there most delicately in order not to flip or jack yourself onto the opposite bank. He'd done this move before with Eric. He did it again. In a horizontal ecstasy he continued down the river, miraculously dodging the trees upsurged through the ice.

Behind him.

In a trance of speed the others sluiced onto what in full moonlight revealed itself as a sloping field. A final drop catapulted their machines at such speed that none of them saw the old barbed-wire fence. Jordan didn't notice when his head was taken off. Charley had thrown his face shield up and was unaware when his smile was sliced back to the hinge in his jaw. The four who were left bounced down the bank, landing well spaced on the ice. It was covered with snow, so they couldn't tell that in places the current had pushed up and made treacherous thin spots. Gary was out of sight. In a state of drunken relief the boys took off their helmets and whooped at the amazing fact that they hadn't wiped out. Their lights down in the blackness between the banks were spooky and intense. They waited for the others, engines idling. They were safe as long as their weight was distributed on their sleds. Eric gathered his wits as best he could. An apprehension seeped into him.

'Where's Charley?' said Travis.

'Have some,' said Kismet, sliding the plate of pecan sandies toward Eric. He put one in his mouth to stop his thoughts. They wouldn't stop. He put a second cookie in his mouth. Then he started ramming the cookies in, crumbs tumbling off his chin. Okay, that was better.

'Wow,' he said, stopping himself. 'Those are good. Did you make them?'

Kismet looked down at the cookies. 'They're just normal cookies, you know. Out of a package.'

His voice sounded teary. He cleared his throat.

'Sorry. They're just, like, really, really good.'

'No they're not,' she said, not looking at Eric. He'd been talking about the party and the accident. He had noticed but not noticed she was there. And what he said was sort of a jumble—what he saw, what he thought Gary thought, their speed down the incline, then mumbling between bites like he was thinking aloud. Yet the picture of what had happened was clear.

'I must be really hungry,' he said, taking the last two cookies.

She got up with the plate and walked toward the back door.

'Wait!' he called.

She looked at him over her shoulder and said that she would get some more cookies.

'No!' he cried. 'No, please!'

She came back to sit at the picnic table. He gave her a stricken look and kept on talking.

Travis jumped off his machine to look for Charley and plunged straight down. He disappeared so suddenly it seemed like a magic trick. Harlan was stepping down too, and tried to stop himself, but he began to slide into the water. Eric could remember his body moving before he knew what to do. He hadn't quite ended up on the river. He was on the bank. He slithered off his snowmobile and onto the ice carefully, spider-crawling toward the dark water, screaming at Knieval to ride off the ice and not stop. Don't stop! Knieval turned around and made for shore.

Harlan somehow managed to kick off his water-logged boots and pull himself toward Eric. 'Breathe,' said Eric to Harlan. 'You've got time. Kick your legs up. Get horizontal.' They locked arms and Harlan clutched hard, but the weight began to drag Eric toward the hole. Eric planted his boots and did the hardest bicep curl of his life. Harlan flopped up and rolled over. 'Keep rolling all the way,' said Eric. Stuffed with coke and adrenaline, Harlan rolled and army-crawled alongside Eric until they managed to reach the bank. Knieval hauled soaking Harlan up on shore. Eric thought Harlan wouldn't have long now and began rummaging around in a mad panic, then slowed himself. He followed his training. Patience now meant survival.

Eric brought the other two around the bend, where there was more cover from the wind. Then he scrounged around, snapped dry twigs off the scruffy trees, found a dead branch and brought it down. He always carried a lighter, not because he regularly smoked, but because a situation might arise where he could need to spark up, though he did not during wrestling season. He used his lighter on a small tipi of bark and added fuel twig by twig until he got larger branches going.

'Yeah, you fuckers,' he said, voice shaking. He

thought of Travis. 'Gonna rag on me for being an Eagle Scout now?'

'No, ma'am,' chattered Harlan. 'Travis.'

Knieval and Eric stripped Harlan to his fleece shirt and made him shed his soggy jeans. Harlan was shuddering, beyond speech now. *Travis!* Eric took off his snowmobile suit, slipped his phone from the zippered pocket, and stuck it in his jeans. He got Harlan into the suit, pushed him right up to the fire.

'Do not burn my suit, you dumb shit,' he said to Harlan. He hugged Harlan, pounded his back.

'Watch him,' said Eric to Knieval. 'Get more branches, dry stuff from the trees, not wet from the ground.'

'Please god,' Eric said and went back to the river. Harlan's machine was still there, idling. Travis's had slid halfway in, enlarging the hole so it was only a matter of time before it swallowed Harlan's too. Eric tried to use his phone, couldn't get a signal until he crawled back to his sled and found a place where he could gun it up the side of the field. Once he was up there, he stopped and pulled his old black down jacket from under the seat. Put it on. Managed on the third try to get in a 911 call that rang and rang. Someone finally answered, wavering out, and Eric's voice scraped in his throat and quit.

What was he seeing? What shape? What meaning? Of course he knew but he wouldn't let himself know. He took a deep breath, turned away and faced into the wind, which had shifted now. Wetter? Drier? Anyway, the temperature was dropping fast. From the northwest where the bad weather came down, it bore upon Eric the dusty fragrance of snow. The dispatcher was still there, her voice clear now. Eric called his own voice back from the edge.

He stammered out their location and what had happened to Travis. 'Stay on the line,' said the dispatcher.

'Godohgod,' said Eric.

'Okay, we got you. Stay where you are.'

They established the location again and Eric told her he'd just sighted someone else in trouble. Had to go.

He ran over to the other form, the one that didn't break his mind, and eased off the helmet, which told him this was Charley, who was choking on his blood. Although it could be a neck injury, Eric had to turn Charley face-down and make space in the snow for him to breathe. At first he thought it was a jugular cut, but if so Charley wouldn't have been alive, so it was something else. He looked more carefully, could barely see. Charley's mouth was way too big, he thought. He gently tried to pinch Charley's lips shut, then pressed snow around the sides of his face. He used a beer can

from Charley's stow chest to hold Charley's forehead
off the snow. Eric thought Charley was unconscious,
but once he stopped choking, Charley began to sob.

'Don't cry, dude. It's gonna work against you.
Hear me?'

Charley gurgled.

'That's better. Stay still. I just called 911. They're on
the way. I gotta go take care of Harlan and Knieval.'

Charley made a question-mark noise.

'You got a bad jaw injury. But the rest of you is
okay. You're gonna be okay. Don't move.' Charley
made another question gurgle.

'Yeah, Travis too.' He opened his mouth to also lie
about Jordan, but he couldn't make a sound.

Eric saw that he hadn't eaten all of his second sandwich, but he jumped to his feet anyway, mumbled his
thanks to Kismet. She was sitting very still, slumped
over a little. She was looking at the table, staring
down and tracing the grain of the wood. Eric looked
sightlessly around and tried to leave, started walking back to his truck. He was lighter and yet much
heavier. Lighter because some of the words and memories were out of him, heavier because he had put at
least some of them on Kismet. He wasn't even sure
what he'd told her and what was spoken, what was

thought. There were other things he should never tell anyone yet he might as well finish. He might as well get this over with. Eric turned on his heel, walked swiftly back to Kismet, who was still staring at the picnic table.

Jordan

E ric made sure Charley still had on his padded gloves and his boots. He pulled the hood of Charley's suit up over his head and tucked it down around his face with tender care. Then Eric glanced over at Jordan's body to make sure there was nothing he could do. His eyes got stuck there. *On my honor,* he thought. *On my honor I will try . . .* He was flooded with thoughts of Jordan's mom, his sisters, his dad. He saw them all. He saw everything. All anyone would ever remember about Jordan's death would be the one thing. The news on TV would lead with it. Jordan and his family deserved some sort of what? He saw an empty thought bubble and later thought, Dignity. Didn't they?

Travis was gone, he knew, and if Jordan was taken

by the river too, it would be a tragedy, yes. But not this. In the stow chest, Eric always kept supplies—rope, hatchet, tarp, all in various containers and plastic bags. He carefully drove his snowmobile counter to the slope and stopped as close as possible to Jordan's body. Then he got down on his knees. He started to pray but then became so angry he heated up. His cheeks burned. He swore as he wrapped the rope around and around underneath Jordan's arms. He could feel that his black parka was soaked with blood. He hitched the rope on and jumped on his Cat. Then jumped off again and put the stupid helmet and what it contained into a white plastic bag that he stowed down by his feet.

I am of course in shock, he thought dispassionately. I'm sorry, Jordan.

He was doing everything just as if he was being instructed by some other Eric who saw this clearly. A higher, coldly enraged Eric who had decided what had to happen. This other Eric steered cautiously, zig-zagging down the bank farther on, and got as close as he could to where Travis had disappeared. The river went from five to thirty-five feet deep depending on the season. Travis had obviously jumped down on a thin deep place. The ice had kept cracking, swallowing Travis's snowmobile, and the water was still open. Eric spread his weight out and slithered to Jordan's body, untied him. Coiled up the rope like a good Scout and stowed it back in his machine's compartment. Then the regular Eric panicked, stalled. Normal to freak out for a moment, thought the clear-minded other Eric, who splayed himself out and brought the white bag to the body. Looking only at the helmet, he saw that it fastened with a chin strap, which he could in turn fasten to a loop on the top of Jordan's zipper. Head in helmet was now in proximity to the right place and Eric somehow felt better. He crawled behind Jordan. Still splayed out he somehow edged him toward the hole, the ice cracking beneath them both until Jordan's body was out where the water was open. Jordan heaved down suddenly in a dive, as if he wanted it this way. The ice floating in the water clicked and swished. Eric heard himself making an awful growling noise. Put his head down. Lifted his face and made the sound again. After a while, Eric wormed himself back to shore. He went up the hill, started Jordan's machine, crept it to the river, and tried to send it down too, but it stopped after a few feet as if it was afraid to follow. He pushed it from behind and slid himself backward. The snowmobile suddenly cracked through, plunged down, taking with it any ice that might have been smeared with blood. Then Eric went around the bend to the fire, where Knieval and Harlan were trying to stay warm; they'd noticed nothing so he closed his mind and waited with them to be rescued.

'I found Charley,' he said. 'But Jordan'—he choked on the lie—'he could've went down to the river farther on.'

'Maybe he's with Gary,' said Knieval.

While they waited, the blizzard started moving in. First the trees began thrashing on the hillside, then some light snow whirled above. They weren't drunk at all anymore and Eric started looking around for better shelter. Also, he kept going to the river and trying to see if either one of them had popped up. No. No. There was just the glowing swales of snow, the black rift quickly sealing. There was the silence around his body, the shriek of wind above his head and up the riverbank.

The visibility was getting worse. A thought of Gary intruded, but Eric allowed the piece of shit just one corner of his brain. The fuck-Gary corner. Who led them across the field? Who quarterbacked them down the downslope? Who knew about the fence and the gap in the fence? Who was missing? Maybe dead or injured, sure, but that was on Gary himself. Of course Eric had made the call not to go after Gary but to stay with the others. But he still had to keep telling himself he'd made the right choice. He was afraid Harlan would lapse into hypothermic shock. Knieval was next to hopeless with the fire. Charley was still up there. Eric went back to Charley twice and was building a windbreak with some branches when at last they heard a high-pitched whine trembling above the low roar of wind. Eric climbed back up the slope, stood over Charley, and sent up a little flare that fizzled comically in the snow. He should have replaced those, he thought, and lit an even older one, which immediately plopped over. It was really snowing now and one of the rescue sleds nearly ran them over.

Even as they were hauled out, Eric struggled to keep thoughts of Gary out of his brain. But the habit of taking care of Gary was impossible to break. And that habit made him pity the oblivious fuck.

Now he heard himself say 'the oblivious . . .' and stopped himself.

The pressure to keep telling this story was so great that he had not been able to stop himself until he came to the f word. And now she knew everything. Kismet was hunched over again, hands clasped underneath her chin, as though she was praying. But her lips weren't moving and her eyes were open. She was frowning, thinking. 'What did you do with the rope?' she asked.

'The rope . . .' He couldn't remember. 'Probably still in that compartment, behind the seat of my snowmobile.'

'Burn it up,' she said. 'Nobody else should ever know what you just told me. I'm glad you did. You did the right thing.'

Now tears went down her cheeks. It was a relief to see someone else cry. After a while, she spoke.

'Nobody else knows?'

'Nobody else knows.'

'Where's your hand?'

'Right here. Don't let go.'

Later she did let go and said, 'You ate, like, a whole bag of cookies.'

'No I didn't.'

'Yeah you did. Two-fisted. You were eating from both hands!'

She actually made him laugh. The relief.

'Eat sugar to grow sugar, that's what Diz says.' Eric smiled in a distracted way. 'I should go now. Thank you for the . . .' He trailed off.

'I am never, ever, going to tell anybody what you said. But you need, like, therapy for it. Don't you think?'

'Yeah. But I'd have to go up to Fargo. That would take a day. I don't wanna go to anyone here, in town.'

'I can see that.'

'They'd say something, you know?'

'You couldn't be comfortable if you thought that.'

'I couldn't. And I couldn't tell it all, anyway, because of sending Jordan . . . yeah.'

'Talk to me if you need to again,' she said in a low voice.

'Gary's the one that needs to talk to you,' said Eric, clearing his throat. 'He's not oblivious, that wasn't right to say, he's under a burden too. Rappatoe told me he was saying crazy things when they pulled him off the river that night. He was way farther down. But now I really gotta go.'

'Okay, Eric, but do me a favor. Stop thinking of Gary.'

After she heard Eric's pickup roar off, Kismet put her head all the way down on the wood and in the darkness beneath her own hands she tried to think. It was hot and a crushing, smothering sensation overcame her, as if she were pressed beneath a heavy tangle of nameless boundless helpless slithering threads. After a while she rose and walked, in a crouch, through the back door and up the stairs to the bedroom. It was only around 5 p.m., yet she crawled into bed. It felt like she'd been felled by heatstroke or a tricky virus. She pulled the bedspread over herself, pressed a button on the remote, and cool air flowed into the room. Her mother's house had one clattering air conditioner so this felt magical. The purr of climate control lulled her but eventually revived her.

She wondered whether the old fencing at the bottom of the pasture had been removed yet. She had been turning over all that Eric had confided, and she knew that in one way or another she might be doing this for who knew how long. She had a sense of how lonely Eric was and it was too big a feeling for her to even cry over.

'He told me to talk to Gary,' she said, rolling out from under the covers. Kismet thought that if she heard the rest of the story from Gary, she could deal with it, because to think of it all in one piece might help her sleep or to forget now and then.

'So get on with it,' she said to herself. But still she couldn't move.

After she heard Gary come into the house, she stirred a bit. When he started slamming cupboards, she got up and went downstairs to feed him. There were brats, poppy seed buns, canned baked beans, coleslaw. This would fix him up pretty good. Once the air cooled off, they'd eat at the picnic table and maybe she would ask him what had happened to him that night. He'd have a beer with supper, and she'd bring him another beer afterward. She would have a cold drink and he'd have a beer and then they'd talk.

'**What happened** after that party where Travis and Jordan died?' she asked.

He stared at her, his face naked with surprise, then desolation. He looked away and said nothing at first, then in a low voice, 'I don't want to talk about it.'

'Okay, well, I'm here if you need to, anytime.'

'*Need* to?'

His voice grated. She shouldn't have said that awful word, need.

'Want to. If you feel like it.'

She spoke lightly, then got up and brought the dishes inside. Over the next few days she didn't refer to it in the slightest way although she thought about it constantly, and thinking about it was intolerable. She thought of the swallows, blue and green, and the black swifts. Then she thought of clouds massing, sailing, or stalled. Things that weren't human. Finally, one night, after they had turned out the lights, he lay next to her and she could feel him brightly awake. Still, she said nothing. She waited. At last, in the black air of the bedroom, tiny in the vast blackness of the farmlands, he began to speak.

The Branch

There was a space of speeding down the river before Gary began to understand. The guys must have slowed down. He couldn't hear them. They also must have turned off their lights. Who knew why they'd do that? It was a good party, wasn't it? He couldn't look behind him—there were so many dangerous snags sticking out of the ice—and he didn't want to slow down. But eventually he did slow and turned off his lights too. Radiance rose from the snow, the black trees tangled down, a gust of wind occasionally threw clumps of snow around as if in celebration. He turned his headlights back on and sped up into the river's soft curves with the charm of shadows racing beside him like ghostly animals. Why would he stop? But he did stop, hit a snag, *crack*, went over the nose as if thrown from a horse. His helmet flew off and he landed on a split branch that tore through the armpit of his suit, not touching his skin, but pinning him to the river.

Gary tried to sit up but he was firmly stuck. The branch was a strong, barbed thing, so he couldn't wiggle off, couldn't even unzip his suit because the zipper was jammed. He tried to pull the zipper harder, but he blacked out. Must have hit his head. Came to. Forgot for a bit where he was but realized that his machine was still running, its lights glaring hard on the other side of the splintered tree. His good ol' Doo. It was sitting there idling, waiting for him.

'Patient pony,' he called, snorting out a laugh. 'Come here, patient pony.'

God he sounded stupid. So glad his friends hadn't heard that. Where were they? With a stab of resentment he pictured them back there lighting a bonfire. They were toasting their feet now, popping more tabs, laughing at what a dick he was charging on alone. Just let him go! Let him be the stupid dick. And what if they knew he was at this very moment stuck on a branch and what if he fucking froze to death stuck on a branch? What would they say then? They would be sorry, sure, but at some point one of them would get very drunk and turn to him and say—what kind of loser gets stuck on a branch? Gary looked over at the branch and renewed his efforts to rip himself free. But no, he had a top-notch suit. It wasn't going to happen. No! He began to yell.

When nothing happened some more, he tried to scream but it took too much breath. He was fading out again, and as he did, the branch with its many fingers reached toward him.

'Kismet?' said Gary. He reached over and turned on the bedside lamp. Kismet slowly turned toward him and propped herself up on her elbow. Gary gazed at her in a way he'd never looked at anyone before. The back of her neck prickled. She'd never seen anyone look this scared. He was sweating. Her heart thumped but she met his eyes and gave a shaky nod. Then he told her more, and as he did his face changed, the skin flattening in fear and the space between them dissolving until they were both there, stuck to the branch on the snowy river.

I Refuse You

When Gary came to, there was someone beside him. Jordan. 'It's about time, asshole,' he said. His brain hurt. Gary hadn't heard Jordan's snowmobile approach. Also, Jordan was dressed in his football uniform. Jordan's number was 43 and the number was upside-down.

'Hey, man,' said Gary, 'can you get me off this tree?'

'Not yet,' said Jordan. 'Sorry. I can, like, sing to you.'

'Fuck no!' Gary had to laugh even though he could feel the heat draining from his body. He was starting to shake in great, sickening shudders. But he still had to laugh because Jordan had the world's worst singing voice. It had always been a joke. Sing to him!

'Dost thou refuse me?' Jordan asked in a serious tone.

Gary couldn't process it. Jordan needed to help

him. Jordan always helped old ladies down the church aisle. He volunteered at the dog pound. He read to kindergarten kids. Suspicion jolted Gary. Was there something about Jordan? What did he mean with dost thou refuse me?

'Christ yes, you pussy! I refuse you!' said Gary, his teeth clacking.

'It's okay,' said Jordan. 'I will stay with your unsorry stinking ass until they get here.'

What was with Jordan? Maybe he'd flipped out. Gary tried to say something normal.

'You guys finally caught up with me, huh?'

'Finally,' said Jordan in a tender voice. He bent toward Gary and looked sweetly into his face.

'Dost thou refuse me?'

'Get off me, bitch!' Gary could hardly get the words out. 'Damn, I'm cold.' Something was just not right. 'How come you're not cold, dude?'

'Cause,' said Jordan, 'I don't get cold anymore.'

'Uh, uh, uh,' cried Gary. 'Get me off this tree!'

He started thrashing.

'That's right, keep moving,' said Jordan. 'It'll warm you.'

'How come you're not cold?'

'Like I said.'

Gary looked at Jordan and his head was off. He was

holding his head on his knee like a helmet and the head kept talking.

'Keep moving, dude, or I swear I'm gonna sing!'

'I'm trying. Jesus,' said Gary. 'Hey Jordan! I am having a really bad hallucination. Maybe the coke was cut with something.'

'Yeah. Speed,' Jordan said. 'Oh the irony.'

He laughed a little. His head was back on.

'Thank god,' said Gary. Nothing was real, was it. 'You put your head back.'

'Keep moving or I'll take it off.'

'Oh no, Jesus, no. Don't do that.'

'Dost thou refuse me?'

Jordan was now pissing Gary off. He struggled.

'Shut up. Jesus. I fucking refuse you, man!'

Jordan leaned down again. His eyes were brilliant and cruel.

'Do not refuse me, you piece of moldy shit.'

'Moldy? What the hell, you weird fuck. Get outta my face!'

'Okay,' laughed Jordan. 'I'll get outta your face, man. But I'm coming in the back door.'

'What's that mean?' Gary cried. He bucked maniacally now. He thought he might be making some progress.

'It means you are mine,' said Jordan. 'It means I will never leave you.'

Jordan stood up and finally said, 'I can hear them!' He went up on his toes and loped off.

As always, Jordan was fast and light on his feet, powerful. Gary twisted around to watch Jordan bounding back down the frozen river—on top of the snow. The snow was deep and soft, Gary knew that. But Jordan was traveling along on the surface the way he'd tiptoe into the end zone, like a ballet dancer. Again he had taken off his head and was carrying it against his body like a football. The head turned toward Gary and cried out suddenly as Jordan rounded a corner. 'Touchdown!'

Everything was terribly wrong, and quiet now, and Gary knew that his friends weren't actually coming for him after all so he went to sleep.

Jordan's Fidelity

G ary went on talking to Kismet about what happened after. He'd run track in spring. As he ran, he knew Jordan was running after him. The guy was lost, under the ice, but there he was chasing Gary. Gary won. He looked back after he crossed the finish line. No Jordan. This happened regularly. Gary took third in the state 200 meter.

Gary said he'd never run track again. He got serious and worked beside Diz. When he worked the fields alone, sometimes Jordan appeared, but only as a speck on the horizon. He could deal with that.

Gary wasn't going to play football the following season, but Jaws sat with him and told him he owed it to his teammates, the living and the dead.

Gary said nothing to Jaws and got in his pickup. As

he was driving home, Jordan was hitchhiking on the side of the road.

'You're kidding me,' said Gary. He passed Jordan. Then there he was again, thumb out. Wearily, Gary stopped and opened the window.

'Get in,' he said. 'I don't refuse you anymore.'

Jordan nodded but didn't get in the truck.

'I saw you,' he said.

'Saw me what?' said Gary.

'Take the gun from the safe.'

'I was only fooling around.'

'No you weren't. Look, man,' said Jordan. 'I know you don't like me always having your back. But I do. I love you, man.'

'Yeah, please.'

'And you know, I'll be here on the other side if you off yourself.'

'Oh fuck me,' said Gary. 'Sincerely, fuck you.'

'You might as well play. Let some steam off.'

Then Jordan gave him a double thumbs-up as he walked backward down the steep ditch and disappeared into a culvert. And so Gary played football, sitting beside the two helmets on the bench. He played well. Once, Jordan caught his Hail Mary pass and scored in the last five seconds. Gary couldn't take it. But who was he going to tell? Jaws? Who made him sit beside his friends' helmets? The guidance counselor who was also Mr. Speck? Some shrink? Or Father Flirty? Don't make me laugh.

Things only changed when he made a move he couldn't understand at first. He started dating Kismet. She wasn't the weird girl—he'd always known that. But she really was different.

'I fell for you,' he said, touching her arm. It was a considered touch, mournful, and he told her that Jordan didn't happen by if she was in the room, in the car, at a game, ever. He told Kismet that was why he'd tried to get her to come to all of his games and why Winnie had offered to drive her to every single one. From the way his mother offered to do that so emphatically, Gary was pretty sure that she knew he was not okay.

'Mom kind of knows,' said Gary. 'She knows that something's wrong. She kind of knows I can't shake Jordan.'

He looked at Kismet as from a deep well, and said, 'Tell me what to do.'

Knotty Pine

As Diz rounded the field and began on the last row, he looked over at his neighbor Pavlecky's expanse and was arrested by what he saw. He was surprised because Bill's soybeans were looking more mature than the Spiral soybeans in a neighboring field. Diz and Gusty didn't plant beans because they had to be harvested at the same time as sugar beets. Pavlecky had planted earlier because his fields dried out faster. For about a decade now, Pavlecky had quit plowing and planting in a normal way, which disturbed Diz without his quite knowing why. He had decided the abnormal actions were due to the fact that Pavlecky was descended of old Bohemian stock and sometimes they just did things differently. But the Pavleckys were solid, no mistake. 'Pavleckys get along good with everybody,' people always said. Eric had always looked out for Gary and Gary for Eric. Even after the accident they had stayed best friends. Or seemed like it anyway. From childhood they'd been pals. Caught the bus together. Old John Pavlecky had built a little bus shelter at the end of their road and all the kids had used it. Pavlecky's grandkids used it now.

Diz glimpsed the bus shelter as he trundled down the highway, wings folded on the sprayer. The little bus shelter was painted the same peach color as the Pavlecky farmhouse. This was because Pavlecky's uncles and dad had bought up gallons and gallons of a high-quality paint ordered for some town project and never picked up. Now that color was the house's traditional color. Peach. Diz always looked at the color and said *different*. Which in Tabor meant *bizarre*. To Diz, white was the only color for a house.

In spite of his care, Diz had a tiny bit of pesticide on his overalls again. Besides beets they had planted corn and wheat. His skin itched, too, and it made him think of his ongoing fight with Winnie about paint colors, a fight that faded into their ongoing fight over pest killers, weed killers, and dirt.

The Geist house had been white when his grandparents built it and, even after renovations, white it still was. Paint colors had almost ruined Diz and Winnie's marriage. Winnie called the Pavlecky color jolly and said she meant to paint their own house the same color as the blooms on the old lilac bushes. Diz had reacted, or overreacted, by forbidding her to even consider it.

'Forbid me? You're *forbidding* me?'

Winnie had decided that if Diz wanted white, he would have it inside as well as out. In a single day when Diz was gone, Winnie painted the knotty pine board in the kitchen and the TV room. When Diz came home and saw what she had done, he had raided the fridge, barricaded himself in his knotty pine den, and refused to come out. He had tried to make her promise to stop painting anything, ever. She would not promise.

This was the original sore point. She couldn't change things in the house or in the way he ran the farm. She told him over and over white was blah and the chemicals he used would come back and bite him in the ass. And not only him, but Gary too.

'Just you try growing to the scale we have a contract for without spraying.'

'We can stop growing beets.'

Diz would shut that down. His family had started growing beets by harvesting with horse-drawn wagons and pitchforking them from the earth. He'd walk away.

'Considering your dad bought my family farm at a steal and bulldozed my childhood home, I damn well think you should let me have my way on this,' she'd call after him.

Then he'd get the silent treatment until he couldn't stand it anymore. Eventually they'd start talking, but they never came to an agreement.

Diz put away the equipment and drove to his favorite indoor spot. The interior of the Tabor Bar was knotty pine and in no danger of being painted. It was a mixture of old varnished pine and cheap wood veneer paneling. The scratched booths were just the right size for four men, and they could hear one another even when the place got crowded. The day was too bright. Diz got out of his truck, walked through the plywood door, and was enfolded in the windowless gloom. Pavlecky and Spiral were sitting in their usual booth. Diz raised his chin to greet them, got a Coors, and sat down. Spiral was saying that the land was young when their great-greats had immigrated. Diz nodded.

'The land was never young,' Pavlecky said.

'He's on *this* again,' said Spiral.

'No, I'm not,' said Pavlecky.

Pavlecky had dropped out of high school to farm after Old Pavlecky died. Though Diz had farming in his bones, he had not only finished high school but actually studied at NDSU so he knew what he was doing.

Diz didn't want Pavlecky to start with deploring the destructive nature of plowing and so on—his neighbor would soon get to what chemical bug killers were doing to the chain of life and they would clear out the bar. Diz diverted that predictable thread.

'Remember the stone boat?' said Diz, then stopped himself as the picture of the old barbed-wire fence flashed into his thoughts. That piece of pasture had once belonged to Winnie's mom and dad.

'Stone boat! Why would you say a thing like that?' Spiral asked. He'd hating picking rocks.

'To keep Bill from yakking on about the bug juice and stuff.'

'Splat. Good play. Yeah, I remember the stone boat,' said Spiral.

Pavlecky groaned. They each had a couple of rocky fields by the river, and as teens they had followed a tractor with the tobogganlike stone boat, picking up the rocks they could lift, rolling the big ones onto the wooden drag. Once, Spiral's younger brother drove the tractor and Diz and Spiral told him where to park it, knowing he'd have to back it up, which was near impossible. Another time Spiral rode the stone boat on the way to the corner where they'd made a cage for the rocks. He was on a big boulder and the damn thing had rolled and broke two ribs, nearly killed him. Diz's two older brothers went into the insurance business, so then Diz and Gusty slowly bought out those brothers. They had some good flat cropland, and also those fields like Winnie's, where they'd picked rocks.

Of course that was after Diz's father had picked up—Diz cringed at even thinking the phrase because Winnie went stiff with fury if she heard it—bought, bought, bought Winnie's family farm. At any rate, for a while they took turns with the stone boats and made the kids pick the yearly harvest of rocks turned up by frost. At last Gusty had given up the war with the ancient habits of the earth and turned those fields into pasture.

Diz hid the pastures from his thoughts, suddenly, thinking of them under snow. He hadn't gone down there since the accident. Why would he?

'I'm gonna show you krauts why a bohunk got his crops in the ground early,' said Bill. 'You asked why my fields dried out and I got no standing water.'

'Drain tiles,' said Spiral.

'Hell no,' said Pavlecky.

'Here we go,' said Diz.

They were three beers in and number four was on its way. Pavlecky took three quart-size canning jars from under his bench. He put the jars on the table just as the beers came. There was also a pitcher.

'I ordered it,' said Pavlecky. 'I went and got a jar of dirt from your field and your field and my field.' He pointed at Diz and Spiral.

'Got?' said Spiral.

'Stole,' said Pavlecky.

'Who's drinking the pitcher?'

'I'll get another for the one whose dirt soaks it up first,' said Pavlecky.

He took the caps off the jars of dirt labeled with the men's names. Pavlecky dribbled some beer into each jar. The dirt in Spiral's and Diz's jars was fine and dustlike. When the beer landed it made droplets and rolled across the surface. Pavlecky's dirt was darker and clumpier. The beer soaked right down.

'Put some more in,' said Diz.

The same thing happened. Only now the beer in Diz's and Spiral's jars penetrated a bit. However, their dirt seemed to be making a sort of layer on top and the beer stayed up while Pavlecky's dirt was darkening to the bottom. They watched through the fourth beer and then started drinking from the pitcher.

'So,' said Diz, pushing himself back. 'This is the upshot of all your preaching.'

'My dirt's soil now,' said Pavlecky.

'I lose track of all the shit-ass crazy things you do,' said Spiral. 'What's next?'

'Seagulls,' said Diz. 'He's gonna raise them for their eggs and train 'em to crap on his fields.'

They kept adding drips of beer to the jars of dirt. Now the dirt in two of the jars had formed a kind of seal and there was a layer of beer on top that wasn't absorbed at all, while the other jar was beer mud. Pavlecky nodded at his jar of mud.

'Now that's farming.'

'You got your dirt drunk,' said Spiral.

'Yours is still sober.'

'I'm not,' said Diz. 'The wife ain't gonna like it.'

This wasn't a bar anybody walked to or wanted to get in trouble for visiting, so there was a pot of coffee on a stand. They shot the breeze a while to sober up and then went their separate ways.

Diz came home and told Winnie about what Pavlecky had done with the dirt, how the soil had soaked up the beer, and Winnie said, 'It makes total and complete sense, Diz, I've been saying that for years. That's how—'

'Don't say it. I don't wanna hear how your mom and dad farmed.'

'They were good farmers, Diz.'

'Oh, this old . . . let's not get into it.'

'Just so we're straight, though. They were good farmers. It was Reagan that wiped us out.'

'Let's leave it be.'

'I'd like to see us suddenly get stuck with an immediate 250K payoff.'

'Okay, we been through this a thousand times. Winnie, I'm sorry.'

'Can't I just say Pavlecky isn't wrong?'

'You can say it,' said Diz, losing patience. His eyes went sort of colorless when he was getting mad. Now they went from ice blue to whitish blue. 'You can say it but saying it doesn't make it so.'

Winnie took a deep breath, held it in, breathed slowly out. She said what she said next in a neutral, reasonable way.

'Diz, just listen. You cut down your shelterbelts. Your dirt's blowin' in the wind. Your fields are lifting off. Gusty won't contour-plow those rises so his dirt's running down into the ditch.'

'The river.'

'I'm not wrong.'

'Okay, well, it was old Sport who plowed your dad and mom's homestead under, sweetheart. It wasn't me. I never would of done it. You know that.'

'It's not about the hand-built house.'

'Oh really? Hand-built?'

'You said you were sorry, okay, I'm just . . .'

They rarely got into this old rut anymore, but when

they did Diz knew words wouldn't solve it. Winnie's loss was bigger than words. And unless he stopped this, she would start on weed killers. He walked up to Winnie and put his big hands on her shoulders. She stood unyielding for a moment, then took a few steps toward him and allowed him to capture her. He slowly, tentatively, hugged. She put her arms up, bent awkwardly, her fists between them. They stood there, Diz with loose-limbed warmth and she militantly apart no matter how close he got. She wouldn't let it go.

'You guys keep using paraquat and glyphosate on pigweed,' she whispered. 'Those are neurotoxins.'

He breathed out and squeezed his eyes shut and tried his best to keep his blood from boiling.

'We're really careful.'

'I know what paraquat smells like and it's on you,' she said, pulling away.

She had a sick look on her face.

'Shed those overalls now and get in the shower.'

'Okay, okay.' He'd forgotten, and he knew it was wrong, but you can't be careful every second of your life.

The Postcards

Gary threw the mail on the table and said, 'There's some for you.'

Hugo had sent a few harmless-looking postcards—Aerial View of Williston, Williston at Night, Williston Main Street. Several of each style.

'What's going on?' Gary said.

'Oh, you can read them,' said Kismet. 'He's just being a pal. Probably homesick.'

'Right,' said Gary.

He went out and Kismet read the postcards.

'Haha' meant *I think about you all the time.* 'It's crazy out here' meant *I'm losing my mind I want you so much.* 'At least I've got a roof over my head' meant *Tonight think about the last time we had sex together.* 'The food out here sucks' meant *I will love you until my dying day.* She didn't have a key to the phrases anymore because after memorizing them she had eaten the little piece of paper they were written on. All of the postcards said: Haha, it's crazy out here. At least I've got a roof over my head. The food out here sucks.

She did think of Hugo constantly. But her thoughts were not of their astonishing wedding-morning rendez-vous. What came back to her were the ordinary times. The way he'd noticed that one of her shoelaces was untied as they sat on a park bench. How he'd knelt at her feet and tied her shoelace. A double knot, the kind her mom used to make for safety when Kismet was in kindergarten. After tying her shoe, Hugo sat beside her again without a break in their conversation. And she liked thinking of the time he'd called her 'duckling' in Estonian. The word *pardipoeg,* they both agreed, was an adorable word. At the Skillet, they'd gently mocked Val Kallinor's naming of signature dishes after lines to 'Spirit in the Sky.' His naming became somewhat pardipoeg. Melly's pigtails were pardipoeg. Kismet's knees were pardipoeg. The T-shirt quilt she gave Hugo was completely pardipoeg. Kismet couldn't find much about her life, at the moment, that was pardipoeg. It was pretty much, she thought, holding the postcards, apocalyptic. She thought about her life before marriage, embezzlement, and now the things she'd been told by

Eric and Gary. Tears shot into her eyes because the past with Hugo all seemed pardipoeg now. Through the blur she read the postcards again. The code had sounded romantic when they thought it up. Now she wished they'd added more phrases, even though she'd have had to eat a bigger piece of paper.

Hugo

More to say would have been nice, thought Hugo. He'd entirely forgotten about pardipoeg. His thoughts were more grandiose, heroic. For instance he'd have liked to describe her collarbone, mystical border, or her eyebrows—her highness and her lowness—they were imperious but one she could raise to ineffable effect and the other lower to ridiculous effect. And if she added the dimple, chaos. Ears, don't get me started. Lips, just kill me. He was resolute about not allowing the distractions of her secretive nipples, her dangerous breasts, or anything more to enter his mind, not at work anyway. He might really die. But her hair was allowed. He could think of her hair all he wanted. And her sturdy ankles. And after work he could cry—had he ever seen her ankles in anklets? Had he ever seen her hair in a straight-line wind? What exactly happened when the sun glanced off her ponytail? Had he ever seen her in braids or a demure devastating ballet bun?

Hugo couldn't help himself from considering the situation with Gary, but the more he thought about it, the more surprisingly bearable he found it. He completely forgave himself for selling Gary the *Sextasy* book. Because after all, he knew that what Gary had to learn about sex wasn't taught in a book. It was taught by Ichor and his mushroom soup (ample dash of cayenne) and Bev's face when Ichor kissed her hand. Both of them when Ichor suddenly fell to his knees one summer day, holding out a little moonstone ring (from downtown Tabor), and asked Bev to marry him again in front of their kids. Bev when she toppled him into the wading pool. Ichor when he pulled her in.

But in fact this comfort with his beloved's temporary capture by another man soon evaporated. Hugo moved away from the Bergs into a tilting little rental house with scabrous siding and a sagging porch, moved in with his friends, who were questionable friends. After getting drunk and telling his so-called friends about what had happened with his girlfriend, he learned he was a cuckaholic, a cow-fucking cockwaffle, a wuss, spineless, a flaccid old carrot, a sissyworm, a simpish zero, a bow-wow coward-candyass, unhung. And this was said with menacing affection by Moss, Hermano, and Florida, who'd grown up on America's penis and was called a shellfish sucker, because what else did men have to do in the oil patch except try not to die, collect large paychecks, and call one another names? There were some who added the search for sex to that list, but Hugo's friends were too cynical, blasted, tired, and antisocial to do that.

The Mudlogger

Bizarre accidents occurred around the mudlogger, and over the weeks Hugo's narrow escapes had made him famous. It was unknown whether it was lucky or unlucky to be around him. He drew shit, for sure, but remained unscathed. Anyway, his good luck did not ricochet and turn to bad luck. Nobody had died because of him, or in his direct vicinity. He was considered safe. More than that. The day before yesterday, red-eyed in his mobile lab from staring at readouts forty-eight hours straight, Hugo had hallucinated an immense gas bubble coming uphole. It would have blown the crew to hell or South Dakota, but fortunately Hugo had understood his hallucination was real. The danger was contained. He'd then slept for sixteen hours straight, and he now sat across from Moss at a popular buffet-style restaurant. Their plates were heaped with steak patties, gravy, carrots in chicken grease, chicken, potatoes in chicken grease, three kinds of bread, butter pats, and creamed spinach for the bowels.

'Living in the close conditions of our household,' said Moss, 'it is important to stay regular.'

'Stop,' said Hugo.

Maybe because of his exposure to danger and the society he kept, Hugo had taken on a strange air. There were bits of yellow fuzz in his roan ponytail. His eyes were more perfectly round than before, always open and staring like cartoon eyes. He was pretending to be in his thirties, but his skin was tight and rosy as a child's. Baby Huey was a nickname he'd tried to shed ever since he'd come to the oil patch.

'After we get home, you're gonna slab out in front of the big-screen, aren't you,' he said to Moss. 'You should read this.' He couldn't help himself. He tried to give his friend *Anna Karenina*, but Moss waved it off.

'No thanks, Professor Baby Huey. A horse gets shot in those pages. Besides, I'm getting wasted.'

Moss had been random-tested that same day and felt the odds were now with him. Hugo gave him a look.

'Okay, sure,' he said.

After they got back to their house, they sat on camp chairs in the yard. Moss revealed that he had some medical-grade marijuana from Colorado. Drawn by his infallible nose, Florida soon joined them. The disturbed earth beside the old house was patchy crust. They were on the edge of town and their house was pretty much condemned. But past the yard, a scraped-over parking lot, and a fence line, a dusty sweetness stirred about. Something of the way this used to be. The sun would be there forever and the earth would be an unhappy husk.

'Door to a better world,' said Moss, looking at a city of clouds on the horizon.

'This is the best of all possible worlds,' said Hugo. 'I've checked out a few other worlds, my friend. Turns out, we are in heaven.'

They laughed peacefully in the booming jeroboam of wind and eventually went back inside. Hugo put on his headlamp, crawled under his super-light black down comforter that never showed grease. His mother had sent it to him. Under the comforter, the quilt from Kismet. This was his talisman. It calmed and soothed him to stroke her T-shirts.

At night you could see the methane burning off from outer space, if you were in outer space. Hugo decided to go there again. He was studying astral projection in order to endure his surroundings. He existed in his flesh on the mattress and soon he would also exist on an ancient plane. Hugo began the deep, slow breathing. Release of contact. His inner organs vibrated and he broke out in a clammy sweat as his bodies separated. There was a gentle tugging sensation, then he floated up through the rattly cheapjohn roof. He pulled upward, kicked off, and shot straight through the roof with such speed that his ponytail flagged comically off the back of his neck. He closed his eyes, tucked his face between his outstretched arms, and was carried away on his personal jet stream. In this current, he relaxed, and floated in orbit around the earth.

The uncapped flares of natural gas in western North Dakota burned brightly as Minneapolis and Chicago. He swerved over to the other side of the state and circled the home of Kismet and Gary. The two were sound asleep, no sign of hanky-panky. Hugo lingered over his childhood home. The warm little house with its one vigilant light on in his sisters' bathroom made him so homesick that he decided to kick his way back like a swimmer. Over the oil fields, Hugo flowed down the silver cord that connected his two bodies. With a feeling of slow, sweet pressure, then a tiny jolt, he reinhabited himself. Long long ago, he had been a contented barge of salted butter. He liked himself better then. Now that he was turning into a fox-colored man you could almost call lanky, he despised himself. Everything around him was ugly, destructive, dangerous, and he was part of it. He strolled to the bathroom, drank a quart of water from a plastic Big Gulp cup beside the sink, then carried the refilled cup into the living room, where a couple of random roughnecks were snoring behind the couch.

Moss glanced at him. Hugo could feel himself swimming back into the present through the sticky glue of his past. Sometimes he got stuck there when he looked down at his home and at the Geist homestead. He balanced on the present moment, sat down in the coveted recliner, and along with Moss motionlessly watched a motionless sandy beach.

Eon, the oil company they worked for, now employed him to read computer printouts and analyze samples taken from five, ten, fifteen, twenty thousand feet below the surface of the earth. It had once blown his mind to see into the earth's deep time this way. But with all they were doing to the present he couldn't help trying to imagine a core sample taken millions of years from now. Humanity's trash heaps of concrete, highways, cars, and skyscrapers, under vast pressure, would become some kind of aggregate stone. And all the trees, plywood, crops, animals, and people would be oil. Everything petrochemical would again be petro. It would all start again. He'd begun to hate what they were doing.

Hermano, rough-faced and pike-jawed, joined Florida. And Moss, young, cut, curious, sauntered over as well. The three stood looking down at Hugo.

'You guys gonna talk to me or whale on me?' asked Hugo at last. He really liked these guys. He wanted to be something to them. They were maybe dangerous, even Moss, who said he'd been a philosophy major, but also they seemed to care about him. They treated him like he was their precocious younger idiot brother.

'Talk to you,' said Florida. And so they talked, talked, and talked, about Hugo's girlfriend and the ignominy of Hugo's situation, until Hugo felt himself begin to crack.

'What do you guys want anyway? What will make you go away?' said Hugo.

'If you take possession of yourself,' said Moss. 'We're trying to build you up to be the man you are.'

Hugo stood and beat on his chest. The men looked at him in amusement but started again with their advice. Hugo slumped into his chair.

'How about I challenge Gary to a duel? Will you guys fuck off then?'

'Right on!' said Florida. 'Make it a cage fight, no?'

'There are rules to a duel,' said Hugo. 'You allow

your opponent to choose the weapon. Then you meet on a field of honor. You draw lots.'

'Lots of what?' asked Hermano.

'Never mind. You flip a coin to see who goes first.'

'Goes,' said Florida. 'Goes as in uses the weapon? That's loser shit. If it's a lethal weapon you get killed.'

'That's the point of a duel,' said Hugo, in a hushed tone. 'One man dies.'

'Excuse me, hero of the republic. I too have an appointment with destiny,' said Moss, meandering off toward his stash.

There was a beat of silence and Hugo got up to leave, saying in a stern voice, 'The stakes are high in a duel.'

'Faded as fuck already,' said Hermano, nodding toward Moss.

Hugo kept ambling backward, talking.

'One man dies, yes, if you choose pistols, or maybe not if you fight with rapiers. I mean swords,' he added swiftly, seeing from Florida's and Hermano's faces where their minds were going.

'I'm beginning to feel a tad queasy,' said Hugo, continuing in reverse motion. Once he was back in his bunk, he closed his eyes and thought about how he was helpless in the tractor beam of love. He didn't mind it. The other day he'd been told that his credentials were being checked. He would definitely get sacked. It was time for him to slide back into Kismet's magnetic current, not just on the astral plane, but for real.

The heat unleashed itself. The wind kicked up a steady stream of grit. Hugo told everyone there was a family emergency, left a forwarding address with the office, packed his meager belongings into his car, and made sure he knew how to access his bank account from home. He tried to drive away, but his car would not start. Moss was off, so Hugo asked him to come take a look. Moss, who had all sorts of work-arounds for car problems, tried to start the car every way he knew. None of his tricks worked. Hugo went to bed with all his stuff still packed and no clue what to do next.

The next morning, he went out to try to start the car again, but the car was gone. Everything he'd packed in it was neatly piled where the 4Runner had been parked. So it didn't seem the car had been stolen.

'Where did you get this car?' asked Florida, who'd come out to say goodbye. Florida had tried to help Moss the night before.

'From a guy.'

'Where'd he get it from?'

'I don't know.'

'Did you get a title, or anything that said, say, there were no liens against it?'

'Liens?'

'Like, somebody else had a hold on your car until you pay your debt.'

'No,' said Hugo.

'And did your guy say where he'd acquired this car?'

'Northland, used, I think he said. Fargo.'

'Oh well, that's it,' said Florida, raising his arm and dropping it against his leg. 'Last night, that was a remote killswitch, my friend. Someone just got around to using it. Your car has been repoed.'

Florida walked back into the house and Hugo stood there staring at the pile of his possessions.

Oafish Words

Kismet opened her phone and wandered outside, turning toward the energy beams of cell towers. At the edge of the shelterbelt, a rogue telecommunication appeared on her phone screen. It was from Hugo.

Storybook, I have returned.

Kismet's heart squeezed shut. He had used the qwerty numbers on his phone to poke out the message. She bent over, thrilled by the sickness and dizziness.

The moon is thin tonight, she wrote. *Park in the ditch. Walk around the outbuildings and enter the shelterbelt. I'll be on the western edge at 2 a.m.*

After she sent this message, Kismet returned to the yard and opened the screen door that Diz had hung so she could enter and exit her garden plot. She sat on the edge of a raised bed and weeded, stopping from time to time to check on the horizon. Her plants were thick and happy. She picked one of the marigolds she'd planted around the tomatoes and crushed the flower, breathing in the sharp scent, rubbing the brilliant petals along her throat. There was something wrong. Her basil was coming up in a crowded line and she thinned the minute plants. Something didn't feel right. She refastened an exuberant tomato plant to its stake. Hugo. She dropped the marigold and frowned across the fields.

Meeting him in secret was such an effort. Maybe feeling sick and dizzy was actually dismay. Hugo totally disregarded her situation. She began to doubt that seeing him was even worth it. Although she loved him, sure, and that didn't feel wrong to her, and maybe Gary was even aware, it would shock Diz and Winnie. She hadn't gotten very far in attempting to leave Gary. It had been easy to get married, because Winnie made the arrangements. Now that Kismet herself had to make all the arrangements, she was finding it very difficult to get divorced. The main thing was that Gary now began to shake when she talked about leaving, and the way he begged her to stay was wrenching. She would have to really harden herself. And now Hugo was making more trouble for her. He had no idea how difficult it was to leave someone who desperately needs you. She also knew by instinct how quickly intense need can turn to rage. She had seen Gary overwhelmed by anger and he'd scared her.

Still, that night she slipped out of bed and down the stairs. There was enough wind so her passage through the house was covered by its low rush and rill. She was wearing her baggy pink cotton pajamas, and she wrapped a knitted afghan around her shoulders. Kismet hooked a couple beers from the fridge, slung them in a scarf she pulled from a hook by the door. She stuck her feet into her yard boots and eased out into the yard. The moon was high, far away, just the clipping of a silver nail. In the heavens a river of concentrated gray cloud moved in a swift flow. Kismet trod through wet grass, slipped along the trail to the western edge with the large cottonwood. In the mild ticking of its leaves she sat to wait.

Not long, and Hugo was beside her, calling her his Storybook. He was skinny. She leaned against him and he wasn't warm anymore. They popped their beers and it felt strange between them. They made the mistake of trying to figure things out and talk about the murky future.

'Why?' asked Kismet. 'How?'

'I am rich,' said Hugo. 'I have twelve thousand dollars.'

'I don't need you to be rich.'

'But it would help,' said Hugo. 'Anyway, I'm only sort of rich, and I lost my car. I'm using my mom's car. And I knew you'd say that. It doesn't matter. Now is our time, my black ribbon, our time.'

'So I should just leave him the way he is?'

'Him?'

Gary had not been discussable before. But after all, she'd been married to Gary for a while now. The truth of that stabbed Hugo hard.

'I suppose you're gonna tell me you love him.'

It was too dark to see her face well, but she made a sound of surprise. He tried to stroke her hair, but Kismet leaned away and gave the last of her beer to the cottonwood. They crushed their cans and curled against the root flare of the great tree. A flood of clear energy coursed in darkness up and down beneath the bark. For a while they breathed in unison and everything was better. Then their thoughts spilled over and they began to argue. It was the first argument they'd ever had but it felt good in a way, like they'd been arguing all their lives.

'I'm just saying that I don't know.'

'And I'm just asking what you do know, I mean, if you know anything.'

'Know, what do I know, you ask if I know anything. Oafish words,' she said, and flung a crushed can at nothing.

Resentment flooded Hugo and she just kept on talking.

'I'm worried about my mom, okay, and I'm worried about Gary's mom, okay, and we both know there's something wrong with Gary and I'm just not . . .'

'Sure? Sure you love him or sure you don't love him?'

Hugo's tone was heated and he felt deliciously mean. He really couldn't help himself, could he, having lived in a refrigerator box and then in a mold-eaten shack in tough company, and at last having caught humiliating and hair-raising rides across North Dakota to get back to her and all she wanted to do was go blah blah blah about Gary. He said all of this, heard himself saying it with horror, tried to hold back and could not hold back. After he finally stopped himself, they were quiet, groping for words, unsure if they wanted to keep fighting after all.

'What's the right thing? What's the right thing to do?'

Kismet sounded like she really wanted to know, so he said that she had only to say the word and he would steal her.

'I can get out of here myself,' said Kismet. 'I don't need you to steal me away. You're talking like you're some kind of knight or hero.'

'I am a hero.'

He said this in a wounded, clogged voice and knew he sounded like a child.

'Well. You came back. Are you off work or something?'

'I quit. I tapped out. Or came to my senses,' he said. 'It's batshit out there. I don't know why you feel sorry for Gary.'

'Uh, because he's Gary?'

'So he's his own punishment, that's on him. Where does that leave me? I'm the one who almost got killed every day.'

'I don't need another guy whose feelings I have to always worry about. I'm not equipped.'

Hugo plunged into a desolate silence.

'Brutal,' he managed to say, then a sob built up in him and he tried to turn his back on her, but she was the one crying now. Possessed by grief, they threw themselves blindly at each other and banged skulls.

'Oh my god.'

'Uhhh, holy shit.'

They lay on their stomachs in the crushed grass, cradling their heads.

'I'm seeing little flashing dots,' said Kismet.

'I'm seeing how unreasonable you are.'

They turned over and tried to stop themselves from screaming with the joy of their sudden alert electricity.

'So, what they call make-up sex. It's real.'

'Yeah, but not now. It's all too much.'

'Agreed. Let's just hold hands and look at the stars.'

So they lay along the tree, the way they had in the back of the bookstore, holding hands, and were at peace. All of a sudden it was morning and they woke at the sound of someone calling in the yard, *Yoo-hoo*. It was Winnie, popping over for her morning coffee.

'Oh dear, we're caught,' said Hugo with a hopeful moan.

'Just drive off. She won't notice,' said Kismet, dusting off her pajamas and walking away.

Ephemera

The finish had worn off Bev's store key. She always found it immediately among the many on her ring. Whenever Bev stepped into her bookstore she paused in the scent of old books—a mellow dusky vanilla. To her, comfort. The humid breath of snake plants in the window had also collected and was strongest at that morning moment when she stepped through the door. She supplied her store from estate sales, old barns of books, library deaccessions, pallets of books she could pick from in the Cities, and books bought from her customers. Her store was overstuffed, as were all stores full of used books. It had to be, because she made as little as a quarter on some paperbacks and at best a few dollars on hardcovers. Selling the older, unusual, rare, often regional books kept her going. She and Hugo sold them

online and split the profits. Hugo had set up her opera-
tion and, now that he was back, he kept things running.
What a relief. She had burst into tears when he dragged
himself to the door, ravenous, gaunt, haggard, actually
looking even older than the age he was trying for. He'd
cried too. Now she felt peace bloom over her working
day. She wrote, 'What a Relief' on a Post-it and stuck
it to one side of her computer screen so that she could
take a deep breath and sigh every time she saw it.

One of the best things about selling old books was
going through them before they went onto the
shelves. She tried not to buy marked-up or under-
lined books, but there were other ways books were
personalized. People kept or left things in books—
quotes, clippings, often about the author, letters
that arrived while they were reading the book, bills
they didn't want to pay, foil gum wrappers, book-
marks from now-closed bookstores, funny drawings from their children, dry autumn leaves, grocery
lists, complaints. She stored these scraps in a manila
envelope marked Ephemera. From another time, another place, the bits had come into her hands. Some
were personal. A bookmark made from dried yarrow flowers arranged between pieces of clear packing
tape had kept the reader's place in *Rosemary's Baby*.

Later, when she looked it up, she found that yarrow was a banishing herb against evil. In a copy of *The Aspern Papers*, she'd found a lock of dark brown hair. A torn envelope printed with the words *Let me go*, hundreds of times, in tiny letters. She'd left the found words *I have never felt such bliss* in yet another book, a very dry study on the properties of land snails. But she wrote the words *I have never felt such bliss* on a bookmark from Books West, in Kalispell, Montana. She slipped it into her envelope and remembered when she and Ichor had been there, buying books on their mountain honeymoon, swimming in glacial lakes, so long ago.

The Mousetrap

C rystal brought in the mail and with sinking spirits opened the invoice from Perfect Advantage. She was going to file it without looking at the numbers, but just to depress herself more she examined the piece of paper. She read it up and down, back and forth, and then she read it again and again. There was no doubt. A large final payment had been made and there were wonderful zeros after the amount owed line. She jumped up and walked quickly out the door.

'**Holy fucking** shit,' cried Jeniver, throwing down the invoice. 'You know I can't touch this, right?'

Crystal snatched up the statement in delirious excitement. 'You never saw this,' she whispered. 'I never showed it to you. It's going back in my purse right now and we are going out for seafood.'

'Are you crazy? This is North Dakota,' said Jeniver, tapping her files into place and setting them aside. 'Steak. Rare.'

She picked up her bag, grinned savagely, and rattled her keys.

At Pookie's Valley Steakhouse, they ordered the works and a bottle of wine. Crystal talked more than she'd talked since the wedding and at some point Jeniver went silent and started glaring from under her roan eyebrows. What Crystal was saying infuriated and disgusted her.

'I'm sooo sad.' Jeniver played a tiny violin on her bicep.

Crystal gulped her wine. Still talking too fast. 'But Martin's doing something to pay me back. Should I—'

'Should you what? If you go back to him, I am charging you my actual rate.'

'There's no mortgage!'

Jeniver leaned toward her, eyes darting right and left.

'Shut your mouth, Crystal. Are you bat-ass nuts? If they knew he paid off your mortgage. . . .'

Crystal clapped her hand over her mouth. 'All right, all right. Too much vino. Here.' She poured half of her third glass into Jeniver's third empty glass.

'That's more like it,' said Jeniver. 'Now zip it. Martin's a goddamn carny and he's taking you on another carnival ride. Yeah. The Mousetrap.'

'Okay okay,' said Crystal. 'Changing subject.'

She switched her pointer finger back and forth between the two of them. 'Attorney-client secret, right?'

'Into the vault,' said Jeniver.

'I have to get Kismet out of there. She had to drive their antique tractor into town a couple months ago. They wouldn't give her a ride. Wouldn't let her borrow a car. Of course, now Gary drives her in from time to time. But what I'm saying is that they keep real close tabs on her.'

Jeniver reared back. Wrinkled her nose in outrage. Shook her head with a disgusted frown, leaned forward, and mimicked pounding the table.

'Not. Acceptable.'

'She made a mistake with that boy. Worst of all, I let it happen. Not acceptable.'

Crystal tapped her chest.

'Ah hell. You're hard on yourself like any mom. I mean Kismet does have a few shreds of common sense. I suppose she made a big deal of her eternal love for loverboy.'

'Well, yes. I should've locked her in her room.'

'You missed your chance. So now we have to strategize. Has she let you in on how he's treating her?'

502 · LOUISE ERDRICH

'No.'

'No? For godsakes gain her trust, Crystal! Be the mom! Force her to confide in you the way I do with Stockton, who hates me.'

They paused, meditatively, and tore into the deep-fried mushrooms when they came.

'Men. Why do we let them tie us in knots?'

'Us?' said Jeniver. 'Do not count me among the us you speak of.' She waved her index finger with its gleaming maroon nail. 'My husband knows he's got gold. So he'd better treat me like a goddamn empress.'

'Oh, no question, without a doubt,' said Crystal.

She looked down at the tabletop and nodded, trying to think of how to change the subject. Both women knew that wasn't true.

'Enough about men, wait, not enough. This FBI guy is kind of, I don't know.'

'Interested in you?'

'Maybe.'

'Or maybe he's trying to trap you into ratting out Martin.'

'Probably.'

'See? That's why you can't say anything about the you-know.'

'The mortgage.'

Jeniver threw her hands out and looked at the ceiling.

'Again, shut up, Crystal. I know the guy you're talking about, your day tail in the white car. He's not bad-looking, but he's a career FBI and they don't make dumbass moves. Usually.'

'I'm having a crisis.'

'You sure are. I know everything about sex. You hit forty and it's a going-out-of-business sale.'

'Me?'

'Yeah, it's hormonal. You're slashing prices. Lowering your standards. Everything must go.'

Crystal gave an exaggerated wince. 'Like my standards were so high. Out-of-work actor, embezzler, and . . .' But she hadn't told a soul that Martin was the Cutie Pie Bandit.

'Yeah, and you have sympathy? It's just hormonal, like I said.'

'Well. Huh, you might have something there,' Crystal said. 'Listen, we have to strategize. . . .'

The Apocalypse Book Club

At 5 p.m. on a mild Thursday afternoon, cars entered the Geists' circular driveway and parked on the edges all around the tarred surface. As always, women emerged, bearing covered pans, squinting in the unfiltered light. The sun-saturated wind was intense and the heat whipped each guest toward the front door. As they paused beneath the peaked entryway, shaded by a small portico, Winnie greeted each woman. She guided them into her air-conditioned living room and gestured past the dog-hair-free couches toward the dining table, an oval with all of its leaves in use, polished by Kismet to a sullen shine. Mary Sotovine, rosy and glowing, extended her plump palms and said, 'Look at your house, it's spotless!'

Kismet rubbed her chapped hands and looked critically at her work. The deep cleaning she had done instead of honeymooning had made it possible to keep up. Winnie had worked alongside her, but Kismet had had to be quite strict to keep her on task. She rubbed a smear off the glass coffee table. Jeniver, Stockton, and Crystal entered. Kismet walked into her mother's arms.

'We're taking you back after this,' said Crystal. 'No argument. Just do what we say.'

Kismet gripped her mother hard, squeezed her eyes shut. Such a wave of happiness poured through her that she started to shake. Stockton pulled Kismet to the dining room table and got her busy pouring wine and lemonade, arranging bowls of chips and pans of three-layer dip. Jeniver started passing food around, chatting, obscuring any questions that the other women might have had about whether Crystal, since the loss of the church renovation fund, was to be included. Crystal had skipped three meetings hoping things would blow over. But no.

'Crystal! What are you doing here?' Karleen asked.

There was a moment of social paralysis. Karleen cocked her head to the side as if puzzled and waited for an answer.

As though electrified by the sight of Karleen, Winnie barreled toward her with a platter of bruschetta. Everyone filled a plate with snacks and sat down. Kismet passed out more lemonade and wine and then sat next to her mother. She had poured herself a paper cup of wine, hoping to calm and fortify herself for whatever was in store. Winnie called the meeting to order, welcomed everyone, applauded their new members, Kismet and Stockton. Winnie went down the checklist and called out names. Nearly everyone was present, as was to be expected since nobody had seen the inside of Winnie's house for over a year. Bev held up *The Road*, chosen by the White twins.

Karleen Krankheit raised her hand. 'I have a question.'

Bev put her fingers on her eyebrows and shook her head.

'I am sure,' muttered Jeniver.

'My question is, are we just going to ignore things?'

'Things? What things?' asked Jeniver.

'You know very well, and so does Crystal. Especially Crystal. Renovation fund, anybody? Who gave? Or have you forgotten?'

'Everybody gave,' said Jeniver. 'Including Crystal.'

Karleen looked around the room, attempting to fix each of the other women with a probing stare. Their eyes slid away from hers to shoot glances at one another. Crystal had roofed her own home and ate weeds, but she was also loved. If she was still here, she wasn't in league with her husband. Kismet sank back into the couch she'd vacuumed, and tried not to hyperventilate. Her mother was still on the edge of her cushion.

'All right, Karleen,' said Jeniver. 'Let's address "things." As Crystal's lawyer . . .'

Jeniver looked around the room and everyone returned her glance.

'I am going to tell you, as Crystal's lawyer, and I am staking my reputation here, that Crystal not only had nothing to do with Martin's theft, but that he included her in his malfeasance. He stole from her too.'

Tiny Johnson, ample and kind, leaned over and patted Crystal's hand.

'Not so fast,' said Karleen. 'He could have stolen from her just to cover up their crime!'

'Oh, for cripes all sake, Karleen,' said Winnie. 'Cripes all sake,' she said again, because she liked the sound of it. 'You sure have an imagination.'

The way Winnie said it, rolling her eyes and dropping her mouth open like a kindergartener, changed the room's vibe. Someone laughed. Winnie's eyes brightened. Her bronze topknot shone with sparkle spray. She was wearing a fuchsia crocheted batwing sweater over a black tank top, black leggings. Her feet were bare, curled in the cool acrylic of the fake sheepskin rug, which was cast over the carpet to be seen beneath the glass coffee table. She could see her toes through the glass top of the coffee table. She'd painted her nails the pale lavender she was hoping to paint the living room walls. Once she began to laugh, the awkwardness disappeared and others laughed along with her. Winnie was a little woozy, with a head start on the wine, and she'd had to drug Poots and Jester with her own Xanax. They were laid out in her bedroom, on their dog pillows, limp and drooling, with the big-screen TV playing a special doggie-soother DVD of classical melodies. What would Karleen say to dog drugging? Winnie was enjoying herself and had no intention of letting Karleen spoil it.

'Everybody's in the same boat,' said Winnie. 'We all gave money. Our money's hijacked. But Crystal didn't do it.'

She passed a pan of Chex Mix down the couch. A general hubbub followed. Everyone dragged out their copy of *The Road*. But the first order of business would still be the problem of Martin.

'So, Martin Poe. Did you, Crystal, or anybody else, notice any warning signs?' Jeniver asked.

She had cleared the question with Crystal before she asked it. Winnie gestured to Kismet and Stockton to go around the room and offer more wine.

'Ichor noticed something,' Bev said. She'd agreed to throw out a diversionary answer. 'And so did Hugo.' She watched Kismet closely, trying to intuit Kismet's level of response to the mention of Hugo. Kismet ducked her head, but it was impossible to know what that meant. The reference to Bev's husband was unexpected. Ichor was rarely discussed—as a problem. More often, his recipes were shared. Martin had been one of Ichor's massage clients.

'I might be violating patient confidentiality, but Martin's muscles were tight as bowstrings. Direct quote. And this was worrisome to Ichor. He noticed about two weeks before Martin disappeared.'

'Tense? He was the one who was tense?' cried Karleen.

'It's not about feeling sorry for Martin,' said Bev. 'It goes to the fact that Martin disappearing wasn't something else, like a kidnapping. He was worried about something, probably the money.'

'Kidnapping. Never thought of that,' said Winnie. Though in fact she knew when it came to kidnapping, she'd been skating the edge with Kismet. She resolved to let her use the car even more than she'd already agreed.

Tight as bowstrings, thought Crystal. But she couldn't remember a time when he hadn't been practically vibrating with tension. Especially before a performance.

'It's an into-thin-air disappearance,' said Jeniver. 'Nobody saw him drive away, nobody knows how he left or has the slightest idea where he is. He hasn't been spotted at a gas station or a truck stop. Anywhere.'

Kismet sipped her warm, paper-tasting wine. She had read *The Road*. Now she was immersed in *Anna Karenina* and was surprised by how much of the book was about farming. She read those parts over and over. With a start, she realized the women were talking about her father. It was odd to listen to everybody try to figure him out. There had been sightings the day before he vanished. It was strange to hear how he'd been glimpsed at the drugstore, at the Skillet, at the fitness center. All over town! Yet she couldn't remember seeing him at all. He hadn't given her a wink, a secret sign, before he vanished. But she hadn't sought him out that day, hadn't paid him much attention. Their questions pierced her. How could he be so visible, then so invisible? Had he ever even cared about her?

Crystal's thoughts mirrored Kismet's. She was ashamed to say that she could not remember when she'd last seen him. There hadn't been a time she suspected that Martin was leaving. They hadn't said goodbye. One thing was true. That he'd been plotting this for quite a while. That he'd become interesting only after he left them was another level of affront. Most of all, he didn't care about either one of them, and it hurt to hear him discussed so casually. She stared at the plate on her knees.

'If anyone sees something, anything, that reminds them of Martin, or a person who looks like Martin, call me immediately,' said Jeniver. 'He needs to be found, for his own good as well as Crystal and Kismet's.'

'And the town's sake!' cried Karleen furiously, but nobody reacted.

'Can we talk about Gusty now?' asked Darva, with a tempestuous shake of her shaggy new haircut. 'I want to bring it up in a positive way. Progress was made. We have of course dealt with his hernia, and now his piles have subsided.'

'Praise be given,' said Karleen, in her indomitable way, 'but let's stick with Martin.'

Darva looked around, her fierce black eyebrows raised. Those eyebrows were short, like little mustaches. 'I amended Gusty's diet and I just want to thank everybody in this room for the help, and Crystal especially for leaving that bag of greens on my front porch.'

'Noted and appreciated,' said Tory White. 'Now. Who's going to kick off the book discussion?'

Karleen opened her mouth, but got shushed by Tania.

'I was just *taken* with this book,' said Tory White. 'I pictured *The Road* as I-29 of course, then 75 all the way up to Winnipeg. Pictured us after the catastrophe.'

'Which catastrophe?' asked several women at once.

There followed a pleasurable babble containing many theories: nuclear winter, the Rapture, aliens, the flu, ozone holes, this thing about the climate, which split members off in subarguments, China conquers us, Russia conquers us, or maybe . . . Tania White waited patiently so that her theory was the last. She stood up and with a smile of satisfaction unrolled a chart of the Yellowstone volcano, the probable epicenter of destruction, as well as the outlying circles of poisonous gas and falling ash.

'So we have here the super-volcano. You see the red circle? Kill zone. Right here, this is us. In the pink zone. We're in the primary ash zone. The secondary ash zone is this peach circle from Lake Superior over to California, taking in the Texas Panhandle. If this volcano erupted, and I guess it's overdue, we get covered in volcano ash. It would be another ice age. Everything in the Upper Midwest would die—just like in the book—only a few random apples left—just like in the book,' said Tania. She paused for maximum effect and tag-teamed Tory, who rose and spoke. 'This is why we wanted to bring it to the club. This book is a very realistic look at the aftermath of the Yellowstone super-volcano.'

'I've read where an asteroid is more likely to hit,' said Mary Sotovine.

'You guys are way off the mark,' said Winnie, pointing out the window, at the fields. 'Look. There's your answer.'

The women leaned sideways or forward to stare out the picture window and saw that, as usual, the wind was sending up curls of earth dust and dust devils were crisscrossing the fields.

'I don't get it,' said Tory.

Across the horizon a band of gray dust wavered. The sun would go down in a bloody stew. Every night was like the end of the world. It was gorgeous!

'What *is* going to happen?' said Mrs. Flossom, excitedly. 'What can we expect?'

Jeniver went over to the table and opened another bottle of white and one of red. Even Karleen had a few sips.

'Don't you see?' said Winnie. 'Every time you look out the window there's dust rising up. That's dirt. We are losing our dirt. No dirt, no food.'

'Okay,' said Karleen, eyes glittering. 'Round that out for us.'

'No dirt, no food, no life. General starvation. My

parents' fields were surrounded by shelterbelts and they left stubble in their fields the way Pavlecky does now. They planted cover crops, but . . . sorry . . . I did some historic reading before Diz and I went to Russia years ago and it curdled my bones. When Stalin made the little farms into humungous collective farms . . .'

'Like the sugar beet collective?' someone asked.

'That's a voluntary collective and a functional one,' said Winnie, with a hint of scorn. 'In Russia it was total and complete retooling where the Soviets kicked out . . . well, starved and murdered, all the landowners and farmers who were growing the wheat and turnips and food crops. Then they tried to organize giant farms, but nobody knew how to farm because most of the farmers-in-charge were dead! It was like when Stalin killed the doctors in Moscow, then he dies because there's nobody to save him!'

'Let's get back to—' Bev started.

Winnie blew right past her. 'Anyway, let's say present practices continue in our case. No dirt. Nothing to eat.'

'Except people,' said Jeniver with a stern, conclusive nod all around, as if they were on *The Road* or on a lifeboat, ready to draw lots. Karleen shrank back. Jeniver's brown hair, held on top of her head by a small golden sword, flashed in the bloody sunset light.

'Correct,' said Winnie, though Jeniver had stolen her punch line. Winnie nodded her head and looked down into her fuchsia lap. 'Starving, that's a bad way to go. You don't just fade out. Extremely painful, and the cravings! One of the worst . . .'

'Not as bad as—' Mary Sotovine began like a pitcher winding up.

'Let's not go there,' Darva cut in.

Once Mary and Darva began competing over worst-case ways to perish, the book club usually spiraled into ghoulish hysteria. Mary's glowing round face flattened in disappointment.

'How about getting pickled?' Jeniver wondered.

'The worst!' Mary shuddered in appreciation.

The other women looked at Jeniver and she held out her empty wineglass.

'Oh, pickled!' The general mood shifted.

'Wasn't that last line of the book really beautiful?' said Tiny Johnson, and the book discussion was soon complete, except that suddenly Bev stood up.

'Listen,' she said. 'While we've been talking about the end of the world like we're looking forward to it, I've been thinking how the world as we know, used to know, it really is ending. I thought of what the world was like even when I was a kid, how it was more . . . it was more full.'

'Last call,' said Tiny. 'I'm bringing out the ice cream.'

'Don't you remember?' Bev went on. 'How there used to be meadowlarks?' She looked around. 'C'mon, when's the last time you heard a meadowlark? You know, our state bird. When I was growing up they were everywhere, in all the ditches, as soon as you got to the edge of town they started. Am I right?'

'She's right,' said Mary Sotovine. 'I'm older, so ten years before Bev remembers, they were in the ditches, as soon as you got to the edge of town. You'd hear them all the time.'

'She's right,' said Winnie. 'There used to be flocks of those cedar birds, cedar waxwings, and bluebirds, even. And bugs, which they ate. Grasshoppers. Mayflies when you went out to the lakes. Now you don't even see grasshoppers. And there's only a mayfly or two. It's the pesticides.'

All of the women suddenly began to talk.

'Do you notice how you look at the grille of your car and there's no bugs? No bugs hit your windshield? And moths. How they used to swirl in the streetlamps?'

'They did. Like snow.'

'And how when it rained the frogs came out and they were everywhere and the grass was thick with frogs?'

'Toads. You could always go out and pick up a toad.'

'Now it's surprising. A toad! It's special!'

'And there were nighthawks, lots of nighthawks swerving around, after the mosquitoes. And bats everywhere and how we used to scream if they dived at us. And flocks of pigeons on the grain elevators.'

'What does it mean that prairie falcons are living in town?' asked Stockton.

Everyone fell silent.

'It means there's less to eat in the country,' said Winnie.

Kismet waved her hand. Winnie recognized her with a nod and called out, 'Kismet has something to say!'

Kismet looked at her mother and said, 'I don't think this book is about the end of the world. That's just the setting, to show what happens between people in extreme situations. The end is about consolation. The father goes to the end of the earth for his son, then dies, satisfied. I mean, it's a really sentimental book. McCarthy's not afraid of that. And it's a brutal adventure book—exciting when they find the food cache, and then there's that cannibal army.'

Jeniver stood up and spoke with urgency. 'This book is about what's most important. You know, this kind of love between a parent and a child.'

Crystal put her arm around her daughter's shoulders, and Kismet leaned on her mother. Winnie saw that Kismet would leave. She thought of Gary and started to cry, wondering how she could possibly save him. All of a sudden she had a thought that dried her tears right up. She'd searched for a way to thank Gary's angel. Well, Kismet was his angel. Oh no! Oh yes! Again she wept. Bev thought about how Hugo had escaped that terrifying pre-apocalyptic landscape, and she also started to cry. Then she thought of Gerta and Trudy, caught by the police last Halloween with a number ten can of creamed corn and jumper cables. They'd been planning to corn cars and jump out of bushes to pinch people with the jumper cables. Mary Sotovine was moved to tears at the thought of the days when she'd see bluebirds in a strip of grassland, now planted in soybeans. Jeniver looked at Stockton, but it was getting damp around them so they air-hugged across the carpet.

Winnie said in a sudden rush, 'Why can't we speak from the heart? That is all I want anymore. For someone to speak to me from the heart.' She vowed that if Kismet spoke she'd thank her profusely.

Everything ceased.

'All right,' Kismet said. 'You have to let me go.'

At the Edge

While Crystal and Jeniver cleaned the kitchen, Stockton went over to the new house with Kismet and together they packed her things. Kismet's wedding dress was in a hanger bag. Stockton brought it outside with other bags of Kismet's things. She put them down and opened the trunk of the car.

Winnie was in the living room making a brave show of wiping off the glass coffee table, plumping couch pillows, making small adjustments to chairs. She stood up, looked out the window, and went to the front door.

'What are you doing?' she called out. Her thoughts whirled because she knew. And she wasn't ready.

'Taking Kismet's things back to Crystal's,' said Stockton, continuing to pack the trunk. Kismet came out lugging her giant black suitcase.

Winnie walked out to the car. She had controlled her weeping but now tears pushed up behind her eyes. 'You don't have to take a big suitcase for an overnight at your mom's house.'

Kismet put the suitcase down with the softest thud possible.

'Everything I brought is in here, Winnie,' she said, giving Winnie a loose hug. 'You'll be all right now, Winnie. You're going to be okay!'

Winnie held up her hands. 'Wait! Wait!'

Jeniver came out and gave the keys to Stockton. 'Kismet is going home now,' said Jeniver with a look that was severe but not unkind, holding Winnie's gaze.

'Home? This, this, this is her home!' Winnie voice rose and her hands began to clutch. 'Listen, Jeniver, she's married, she actually is happy, she has a garden, she's so good for Gary. And you know, we really need Kismet. Diz loves and adores her and so do I, really I love her. We'll do whatever she needs.'

'She needs to leave,' said Jeniver.

Suddenly Winnie's tone shifted, her voice became strained, and she wrenched back from Jeniver. She wanted to thank Gary's angel by opening her arms but instead her fingers clutched.

'Then, then,' said Winnie in a lost tone, 'I'll sue.'

'I'll be in my office,' said Jeniver, lowering her voice

and looking at Winnie with polite regard, 'and I'll be sure to take your call.'

'I will call.' Winnie's chin jutted but her eyes were shining with tears now as Jeniver walked to the door.

'Where's . . ,' said Jeniver, turning in the doorway. 'Oh, Kismet . . .'

Kismet came around the car to Winnie. 'You wanted me to speak from the heart.'

'I didn't think you'd go,' Winnie gasped, eyes closed.

'It will be okay,' said Kismet. 'I just want to say take care of the garden. It's yours now.'

Winnie put her hands up to her face and gave a child's sob. Then she righted herself, pulled her dignity around her, and pressed her hands to her worn face.

'Thank you,' she said with a decisive nod.

Later, hoping to get a call from Kismet, she said to Gary and Diz, when they asked where Kismet was, only, 'She's at her mom's. I'll have to make those breakfasts tomorrow morning.'

Martin

Martin was riding his bicycle along Highway 2, reveling in the air and, after the flat grounds of the air force base, appreciating the occasional prairie pothole shining deep blue along the road. He'd become blond and blond-bearded, even more nondescript. At last he stopped at a rest area. The shelter was a former ferryboat that had been hauled there and refurbished into a pleasantly windowed lounge with clean bathrooms tiled in red and white. Martin had scouted this rest stop before. He parked his bicycle in thick brush overlooking a tiny slough and went into the bathroom, where he fitted a plastic carry bag into his bike helmet and made himself an instant basin. He took a leisurely dab bath in a stall.

Martin had mailed most of the cash to mailboxes he

had set up in towns along or just off Highway 2, running along the northern tier of North Dakota and Montana. There was quite a lot in Havre and some in Whitefish. Not that robbing banks was big business the way he did it. The robberies had simply been the highest use of his talents, the greatest performances of his career. He'd known all along that tellers didn't keep much available money. He hadn't done it for the money. The last of the cash he'd robbed was in Idaho, where he also planned to visit a religious group. He planned to join this cult and thus gain entry to its mysteries. He would take notes and when he left the cult—or rather, if he wanted to and was able to leave the cult—he'd write a play about his experience. He would remain ever elusive. Most important, he'd paid off the mortgage on Crystal's house. He'd also hidden the renovation fund accounts and taken the passwords with him so that nobody could sell the stock, which remained steady and would most certainly surpass its present value. As he washed, he heard some men enter the bathroom, gathered that they were law enforcement. He froze, then did his calming exercises and flushed the toilet. They did their business and departed. After he heard several cars drive off, he went out. The officers were talking to a couple of leathered bikers in the parking lot and they didn't notice him. He went out back of the building, past the bushy Russian olives, waded soundlessly into some cattails, and sank himself. He'd brought along a snorkel for this eventuality, even painted and dulled the plastic to mimic sludge. He'd done this once before to escape detection. Everything inside his backpack was snugly ziplocked. He wondered if they'd find and confiscate his bike. He hoped not, for his pup tent and camp stove were stashed in the saddlebag.

While underwater, holding the bases of cattails to keep from floating up, he timed his breaths to his beating heart. He enjoyed that his heart was beating and the water wasn't as cold as he'd feared. These were the times you could usefully employ reviewing your performances, and he did so. Martin had used various bicycles to make his getaways, stashing the money first in trash cans on no-pickup days, wobbling along slowly, white haired and earnest, even giving a false report of a bank robber sighting once. He thought of these bicycles now with affection and was careful not to smile, not to admit a drop of the rank slough water. A gastrointestinal bug could wreck his plans.

Watching his debut as Cutie Pie had brought tears to his eyes. What an audience! The appreciation! His triumph as Cutie Pie had required a year of practice to perfect a crouching sort of walk with upright torso to reduce his height. That had been the caper he'd emerged from as the elderly bicyclist by unfolding himself, pulling off his robe, and lifting off his gnomish hat. He'd stashed the money and pedaled back, yes back, to the bank. It had worked so well that he'd used the ploy again and again: the earnest customer (himself) appears, carefully chains his bicycle to a post, notices there is something amiss. Waits for a chance to cash a check and is disappointed. Has a story for the local residents at the ready, some explanation of his presence, some knowledge of the various folks he might know or work for. It took research! But research gives depth to a portrayal, he always told his students. He also told them to dream big and gave them tips on overcoming attacks of nerves. How he wished that he'd been able to acknowledge them. They would have been so proud.

His Rasputin. Now *that* part had meaning. Historical, of course, also just in terms of the sheer menace he'd developed in his voice, his walk, his gaze. Rasputin's eyes had mesmerized, terrified, seduced. Perhaps Martin would start a cult himself once he reached his terminus. His toes were going numb. He did some foot exercises. Hundreds of dollars were stashed in his shoes. He'd have to dry out the bills. They were not marked money. If his bicycle had been impounded, he'd still have money, anyway. He wasn't that far from a town and could walk if he had to. Bikes were cheap. He could sleep rough for a little while.

At last he emerged and found his bicycle had not been disturbed. He went back into the rest stop and warmed himself as best he could at the electric hand dryers. When he was presentable, he clipped on his bicycle lights, connected the batteries on his flashing bike helmet. He got back on, pedaled off, and made his way meekly toward the edge of the world.

At the Edge

So did Kismet say she'd be back this morning?' asked Gary as he sat in his parents' house eating a bowl of cereal for breakfast. 'Or maybe this afternoon?'

Winnie had agonized over what to tell Gary and decided it had to be the truth.

'No, Gary. She was going to call last night but she didn't. I think Kismet's gone.' Winnie sat down at the table and pretended to think. 'Actually, Gary, I think she went home for a while. Can you call her and convince her to come back?'

Winnie went out to the living room and settled herself, propping pillows under her knees, folding her hands on her stomach, staring at the ceiling. Diz had already left the house, upset. Poots and Jester curled around her. Gary touched his mother's shoulder, then he picked up Poots, put his face against his wiry, salt-smelling coat. Next he held Jester and scratched his ears. Gary put the dogs down and went over to his house, up to their bedroom, sat and stared at his phone. After a while he called Kismet.

'No, I'm not coming back,' she said.

'Okay,' he said, 'why don't you stay a week?'

'I'm sorry, really, Gary,' said Kismet 'I can't fix everything.'

'You fixed me! I love you so . . .'

'You need help.'

'Then help me.'

'I'm not equipped.' He could hear that Kismet was faltering and hope glimmered. But a hollow quiet fell and he pictured her deciding. She gathered herself and said in a firm voice, repeating some words she'd seized on, 'I'm not equipped, truly, I don't have a clue.'

'You do have a clue. You're . . .'

'It was just too fast, Gary. I should have stepped back before I said I do.'

'You do, you do, you do.'

His voice rose like a siren and he took it back down, then he heard himself chanting in a lower voice, tried to make it a sexy compelling voice, *You do, you do, you do.*

Kismet felt herself teetering.

'Gary, I gotta go.'

She hung up. Gary knelt on the carpet and toppled over like a child, his legs curled and his arms guarding his ears. He hadn't slept the night before. Now he dozed in fits and starts, half conscious although he couldn't move. At last he got up off the floor. He took his bison tooth from its glass dome. He put the tooth in his pocket and stumbled down the stairs, out into the yard. Jordan was walking toward him with the mail.

Gary cut around back of the house, jumped in his truck, and began to drive. He powered out along the highway, then crossed the railroad track and took a surprise turn, glancing in his mirrors to see if Jordan was following. Once, he thought he saw Jordan a few miles ahead but it was Pavlecky checking one of his fields. They waved at each other. Gary tried for a jaunty salute but it only made him feel more alone, cut off from the world of normal doings. He longed for the hours before the party when he was allowed to make a stupid mistake or two, allowed to be a stupid asshole. He hadn't had to think. There had been nobody to avoid. It seemed to him that he'd been a child, full of joy, though he knew he'd been the jocky top dog, irritable or scornful, conceited, and probably, yes, for sure, spoiled. Everybody said so. Now he guessed it could be true. But in those days he hadn't killed Jordan and Travis yet, so those times must have been extraordinary. It must have been a beautiful life he had back then.

Gary swept along the green croplands glimmering in the sun. They were uncannily saturated with meaning this morning. He noticed in amazement the puffy soybean plants, elegant spears of corn leaves beginning their downward arcs, wavery plump sugar beet greens in perfect stands, the promising bristles of wheat. Tremendous life was endowed here, and there, golden life. A soft benign invisible touch as of a stroking hand lowered to his shoulder in the quiet roar. You'll be okay, he repeated to himself. Be okay, Gary. He kept driving, quieted and calmed.

A sweetness that he'd known sometimes as a child when his birthday was the next day, or something very good was about to happen, came upon him. He remembered the way he'd felt when he'd fallen into the bin of fragrant heady grain and lay sprawled on top as something lifted him from underneath. And then over the edge of the treacherous (but he didn't know that) grain, his father's face had appeared and his down-stretched arm. That was the first time. When the tiger had approached on the inside of the fence, padding along in silent power, Gary knew he was safe and sat down. The great creature encircled him and made itself comfortable with a grunt of satisfaction. Gary sank back against its cushiony body and fell asleep within the cowl of its resounding purr. Other times he'd fallen heavily but swayed downward, light and insubstantial as a leaf, and landed in the yard. Then sat there quietly until Winnie noticed him.

Yes, there was lightness, a soaring heart, a happy moment approaching. From the intense glow emanating from each field and tree, Gary knew. He would be all right because he knew where he was going now. Gary turned down the section road, the boundary of Winnie's family fields that now were Gusty's fields. He continued driving toward the pasture at the end.

Ichor

Although he got farmers to use them all the time, Ichor didn't like crop protection chemicals, the 'cides—fungicides, molluscicides, insecticides, rodenticides, bactericides, larvicides, and, most of all, herbicides. The world needed food, but farmers couldn't keep going this way, ratcheting up the kill strength, adding layers of product. No chemical could be precise and there was no way to really quantify the overall effect. Nobody could adequately factor in the big picture, which was really big, being all of creation. Sometimes he woke at 3 a.m., sweating, having absorbed, say, a new study about the link between the herbicide paraquat and Parkinson's disease. Glyphosate and depression. Insecticides and schizophrenia. The plunge in insect life was disturbing. The velocity of loss was exponential. He kept going by hoping better things than more chemicals were coming along. He saw no way for things to end well unless they changed course. Most farmers knew this or were becoming aware of it or even agreed, but nobody liked anyone not trying to survive off farming to tell them what to do.

There were other ways to manage the most pernicious weeds around. In fact there were some methods that made him happy. Take for instance the nemesis of pastures—leafy spurge—a plant to reckon with, sinking roots down fifteen feet and spreading top root systems too, shooting seeds out over twenty feet. The spurge had been considered almost ineradicable, it had taken over whole pastures, crowded out the good forage, killed cows and horses. Poisons had to be applied and reapplied, to only modest effect. Then Ichor started hearing about how leafy spurge beetles went to town on the spurge. Season by season you could see those yellow pastures turn green.

A while ago, Ichor had been to a barbecue hosted by another weed control officer, Ron Manson Jr. There he ate famously well and took home a cooler of those beetles. Now Ichor was turning those caramel-colored beetles loose regularly on all the pastures in his county, and beyond, too. The beetles went wild eating the stuff they were named for, and better yet, multiplied and sent their larvae down to eat the roots. Every year Ron, and now Ichor too, express-mailed tens of thousands of beetles to farmers and ranchers with infested ranges. The rancher would open the cooler of leafy spurge beetles, release them out onto his problem, and bugs would start eating the problem. After a few years the bugs would be so numerous that Ichor would drive over to shake them off the plants into his tarps. The pasture he was going to was even restoring a section of the river it sloped down to meet. One thing he especially liked about the beetles was that they controlled the weeds but never quite ate all of the spurge, never ate themselves entirely out of existence. They weren't like people. They respected their existential limits.

Over the Edge

Gary parked his truck at the turnoff to the pasture and put on a pair of old boots thrown behind the seat. He got out and stood in the warm, dry breeze. He took the bison tooth from his pocket, regarded it lovingly, and closed his eyes. The wind touched his face. Sun on grass. He pressed the indented tops of the big squarish tooth and ran his thumb along the rippled sides and forked root. Gary walked down, past where he'd stopped his snowmobile to clean off his face shield. He could have just turned around and gone back home to party. But no, he'd kept revving up, speeding along past this level area. Again he saw Jordan off to his left, racing him, and he'd tried to wave Jordan over his way to the gap in the fence. Hadn't he? No, yes, no, yes.

His heart remembered the velocity. Gary's steps began to jounce, his hair flopped side to side as he made his way down the hill. It was so steep and when it had been covered with slick snow . . . but that was past. No going back, only forward into the fresh, clean mixed pasture grasses, into prairie sage, asters, and wild roses. Gary calmly strode to the river. He walked down the bank, over cracked sediment. He trudged through muck stinking with life. He thrust the bison tooth before him in his fist. Then waded into the easy brown summer water.

The Red River hasn't cut a steep channel in the land like other rivers. It meanders on the flat bed of a lake that vanished only ten thousand years ago. The landmass it runs through is one of the youngest on the continent. Because the Red River flows north, the southern end of the river thaws first and that water runs into winter ice, backs up on itself, turns exuberant, deep, dangerous, and floods. But when the flood is over, the river shrinks. Gary kept walking into the river but the water had stalled to a lazy curl and was only as deep as his heart. Nevertheless, Gary folded himself into the water. He was holding on to his peace in order to drown himself, turning his eyes up to see sky through the river's murky lens. He was trying to open his mouth when Jordan leaned over. He distinctly heard Jordan say, *Don't you get it, brother? I've got you now. I'm here for you. I'm your tiger. I'm not mad anymore.*

Ichor

Ichor bundled the tarps in his arms and started his walk down into Gusty's field to collect his weed-eating beetles. On the way he stopped to observe a spurge hawkmoth, rosy pink underwings, cream and brown streaks, a lovely creature. On his way across the pasture, where he intended to collect the beetles, he stopped to listen to some birdsong and saw Gary. It bothered Ichor almost immediately that Gary was alone and walking with such eager purpose toward the river. He put his tarps down and ran when he saw Gary enter the water.

When he pulled Gary out, Gary said with a sort of wonder, 'I got you too!'

He staggered out with Ichor, breathless, then talking.

'Jordan's not mad anymore. I couldn't make myself breathe in the water!'

They sat down in the weeds. Ichor pressed his hand to his chest and bent double.

'Oh, thank god,' Ichor said in a muffled croak.

'For what?' said Gary. His manner became false and subdued. 'I mean I wasn't gonna— No, you can't mean . . . is that what you thought?'

'What else would I think?'

Gary felt the sun on his back, and he'd always loved that feeling. It pressed on his shoulder blades.

'I was taking a swim.'

'In your boots, yeah, you bet. You were trying to drown yourself.'

'No, no, it's a sin, I wouldn't do it.'

But even Gary could hear how fake his voice sounded. Sitting there, the two fell into a sort of trance. Lush shadows lay across the waters. Here, the river below the pasture was fringed by alders and box elders. Some kind of fish strove upward and splashed back. A kingfisher chattered as it darted from an over-hanging branch. Farther upriver a small dark furred creature wagged and rippled as it swam. A yearling buck emerged to drink, its hooves piercing the mud.

'They usually don't come out in daytime,' said Ichor.

Gary caught his breath. He knew that was true and

believed that his favorite creature had come to remind him why he should stay alive.

'Young man, what's going on with you?' asked Ichor.

He said it like he really wanted to know. Gary told him everything. He told the truth about the party and how he acted, how he led his friends down the hill, how he hadn't looked back, how he knew the way to turn at the river before you smashed into the opposite bank, how Charley would not have hit that fence, Jordan and Travis would not have gone through the ice, if Gary had only turned back. Instead he'd kept racing down the river until he snagged on that branch. He told Ichor that Jordan had visited him on the river and kept visiting after that. He told why he had married Kismet and how she had decided to leave. He told Ichor that when he'd bent over to save him, Gary had seen Jordan. He told what Jordan had said.

'Do you think Jordan's real?' asked Gary.

'Anything you see with your own eyes is real,' said Ichor.

Gary sat paralyzed for a moment. Hearing that what he saw was real was a frightful sort of comfort. He spoke with difficulty.

'So did he mean what he said?'

'What do you think?'

Gary plucked a piece of grass and shredded it.

'Maybe,' he said at last. 'He was that kinda guy. I mean he never held it against anybody if he got knocked down, even as a kid when he was little. Nobody knocked him down when he got older. Man, he got his growth and nobody knocked him down! But even when he was a scrawny little runt I never did anything like that. I was always his friend, always looked out for him, me and Eric. Knieval and Harlan used to mess him up. I wish I could go back in time, Mr. Dumach. Every single day I wish I could go back in time.'

'I know,' said Ichor.

The breeze had come up in the trees. The leaves turned over and flashed like coins. The reeds along the shore clattered and ticked. Sometimes there was absolute silence. Sometimes the blackbirds trilled. After a while Ichor said, 'Just think. If I had come down to the river ten minutes later, I would be thinking the same thing as you do. I would have been too late. I would have thought about how slow I was, how I was parking my truck just right, drinking that water from my water bottle, bundling up my tarps just so, watching that hawkmoth. I would never have forgiven myself for stopping to listen to some redwing blackbirds, too, don't you love their song? I would have been thinking, right now, If only I could go back in time.'

Gary glanced over at him then ducked his head.

'Suicide always leaves someone else holding your pain,' said Ichor. 'There's no reasoning out what happened, Gary, why the ice was rotten right there. You'll never get an answer.'

Gary kept his head down and said, 'I don't know what to do.'

They sat there for quite a long while, watching the river. Finally, Ichor spoke.

'I'm gonna sound like a kindergarten teacher, but you could start by saying you're sorry. Say it to everybody who was with you, and to their families, and to their friends. And say it to Jordan. Trust me, it will help. And it's what a man would do.'

'Okay,' said Gary, slowly, for now his terror was different and he didn't know if he could accomplish what his savior had asked.

'And then after that, there's the next step, and the next after that. The way back up that hill—' Ichor tipped his head up the slope.

Ichor turned down his mouth. 'Oh geez, listen to me. I was going to say the way back up the hill is longer than it looks. But it isn't. It's exactly how it looks.' For the first time, he looked directly at Gary. 'I promise you it's going to get better.'

Gary nodded, still looking down at his knees, and asked, 'What were you doing down here?'

'Collecting spurge beetles off your uncle's pasture.'

'Used to be my mom's pasture.'

'I know.'

'She talks about how farming's going off a cliff; she wants to farm like her dad and mom farmed, more like Eric's dad and mom.'

'What's your dad think?'

'He won't say it to her, but I know he thinks it's bullshit. It won't work at the scale we're farming.'

'What do you think?' asked Ichor.

'Me? Nobody asks.' Gary cleared his throat. 'But I read stuff. They're both right. First, I'd get out of beets, over time because we have a contract. I'd plant nitrogen-fixing crops, plowing them back in, using less fertilizer. I wouldn't go full-on organic, not for a while, but for every problem that comes at us I'd look for a solution that gets us further along, like toward a goal of getting certified. I think the fastest-growing market's in organics, so I want to get in there. I haven't told anybody.'

It took a second for Ichor to ask, 'Why not?'

'Obviously,' Gary said, 'I'm a dumb jock.'

Aftermarriages

Cottonwoods Are the Kindest Tree

Travis was modest, even humble, so the river immediately snagged him on a simple car door. But as if it knew Jordan's legendary status, the river bore him along ceremonially. He was carried like a king through black hills. Traveling swiftly in repose, as though just ahead of enemies, he was borne by many arms. This went on for miles. Then, at a confluence of darknesses, the water seemed to argue with itself about which way to take him. At last the current turned Jordan over, wagged him this way and that, jostled him fretfully and finally dropped him. Now he was pulled smoothly down into a lateral current near the bottom. Everything slowed. A young sturgeon nosed against him, companionably swam at his heels like an honor guard. Again he bobbed forward and was carried in state. The sturgeon, with its small dark pebbles of eyes and wise whiskers, veered off. Jordan was next attended by some sleepy perch. An old pike grazed him suspiciously with its underslung jaw. The procession continued north, the banks at last flanked by giant cottonwoods grown up since the days of steamboats, when the river's banks had been cut bare for fuel. In some places gnarled deadfalls reached far into the river as it oxbowed. Beneath the ice they made snake balls and tangled caves. Jordan slid toward a narrow tunnel, paused politely at the entrance, was at last admitted and gently bound into the mass. Once spring came, a ton of muck surged across the aperture. Jordan became a citizen of the riverbank and was much celebrated by a vast population of tiny forms of life.

Coal Black, Diesel Black

North Dakota has the largest lignite coal mine in the country. Almost every week, 132 cars of coal were unloaded and the coal was moved from the train to piles near the boilers at the sugar beet plant.

'That soft coal's shit,' said Dale one day while he and Crystal were waiting for their turn to unload. 'I used to operate a dragline at the surface mines out west. It gives off so much worse stuff when it's burned. Nobody in this extraction state will talk about it.' He stubbed out a cigarette and Crystal raised her eyebrows.

'I'd take you more seriously if you weren't sucking down toxins.'

'I'm hooked,' said Dale. 'It's not my fault.'

'I love when people say that,' said Crystal. 'Hey, did you ever stop to think how much sugar we've hauled?'

'I guess I could go back,' said Dale, 'and look at my calendar. I mark my shifts on there. I mean, we could estimate our loads, thirty-two tons about, eighteen percent sugar.'

Dale sounded dreamy. 'And there's about eighteen trucks going all the time just at this one plant. And at the Crystal plant, who knows? At least, for once we're keeping the money in state.'

They shuffled. It was getting cold and the line was moving. Dale tapped out a cigarette and said, fake solemn, 'We're part of something bigger than ourselves. Sugar. And I don't even eat it, almost ever, and that's the reason I am still alive.'

Martin

2011

On the same day as a letter with typed numbers reached Crystal, a letter with typed numbers and alphabetical signs reached Father Flirty. The letters had been dropped off by person or persons unknown. A typed notation counseled Crystal and Father Flirty to consult each other. They quickly realized that the numbers were bank accounts and the complicated combinations of signifiers were passwords. When the two of them were able to access the accounts, they found the renovation fund had swelled to almost two million.

'God bless him, God bless him,' cried Father Flirty, weeping.

You fucker, thought Crystal, relief brightening her heart.

She was the reason. Panicked with anxiety in September 2008, Martin had gathered his wits and gone into a state of deep and unprecedented consideration. He had beseeched both St. Matthew and St. Homobonus, patrons of stock traders and of business. He had watched his wife and daughter. Thought about their choices. Extrapolated from their choices. They shopped at Dollar Tree. He bought Dollar Tree stock. They talked about McDonald's like it was a big treat. He bought it. Then kept going and bought Walmart and Amazon and everything else he could think of that was a go-to during times of stress and poverty. He bought stocks that were inordinately cruel or cheap or rapacious or environmentally destructive. He'd lost his ideals when he took charge of the fund. He bought Monsanto and sold it just in time. He bought eBay and felt better somehow. He should never have taken on this task. He wasn't cut out for investing money. He was supposed to be free as a barn swallow, his life a wing and a prayer. An inky swift's wing and a blue Hail Mary. He'd had to mortgage the house to fund his plans. Then he'd robbed banks to satisfy his soul and unmortgage Crystal's house. He'd had to work straight jobs once he got out west. The cult had rejected him for being a Catholic because they didn't accept people who already belonged to a cult.

Charley

Few people knew how much he liked to fish. While his friends were chasing girls and drinking beer around Ottertail or Detroit lakes, he was always fishing. He would fish for anything. He liked the long wait, the art of reeling in a fish, letting it go or not, and starting over. He even liked the tedium of ice fishing. People thought he would go to L.A. or New York, but he had no interest.

Charley headed out to Montana and took a series of jobs. First he apprenticed to some wilderness people, helped guide hiking and fishing trips. After a few years, he took courses in wilderness rescue. Over time he realized that what had happened to his friends was just what happened in the course of things when you were drunk and unlucky. Eric had told Charley how fast Travis had disappeared and now he knew why. The shock of such cold water had forced Travis to take a deep breath, drowning him immediately, before he could get his boots off. At least it had happened fast, before Travis had a chance to be afraid.

Charley had rescued sober people with splintered bones from the bottoms of cliffs, plucked drunk people from rapids, found some alive and some dead after days of suffering. He thought he knew how to act around bears but had gotten charged and was not as calm as he imagined he'd be in that situation. He'd gotten lost himself because he hadn't admitted until too late that he was lost, and couldn't backtrack, and by then he should have known better. That was how everyone got lost. He felt like a fool, but the woman who rescued him said, 'You're too good-looking to die,' and married him.

While he was lost he wasn't terribly uncomfortable. He knew the worst thing he could do was keep chasing false clues, so he built himself a brush shelter, settling near a tiny lake. He had a LifeStraw with him, so he wasn't even thirsty. He rationed the food he had and knew he could do without food for about three weeks. He had a knife and some wax-tipped matches. He hoped that eventually, in the evenings, someone would notice the smoke. But every night he banked his fire and when he woke he was still alone. The days wore on until he was so hungry that everything began to hurt. He had no fishing line, no hooks, but he had a lot of time and knew that if he found the right spot, moved slowly, and allowed a fish to get used to his fingers, he could catch one by hand. He caught a small trout, a Rocky Mountain whitefish, more trout. He was getting pretty good. Most of the time he thought about Travis. They'd been neighbors, gone fishing together as kids, on the river, caught bullheads mostly. Charley had a cruel father. Once, Charley's father had grabbed him behind the neck like a cat and lifted him off the ground, then slammed him down. Travis had seen it and challenged his dad to a fight. Another time, Travis had called the police, but nothing came of that except more hurt. Charley was fearless because he had no hope and Travis was fearless because he'd never been hurt. They figured out a way to kill Charley's father.

Charley had started fishing because of his father. He'd had some hope once. They lived by the river and had a little fishing boat with an outboard motor, very old school. Charley's father could not swim. He'd never taken Red Cross lessons. The boys decided to dump him off the boat and drown him. They were strong by then and had practiced upending each other by heaving up on a foot and keeping their heads clear. They chose the widest and deepest stretch they could find and the trick worked extremely well. What was hard was starting up the motor and racing away. Travis did that. When they got farther down the river, they tied up the boat and ran to the nearest person they found and told about how Charley's dad had gone straight down.

Because of what they had done, and the lie they told, Charley believed that the river took his friend. He believed that he had sacrificed his father to those waters, but Travis paid the price. Of course, the river should have taken Charley, and after Travis died, Charley had suffered greatly. He went to the river often during the worst of it, and talked to Travis, saying he was sorry over and over, also thanking him because he'd had six years of living free without his father. And because he'd seen his mother's face when they told her, and he knew that her eyes darting rapidly from side to side, her trembling jaw, her lips working strangely, were not signs of temporary insanity as people had said, but attempts to hide relief and joy. But he wished he could talk to Travis, because he'd not had the clarity of mind to thank him with all the words he had now.

Only Eric knew that Charley kept a school photo of Travis and one of Jordan in his wallet. Eric knew because he kept photos of them too, only his were from fourth grade and Charley's were from fifth. After those grades, guys didn't trade photos, in fact, kids probably didn't even do that at all anymore. Charley had kept Travis's photo in a waterproof hiking wallet with his money and identification. And he was glad when he was lost because this way he could look at Travis as he talked to him. Travis was part Ojibwe, like Kismet, and he'd always laughed when teased about his special powers.

'For good, not evil,' he always said. 'But not *that* good.'

They'd learned together in football not to make excuses, not to get distracted, and not to blame the other guy. 'Mii go maano,' Travis always said, meaning 'let it go.' He hadn't sweated it out after the murder; he'd never told a soul, nor had Charley. There had been just the two of them to talk about it. Now there was only Charley and the picture. The photograph looked at him shyly with warm brown eyes, a funny sort of half smile, and from the way the photo's brow creased a bit, in the middle, it seemed that Travis knew what they were going to do and that they might even have to die. But still he was calm enough to go ahead, whatever might happen, because he knew Charley was in trouble and it was the only way.

Sweetness

2012

You are every atom of glitter in this sugary hill. The vanishment of bitterness. You. What is this sweetness? C_{12}, H_{22}, O_{11}.
Carbon. Hydrogen. Oxygen. Sugar.

1

As the line of radiance along the eastern horizon intensified, Crystal was completing her final haul. It wasn't just another dawn in her night haul career. She'd given notice. She was finished. She had decided to get out because nothing—not acetaminophen, ibuprofen, Voltaren—worked for her back. Weed didn't work and the stronger painkillers made her sick. She had decided to wait a couple months before her next job—whatever that might be. She planned to walk seven miles every day, do yoga from videos, and mess around in her garden. Kismet was taking classes in biotechnology and weed science at NDSU in Fargo, but she decided on a semester off, to go with her mom.

They would hike the badlands, the Sheyenne Grasslands, the parks here and there through North Dakota and maybe over in Minnesota. Once they were tired out, she'd decide what came next. Crystal and Kismet were so relieved to be single that they aimed, at least for a while, to keep their distance from men.

'Let's not go repeating our mistakes until we get them wrong again,' Kismet had said. She leaned her head on her mother's shoulder. After her repeated refusals to marry him, Hugo was seeing someone else. So much for deathless romantic love.

As Crystal drove her last miles, she remembered the night she'd seen the mountain lion and hoped it would vault across the road again.

The mountain lion did not reappear, but Crystal was sure now that she and Kismet had their own guardians—angels, people, ancestors, saints, and spirits, even the ones in secondhand dresses. Overhead there was Orion, bright and clear. Not a hunter but a dress on a hanger. So her last haul was not an anticlimax after all. After she turned her truck in and went home, closed her door, and fell asleep in the peace of the morning, Crystal relaxed so utterly that there was no pain in her body when she awakened. Everything was perfect and she was perfectly alone. She suddenly realized that she had done a magnificent thing. She had raised and supported her daughter. She had used her secret stash of money to nearly put Kismet through college. She had survived the long haul. So why was it that she felt an unbearable pressure, a sense that she should weep but that weeping would never be enough? Although she'd been troubled sometimes at night, it seemed that she had ignored an altogether vaster grief or, perhaps, missed a vaster joy.

Crystal put on her spongy shoes and went walking along the top of the levee by the river. She didn't have to worry about time now. She just kept walking, crossing someone's yard and a straggly area of floodplain, until she was looking at an area of a tributary river where water rushed over the lip of a low dam. Below the dam there was a deep, lucid spot where the water swirled. In that place, enormous gray shadows moved. They were sturgeon, prehistoric fish that once grew ten feet long in this river and weighed one hundred pounds and could live that long too. They'd been designed seventy-eight million years ago. She couldn't see their tiny black eyes, or their detailing, the cartilage barbels beneath the narrow heads, but she watched them mull around in the dim spring runnels off the dam and her heart was consoled.

2

One afternoon, washing dishes at the sink beneath the kitchen window, Crystal looked out and saw Martin rolling his bicycle, a scratched blue woman's Schwinn, into the shed behind the house. She lifted her hands out of the soapy water, drained the sink, dried her hands, and walked out into the yard. When he finally came out of the shed, she saw that he was wearing a set of ordinary unspiffy clothes. Nothing he would ever have worn in the time before. Crystal felt only mild surprise at seeing Martin, but she was mystified by the floppy jeans and soft old plaid shirt, untucked. The plaid was gold, turquoise, white, and brown. His hair had grown out of its cut and curled around his ears.

He stood before her and took her hands in his, startling Crystal. She had never know his hands to be hard and callused.

'Where were you?' she asked, unsmiling.

'All around,' he said. 'I biked through snow in the Rockies.'

'I have to go to work.'

'What? Isn't the campaign over?'

'I've got some other jobs.'

'Where?'

'Tonight, I'm at a library meeting. Day after tomorrow, the Skillet. And I fill in for Bev at the bookstore. I don't get paid much but you know me, low overhead.'

Martin pressed his hands into his pockets and looked down at his feet, which, Crystal saw with astonishment, were wearing a pair of mismatched flip-flops. She stepped backward and pointed at his feet, her hand over her mouth.

'Somehow I got to a beach in Yucatán,' he said. 'Mounds of free flip-flops on the beaches.'

'Are you still a Catholic?' she asked.

'No, I left that behind in the Rockies.'

'And do you have a job?'

'I'm going to get a job.'

She nodded, thoughtful, and said at last, 'You can come in. I guess I can be late.'

They entered through the kitchen door and went into the living room.

'Gosh,' he said. 'I like what you've done with the place. It's spare.'

'I got rid of your things.'

'My silk ties?'

'Especially your silk ties.'

'That's okay. I was just hoping there might be a pair of pants left, a shirt, maybe a jacket.'

'No. Where's your carry-around stuff? Your suitcase, toiletry bag, your special snacks, travel coffeepot, nose hair scissors, Q-tips?'

'I don't have those things. I've just got a saddle pack. There's a tent in it.'

She assessed him.

'So. What kind of job are you going to get?'

'Bank teller.'

They gazed at each other.

'I've got excellent references,' he said.

'How did you get away after the robberies?' she asked him.

'That's pillow talk.'

'Where's your special pillow, Martin?'

'I don't need it anymore.'

She smiled.

Evolution

2023

Diz said to Gusty, 'Follow me.' They drove out to the field that had been the first field where they had used the Roundup Ready sugar beet seeds. He'd never forgotten how after spraying that year, 2009, there just wasn't a weed in sight, and how the weedless wonder continued until they'd lifted out the beets. Since then, they had rotated the beets every three years with barley. Every time they planted beets the seeds lost some magic.

'Remember?' Diz asked.

'I do,' said Gusty.

They walked out to the rows. Here and there dead pigweed had nearly melted into the earth. But also, here and there something else was happening. Some of the dead plants were turning green again. A few were lifting their heads. Across the field, as the brothers turned their great bodies, faces keen, eyes implacable in the shade of their caps, hands cupped at their hips, Diz and Gusty saw the resurrection. Silhouetted against the white haze of August heat there were spears of Palmer amaranth. Just here and there. But those plants could mean a million next year.

'The goddamn stinkers just pretended to die,' said Diz. 'They were dead a week ago, I swear. But now it's their Easter Sunday out there. Pardon my'—he choked a little on his words—'irreverence,' he mumbled.

'It's just a fuckin' dickens of an outrage,' said Gusty.

Diz grabbed his hat and threw it on the ground and stamped on it. 'There. I feel better,' he said. He reached down to pick it up. Gusty noticed how his hand shook. Diz dusted the hat off by slapping it on his thigh. He put the hat back on his head. Put his hands in his pockets to try and still them.

'If we could grow that monster,' said Gusty, almost in admiration, 'bombproof crop.'

'Maybe,' said Diz, as they walked back to the truck. 'Soon as we figured out a market for it, yeah. I think it's something like quinoa. Quinoa ain't sugar. And there's nothing on it like a price protection.'

'Sure not. Soon as we tried to grow it, some bug would come along and clean it out anyway.'

'I know,' said Diz. 'Nobody ever said farming was easy.'

'It's not for dummies,' said Gusty.

They laughed silently because they'd said exactly this a thousand times before. To outwit nature for even a few years, you had to be a brilliant SOB.

'I can see a lot of steps ahead and this weed is gonna win.' Gusty plodded along, kicking at the half-living weeds.

'Ichor says it's actually metabolizing the poison now. Just eating it. Whatever you throw at this thing, it can break it down. We're gonna have to handpick. Pay a church group or a football team or hire a bunch of kids and migrant labor like back in the day.'

'Darva's book group,' said Gusty.

'Oh. wouldn't that be . . . didn't Darva hoe beets when she was a kid?'

'Didn't everybody?'

'What goes around . . .'

'What does go around?'

'Weeds.'

'Believe it.'

———————

That night Diz lay awake staring into the bedroom gloom, Winnie softly burbling and snorting beside him. He saw himself running the thresher on one of those bright cool fall days and the obedient crop was falling into the rolling blades and the amaranth seeds were hissing onto the conveyer belt and down into the bed of a giant grain truck. He and Gusty were slapping their hands together, the way they did that time they'd temporarily beat the weeds. He was talking to Gary at the screen of a computer and they were looking at drone footage of the Red River Valley covered with amaranth. Field to field, that was all there was. His arm was big, a smooth honey bear arm, but he had the sudden childish sense of how tiny their farm was on its plot of earth, and on that plot a house, and in that house a bed with two people on it no bigger than gnats. He felt the weight of all he couldn't control, tiny little human that he was, working and striving, without really knowing how big it all might be. Winnie mumbled. He held her and at least there was the calm of her, the warmth of her, the goodness of her sleeping and the annoyance of the two little dogs. Apparently there would always be two little dogs that never slept. They growled and tried to bite him when he kicked at them. But their teeth got stuck in the woven coverlet.

Evolution

2024

Look at this,' said Winnie. She pulled up an issue of *Agweek* on the computer. The magazine featured a firm of young fellows from the Northwest, based in Fargo now, who'd programmed their robots to recognize weeds and leave crop plants alone. There was a video of the robots plucking weeds out early on at the sugar beet two leaf stage. Winnie called Gary over. Grace came too, her wan crooked little face round now, her eyes bright, cheeks apple red and shiny.

'We should hire these guys,' Gary said to Grace.

'Probably an arm and a leg,' said Diz from his chair.

He had a special weighted coffee cup because his tremor was getting worse.

'I bet you get a good deal for being one of the first,' said Winnie. 'And you'll cut down, maybe cut out, dicamba or whatever.'

'Why not call Ichor?' said Grace. 'He must know.'

'Weed resistance,' said Ichor. 'Give it a try.'

Diz and Gusty talked about the pigweed resurrection and decided why not.

A few weeks later, they invited people over. Eric held hands tightly with Orelia DeSouza, whom he'd met in college, and Bill and Bonnie stood together with their arms crossed, grinning. Spiral pulled up honking. Ichor brought a pan of bumble bars. Everyone stood at the end of the field watching the robot van pull into the yard. Two thin young men with an urban vibe shook hands all around, then rolled up the back of the van and attached a ramp. Three smallish contraptions came rolling out. The technicians tapped information into their laptops, then guided the robotic weeders onto the first field, ninety acres of beets. There was something appealing about the mechanisms as they trundled along, something earnest, sturdy, slightly comical. The watchers nodded, laughed, broke out in soft applause.

Again

One spring night two nearly middle-aged lovers, Kismet and Hugo, walked in the park among the wild geese, who wandered around restlessly, some complaining, others issuing commands. Someone in the park or city administration had cut down the last of the ancient cottonwoods. The mournful honks of the geese sounded in the dusky air like the spirits of the slain giants. The two sat together on a huge stump, holding hands.

'I'm suing the city about this. Stockton's helping me. They gave a contract to someone who thinks the life of a tree is fifty years.'

Kismet stroked the tree stump. '*L'amour de ma vie*, these trees were here when my great-greats camped around this exact place. They were, you know, Métis and French Canadian guides and such.'

'Do I know? You've only mentioned it a thousand times,' said Hugo.

'You keep forgetting,' said Kismet.

'Oh do I? Well, apparently an ancestor of mine was forced to surrender a weapon he'd used at Culloden to an ancestor of yours. It's in a book.'

'A righteous theft,' said Kismet.

'No theft is righteous.'

'Did your ancestor get his hundred chains of our land?'

'For all the good it did him,' said Hugo.

Hugo's Scottish forebears had come to the Red River Valley in the mid-nineteenth century with Lord Selkirk's settlement because they had lost their livings, their homes, and wanted to leave Culloden and their status as outsiders in their own realm behind. But they landed in the middle of a deadly struggle between rival fur traders, between the Métis, the Ojibwe, and the Sioux, and besides that the Scots were subjected to prairie fires, crop-annihilating grasshoppers, and a depth of cold they couldn't have imagined. About half of the first settlers died wretchedly, but eventually others brought the first sheep to the Red River Valley knowing they would have to contend with panthers, wolves, grizzlies, and obliteration by blizzards.

'Sheep farms didn't exactly take off,' Hugo said. 'But did you know they tried to make buffalo wool a thing?'

'I bet it was scratchy,' said Kismet.

They were sure that in other forms and other lives they'd met in Pembina, which attracted a lot of Michifs even as the fur trade faltered. How else to explain why through the years they kept circling back to each other? The sky turned a deep soul-blue twilight green. They drew close, night flowed off the river, and the stars fell into an alignment that told the geese what to do. Something happened to Kismet and Hugo when they sat together on the stump of a tree that might have been a sapling when their ancestors had nearly starved and then been saved by the ancestors of those returning geese. Kismet put her arm around Hugo, who was chubby and warm again. He'd driven her insane with grief, once, when he'd gotten married for a while. But she'd recovered. Time shifted back and forth as they leaned against each other and closed their eyes. It seemed that they were going somewhere that wasn't a place. It felt to Kismet like a slow arrival. To Hugo it was one stop on a longer journey. He'd taken everything he'd learned about fracking and applied it to accessing geothermal energy. He was working out in western Utah on an actual repurposed oil rig trans-planted from North Dakota. Now he was going to try doing the same thing here. He hadn't seen Kismet for almost a year this time, but it felt like yesterday. When they finally stood up, they pressed together. Arm in arm, they walked out of the park, toward a buzzing streetlamp. Kismet bent over as they crossed the river. She said, 'I don't know what is happening.'

Hugo crouched beside her and looked into her smeary night face. 'It's okay, dear leaf,' he said. 'It's just that we're in love. You keep forgetting.'

A tiny vial behind her heart that had been sealed since before birth cracked open.

'This time it really hurts,' she said, rubbing her chest. 'Ow.'

The geese on the oxbow and those who'd been graz-ing on the cropped grass began a loud discussion that surged into sudden rapturous agreement. They took off in a wild rush, flapping up over the water, wheel-ing and at last arranging themselves in an ecstatic for-mation. They flowed north with the river, guided by its mystery, toward the giant puddle at the top of the world.

'Ah, they're gone now,' said Kismet.

Once the language of the geese had faded, the two lovers who were the best of friends walked toward the streetlamps, twining their fingers together, sometimes stopping to sit on metal benches beside small new trees on the quiet main street. When they talked about signing papers to get legally married, they started laughing and soon lost all dignity and choked, snorted, burped, wheezed, even farted, adding to helpless hilarity, which made them ever more hysterical. In the year that followed they did not get married. They just kept making jokes about it, even when Kismet got pregnant. Everything was still funny until Kismet went into labor. Then for a while nothing was funny. It was a crisis. But after the baby was born things gradually appeared in a ridiculous light once again, also an absorbing silent light, and the times were pleasant but also desperate. This was the world.

Acknowledgments

I am grateful to friends and family in the Red River Valley of North Dakota. My brother Ralph Erdrich Jr., my niece Jalina Erdrich, and my high school friend Vern Shasky helped me sort out many aspects of the cars, birds, and football culture in this book. Thanks to my sisters Angela, Heid E., and Lise Erdrich, my daughter Persia, and my mother, Rita Gourneau Erdrich, for your support during the writing of this book. Thank you, Steve Berger and Vicky Radel, for creating Redpath Retreat, a prairie haven for people, birds, and the vesper flights of swallows. Bruce Eckre, thank you for your guardianship of civic libraries and landscape.

Ron Manson Jr., weed control officer for Stutsman County, many thanks. Also, Jim Stark, for a conversation about the geology of the Red River Valley. Sarah

Vogel, thank you for *The Farmer's Lawyer*. Quincy Law, invasive and noxious weed specialist at NDSU, thank you for responding to my questions.

Thank you to the editors and writers at the *Daily News*, for tending to the life of Wahpeton and Breckenridge. Also I'm grateful to you for archiving old issues of local newspapers in the back of your building, so that local people can read vibrant accounts of the doings of life in the Red River Valley, past, present, and, I dearly hope, on into the future. That said, this book is in no way about any town or farm in the valley, nor are any of the characters based on real people.

To my daughters Pallas and Nenaa'ikiizhikok, love and thanks for endlessly discussing farming, sugar, the climate, and characters in this book. To my daughter Aza Abe, thank you for the cover of this book. To those who have been invaluable in its publication, my superlative longtime editor Terry Karten, my matchless longtime copy editor Trent Duffy, Lydia Weaver, Andrew Wylie, Jin Auh, and so many others at the Wylie Agency and HarperCollins, grateful regards.

I particularly want to thank Clyde Johnson, a sugar beet truck driver and friend of the family. For the past twenty-two years, Clyde has hauled sugar beets in the Red River Valley. He has kept track of the number of loads he hauls every night, as well as his mileage. Clyde can extrapolate from his numbers a great deal of information about this aspect of the cost of making sugar. As of February 29, 2024, Clyde has driven 1,236,172 miles and hauled 26,052 loads of sugar beets, totaling 744,932 tons. At 18 percent sugar per ton, he is responsible for 134,088 tons of processed sugar, plus an unknown amount of beet by-products—cattle feed and food-grade yeast. At 5 miles per gallon, his trucks have used approximately 247,234 gallons of diesel fuel, equal to 30.9 oil tankers holding 8,000 gallons each. Day and night during the harvest, eighteen to twenty-two trucks will be on the road for this one sugar beet plant. Over the course of more than 35,640 working hours, Clyde has lunched on thousands of sandwiches and a lot of fruit—about 14,350 bananas, oranges, and apples. Haralson apples are his favorite variety.

About the Author

LOUISE ERDRICH, a member of the Turtle Mountain Band of Chippewa, is the award-winning author of many novels as well as volumes of poetry, children's books, and a memoir of early motherhood. Erdrich lives in Minnesota with her daughters and is the owner of Birchbark Books, a small independent bookstore.